MONSTRUM

KAT ROSS

Cover design by Damonza

Map design by Robert Altbauer at fantasy-map.net

ISBN: 978-0-9990481-6-0

For the dreamers and the slackers

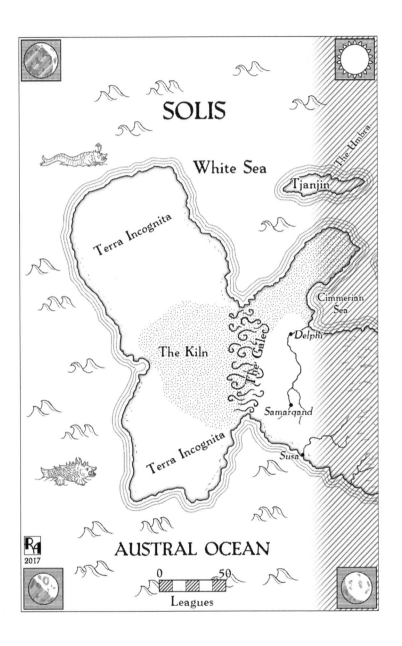

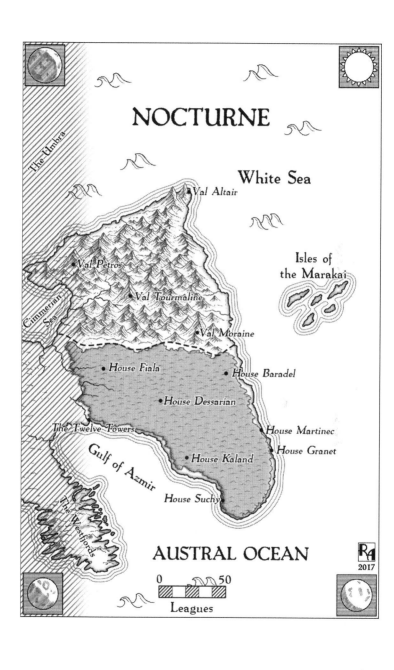

NOCTURNE

White Sea

The Umbra

•Val Altair

•Val Petros

Cimmerian Sea

•Val Tourmaline

Isles of
the Marakai

•Val Moraine

•House Fiala

•House Baradel

•House Dessarian

The Twelve Towers

House Martinec

•House Granet

Gulf of Azmir

•House Kaland

House Suchy•

The Westfjords

AUSTRAL OCEAN

RA
2017

0   50

Leagues

CONTENTS

FOREWORD

Hi Dear Readers, just a quick note to say I decided to include a brief character guide in addition to the glossary, since the cast keeps expanding and I figured it couldn't hurt. If you're anything like me, once a few months have passed between books, I'm like, wait, who the heck are *you* again? So maybe you'll find it helpful, at least for the family relationships and minor characters.

And now, on to Monstrum...

MOTHER OF STORMS

M eb tipped the bucket of fish guts over the rail and watched them vanish into the black water. The guts would make a tasty meal for *something*. A silverside, maybe, or a dragonet. If she'd been alone, Meb might drop a hook to see what showed up. But the current master of the *Asperta* stood braced on the deck a few paces away, eyes tight with concentration as he guided the vessel through heavy seas. Salt spray lashed his bare arms. The left one sported a tattoo of a small grey cat, her striped tail curling around his biceps. He appeared oblivious to Meb's presence—she was beneath notice—but he'd know if she shirked her chores. They always did. And she wasn't supposed to be fishing. She was supposed to be *cleaning* fish.

Meb scowled and grabbed a barreleye from another bucket. It had a smooth, almost featureless body, like a potato with fins. Barreleyes were deep-water fish. This one had been hauled up into the moonlight by the power and still wore a startled look on its face. With a practiced flick of the wrist, Meb slit its belly open and poked through the innards. Sometimes she found smaller fish. On one exciting occasion, she'd plucked out a perfect black pearl, which she traded in Tjanjin for a better knife. But this barreleye hadn't eaten anything interesting. She discarded the innards and used her knife to scrape the scales off.

Six more buckets of fish waited on the deck. Meb blew out a breath. The fan-like sails of the *Asperta* trembled in a sudden northerly gust.

"Mebetimmunedjem!"

Captain Kasaika's voice cut straight through the wind. She had years of practice at that, the captain did. Meb tensed, instantly wary. The captain only used her full name when she was displeased or worried. Had the cook told on her for sneaking an extra helping at breakfast? Or was it the slop bucket she'd spilled in the galley? She'd cleaned that up all right, though the smell lingered. Well, there was no ignoring the summons, or whatever punishment she got would be doubled.

Meb flew to the wheelhouse, scrawny limbs moving with apelike agility across the pitching deck. She looked younger than her twelve years, with furtive brown eyes nearly hidden by a mop of kinky curls. She couldn't be bothered to comb it and nobody made her.

The *Asperta* had sailed from the mortal city of Delphi across the Cimmerian Sea to Val Altair at the northern tip of Nocturne, where Captain Kasaika traded a cargo of copper plates and brass buckles for chests of raw gemstones. Now they were headed south, back to the Isles of the Marakai. Meb wondered if she would ever see Delphi again. All the Marakai ships had hoisted their sails and left the same day the Oracle issued a new prophecy. Meb didn't know what it was, not then, but she'd felt the cold stares of the men at the port. Like she was a rabid dog who might bite at any moment.

Captain Kasaika hadn't told her anything—no one ever did— but Meb was an accomplished sneak and overheard her talking to the current master after they left the harbor. Captain Kasaika said the Oracle wanted an excuse to wage war on the Persians. That she hated magic. Meb didn't see how you could hate magic. That would be like hating the sun or the stars. But mortals were strange. Captain Kasaika said the Five would deal with the Oracle. The *Asperta* would continue to make trade runs, perhaps to Tjanjin next. The seas belonged to the Marakai whether the Oracle liked it or not.

Now the captain gave her a stern look.

"I need you to check on Anuketmatma."

Meb froze. "Me?"

"Yes, you," the captain snapped. Her strong hands rested lightly on the wooden rail that enclosed the quarterdeck. "I'm not crazy about the idea either, but there's no one else."

One of the water barrels had somehow gotten contaminated and most of the *Asperta*'s crew were moaning in their hammocks. Those still standing were all working triple duty.

"But—"

Captain Kasaika's eyes narrowed. "Are you arguing with me, Mebetimmunedjem?"

Meb hunched her shoulders. "No, captain."

"Good. It's a simple job—so simple I doubt even *you* can muck it up."

Meb stared at her knobby toes. She was cautious by nature— one of the reasons they called her Meb the Mouse. She knew how to pass unnoticed, how to fade into the background. It was a habit acquired at an early age when she first realized how different she was. Unlike every other Marakai she'd ever met, Meb could hardly work water at all, nor could she read the weather beyond looking up at the sky and noting whether it was clear or cloudy. Navigating the Great Green required a subtle understanding of the currents and tides, of the surface swells and churning movements hidden in the depths. A sailor unable to commune with the sea was worse than useless.

After her parents vanished, she'd been turned over to Captain Kasaika. The captain didn't know what to do with Meb, so she was given menial jobs like cleaning fish and scrubbing things. Meb found these tasks boring so she was always daydreaming, which led to getting yelled at. She liked to imagine her parents would come back someday, but she was also a realist and expected they were probably dead.

"No time to waste," the captain growled when Meb failed to move. "It's already two bells past her suppertime. We have enough problems without...."

She didn't finish the sentence but Meb knew what she meant to say.

Without Anuketmatma waking up hungry and mad.

"Yes, captain," Meb mumbled, slouching for the nearest hatch. She slid down the ladder into darkness.

It smelled bad below decks, like sick and overflowing latrines. Physical maladies were rare among her people. Never had everyone come down with such vile humors at once, too many to attempt healing. Meb wondered if the Greeks had poisoned their water.

She crept down the corridor, one hand trailing the wall for balance, to a hatch at the very end. Anuketmatma got her own berth, according to the contract. Meb cautiously cracked the hatch and peered inside.

Moonlight spilled through a square porthole with brass fittings, illuminating a nest of blankets on the floor. Curled up in the center of the nest was a small grey cat with dark stripes. Her eyes were closed. The rumble of her purring filled the cabin.

Meb heaved a sigh of relief. She sidled inside and rooted carefully through the blankets until she located an empty bowl. Then she slipped down the hall to the galley. It smelled of black kelp and fish. The cook arched an eyebrow when Meb handed him the bowl.

"Captain sent me," she said briskly, trying to sound as if she did this sort of thing all the time. "I'm to care for Her."

The cook stroked his beard. He was big, with hands roughened from saltwater and a voice like distant thunder. He wore his tattoo on the left cheek. Meb was a little afraid of him because he had a short temper and threw things when he got angry.

"What about my fish?" he demanded.

"I'll finish it after," she said quickly. "I was almost done anyway."

That was a lie, but she could gut and scale with great efficiency when she wanted to, which was rarely.

The cook grunted. "See that you do. Not many's eating, but I still need a meal for the rest of us." He took a skin bag from under his leather vest, where it nestled against his chest, and squeezed milk into the bowl.

"She likes it warm," he said. "Cold is bad." A pause. "Very bad. So don't dawdle."

Meb nodded and cupped the bowl carefully in her hands. The *Asperta* wallowed through a series of deep troughs as she made her way back down the corridor. She was starting to feel better—proud, even, that she'd been given such an important job. Though Meb worked hard to be invisible, it made for a lonely life. No one treated her cruelly. Captain Kasaika was tough, but that was to be expected. She was captain. And she kept Meb's weakness a secret. Still, Meb knew she had no future with the *Asperta* or any other ship. She wondered if Captain Kasaika would even let her get tattoos. Other Selk kids got theirs at thirteen, but with her inability to work water, Meb worried she might be forever barred, which would be beyond humiliating.

She reached the cabin and nudged it open with one foot, knees bent to absorb the rolling of the ship. Anuketmatma's striped tail was snugged over her nose like a scarf. She looked soft. Meb had a sudden urge to pet her but didn't dare.

The little grey cat was the mother of storms. As long as she was content, the weather would stay fair. But if she got angry or hungry, things could deteriorate quickly. The Selk fleet took turns carrying her. Anuketmatma had been on the *Asperta* for the last month. When they reached the Isles, she would become the blessing and burden of another ship.

Meb approached the blankets, the bowl in her hands. Should she leave it on the floor? But it would grow cold if Anuketmatma didn't wake soon. And the cook said she'd be upset if she found cold milk.

I better sit and wait to see what she does.

Meb took up a cross-legged position at the edge of the blankets, cupping the bowl to keep it warm. She felt nervous being so close to the mother of storms, but it was still better than cleaning fish. If she stayed here, no one would bother her to do some dirty chore they didn't want to do themselves. She gazed out the porthole at the sea. She'd spent the last year on the ocean, working for Captain Kasaika, yet it still scared her. It must be different for the Marakai who could wield water, but Meb felt no connection to the sea. It was unpredictable, violent and merciless. Most likely, the sea had taken her parents.

She had no brothers or sisters. There was an old woman she'd visited once when she was little, some distant ancestor. The woman asked her a lot of questions and tried to make her do things with water. It was clearly a test, and just as clearly, Meb failed it. She never saw the old woman again.

Now she opened herself to the Nexus and felt the rush of the wind outside, the creaking of the wooden planks beneath her. Air and earth came more easily, although she wasn't strong in either. Water was the most unreliable element of all, which is why Meb had no warning when a rogue wave suddenly lifted the *Asperta* in a dizzying ascent and dashed it back down again like a frustrated child hurling a toy.

The bowl of milk in her hands splashed straight into Anuketmatma's whiskered face.

Meb froze. The cat's yellow-green eyes opened to slits. The fur on her back rose up. Her striped tail gave an angry lash.

"Oh, shit," Meb whispered.

❦ 2 ❦

SHE COMES FROM THE DEPTHS

Bitter cold shrouded the *Chione* as she sailed around
Nocturne's southern cape and took a northerly course for
the Isles of the Marakai. Ice rimed the rigging and slicked the
twin masts. Even the stars above looked frozen in place. Somewhere over the western horizon, past the Great Forest and the
Umbra and the mortal cities, the sun beat down on a trackless
desert, but in the far reaches of the Austral Ocean its light and
warmth were a distant memory. Here, the three pale queens of
night reigned supreme.

In her small berth, Nazafareen curled beneath a mountain of
blankets. Darius lay at her side, his breathing deep and even. He
slept peacefully now, though a short while before he'd woken her
with panicky mutterings, twisting and clawing at his throat. He
would have drawn blood if she hadn't pinned his hands. She spoke
to him, empty, reassuring words, and he grew calmer, finally
passing into normal sleep. It was a nightly ritual. He never seemed
to remember when he woke and Nazafareen hadn't told him.

Sometimes he whispered a name.

Thena.

Nazafareen's bond with Darius broke when the *Chione* passed beyond the Umbra, but she didn't need it to sense the fear contained in that single word. Thena must be the one who'd punished him with the iron collar. He still refused to speak in any detail of what had happened to him at the Temple of Apollo and Nazafareen didn't press. But she thought often of this faceless woman, and how much she would like to meet her someday.

This invariably led to brooding about the Pythia. Her pitiless blue eyes and the bellowing shrieks of the brazen bull. Now the Oracle sought the daēva talismans, to collar and enslave them.

Captain Mafuone said they'd reach the Isles within two days. Then Kallisto would try to find a bird who knew Sakhet-ra-katme and send her a message. Apparently, Sakhet knew a great deal about the talismans, more than anyone living. Nazafareen harbored secret hopes Sakhet might know how to restore her memories too, but she kept those to herself.

During their time together on the *Chione*, Darius had told her more about her life before Nocturne. About a woman named Tijah, who had been their comrade in the Water Dogs, and her bonded daēva, Myrri. Nazafareen asked every question she could think of and Darius dug out scraps he thought he'd forgotten, and it all left her both intrigued and deeply bitter because it was like hearing a grand adventure story about somebody else.

The truth of their past troubled her, as he'd known it would. Before the bond broke, she felt his power and the awareness she could sever him from it if she chose to. As much as Nazafareen enjoyed the intimate connection with him, it seemed too much like a form of slavery. The cuffs were designed for the express purpose of domination. For humans to control a power not meant for them.

In the bright moonlight coming through the porthole, she studied the gold cuff circling the stump of her right wrist. It was engraved with a snarling griffin—a winged lion—and had a lock with a small keyhole. The magus who first bonded them had kept the key, though it must be long gone now. Nazafareen tucked her arm under the pillow again, snuggling against Darius's warm body.

His left arm appeared smooth and unblemished now, but it would wither again if they entered Solis. Darius had explained how the bond took a piece of him and trapped it in the cuff, and that—plus the element of fire—was what made the bond work. Every daēva suffered a different infirmity. Some lost tongues or eyes. Others had crooked backs and twisted legs. Nazafareen scowled. It all seemed utterly barbaric.

But their bond was gone in the darklands, and so was her negatory magic. Nazafareen felt naked without it, vulnerable and exposed. Darius said it drew on the power of the void, but where did *that* come from? Not the Nexus. Breaking magic was an inborn trait and one so rare Nazafareen didn't know of anyone else who had it—or what ultimately became of them.

She pondered these things as she lay in the bunk, listening to the wind in the rigging. It had blown steady for days from the south, but now she heard intermittent stronger gusts that made the sails flap madly, as if the breeze couldn't decide which way to go. Nazafareen touched Darius's shoulder and his blue eyes flew open, wary and tense. He unconsciously reached for his elemental power, as he always did upon waking, as if to reassure himself it was still there.

His gaze softened when he saw her. She cupped his chin and ran a thumb across the dark stubble. It had been rough when it first grew in, chafing when he kissed her, but now it felt soft and silky.

"I like you with a beard," she said. "You look distinguished, like Herodotus."

He frowned. "It itches. But I'm not sure I want to try shaving on the Austral Ocean. You might not like me so much with one ear."

"I'd like you with no ears at all," she said seriously. "But listen, Darius. I think the weather is changing."

He sat up and looked out the porthole, studying the sea and sky.

"Storm coming," he said softly. "A bad one, I'd reckon."

She leaned over him and pressed her face against the thick glass. It was too dark to see much, though his daēva eyes were keener.

"How bad?" she asked.

"We ought to ask the captain," Darius replied. "She'll have a good sense of it."

Nazafareen had spent hours on deck observing the Marakai sailors and was deeply impressed by their grace and agility. They seemed to anticipate every swell and gust of wind. The *Chione* rode the waves like a water bird, perfectly at ease. And Nazafareen found herself reveling in the salt spray cast across the bow, the rush of water beneath the hull and sense of tremendous space all around, of being a tiny speck hurtling along beneath the vast starry sky. What a wonderful life, she'd thought, to sail free on the oceans!

But now she felt the power of the coming storm and was afraid.

"Better to know what we're getting into," she agreed. "I only hope it doesn't delay us too much."

With some reluctance, Nazafareen crawled out from the blankets and donned her fur-lined cloak. Darius, who seemed indifferent to the chill, pulled a tunic on and they headed up to the deck, where they found Captain Mafuone at the bow. As they approached, a gull flew past, making hard for the west.

"Rough weather ahead, captain?" Darius called.

Nazafareen gazed out at the water. It was choppy and streaked with white spindrift, but no worse than yesterday. The skies looked clear.

Captain Mafuone turned to them, calm and commanding. She wore her hair in rows of tight braids that accentuated a high forehead and enviable cheekbones. "Do you see the moon?" She pointed at Hecate, which was surrounded by a bright yellow halo. "The corona is a sure sign. And the birds know. They're headed for shore." Her face grew thoughtful. "This storm, it isn't natural. It appeared out of nowhere."

"What does that mean?" Nazafareen asked. "Someone conjured it up with magic?"

The captain shook her head. Despite the cold, she wore a sleeveless leather vest and baggy trousers cinched at the ankles with cords of shell. The tattoo of Sat-bu, She With No Face and Many Arms, seemed to writhe as her lean biceps flexed. "I'm not sure. But we have a few hours yet to prepare. Go tell your friends to stay in their cabins."

The crew was already reefing the sails and lashing down anything loose. They moved quickly and efficiently, each focused on the task at hand. None looked especially worried, which Nazafareen found reassuring. She threw a last glance at the sea. The wind had shifted again, driving long lines of swells from the north. In the thickening haze above, Hecate's outline looked gauzy and indistinct. She clasped Darius's hand and they hurried below, splitting up when they reached the companionway leading to the passenger quarters.

"What?" Megaera demanded grumpily in response to Nazafareen's pounding. A blanket lay across her broad shoulders and her dark hair hung in a messy braid. Like Herodotus and Rhea, the lateral rolling of the ship made her ill and she'd been in a foul humor for days. Nazafareen tried not to recoil at the unpleasant aroma wafting from the small cabin.

"Storm's coming," she said. "Captain says everyone should prepare for rough seas."

"Rough seas?" Megaera laughed darkly, one hand braced on the door. "What does she call this?"

"It's going to get worse."

An instant later, Cyrene and Charis crowded the doorway. Cyrene's pretty almond eyes were bleary and red-rimmed. Only

Charis looked alert, gripping her staff as if she expected to confront a boarding party of pirates.

Nazafareen had lived in Nocturne and easily judged time by the moons, but for her companions from Solis, the constant darkness played havoc with their natural rhythms of rest and wakefulness. As a result, some of the Maenads slept all the time and others hardly at all. The seasickness didn't help. Nazafareen heard a loathsome retching sound from the dim recesses of the cabin that must have come from Rhea.

Lightning flickered through the porthole, though it was still far away. Down the corridor, Darius spoke in a quiet voice to Herodotus and Kallisto.

"Don't worry," Nazafareen said confidently, "the captain knows what she's doing. I figured we were bound to hit bad weather eventually. Just sit tight."

"As if we had any choice," Megaera muttered, wincing as the ship gave a slow roll.

"Oh, quit complaining," Charis snapped. "At least you're not sharing a bunk with Rhea. If I'd known she had such a delicate stomach, I would have asked to sleep in the cargo hold!"

Rhea snarled something vicious from her bunk and Nazafareen used the distraction to slip away and leave them to their squabbling. She did sympathize. It must be difficult for four women to share a cabin, especially when two of them were sick half the time. Darius had offered to give his up since he spent most of his time on deck or with Nazafareen, but despite Cyrene's constant harping, she'd chosen to stay with her sisters. Nazafareen wondered if it had to do with the twins, Adeia and Alcippe. She knew the Maenads still mourned them, as she did too. Perhaps it was a comfort to stick together.

Curiosity drew her and Darius back up to the deck. Captain Mafuone gave them a hard look but didn't insist they go below—not yet, at least. This was her first real storm at sea, and Nazafareen wanted to see it for herself. They moved to the stern, out of the crew's way, and leaned against the taffrail.

"How many times have you been on a ship, Darius?" she asked.

"Twice, counting this one," he replied.

"Was there a storm?"

Darius pulled a bruised apple from his pocket and bit into it. "Not then. We crossed the Midnight Sea, but it wasn't nearly as rough as this." He chewed thoughtfully. "We did ride through a sandstorm in the desert once. I don't think anything could be worse than that."

They watched in silence as Selene crept above the horizon. In her buttery yellow light, Nazafareen could see clouds shaped like mare's tales trailing off to the southwest. Then the wind died. The *Chione* sped along swiftly because the Marakai were working invisible currents in the water, although the air felt thick and oppressive.

"Perhaps the storm turned away from us," she said to Darius.

He shook his head. "This is the prelude," he said quietly.

And of course, he was right. Within an hour, an impenetrable blackness covered the northern horizon. One by one, the stars winked out, as if devoured by some slouching celestial beast. They stood together as the *Chione* hurtled into the teeth of the gale and Nazafareen's heart stirred with a strange exhilaration. She'd always thought earth to be the strongest element, but the spectacle of air and water clashing together in all their fury quickly disabused her of that notion. Never had she felt so small and helpless. But the bravery of the Marakai crew, who clung to the rigging like a flock of dark birds and laughed in the face of the storm, gave her courage.

Due north they ran. The seas grew heavier. Lightning forked overhead.

"Get below," Captain Mafuone ordered. She stood on the

quarterdeck, arms crossed and legs spread. "It will be upon us in minutes."

Neither Nazafareen nor Darius put up an argument. They retreated to her cabin and huddled on the bunk as the storm broke with shocking suddenness. Rain hissed against the port-hole, and the darkness was absolute except for flashes of blue-white lightning. Deafening booms of thunder shook the timbers of the ship. As the hours passed, the waves grew so mountainous they overtopped the deck and burst through into the companion-ways of the vessel. Freezing water crept beneath the door. Nazafa-reen gripped the rails around the bunk as the ship pitched and rolled, sending her belongings tumbling about the cabin. The roar of the tempest drowned out any attempts at speech so she and Darius simply held each other, waiting to see what would happen next.

As the storm reached its zenith, a terrible crack rang out. She thought it could only be one of the masts breaking in half. This was followed by the clatter of hailstones the size of oranges pummeling the deck. Nazafareen didn't think the *Chione* could survive another minute, but somehow the ship stayed afloat.

It was the darkness she hated the most. Since her encounter with the snake that long-ago night in the forest, Nazafareen dreaded the lacuna—the period when none of Noctune's three moons were visible. The daēvas called it True Night. If the stars were obscured by clouds, the blackness felt crushing, dense and solid. But the lacuna usually lasted a few minutes. *This* darkness had persisted for hours. Each sloshing roll might be the last if the ship capsized, and Nazafareen knew she'd never make it out if that happened.

Finally, with the water steadily rising, she and Darius reached an unspoken agreement that they'd rather be drowned above than below, so they clawed their way through frigid knee-deep water up the ladder to the deck. As Nazafareen poked her head out of the shattered hatch, the ship climbed a great, curling wave and scudded down the back side with a sickening lurch. Wind whistled in her ears. It whipped froth from the surface into the curtains of rain so one could hardly tell where the sea ended and the skies began. She seized a bit of rope and held tight as a fork of lightning illuminated the scene of devastation.

Both masts had cracked, the top halves swept clean away. Bits of shredded sail flapped in the rigging. Water rushed everywhere, pouring into cracks where the hail had smashed through the deck. A knot of Marakai sailors huddled with Captain Mafuone, all of them soaked to the skin. Nazafareen hauled herself along the rope, reaching forward with her left hand and then using the crook of her right arm to keep from being flung overboard. She felt Darius's fist gripping the back of her tunic.

"How much more of this?" Nazafareen yelled when she was close enough to be heard.

Captain Mafuone turned. "The storm is big," she yelled back. "The outer edge is still a day away."

Nazafareen blinked stinging saltwater from her eyes and shared a grim look with Darius. A day?

The captain muttered something to herself, then conferred with the daēva Nazafareen knew to be her current master. An order was quickly relayed to the crew, who began hauling up the cargo from the hold and tossing it over the side. Barrels and crates, chests and clay amphorae, all vanished into the heaving waters. Captain Mafuone held her arms to the sky and chanted something in a strange tongue.

"What are they doing?" Nazafareen shouted to Darius.

He shook his head, hair plastered against his pale face. "I've no idea!"

With the cargo gone, the ship had almost no ballast and the waves flung her about even more violently. It made no sense. Nazafareen feared the Marakai were carrying out some final ritual in preparation for the certain death that awaited them all. Then she felt Darius's hand tighten on her arm. She followed his gaze toward the horizon. A patch of darkness lurked there even blacker than the sky. He drew her close and they clung together like children.

"What *is* that?" she whispered.

His eyes narrowed, the irises glowing an eerie blue. "I think it's a wave," he said faintly.

"The rope!" she cried.

He seized the end and wound it around them, tying it off in a quick knot.

The sea began to rise like an incoming tide, lifting the *Chione* higher and higher. Darius was wrong, she decided. This thing rushing toward them was not simply a *wave*. It had no slope at all —the face appeared vertical. The top, which towered at a hideous height above, did not curl, although a thin white line ran along the crest and streaks of froth poured down the face like a water-fall. In no time at all, the smasher was upon them and the *Chione*'s bow lifted to meet it.

We're going to capsize, Nazafareen thought with the perfect clarity of the damned.

Up and up the ship tilted, until the sky became the new horizon. Nazafareen pressed her face to Darius's chest, the rope biting painfully into her back. And then the *Chione* gave a sudden, violent lurch. The ropes slackened and pulled tight again as the vessel righted itself and pitched forward. Nazafareen's eyes flew open. A grey tentacle extended from the wave, coiling around the hull and lifting the *Chione* clear as the smasher passed beneath her. More tentacles—thick as the boles of an ancient oak—encircled the quarter deck and forecastle. Nazafareen gasped as one slithered past her foot. It had a smooth gray hide with tiny pale suckers on the underside. She couldn't begin to fathom the size of the creature they belonged to. She had just decided they'd traded one gruesome end for another when the crew gave a ragged cheer.

"She has accepted our offering," Captain Mafuone shouted. "The price is paid. The bargain struck."

Far below, the sea continued to rage and boil, but the monster held the *Chione* as gently as a babe in arms. She swam smoothly through the water, only her powerful tentacles visible against the waves. Nazafareen and Darius shared a look of awe.

"It must be Sat-bu!" Nazafareen whispered, thinking of the tattoos of the faceless monster worn by the crew.

"They might have called on her a bit earlier," Darius replied with a shaky grin. "Though I suppose the captain didn't wish to part with her cargo until she had no choice."

The rain still beat down, but from her vantage point high above the waves, Nazafareen's terror began to ebb and she peered at the sea, hoping for a glimpse of the creature's face.

"I wondered if these sea gods they worship were real or made up, like the Greek ones," she mused. "Do you think it's just tentacles?"

"I don't know. They must be attached to something...else."

But whatever the rest of the creature looked like would remain a mystery. She carried them for many leagues to the edge of the storm, where she deposited them back into the sea and sank into the depths. Water streamed from the portholes as the Marakai used the power to drain the ship and effect hasty repairs to the hull. Darius's skill with wood came in handy, and they both pitched in until it was certain the *Chione* would stay afloat. Then they crawled below and fell into a sodden, dreamless sleep.

When Nazafareen woke, the sky had cleared and the moons shone down, but the sea was still rough and driven by strong winds. Darius had already gone. He seemed to dislike the cramped confines of the cabin and rarely stayed below more than a few hours. She found him with the Maenads and Herodotus on deck, the latter looking bruised and tired but glad to be alive.

"If there's a gate to the underworld in the Isles, just push me through when we get there," Megaera declared as Nazafareen approached. "I'd rather brave the harpies than set foot on a ship again."

"At least my sickness is passed," Rhea put in. The tallest of the group, she stood regally at the bow, her pinecone-tipped staff in hand. "I think the storm beat it right out of me."

Nazafareen eyed Herodotus, whose pockets bristled with rolled up parchment like the quills of a porcupine. "I clung to a ladder all night," he confessed. "But I kept them dry. A record of all our adventures so far. I plan to write a book, you see, perhaps more than one—"

"Did you see it?" Charis interrupted, her eyes shining with wonder. "The beast?"

"Not *it*," Captain Mafuone corrected tartly, striding over. "Her. And She hears all, so you'd best guard your tongue."

Charis snapped her mouth shut and made the sign of forked fingers to ward off ill luck.

"No disrespect meant, Captain," she muttered.

"None taken," Mafuone said grudgingly.

Nazafareen joined Darius, wrapping her arm around his waist. He scanned the sea. "Where are we?"

"Not far from the Isles," Captain Mafuone replied. "But thanks to the gracious intervention of Sat-bu, there's no need to go there." She shared a look with Kallisto, who nodded, excitement in her eyes.

In the distance, Nazafareen saw a thick grey line, though to her relief it didn't appear to be moving.

"That is the place we seek," Kallisto said, following her gaze. "The home of Sakhet-ra-katme."

"What's in there?" Nazafareen asked. "An island?"

Kallisto smiled. "You'll see shortly. It's lucky Sat-bu brought us here."

"More than luck, I think," Captain Mafuone said. "They say one must have great need to find Sakhet. Perhaps the goddess knew this and helped us."

"Then we owe her a debt," Rhea said solemnly.

Mafuone smiled. "She likes pretty things, or objects of sentimental value. If you wish, you may offer something to the waves. But Sat-bu's price has been paid. The treaty honored."

She turned away and signaled to the crew. A squall brought fresh curtains of rain and they all drew up their hoods. Scraps of sail rattled like pennants from a bloody battle.

"I've never lost a ship yet," the captain muttered. "But if we don't reach port soon, we may all be swimming with Sat-bu."

And so the *Chione* lurched forward, drawn on swift currents toward the line of grey mist.

❧ 3 ❧

HYENA AT THE FEAST

The flat-roofed houseboat drifted on water as stagnant as a swamp. It had been painted in bold colors, red and yellow and blue, though the stretch along the waterline showed signs of peeling. Curtains hung limply in four square windows. The banks of fog enfolding the houseboat never came closer than fifty paces, leaving a clear eye at the center. Beyond the outer edges of the fog, the White Sea raged. Waves crashed and foamed. The wind howled like a banshee. But the waters within this calm eye were as still as a dark mirror, reflecting the quilt of stars overhead.

A woman sat on the deck, thin legs folded beneath her. She had large calloused feet with long, pointed toenails. She wore a leather vest and wide, loose trousers. A tattoo of a grey cat marked one wrinkled cheek, so faded with time the lines had grown blurry. The other cheek bore a similarly weathered image of a fanged eel.

On the placid surface, a net twitched. Moments later, a drag-onet swam into the meshed strands. With a jerk, hands the color of strong tea yanked the net into the boat.

Sakhet-ra-katme examined the fish with satisfaction. She

whispered a word of thanks to Khaf-Hor, who would welcome the dragonet home to his sinuous embrace, and used her knife to swiftly cut its head off. Sakhet ate half herself and gave the other half to a young pelican who waited patiently at her side. She tossed the head to a stormy petrel. Once she would have kept this delicate morsel for herself, but her appetite wasn't what it used to be.

Dozens more birds crowded the small deck and flat roof. Murres, puffins and guillemots. Auks and terns and cormorants and gannets. They watched her with bright, clever eyes. There were always birds hanging about. The houseboat of Sakhet-ra-katme offered a place of safety in their long migration across the sea. When storms blew them far off course, the birds knew that if they could find the fogbank, they would be given sanctuary. The old daēva shared her fish and let them rest. In turn, they carried the occasional message and allowed her to see through their eyes. Sakhet-ra-katme traveled the world this way without leaving her houseboat, though she glimpsed things in disjointed bits and pieces and usually from high above.

In all, it was a happy arrangement. It took a great deal of power to maintain the fog and quiet place in the White Sea, but the great eel Khaf-Hor loved Sakhet and had made it his gift to her long before when she decided to live apart.

She used a fishbone to pick her teeth clean and hauled up another catch—a pair of blue tang this time—which she gave to her companions. The newly arrived birds were all battered and bedraggled. Sakhet sensed a monstrous storm system to the southeast that was just beginning to tire itself out, like a child after a temper tantrum. Apparently, someone had pissed off Anuketmatma. Sakhet had great respect for the little cat—one would be foolish not to—but in her heart she'd always preferred Khaf-Hor, who might not be cute but was much less temperamental.

Each day, she watched Artemis grow closer. The restless moon spent most of her year-long orbit traveling the inky depths of space, but she was well into her return journey now and soon she would fill the sky with ethereal white light, exerting her powerful pull on the tides.

The Marakai welcomed Artemis with caution. Her influence, combined with the other two moons, could generate ocean swells to rival the Valkirin range. But tucked away in her fog-shrouded pond, Sakhet still enjoyed seeing Artemis in all her glory. She might not bother counting the years anymore, but the Wanderer was the only visible sign of the passing seasons.

Now she lowered the net and listened. With her sharply pointed nose and plumage of white hair, Sakhet-ra-katme looked like a bird herself, an impression enhanced by the sudden cocking of her head and perfect stillness of her limbs. Something was coming through the fog. Sakhet could feel the ripples in the Nexus.

Friend or foe?

She stirred a handful of black kelp into a pot and swirled it around, watching as the chai steeped and grew darker. In her pocket was a packet of powder, but she did not add it to the pot. Not yet.

Sakhet held out her palm. One by the one, the birds hopped up to her hand and accepted a thought-message. Some would go to Halldóra at Val Tourmaline, others to Tethys Dessarian of the Danai, and the last to Kallisto of the Cult of Dionysius in Delphi. Sakhet sent three birds to each woman to ensure at least one would get through to deliver the message.

She considered sending one to Mebetimmunedjem too, but that might bring even greater danger to the girl and she wouldn't understand the message anyway. Meb's only shield was her ignorance. No one knew who she truly was—no one except for Sakhet herself. As a precaution, she had arranged for Meb to be taken from her birth parents and given to another family to raise. They were never told who. And Meb herself knew nothing at all.

Just once had Sakhet seen Meb face-to-face and that was for the testing. There was no way around it. The inheritance of the gift was arbitrary and the only way to know which of her descendants had it was to determine who was weak in the element of water. When the gifted one was old enough, at least fifty, Sakhet would reveal the truth. He or she would keep it a close secret until they bore their own children, when the gift would in turn pass down again and the process would begin anew. The Drowned Lady had told Sakhet-ra-katme it must be so.

But Meb was not nearly old enough to be told. Had Sakhet taken the girl under her personal protection, those who sought Meb could have tracked her all too easily. A secret was safe in direct proportion to the number of people who knew about it.

But Sakhet had watched Meb from afar through her birds. The girl was cautious and sneaky, which was good. The only person Sakhet trusted implicitly was Kallisto. The other clans would need to protect their own talismans, but Kallisto could protect Meb.

The original talismans of the Danai and the Valkirins were long dead. They might have taken the secret to their graves for all Sakhet knew. The last time she set foot on solid land was when the three of them joined their gifts to make the Gale and turn back the Vatras. The war had ended, the world sundered into light and dark. But as soon as Sakhet bore a child, her gift had vanished, passed on to the next generation, and the next, and the next, for a thousand years.

Now she stirred the leaves, waiting to see who was coming through the fog.

It might be Kallisto. Sakhet had received a message from her that morning, warning of grave danger.

Or it might be the other. The one she'd dreamt of.

A gull perched on the roof gave a rusty cry of alarm.

Out of the mist, a small boat appeared. It was a humble vessel and built in the shallow-draft style of Tjanjin, with sails reefed against the fury of the storm roiling the sea beyond her safe place. It drifted slowly towards her, leaving faint ripples in its wake. A man with copper hair stood at the bow, white shirt plastered wetly to his chest. His mouth had a gentle cast, yet his eyes reminded her of a barracuda. A creature of contradictions.

So that's how it was.

Sakhet quickly slipped the packet of powder into the kelp tea and swirled it around until it dissolved.

"Fire child," she called. The fog dampened her voice like the walls of a cave. It didn't quaver despite the fear coiling around her spine. "What brings you to the middle of the White Sea on a night such as this?"

He inclined his head, appearing to consider his reply.

"I have some questions for you," he called.

His boat drifted closer. The birds watched with eyes like polished sea-glass.

"How did you escape the Kiln?" she inquired.

He smiled then, a disarming smile full of white teeth.

"It's quite a tale. May I come aboard?"

A cloud veiling Selene passed then and the light grew brighter. She could see his features clearly. He was well-fed but still had a starving look, a bottomless hunger etched into the lines of his face. The hyena at the feast.

"If I refuse?" she said mildly.

He didn't bother to answer this foolish question, watching her with eyes the color of the depths on a moonlit night.

Sakhet gave the barest nod. Why not? She had nowhere to run. Her gift was long gone. She would be no match for him and they both knew it.

A moment later, he leapt lightly across the gap between their two boats, a line in his hand. He tied it to a cleat and sat down cross-legged opposite her, close enough for her to feel the heat rolling off him in waves. A network of pink scars was visible though the thin material of his shirt.

"Well, this is cozy," he said, looking around.

"Kelp chai?" She held up the pot.

He smiled. "Thank you, no."

She poured herself a cup and cradled it in her hands, but she did not drink. Not yet. There were things she wished to know first.

"How did you find me?"

He rubbed his forehead, slicking his wet hair back. "It wasn't easy. I've been looking for two years. Not all of the time, and not very hard. Until recently." His mouth split in a charming grin. "And now I've found you."

"The Gale." She swallowed, her mouth dry. "Is it....?"

"Down? No, not yet. Not yet." He picked up her fish knife and twirled it through his fingers like a conjuror performing a trick. "I found another way."

She let out a breath. "What way?"

"An answer for an answer."

"What is your question then?"

He studied her closely. "Where to start? I have so many." The knife flashed and spun. "All right, here's one. Why are the talismans weak in their clan's power?"

"So they cannot abuse it as your own King Gaius did."

He nodded, a finger tracing aimless patterns in the blood staining the deck.

"My turn. How did you get through?" she asked.

"All the gates west of Samarqand were damaged in the sundering. The coastline is surrounded by reefs—not that we have wood to build ships. There isn't a single tree in the Kiln. Not one. But I suppose you know that already."

She frowned. "There were oases."

"Before the sundering. They all dried up. We can't tunnel under the Gale because the sands are too unstable. The barrier is warded so no talisman can penetrate it. So...take a guess!"

She thought for a moment. "You said the gates were damaged, not destroyed."

"Very good. But gates need water, you see. And we have none save what falls from the sky."

Sakhet suppressed a shiver. No water? She felt a moment's pity until she remembered the Marakai ships burning in the harbors.

"Yet it had to be the gates," he continued. "So twenty of us went east to find one. Seven survived the journey."

"Just seven?"

"The Vatras are not the only wildlife in the Kiln," he said lightly. "There are many other creatures. They've adapted remarkably well. I wish you could meet them." He stared out at the fog and his voice grew soft. "We did find a gate eventually, not far from the Gale. But it was dead, half buried in sand. Our water was gone. We waited a week, hoping it might rain." He turned to her. "I don't imagine you've ever suffered from thirst. It's far worse than hunger. Your tongue swells up. The agony is...maddening. Then I had an idea."

Sakhet said nothing, though her fingers tightened around the cup.

"We bled ourselves until the sands were soaked crimson. It turns out gates like blood. They like *wet*. I was the first through."

"So there are seven of you here?" she managed.

He shook his head. "One other. The rest died when the gate failed again moments later." He gave her a mirthless smile. "Don't worry, they're better off. Do you know how we live in the Kiln?"

In the beginning, Sakhet had often wondered what became of the Vatras. She assumed some of them survived the flight across the desert. But as the years passed with no sign either way, she'd thought of them less and less. She hoped they were gone forever. Yet she had maintained her precautions with the heir to the power.

"It must be difficult," she said.

He cocked his head, blue eyes narrowing. "Difficult? Yes. There is no food. No shade or water."

"That was not our intention—"

"No? What was your intention?"

"To lock you away where you could do no more harm."

Rage flashed across his face, there and gone in an instant.

"It's my turn for a question. How do I access the talisman's true power?"

And now they had come to it. Sakhet sipped her tea, trying not to grimace at the taste.

"How would you use the talisman?" she asked to buy herself some time.

"She will bring down the Gale."

She. What did he know?

Sakhet shook her head. "It would take all three working together to do such a thing."

"Would it? I don't think anyone knows."

This much was true. She took another sip of tea.

"You're young," she observed.

"I was born in the Kiln."

"So you don't remember what Gaius did. Does he live?"

He ignored this question.

"You were one of them," he said. "One of the three."

Why deny it now? she thought. "Yes."

The memory came with sudden, vivid force. Gaius sending a wall of flame racing toward the clans as they came to parley at the Vatras' capital. The channel of power opening inside her, weaving together with the others to sweep the fire back at the Vatras. The terrible roar of the elements, a thousand times greater than any of them could have wielded alone.

"Where did the power come from?" he demanded. "Who gave it to you?"

A lance of pain stabbed her belly, but Sakhet kept her face smooth.

"It was all a long time ago, fire child. I can hardly remember."

He seized her wrist in a powerful grip, grinding the bones together. The ferocious heat of his skin repelled her, but she refused to give him the satisfaction of knowing it.

"The time for lies is past, old woman," he grated. "I'll burn you to cinders, but I won't do it quickly. Dying can take a very long time indeed and I'll have the truth out of you in the end."

Sakhet thought of Khaf-Hor and his needle teeth, each the length of a ship's mast. Now would be a good time to come along and eat this man, she thought.

But the great eel must have been occupied elsewhere, for he did not appear.

"You'll never find her," she said.

He thrust a hand into his pocket and pulled out a tern. Its head drooped brokenly against one grey wing. "You think so?"

Sakhet felt a sickening jolt.

"This bird carried an image of a Selk ship." He paused. "And a young girl. Give me the name of her ship and I'll let you live. I'll find her anyway, but it would save me some time."

"She'll be useless to you, fire child," Sakhet whispered, darkness sucking her down like an inrushing tide.

"Useless?" He jerked her closer until his face was inches away. "What do you mean?"

The fog roiled. "Leave her be. Without the fourth talisman, you will never touch her power. And even I do not know what it is."

He glared at her, realization dawning. "What have you done?"

The cup fell from her hands, the dregs tipping to the deck. Black sludge with traces of grey powder.

"The chai," he hissed. "You poisoned it."

The birds flew at him then, pecking at his eyes, battering him with their wings. He let her go and threw his hands up. A din of terrified squawking filled the air as they erupted in flames. With her last ounce of strength, Sakhet threw herself into the sea.

As the frigid waters closed over her head, she saw his face backlit against the moons, fire boiling in his eyes.

NICODEMUS COULDN'T TAMP DOWN HIS FURY AT LOSING THE old woman before he was done with her—and on *her* terms rather than his. With an almost sensual shiver, he released the molten heat building in his veins. Sheets of flame swept across the houseboat, licking at the paint and devouring the curtains. Wood splintered and cracked. The flames burned unnaturally hot, red and yellow and, at their heart, a kinetic blue that was reflected in the dark mirror of the sea so it looked as if the water itself was burning.

Gaius said the other elements could be diluted, contaminated. Only fire was pure. Only fire *transformed*.

Nico's legs trembled as he pocketed Sakhet's knife. He barely managed to reach his own boat and shove off before a wayward spark set the sail alight. From a safe distance, he watched her houseboat burn and sink into the sea. She didn't resurface and when the last of it was gone, he called a breeze to propel him into the fog.

The cool mist helped calm him. He'd gotten what he came for. He didn't need the girl's name. He knew what she looked like now and he knew she was part of the Selk fleet. He'd recognized the image of a small grey cat painted on the sail. He'd also seen a woman, the one the message was meant for. A mortal with grey-streaked braids and a staff in her hand. Again, he didn't know her name—names meant nothing to birds—but her face was clear enough. He got the sense she was supposed to protect the girl, though it seemed odd Sakhet would entrust this task to a mortal.

Good luck with *that*, he thought.

Nico had to find her ship, but the whole Selk fleet numbered a few dozen. As his boat drifted through the fog, Nicodemus unwrapped the globe and blew softly on the runes until they glowed a faint blue. The view changed as it sped across the sea. It entered the twilight realm of the Cimmerian Sea and passed the port of Delphi, swooping across the whitewashed buildings of the city and over the great hill of the Acropolis to the Temple of Apollo, through silent torch-lit corridors and finally, the innermost chamber called the adyton.

A woman with hair the color of freshly spilled blood paced up and down before a tripod. Steam drifted from cracks in the stone beneath her bare feet. She had sternly handsome features and wore a white gown with a serpent brooch at the shoulder. She turned as his presence grew near and hurried over to a hidden niche in the wall, withdrawing her own globe. Pale eyes locked with his own.

"What took you so long?" she demanded coldly.

Nicodemus smiled. "I had no news to share. Now I do."

Her mouth drew into a tight line. Domitia couldn't use her globe to find him anymore, although it was her own fault. She'd thrown a fit a while back and partly melted the base. It couldn't be used to Seek so she was forced to wait for Nicodemus to contact her. This drove Domitia crazy, though he couldn't be happier. Before she broke her globe, she used to hound him on a daily basis.

"I needed your help weeks ago," she snapped. "Where have you been?"

"Sakhet-ra-katme is dead," he said.

Her nostrils flared as she drew a sharp breath. Nico knew how much she hated the old Marakai. Gaius said Sakhet had been a leader of the faction whose jealousy of the Vatras led to the sundering and banishment. That she'd sold her soul for dark magic.

"And the heir?"

"A young Selk. I know what she looks like. It won't be long now."

Domitia considered this. "Once she's collared and broken, we might not need another. One could be enough to unravel the Gale, especially if she's Marakai. The storms feed on water."

The Gale. The gate to the Vatras' prison. Nicodemus had glimpsed it when they made the pilgrimage across the desert. A howling wall of sand that sustained itself through the powerful wards the three talismans had conjured a thousand years ago.

But what could be made could also be destroyed.

"I ordered the Polemarch to close the ports of Delphi to the Marakai," Domitia said with satisfaction. "They're gathering in the Isles. You'll find the girl there." She pursed her lips. "There's another matter we need to discuss. A mortal. She has a rare power the philosophers call negatory magic. I set chimera on her and she dissolved them. I felt them die."

"Huo mofa," Nicodemus said after a moment.

"What?"

"That's what the alchemists in Tjanjin call it. Huo mofa. Fire magic."

She frowned. "Like ours?"

He shook his head. "It needs fire to work, but the source is inside the wielder. I've never met one." How to explain? Domitia always thought in literal terms. "It's less magic, I think, than a concentrated *absence* of magic."

"I know that," she said dismissively. "But there's a weakness. She can only use it in Solis. I ordered the chimera to wait until she'd passed fully into the darklands, but they're stupid creatures. They must have attacked too soon."

Nico leaned against the mast, tendrils of mist curling around his cloak. "Who cares?"

"She broke my gate," Domitia said flatly.

He raised an eyebrow.

"She's with a bunch of Greek women who call themselves the

Cult of Dionysius. They're impervious to fire. They helped this woman free two prisoners. And they have a connection with the talismans."

Nico thought for a moment. "I intercepted a message from Sakhet-ra-katme," he said. "It was to a woman with grey-streaked hair and braids. She carried a staff."

"That's their leader." Domitia's face darkened in rage.

"What exactly happened?"

"I planned to execute two mortals. A Greek and a Persian. The Greek had knowledge he refused to disclose. Something about a *fourth* talisman."

"Sakhet said the same," Nico replied. "I thought she was lying."

Domitia leaned forward eagerly. "What did she say?"

"That even if I found the Marakai girl, she would be useless without the fourth talisman."

"Well, what is it?"

"I don't know. She didn't say."

"And you killed her?" Her voice choked with rage.

"She drank poisoned tea," he admitted. "I didn't know until it was too late."

Domitia hissed out a breath. "I wish you'd kept that old monster alive. She might be the only one who knows the truth. Why are the talismans weak in the element of their clan? How do their powers work?"

Nicodemus had often wondered the same thing, but he shrugged.

"Calm yourself, Domitia. There's nothing we can do about it now. Most likely it's a mental block. You know how to break those. Perhaps we need all three together, perhaps not. We'll find out soon enough."

Domitia sat down on the tripod, her back hunched. He could see torches flaring in the background. "When you get to Selk, keep an eye out. I sent some Shields of Apollo to Susa to sniff out the trail of this woman. The one with negatory magic. She took a ship to the Isles of the Marakai. If you see her, kill her."

A wielder of huo mofa. Nicodemus mulled over the possibilities for a moment.

"If she can shatter magic, why not capture her and bring her to the Gale?"

Domitia gave him a pitying look. "Because it's in Solis, you fool. We'd have no means of controlling her power. She's mortal so the collars won't work on her. No, best to just catch the Marakai girl and get rid of the Breaker if she crosses your path. She's helpless in the darklands."

Domitia's head turned at a soft knock on the door of the adyton. Her hand flew to the serpent brooch and its eyes flared red for an instant. Her copper hair changed instantly to black. Nicodemus gave a thin smile. Domitia always did love intrigues.

"Just do it," she snapped, severing the connection.

The view inside the globe grew cloudy. Nicodemus wrapped it up and stowed it away.

He knew the Marakai talisman was an orphan. A year before, the globe had led him to her adopted parents. Whatever warding protected her didn't extend to her family. Before they died, they admitted they'd been given a child by Sakhet-ra-katme. They told him other things too. The father said he called her Jem. But no one knew any girl by that name. If fact, no one he spoke with later knew the two Marakai had sheltered a child at all.

Questioning her parents was the first time Nicodemus saw what fire did to the other clans. He'd been fresh from the Kiln and his own power was new to him, an explosive, unwieldy thing that erupted without warning. He hadn't meant to kill them, but he'd gotten angry. Flame had dripped from his tongue and though it hadn't touched the two Marakai, they'd been unable to resist reaching for the fourth element and charred themselves to husks.

At least it had happened away from the house. He'd buried the remains in a crevice of rock and no one ever knew what became of them.

Nicodemus examined the fish knife he'd taken from the old Marakai. A fanged eel coiled around the hilt, needle teeth bared in a ghoulish grin. His own lips curved in a smile. The knife would be his private joke. He tucked it into his belt and set a course for the Isles, the fog slowly dissipating around him.

❦ 4 ❧

SOL INVICTUS

The raven circled the mountaintop keep of Val Moraine, a coal-black shadow against the lofty snowbound heights. It had flown hard from the forests of the Danai bearing a thought-message from Tethys Dessarian to her son, Victor. Unlike her first four missives, which were lengthy rants about his unsanctioned invasion of Valkirin lands, this one was short and dire. The raven brought word of dark goings-on in Delphi. Of an assault on the Acropolis to be led by Victor's wife, Delilah. Chill gusts battered the bird, ruffling glossy feathers as it swept along the carapace of ice. Thrice it circled the holdfast, but there was not a single crack or crevice in the glacier, and the raven finally flew off, the message already fading from its mind. These were killing mountains and it had no intention of lingering.

In a darkened room on the other side of the ice, Victor Dessarian sat in the chair once occupied by his old enemy, Eirik Kafsnjór. He wore the same white leathers the previous master of Val Moraine had worn, and around his neck hung the massive white diamond that had triggered the keep's defenses. Victor clutched it in his fist, the facets digging into his palm nearly to the point of drawing blood, although he was unaware of this.

He stared moodily at the exterior wall, where not even a hint of moonlight trickled through. The keep struck him as grim before, but in fact it had been downright cheerful compared to how oppressive it was now. Victor couldn't shake the weight of claustrophobia, the feeling of being trapped in the belly of a stone beast.

The wall opposite was once open to the sky, protected from the flaying winds by a shield of air, but that had been transformed to solid ice twenty paces thick. The other three walls were naked granite. Maps of the Valkirin range lay unfurled on a large table in the center of the room. Mithre, his closest companion, sprawled in another metal chair, somewhat smaller than Victor's if equally grotesque. He too wore fur-lined Valkirin leathers and carried a sword at his hip. Coarse waist-length black hair hung loose down his back. Mithre usually affected an attitude of mordant wit, but his wolfish features were settled into serious lines today.

"Rafel is the only one I trust," Mithre was saying. "He's a Dessarian. And the man is clearly anguished that his sister is still held captive by this Oracle in Delphi. But the others?" He shook his head. "Let's start with the big Valkirin. Halldóra's grandson. There's something off about him. He's too calm, for one thing. He hardly seems angry about his ordeal."

"Maybe he's the stoic type," Victor said.

"Valkirin pride? Perhaps," Mithre conceded. "And he arrived to find Val Moraine in Danai hands. We're hardly his friends." He tapped blunt fingers on the armrest. "I've tried speaking to him, but he's vague about how many daēvas are being held hostage. Says he was kept isolated from the others, which could be true. But just before I came here, I found him in the armory looking over the weapons. We need to do something."

Victor gazed at the diamond in his fist, turning it this way and that to catch the dim light.

"Are you even listening?" Mithre demanded with some asperity.

"I'm listening." Victor's jaw hardened. "Put him with Gerda."

Mithre arched an eyebrow. "That seems a bit vicious even for you," he said mildly. "I don't think he should be running loose but—"

"Better to keep our enemies in one place. We'll give him back to Halldóra if she agrees to our terms."

Mithre shrugged. "What about Culach?"

Victor gave a mirthless laugh. "I trust Culach more than I do the others, Gods help me. He's blind and incapable of doing much harm. And he helped us. I made a deal and I mean to keep it." Victor glanced at the pair of slender gold bracelets sitting in the center of the map. They were unadorned except for elaborate clasps in the image of Sol Invictus, the Conquering Sun. "What do you make of those?"

Mithre eyed them with deep revulsion. "They appear identical to the ones forged by the magi, in purpose if not form. A talisman to leash daēvas, though they don't appear to cause a deformity."

"But where did they come from? How did the mortals discover their making?"

It was obviously a rhetorical question and Mithre remained silent.

"And those collars," Victor muttered. "They're even more barbaric than the cuffs we wore."

All efforts to open the iron collars had failed. Whatever magic warded them, it had survived the passage from the sunlands to Nocturne, even if the bond itself had broken.

"I want to talk to those women again," Victor said, tucking the diamond into his coat.

"You've already questioned them," Mithre pointed out. "Repeatedly. Their story hasn't changed."

"Do you believe it?"

Mithre blew out a breath. "I don't know. Rafel and Daníel back them up. Why would they lie?"

"Why indeed?" Victor murmured.

"It's not unheard of for mortals to show compassion for our kind. Look at Nazafareen."

A flash of pain crossed Victor's face. Neither of them knew if she or Darius were still alive and the odds seemed slim.

"We need to get word to the other clans," Victor said. "That includes the Valkirins. I won't see the rise of another Empire. If that means distasteful alliances, so be it."

"Agreed. But digging a tunnel out is proving more difficult than I expected." Mithre looked at the wall of ice, gleaming softly in the faint moonlight. "It's compressed and hard as stone. If we use earth power, we risk shattering the whole face. But hacking through by hand will be a grueling task."

"I have an idea about that," Victor growled. "But first bring those women in." He stared moodily at the map. "Do you remember when the Numerators would visit Gorgon e-Gaz?"

Mithre was quiet for a long moment. They rarely discussed the Empire beyond the gates and what had been done to them there, though Mithre still thought of it often. When they'd been bonded to the king's cuffs, Victor's infirmity was relatively minor —a few missing fingers. Unlike every other daēva there, Mithre's damage hadn't even been visible. But the bond did something to his brain that caused debilitating headaches. He would see a shimmering corona out of the corner of his eye that would grow brighter and larger, blurring his vision. The corona was the first sign. Within hours, or sometimes minutes, a blinding pain would follow.

Then an old magus had shown him a pressure point in the webbing between the left thumb and forefinger that helped eased the pain. When his bond had broken, the headaches went away, but he'd retained the habit of massaging the spot in times of stress, as he did now.

"I remember," he said.

"They were masters at extracting information. Dig down until you find a crack and then pry it open."

"I hope you're not suggesting physical torture."

"Gods, no. There are other ways of discovering the truth."

"Perhaps. But I lied to the Numerators repeatedly. So did you. Keep asking and eventually people just tell you what you want to hear."

Victor caressed his thumb along the diamond's sharp outer facet. "Always assume the worst," he said darkly. "You'll rarely be disappointed."

THENA LEAPT TO HER FEET AS THE BOLT SHOT OPEN AND THE iron door swung wide. It was the witch with topaz eyes and long dark hair who brought them food and water. His gaze raked the small room she shared with Korinna, who visibly flinched—as she did each time he came. For all her bluster when they were initiates together at the Temple of Apollo, Korinna had turned out to be spineless. She spent most of her time either crying in bed or carping about what a terrible mistake they'd made in coming to Val Moraine.

"Come with me," the witch commanded.

Dusky skin accentuated his eerie catlike eyes and Thena suppressed a shiver of revulsion, smoothing her dress and standing obediently. When Korinna didn't move, Thena shot her a murderous look behind the witch's back. The other girl rose with a grim expression and they followed him into the corridor.

Thena still didn't know any of the witches' names. Sometimes they interrogated her and Korinna together, sometimes separately. They asked the same questions over and over, with subtle changes in the phrasing, clearly hoping to catch her in a contradiction. She'd seen little beyond her room, which was really a cell, and the place where they questioned her. The keep was gloomy, illuminated by crystals in the walls every twenty paces or so, which gave off a chill blue light and only sprang to life when someone came near. As Thena followed the witch down endless, echoing passages, a fragile pocket of light enveloped them, leaving the space ahead and behind in perfect darkness.

All those empty rooms! She thought Val Moraine must once have housed hundreds of witches. They seemed to be gone now, but the thought of so many in one place still made her skin crawl. Sometimes she fancied she heard things in the darkness, just beyond the edge of the light. Whispers and dry rasping sounds. Her imagination conjured up images of mortally wounded soldiers dragging themselves along the floor, hands out in supplication, trails of blood and gore staining the stone in their wake....

Thena hurried to catch up with their escort, whose long strides had led him ahead. The blisters on her thighs still stung, but at least they no longer wept pus. Thena silently thanked Apollo for the second chance she'd been given.

May the light shine on us all. Even Korinna.

They reached the usual room and her escort threw the door wide.

The big black-eyed witch sprawled in a huge metal chair like it was some kind of throne, his bulky frame taking up every inch. As usual, Thena and Korinna were left to stand. He believed their story to the extent he hadn't killed them, but she could tell he had serious doubts.

"You claim you lost this Talisman of Folding." His gaze picked her apart, piece by piece, like a hungry vulture. "We've searched the well and found nothing. Where is it?"

"I told you. I must have dropped it in the between-place," she said, daring a quick glance at him through her lashes.

"Tell me again," the witch said harshly. "Different words this time."

"It looks like a disc. Daniel said the talisman cuts a hole into some plane of the shadowlands." She pressed her fingertips together. "Like a shortcut. You can travel from one spot to another if you've been there before." She gave a shiver that was only partly for theatrics. The passage from Delphi to Val Moraine had been like swimming through blood. Some substance thicker than water and warm. She'd held tight to Daniel, terrified that if she let go, if she lost him in the murk, she might never find the way out. "I thought I had it in my hand, but I must have dropped it then."

Of course, Thena knew exactly where it was. She'd buried it beneath the roots of an apple tree not far from the well they'd emerged from. But she wouldn't use it until she had something useful to bring the Pythia.

"This talisman would be priceless if we could find it." He scowled. "Tell me about the Oracle."

"She despises daēvas," Thena replied promptly. "She calls them witches."

The witch gave her a grim smile. "How many does she hold captive?"

"Only three now, since we helped Daniel and Rafel escape." She paused and assumed a stricken expression. "Five died in her custody."

His face darkened. "Where does she keep them?"

"At the Temple of Apollo."

"For what purpose?"

"She hopes to build an army against the Persians."

The two witches exchanged a look. Her inquisitor leaned over and whispered a few words she couldn't make out. She studied his profile. Again, something about him seemed maddeningly familiar. The bold line of his nose and weight of his shoulders. The curve of his mouth.

And just like that, she was back in a room with golden sunlight pouring through the window and heavy manacles dangling from the stone wall.

What's your name?

Thena, she had whispered...

The black-eyed witch turned back to her and she realized what it was.

He reminded her of Andros.

Just the name sent a flash of rage coursing through her. Those weeks with him seemed a nightmare now. He shouldn't have been able to touch his magic yet he'd somehow bewitched her. Clouded her mind. She set him free believing it was what the god commanded, but then everything had fallen apart. She couldn't remember precisely what happened next, but she knew Apollo had punished her betrayal. The blisters on her legs were proof of that.

Now she knew the truth. The witches were demons. Thena wouldn't rest until they were all wiped out or collared, and she had Andros on his leash again.

"Who does this Oracle hold prisoner?" he demanded.

Thena told him, naming Rafel's sister, Ysabel, and two Valkirins, one from Val Petros and one from Val Altair. She did not mention Andros.

"Where did the collars come from?" the other witch demanded. "Who made them?"

"The Pythia. She said the god led her to them."

And that was the truth.

"Who is she? Where does she come from?"

Thena opened her mouth to reply, but Victor held up a hand. He stared at Korinna. "No. I would hear it from her."

Korinna squirmed and Thena resisted an impulse to pinch her.

"I...I don't know," she stammered. "No one knows. She just appeared one day."

"When?"

Thena and Korinna exchanged a look.

"About two years ago," Thena said.

"And why was she appointed Oracle?"

"I don't know. The Archons decide that."

"Who else knows what she's done?"

"The Archons, of course. And the Polemarch. The Shields of Apollo. And a few of the initiates."

"How has she managed to keep this secret?"

"We—they—are all afraid of her. Her word is law."

And that too was the truth.

The witch stared at them both for an interminable moment. Then he made a motion of dismissal. Korinna practically ran to the door. The other escorted them back to their room and locked the door.

"That went well," Thena said, sitting down on the bed.

"Well?" Korinna hissed. "We are inches from being discovered and executed."

"Don't be so melodramatic. There's no proof we did anything wrong. We're heroes. He will accept it in time."

"The proof is Daníel and Rafel," Korinna spat back.

At least she was remembering to call them by their real names and not their slave names. Thena sensed the witches, especially the big one, would be enraged if they knew. There had been some near fatal slips until Thena took matters in hand. Now Korinna sported bruises beneath her acolyte's gown and Thena felt certain she would never make that mistake again.

"They've both played their parts," Thena replied with a frown.

"For now, yes. I trust Daníel. He worships you. But Rafel?" Korinna gave a hollow laugh. "He keeps our secret for the sake of his sister and what the Pythia would do to her. But he despises us both, I can see it in his eyes."

Thena strode over and took Korinna's hands. "Be at ease, sister. The god watches over us. He will show us the way. You must have faith."

"Faith," Korinna muttered. "I try, but it's not easy in this frozen pigsty."

Thena didn't like it either. She'd had only a brief glimpse of the outside world—mountains and stars and the moons—before the shroud of ice closed around them.

Neither she nor Korinna understood why the dark-haired forest witches held the keep belonging to the mountain witches. Thena sensed the two clans hated each other, but not why. She wanted desperately to see Daníel. He was a base, defiled creature, but he loved her.

Thena thought of the day in the yard Daníel wielded his power for the Archon Basileus. The sheer exhilaration of it sweeping through her, how she and Maia had exchanged a knowing look, trying so hard to contain themselves in the intimidating presence of the red-cloaked Archon. But then he'd brought out those criminals from the dungeons, and the thing happened with Maia, blood running from her nose....

"Let us pray together," Thena said, dragging Korinna to her knees.

She pushed the memory back into the depths. Andros claimed magic was a natural gift, but every word he spoke was a lie. Magic was wicked. Sinful. Apollo stood for reason and logic, for the industrious works of humanity against the corrosive power of the witches and alchemists. She had seen the consequences with her own eyes.

"It's cold," Korinna complained, shivering on the bare stone.

"And it will be even colder in the pits of Tartarus if we fail in our mission," Thena hissed. "Let the light fill you, sister. Let His will be done."

And so they prayed together, until Korinna's lips were blue. Thena tucked her into bed like a child and soon the yellow-haired girl fell asleep. Thena stayed awake for a long time after, whispering with the god. And when she slept, she dreamed of the brazen bull, but it was not her screaming inside.

It was the Pythia.

❧ 5 ❧

VICTOR'S STUPID PLAN

Of the odd collection of daēvas and mortals trapped within the oppressive confines of the Maiden Keep, Culach No-Name, formerly Culach Kafsnjór, was the only one who didn't mind the cold and dark. It made no difference to him whether moonlight penetrated the walls, and his Valkirin blood could withstand temperatures most would deem unbearable. In fact, Culach's circumstances had improved drastically since Victor released him from the cold cells and gave him his old chamber back.

He'd felt nothing when the keep's magical defenses were deployed. He could no longer touch the Nexus or the elements. But his finely tuned senses detected other changes, such as the dulling of sound within the walls and the complete silence outside. For the first time in his long life, he drifted off to sleep without the wind singing against the shields of air.

In truth, he found the quiet a bit eerie. The Iron Wars—the last time his father had deployed the diamond—ended shortly after his birth. He'd heard stories, of course, but it wasn't the same. That siege had lasted nearly a year before the other hold-fasts gave up and flew home.

Now he lay in bed thinking about Mina and what she'd told him about her son, Galen. How he was pathetically weak in earth power even though his father Victor was the strongest of his clan. Mina had confessed she was once weak in earth too, but she'd grown strong again after Galen was born. She always hoped the same might happen for him someday, but didn't want to give him false hope so she never told him.

Part of Culach resisted believing it. The boy was a snake. Culach loved Mina passionately and wouldn't say so to her face, but it seemed monstrous such a man would have such a gift.

Yet it nagged at him, the possibility that Galen could be one of these talismans Gerda spoke of.

He'd seen them himself, the three daēvas, in his dreams, although he was no closer to understanding what it all meant. Twice in the last week he'd relived Farrumohr's gruesome death buried alive in the sands of the Kiln. The slow suffocation lasted for days and Culach felt every excruciating moment of it.

Then there were the new arrivals.

Two mortals, a Valkirin and a Danai. Mina told him about them. He knew Daníel of Val Tourmaline reasonably well. A bit of a loner who'd seemed to love his mount more than anything else. When he went missing, Culach assumed he'd had an accident. The mountains were dangerous even for seasoned flyers like Daníel. But now he was here, claiming to have escaped the Oracle of Delphi.

The mortal cities had never held any interest for Culach. The Marakai took the Valkirins' raw ore and brought it back as swords and shields and whatever else the holdfasts asked for. Culach had never even seen a mortal until that cursed girl, Nazafareen.

He wondered if the chimera had found her yet. He had no regrets on that score. She'd killed most of his holdfast and left him blind. Culach would not mourn her death. He felt sorrier about Darius now that he knew Victor's son was innocent of killing Petur, but what was done couldn't be taken back.

Culach threw off the fur blankets and dressed in a coat and trousers of fur-lined leather. He'd kept to his room since the keep was sealed and Victor Dessarian hadn't summoned him. His world now consisted of two things: Mina, who was lovely, and his dreams, which weren't. What they meant and if they would ever stop. He suspected they had something to do with that day at the lake when he was burned since they began not long afterwards, but the connection eluded him.

Culach scrubbed a hand across his silver stubble. He found a bowl of water and cracked the thin layer of ice, then splashed it on his cheeks and scraped them clean with a blade. Feeling more awake, he set off for Gerda's tower. He hadn't been to see her since their argument over the Vatras, but she *was* the only other living Kafsnjór and he felt it was his duty to see how she was faring. Besides which, sparring with Gerda was one of the last entertainments available.

The guards at her door let him pass without comment. Culach was no longer a prisoner in the strict sense of the word. His bargain to tame the abbadax allowed him the run of the keep, though in reality, they were all inmates of Victor's asylum.

"Well, well," Gerda said by way of greeting. "What do you want, traitor?"

Her stiff leather gown creaked somewhere off to his left.

"You're one to talk." Culach gave a thin smile. "You told them where the food was."

She grunted. "We'd all be starving if I hadn't."

"I struck a bargain for your and Katrin's freedom. You chose not to take it. Why?"

"I won't be forced out of my own home."

"I don't believe you."

"And I don't care."

Culach inched forward until his knees smacked into a piece of furniture. It turned out to be a chair so he sat down. Traces of the foul brew she called wine hung in the air. This time, she didn't offer him any.

"I hear you and the idiot are friends now," she said.

"Hardly. I did what I had to. There's nothing left to salvage, if you haven't noticed."

"Your father would be appalled."

Culach didn't bother responding. He'd expected Gerda to be rude, that was simply a given, but he had the odd feeling she was putting on a bit of a show. In fact, if he had to peg her mood, he'd say she sounded happy, which made no sense at all. The trick would be to find out what she knew without revealing anything of importance.

"I'm still having those dreams about the Vatras. I thought you might help me understand—"

"Oh, now you want my help?"

Culach let the silence hang there for a moment. She tried to conceal it, but he heard a note of curiosity in her voice.

"Well?" she demanded.

"I'm wondering about the talismans." He chose his words with care. "This weakness you spoke of. Are you certain that's the sign?"

"Without doubt. Have you dreamt of them?" she asked eagerly. "Who is it?"

"I've no idea," he lied. "I only see the past."

"Oh. Well, that's not worth much, is it?"

"What about Farrumohr? The Viper."

"Didn't you say he was dead?"

Culach thought briefly of the horrid dream. "Most definitely. He helped Gaius gain the Vatra throne and poisoned him against the other clans. I don't know why Farrumohr hated them so much, but he convinced Gaius to woo a Danai who was already in love with another. That's what started the whole thing."

"Well good for him."

Culach decided to play along, creasing his face in a mystified frown.

"You can't mean it, grandmother."

"I certainly can. What have the others ever done for us?"

He sighed. "That's not the point. It's like asking the wolf to save you from the icebjorn. They both want the same thing in the end. To rip your throat out."

"Don't be melodramatic." She bit into something crunchy and chewed with gusto. "Look, kid. I'm sorry for what happened to you, but it's time to choose sides. We're the last ones left. So tell me, can you still get it up?"

Culach blinked. "Pardon?"

"Don't play dumb. You know what I mean. It's your duty to bear as many children as possible. Katrin would have been my first choice, but we'll find you a nice girl from one of the other holdfasts—"

"Bloody hell," Culach muttered.

"Your mother knew she was going to die birthing you," Gerda continued mercilessly. "She knew something was wrong. She could have gotten rid of you and your sister. But she told me she was willing to give her life so the Kafsnjór bloodline would continue. Does that mean nothing?"

The woman knew precisely where to slide the knife in, Culach had to give her that.

"Of course it does," he said, seeming to mull it over. "Perhaps you're right. But what can we do?"

She lowered her voice. "Sit tight. Help is coming."

"What help?" he whispered.

"Let's just say all that ice will be naked stone when—"

Culach turned as the door creaked open. He assumed someone realized he had no explicit visitation rights with his cantankerous ancestor. But the guards turned out to be there for another reason entirely.

"Go on," one of them said, in the firm but not unkind tone

one might take with a child being ordered to mount a hissing abbadax for the first time.

A third set of footsteps entered the room. A man roughly his own size judging by the stride.

"Why am I here?" a deep and unfamiliar voice asked.

"Your new quarters," the second guard replied, and Culach heard a note of pity.

New quarters? Culach thought. Had one of the Danai committed a sin so unforgiveable that Victor would banish him to the hinterlands of Gerda's tower?

"Why?" the man asked.

"Victor thought you'd be more comfortable with your own kin."

"He's not my kin," Gerda cut in acidly. "What is this?"

"Sorry," one of the guards muttered, though Culach had the feeling he was speaking to the new arrival rather than Gerda.

"Who the hell are you?" she demanded.

There was a freighted pause. "I'm from Val Tourmaline."

Culach's mouth dropped open.

The door slammed shut.

CULACH DIDN'T LINGER LONG AFTER THAT. HE HAD NO burning desire to speak with Halldóra's grandson, and Gerda's fury had been more than he cared to endure. So he made the guards let him out and hurried down the winding stairs as fast as he could go without falling on his face.

When he returned to his chamber, he found Mina sitting in her old chair. She smelled of clean wool and herself. He ran his fingers down her long braid and gave it a gentle tug. She was the one decent thing in his life. It still amazed him she seemed to care for him after the way he'd treated her for years. It was almost worth giving up his sight for that.

"I went to see my grandmother," he murmured in her ear.

"And?"

"She's insane as ever. But she confirmed the daēva talismans would be weak in the power."

Her shoulders tensed. "Should we tell Galen?"

"What good would it do? And I'm not entirely sure I trust her. This is Gerda we're talking about." Culach lifted Mina up and carried her to the bed. She swatted at him, but her heart wasn't in it.

"It seems wrong not to tell him," she muttered as Culach began undoing the tiny buttons down her back. He discovered a sliver of silky skin and kissed it reverently.

"Go ahead, then." Culach traced a finger along her spine and Mina shivered.

"That tickles," she murmured.

"Tell your son he inherited some extraordinary power, but instead of making him lord of the Danai, it's left him a sad cripple like me."

Mina snorted.

"Tell him you have no idea how it works or what it means, and in fact, it's probably the result of incestuous inbreeding—"

"You have a filthy mind."

"—going back generations, but you still love him and wish him luck. I'm sure he'll take the news well. It's not as if his mental state is fragile in any way."

Mina slid her hand along his thigh. "You may have a point."

Culach felt a pleasant twinge in his lower abdomen. "There's something else. Gerda said help was coming and I don't think she meant the other holdfasts."

"Who then?"

The final button gave way. Culach slid the dress to her shoulders and nuzzled the nape of her neck. "What if she meant the Vatras?" he whispered.

Mina laughed. "You said it yourself. She's insane."

"Well, yes. But she's more devious crazy than deluded crazy. And she seemed convinced."

He eased the dress down another few inches and cupped her small yet spectacular breasts.

"But she's stuck up in that tower with guards at the door," Mina objected, arching into his hands. "How could she know what's going on outside?"

"I'm not sure. Oh, and I didn't tell you the other thing. They've put Daníel in with Gerda." Culach laughed softly. "That poor bastard."

She twisted to face him, nipping at his full lower lip. "I have a bad feeling about all this."

"Oh, I do too," he murmured. "Very bad."

She stood and let the dress fall, then pressed her naked body against his leather coat. Nimble fingers plucked at the fastenings on his trousers.

"Why do I like you again?" Mina asked rhetorically.

"Because," he gasped. "Yes. That."

"It's time you earned your keep."

Shadows obscured Victor's face, but there was no mistaking the contempt in his voice. The half dozen daēvas arrayed behind the table stared at Galen, silent as wraiths. Only Mithre didn't seem to despise him. If anything, Victor's second-in-command looked troubled.

The Danai named Rafel stood apart from the others, watching with an unreadable expression. Galen remembered him, though they'd never been friends. Rafel went missing a few months before Victor returned, vanishing without a trace in the forest with his sister, Ysabel. Now he was back, with an iron collar around his throat and a haunted look in his dark eyes.

"All right," Galen said evenly. "What do you want?"

His gaze flicked to the diamond hanging from a chain around his father's neck. It gathered the faint light, glowing with a chill radiance. In his Valkirin leathers, Victor looked grimly at home in Eirik's chair. He seemed to have forgotten that Galen fought at his side when the emissaries came from the other holdfasts. Or maybe it had never mattered at all.

"I'm putting you on ice duty," Victor said. "We have to hack out a tunnel to the outside, but you can't use the power. That might cause the whole shelf to collapse. You'll do it by hand."

Galen nodded. If Victor thought this would be some kind of punishment, he was mistaken. It came as a relief. Galen lacked the strength to carry out the task any other way.

"No one wants to take a shift with you and I can't say I blame them," Victor continued. "But you'll dig until that tunnel is finished." He glanced at Galen's ill-fitting boots. "Or I'll see to it you lose the rest of your toes."

The others smirked. Heat crept up Galen's neck.

"Fine. I'll start now," he said, eager to be gone.

"I'll take him to the stables," Mithre offered.

"Good. Just get him out of my sight," Victor growled.

They turned to leave when Rafel stepped forward.

"I'll help," he said quietly. "The work will go faster with two."

Victor looked at him in surprise, then nodded. "There are picks and axes in the armory."

Galen felt the heat of his father's gaze on his back as they left the study. His gait was still awkward from the loss of four toes to frostbite. When the wounds had healed, he'd stuffed rags into the tips of his boots, which helped some. The toes still ached in the cold sometimes. Phantom reminders of his shitty judgment, Galen thought morosely.

Mina had told him about Rafel and Daníel, and the mortal women who accompanied them. It all seemed bizarre. What did the Oracle want with captive daēvas? She must be mad.

They stopped at the armory and silently gathered a collection of picks and axes. Then Mithre escorted them to the stables. The abbadax screeched in irritation when the door opened but soon settled back on their nests. Galen's breath frosted the air, but it was warmer without the biting wind. A wall of deep blue ice ran the entire length of the pens.

"I'm not sure how thick it is," Mithre said, resting his hand on Galen's shoulder for a moment. "But I'm sure you're equal to the task."

Galen nodded, surprised and grateful for his kindness.

"Personally, I don't intend to stay in this desolate hole a moment longer than necessary," Mithre told them both. "The sooner we can make contact and reach an agreement with the other holdfasts, the better."

"So Victor will give up Val Moraine?" Galen asked.

"Your father has a plan," Mithre said. "It's stupid, but it might actually work. Just make sure the tunnel is wide enough for a single abbadax, no more."

Galen glanced at Rafel, who gave the barest nod of acknowledgement.

"I'll check on you lads in a few hours," Mithre said, heading for the great oaken door. "Good luck."

Galen took a position to Rafel's right and started hacking with his pick. Tiny slivers of ice flew off at each blow, but far fewer than he expected. This was not normal ice. His heart sank. It was going to be a monumental task.

Galen's shoulders burned as he hefted the pick again and again. He used to be strong, but weeks of bitter cold and inactivity had taken their toll. After ten minutes, he thought he'd fall over from exhaustion. A few paces away, Rafel hacked methodically at his patch of ice. He'd actually managed to make a dent and Galen's pride forced him to push through the misery and keep going. After a while, he found a rhythm. His muscles would be screaming by the next day, but the work was also oddly soothing. The sharp *crack* and *tinkle* of the ice as it hit the stone floor.

The rush of steaming breath as he brought the pick back and slammed it into the glacier.

Huddled on their nests, the abbadax watched them in slit-eyed silence. The beasts seemed to have adjusted to their new conditions, though every now and then one of them gave a soft hiss.

Hours passed. Mithre returned, surveyed their pathetic progress, and left again, presumably to report to Victor. Finally, Rafel dropped his pick and departed without a word. Galen thought he'd quit but he returned a few minutes later with a jug of water. He drank deeply, then handed it to Galen.

"You look exactly like your father," Rafel observed. "It's uncanny."

Galen turned away, his reflection swimming darkly in the ice. With his raven hair and heavy build, he knew he was the spitting image. Once, he'd relished the resemblance. Now he found he hated it.

"How long do you think it'll take?" he asked.

"To break through?" Rafel shrugged. "A week. Maybe more."

That seemed to exhaust their conversational prospects. Galen certainly wasn't going to ask about the Oracle of Delphi. Or about the collar. He made a point of ignoring it, though when Rafel's gaze was turned, he couldn't help sneaking a peek. Gods, it was a vicious thing. Galen couldn't imagine forcing an animal to wear it, let alone a person. The skin at the edges looked raw and chapped. For the first time in recent memory, he felt pity for someone other than himself.

They grabbed their picks and worked in silence. Gradually, the shallow outline of a tunnel six paces wide and five high emerged. Rafel used the flat end of his pick to sweep away the pulverized ice.

"Better get some rest," he muttered, taking a swig from the water jug and handing it to Galen.

Rafel started for the door, then turned back when Galen failed to join him. "Aren't you coming? We've done what we could for today."

"I'll be along soon."

Rafel shrugged. "See you tomorrow."

Galen stayed until he could barely lift his arms. He returned to his chamber, gingerly unwrapping his feet and removing the rags from the toes of his boots. Then he lay back on the bed and pulled the furs over himself. He often wondered who the former occupant had been. A chair positioned next to the arched window held a half-finished coat with needle and thread set neatly on top, and Galen imagined a Valkirin sitting there sewing, gazing out at the starry night (now hidden by the ice, of course). The dried-out core of a pear sat on the sill. He pictured whoever it was absently setting it there, not knowing it was one of the last things they'd ever do.

What was your name? he thought. *Were you a man or woman?*

A dressing table held boxes overflowing with silver rings and brooches and jeweled hairpins, but this meant little since Valkirins of both sexes enjoying adorning themselves. He hadn't touched the jewelry or any of the other personal belongings, except for a few linen undershirts, which he tore up to stuff his boots.

Galen had deliberately stayed in the tunnel until he was nearly dead with exhaustion, but it didn't stop the dreams later. His old friend Ellard, trapped in a prison of ice, a brace of dead rabbits hanging at his side. Galen chopped at it until his hands bled but never seemed to get any closer. Somewhere nearby he could hear the howling of wolves.

"It's all right," Ellard whispered, a white palm pressed against the frozen barrier. "We'll just stay here, Galen. Forever and always."

He woke glassy-eyed and trembling with weariness some hours later. Rafel was already going at it with feverish intensity when Galen arrived at the stables. He didn't look much better. After a terse greeting, neither of them spoke at all. But inch by inch, the tunnel grew larger.

And Galen found himself wondering what they would find waiting on the other side.

BLINDING SNOW BATTERED KATRIN'S ABBADAX AS SHE SPED through a narrow pass. She'd reached Val Tourmaline only to discover Halldóra had left for Val Moraine with a large contingent of riders, bent on Victor Dessarian's destruction. They'd probably passed each other and not even noticed in the storm. So now she was headed back to the Maiden Keep, gloved hands lightly cupping the reins. Berglaug knew the way and needed no guidance.

Katrin peered into the darkness ahead, hood cinched tight around her face. Beneath it she wore another layer to fend off the bitter wind. Mountain passes sped by beneath, deep, purple-shadowed ravines and blue-tinged glaciers. The beauty of the northern range stirred her, especially after days in a cell listening to Culach's nightmares.

It still infuriated Katrin to have been taken alive and she intended to exact the appropriate measure of revenge. She was a warrior, the best Eirik had, but all those years of sacrifice and discipline meant nothing when the Danai used the power against her. If only she had been stronger, faster. Katrin's jaw clenched. She would be ready for them next time. Halldóra *had* to take her. If not, she would loose her buckles and embrace the final fall.

She urged Berglaug to greater speed. Sensing its rider's mood, the abbadax shrieked in fury, great wings slashing the night. And then Katrin saw a phalanx of flyers passing over the mighty glacier of Mýrdalsjökull. She bent low, turning her cheek to Berglaug's neck, and whispered words of encouragement. They were downwind and he'd already caught the scent of the abbadax from Val Tourmaline. Berglaug snapped his beak and bent his will to overtaking them.

The riders drew closer. Katrin shouted and she thought the wind snatched her voice away, but the last rider turned and saw her, reining in abruptly. The news traveled swiftly through the ranks. The rest of the abbadax wheeled around in a hard bank, their hooded riders signaling to Katrin that she should land in a sheltered pass. Berglaug screamed defiantly, but when Katrin failed to give the attack command, he settled his razor-sharp feathers and dove for the narrow saddle between two peaks.

One by one, the mounts alit in skidding puffs of snow. Katrin leapt from the saddle and threw her hood back so they could see her face. Fifty pairs of stony eyes followed her as she waded through the snow toward the tall, imperious woman who had led the tip of the phalanx and was the last to land.

"Katrin!" Halldóra exclaimed, undoing her buckles and sliding to the ground.

"I just missed you at Val Tourmaline," she said grimly. "Victor Dessarian deployed the defenses."

Halldóra's face hardened. "This is dire news. How did he find the diamond?"

Katrin felt bad, but she wouldn't lie. "Culach traded my freedom for it."

Halldóra cursed under her breath. "So he lives. What about the others?"

"All dead," Katrin replied. "Eirik too."

Halldóra's shrewd green eyes narrowed. "I assumed as much. Why did the Dessarians spare his son?"

Katrin shrugged. "He's blind. I don't think they had the stomach to kill him."

"What a mess," Halldóra muttered.

Katrin knelt at the older woman's feet.

"I would pledge my life and honor to Val Tourmaline," she said, looking Halldóra in the eye, heart drumming in her chest. "If you take back Val Moraine from those Dessarian dogs, I swear to aid you in the attempt, even if takes a hundred years."

Halldóra peered down at her, silver-white hair whipping in the wind. Then she pulled Katrin to her feet and kissed her on both cheeks.

"I welcome you, Katrin Aigirsdottir." She raised her voice so the rest of the company could hear. "Victor Dessarian holds the Maiden Keep. She wears her girdle of ice. Should we turn back and let the Danai keep the holdfast?"

The answer came as a resounding roar that cut through the howling storm.

"To war then," Halldóra cried. "We will teach them why the first mortals named our realm Niflheim, the coldest hell!"

Katrin felt tears sting her eyes. There was hope yet. A purpose greater than her own faults. She climbed onto Berglaug's back and they soared into the darkness.

❧ 6 ❧

HUNTRESS MOON

G erda stared at the Valkirin who'd been unceremoniously dumped in her room. He didn't look very clean. Some kind of collar ringed his muscular neck, secured by a heavy lock. His leathers fit awkwardly, the trousers too short and the coat too tight, as if borrowed from a smaller man. Gerda sensed immediately something was wrong with him. His eyes had a weird blankness.

"What the hell happened to you?" she asked after a long, uncomfortable silence.

He didn't reply. Gerda scowled. She'd removed her bed years ago and slept in little catnaps sitting upright in her favorite hard chair. It faced the mountains so she could watch the moons drift across the sky and enjoy the beauty of the snow-clad peaks. On a clear night, she might see all the way to the White Sea. Now her view was obscured by a slab of ice. She hated it. But to be confined with a stranger? That was far worse.

"They can't expect you to stay here," she muttered. "It's an outrage. The keep has a hundred empty rooms." Then she understood. The idiot was punishing her. Stripping away her last vestige of privacy.

"Hey," she snarled. "Whatever your name is. Sit down."

He turned to her and Gerda shrank back from his empty gaze. It took a moment, but she recognized him now. Halldóra's grandson. She hadn't seen him in years. He'd come to the keep for a wedding between her great-nephew Hinrik and some woman from Val Tourmaline. Gerda danced with him in the Great Hall to the strains of a langspil, which was a kind of zither. Daníel was quick-footed and full of an easy, infectious happiness, though he'd seemed relieved when the festivities were over, probably because Halldóra had been eyeing potential wives for him.

Except for the basics—eyes, nose, mouth—the man standing before her bore little resemblance to the youth in the prime of his life that Gerda remembered.

"What's that thing around your neck?" she demanded. "How did you come here?" She sniffed when this failed to garner a response. "Well, don't expect me to share my wine. I've little enough left as it is."

Daníel turned away and began prowling around the room like a caged beast. His eyes flicked over her chest of drawers and the tall cabinet in the corner where she kept her most precious possessions: a spinelstone and other gems, some gold jewelry, a small ivory carving of her late husband Albert, and of course, the talisman of seeking.

Gerda ground her teeth in frustration. How was she supposed to use the globe with Daníel there? She'd been speaking regularly with the charismatic Vatra. His name was Nicodemus. He said he was on an important mission in the Isles of the Marakai, but promised to liberate Val Moraine from the invaders as soon as he could. Gerda found their secret liaisons terribly exciting, even a bit romantic. She'd taken to doing up her hair and putting on her nicest earrings before calling him on the globe. The fact was, her life had grown tedious before the idiot invaded. No one ever came to visit. She'd taken to having long, one-sided conversations with Albert about days past, when they were both young and the keep was full of life.

Val Moraine might have withstood the long siege of the Iron Wars, but a pall had lingered over the holdfast that never went away. Near the end of the final year, Ygraine died birthing Culach and his sister Neblis, and Eirik wasn't the same. He'd loved Ygraine fiercely and part of him blamed the mewling creatures she left behind, even if he'd never admit it.

But it was more than that. Gerda always suspected the change in him had something to do with the diamond. Eirik had discovered it in a trove of talismans sealed behind a wall in the lower section of the keep, near the oldest crypts. He'd been fortifying the tunnels and found a secret chamber. Of course, he'd ignored all the runes carved into the walls warning anyone who found it that the talismans were unpredictable and shouldn't be used under any circumstances. Gerda snorted. No, they only encouraged Eirik, frost-brained fool that he was. He grew convinced the trove belonged to the founder of Val Moraine, an enigmatic man known as Magnus the Merciless (though rumor claimed his wife called him Magnus the Rather Unpleasant because he was more irritable than truly vicious), and whose body was conspicuously missing from the catacombs.

The diamond saved them from the other holdfasts, but Eirik became possessive of it long after the threat was vanquished, wearing it on a chain around his neck. His bitterness and isolation grew. Eirik was gentler with Neblis, but Culach had borne the worst of it. Gerda retreated to her tower. The last time she'd gone to see Eirik, he was sitting in his study, staring into the faceted depths of the diamond, and nearly tore her head off when she announced herself.

Now Victor Dessarian had it.

She smiled grimly.

Let it destroy him as it did my grandson.

Her thoughts turned to Nicodemus. She'd told him about

Culach and his dreams, though Nicodemus didn't seem to know what they meant either. He said the Gale had to be brought down so the rest of his clan could gain their freedom.

But when Halldóra came, Gerda felt sure she could make her see reason. The Vatras weren't their enemies. Fire and air were kindred elements. Fire fed on air, just as earth and water stood in opposition. The Valkirins and the Vatras were clearly destined to rule together. Gerda held no special grudge against the Marakai—they had their uses—but the Danai? Who needed them? She despised wood, as all proper Valkirins did. And how wonderful it would be to have the makers of talismans back! A return to the glory days.

Gerda fingered the emeralds on her dress. Albert had died in a mining cave-in nearly a hundred years before. He had a special talent for finding emeralds. The ones sewn into her collar and sleeves were all gifts from him. Gerda felt certain Albert would agree with her. A new age would dawn of peace and harmony—and the utter annihilation of the Danai.

Lost in her happy reverie, Gerda nearly forgot about the Valkirin wandering around her chamber.

"Hey!" she barked, as Daníel opened the ornate brass wardrobe and stuck his head inside. "Get out of there!"

To her surprise, he obeyed at once.

"Sit down," she ordered, pointing imperiously at the chair Culach had vacated. "Where's Halldóra? What happened to the rest of you? Go on, boy. Speak!"

He settled into the chair and seemed to truly see her for the first time.

"I don't know," he replied mildly.

"How can you not know? Those Danai dogs caught you, didn't they?"

He frowned in apparent confusion. "No, no."

He must have taken a blow to the head, she decided. She

didn't recall Daníel as dim-witted, quite the opposite. Yes, that must be it. Though it didn't explain the ill-fitting clothes.

"You'll have to sleep on the floor," she said tartly. "And I don't have any blankets. Don't believe in 'em." She thumped her chest. "It's the cold makes us strong."

She looked him over. He was weird, all right. Daníel put a crimp in her plans, but it might not be so bad having company. He could fetch her things.

"My old bones are aching," she said pensively. "You see that bottle over there? The green one? Pour me a glass of it."

He did as ordered, which pleased her.

"When are the others coming?" she asked.

His hand went to the collar and an unfathomable look crossed his face. Something close to longing.

"Others?"

"The other holdfasts! Blind me with the blazing sun, you *did* come from Val Tourmaline. Tell me what's happening!"

"You misunderstand. I came from Delphi."

She choked on her wine. "Delphi?"

His green eyes flickered uncertainly. "They didn't tell you?"

"They tell me nothing, boy. Now, what madness is this?"

Gerda listened in mounting disbelief as Daníel related his tale.

"Never trust a mortal," she spat. "We should have wiped them out years ago."

"But she saved me," he replied dreamily.

"Who? This girl from the Temple? Pah! You said she had you for a year. Why didn't she help you before?"

He had no reply for this.

"Well, you're with me now," she said soothingly, feeling a pang in her chest. Gerda feared she might be having a heart attack, but then she realized it was merely an unfamiliar emotion: Pity. It's the ill-fitting clothes, she thought. They made him look like a neglected, overgrown child.

"I have some things of Albert's you could wear," she said. "You're about the same size."

She set her goblet aside and went to a silver chest, where she dug out a coat and trousers. They were a bit musty and out of fashion, but otherwise serviceable.

"Put these on," she said, thrusting the bundle into his hands. "Go on, don't be shy. I've seen plenty of naked men, believe me."

Daníel nodded his thanks and donned the new outfit. She looked him over with a critical eye. He was a bit broader in the shoulders than Albert, but at least the pants didn't stop short of his ankles.

"Go ahead, have a glass if you want," she said expansively, pointing to the bottle. "I guess you've been through hell. A little drink won't hurt."

Again, he did as he was told. Gerda warmed to him even more.

"A toast," she said. "To the Huntress moon. The Conqueror and the Redeemer! May her cold fires burn bright."

They clinked their goblets together.

THENA COULDN'T STOP THINKING ABOUT THE BLACK-EYED witch. In particular, how much he looked like Andros, although the resemblance was subtle. Andros had wavy brown hair and blue eyes. He wasn't nearly as tall. But there was something in the way they both moved. In fleeting expressions.

It intrigued her.

Despite her constant reassurances to Korinna, they weren't making any progress in finding the Danai talisman. The Pythia said they'd be given a hero's welcome, but these witches weren't so trusting. Rafel might have learned something, but she hadn't seen him or Daníel since they first arrived.

It was time to take matters in hand, Thena decided.

She glanced at Korinna, who lay curled on the bed, staring at the wall. The stupid girl had given up. She reminded Thena of poor, vacant Maia. Thena wondered how Maia was faring back at the Temple. It would be a mercy if she'd died. Whatever the witch had done in the yard that awful day with the Archon Basileus, it left her an empty husk. Hardly human anymore. Thena stared at Korinna's long blonde hair. It streamed across the smelly furs in a tangled mess. A mercy, really....

Time seemed to stretch and stand still at the same time. She felt a blankness come over her, heavy and languid. Disjointed images tumbled through her mind. The crash of waves on a shore. Coming and braiding Maia's hair. A pillow in her hands....

Thena returned to herself uncertain how long she'd been standing there. She was closer to the bed but couldn't remember walking over. Korinna had fallen asleep. She snored softly, one slender arm thrown over her face.

Thena clenched her fists and felt the blood rush back to limbs grown stiff and cold.

Andros. That's who she'd been thinking of.

Where are you now? she wondered. Where did you run to? Do you still think of me?

Thena had a feeling he did. They'd shared a great deal, after all, even if he'd never given up his name. But she had come to know him intimately in other ways. Someday, she would have him back. And he would *beg* to do her bidding.

She banged her fist against the door. Korinna rolled over sleepily, her expression turning to alarm when she saw Thena.

"What are you doing?" she hissed.

"Just stay here and keep your mouth shut," Thena snapped.

Korinna started to reply, then changed her mind. She'd learned the hard way what happened when she argued.

Thena told the witch who opened the door—a different one— that she'd remembered some important information they might wish to hear. He told her to wait and returned a few minutes later.

"Come," he said.

The black-eyed witch was waiting in the usual dark, high-ceilinged room, a diamond in his fist. She pulled her cloak tighter around herself. He looked gaunt and she saw lines of bitterness along his mouth that seemed new.

"What is it?" he asked brusquely.

"I was talking with Korinna, trying hard to remember anything that could help," she said. "I think the Pythia has another one of your clan, though I only caught a quick glimpse of him."

His cool stare bored into her.

"I wasn't sure, you see, because he looks different from the others," she said. "The Shields had him. They were dragging across him a courtyard."

"Different how?"

She pretended to think on it. "Well, he looked like he could be a Danai, but with blue eyes. That's a rarity among your people, isn't it?"

The witch's gaze hardened. "Blue eyes?"

"Yes. Very blue. I noticed them from a distance." She paused. "Come to think of it, he had your build, although he was shorter."

Thena's heart beat faster at the witch's reaction. He leaned forward, gripping the armrests of his chair.

"When did you see him?" he asked hoarsely.

"Only a month or so gone, I suppose. I never saw him again except for the one time." She kept her face smooth. "Do you know him?"

The witch ignored this question, to her intense frustration. He seemed to be working through something in his mind, eyes moving restlessly but without seeing.

"If you told me his name, I may have heard someone mention it." She tried to mimic the sultry smile she'd seen Korinna bestow on the handsomest Shield of Apollo, a lithe young man named Agytus. Thena knew she was beautiful, the cook always said so, though the witch didn't seem to be paying her the least bit of attention.

"But Darius went to Samarqand," he murmured. "It can't be."

Darius.

Thena clasped her hands to keep them from shaking. How many times had she asked for his name and received a mocking reply? A hundred? A thousand? She'd nearly killed him for it. And always, always, he had won.

Darius.

She pictured him saying it. Pictured his lips forming the word.

Mine now. I have your true name.

"Well?"

Thena came back with a start. The black-eyed witch had been speaking to her, though she hadn't heard a word of it.

"I'm sorry," she said. "I was....trying to...."

He slammed a hand down on the table with sudden violence.

"How could you not remember this before?" he demanded, livid with rage.

Thena took a step back. "I...I thought...."

But she couldn't get the words out. He rose from the chair and she thought he might kill her then and there, except that the other witch, the long-haired one, laid a hand on his arm.

"Peace, Victor," he said sternly. "It might not be him."

Victor. Thena registered this second piece of information even as her legs felt like they might buckle at any moment.

Poke a tiger with a stick, her mother used to say, and don't be surprised when it bites.

Victor drew a slow breath. "What was he wearing? What did he carry?"

"I...I think he was unarmed," she said quickly. "He wore a plain tunic and trousers."

"This Pythia will pay dearly if she's interfered with my son," he grated.

They kept her for a while after that, but she had little more to say. When the long-haired witch walked her back, she asked him if she might be able to see Daniel, just for a little while. He seemed to feel a bit sorry that Victor had taken his anger out on her and said he'd see what he could do.

As soon as Thena was safely back in her room, she impulsively rushed over to Korinna and gave her a hug. Korinna pulled back, staring at her like she'd grown a second head.

"What are you so happy about?" she demanded.

"I learned Andros's true name," Thena confided. "It's Darius."

"So?"

Thena's face fell. "Aren't you happy for me?"

Korinna pushed her away. "What good does it do us? We'll never get out of here!" Her mouth turned down and she looked as if she might cry. "You're putting us all at risk with your stupid games."

Thena felt a blind rage come over her. "I will tell the Pythia all about you when we get back," she snarled. "And she'll burn you up in the bull."

Korinna gave a mocking laugh. "When we get back? We're never getting back. You're out of your mind." Her voice rose a notch. "I know what you did. Everyone does! You let Andros go. You—"

She didn't get any further because Thena leapt at her. They tumbled to the bed, clawing and tearing at each other's hair. Korinna was taller but Thena had grown up with older sisters and knew how to fight dirty. In the end, Thena sat atop her, pinning Korinna's arms beneath her knees. Korinna struggled uselessly, trying to buck her off, until she ran out of energy and fell quiet.

"She'll burn you to a crisp," Thena whispered. "The first thing that happens is your eyes start to bubble and turn to liquid. They'll run right down those pretty cheeks like tears. You'll smell your own hair burning. Then your skin will turn black and start peeling off—"

"Shut up!"

"Say you're happy."

Korinna gave a last half-hearted buck. "I hate you."

"Say it."

Venom twisted her mouth. "I'm happy for you," she muttered.

"That's all I wanted." Thena stood up, pushing the hair from her eyes. She smiled, showing her dimples. "And now we'll be friends again, won't we?"

AND SO IT HAPPENED THAT LATER THE SAME DAY, A WITCH brought Thena to a part of the keep she had never seen before. It was high up and reached by many long, winding staircases, some of them wide and sweeping and others cramped and narrow. She found she actually missed Daníel and wondered if he would be changed. She felt a bit afraid, though he must still be loyal to her or she would be dead. Unlike Rafel, whose obedience was purchased with the threat of his sister's torture, nothing prevented Daníel from exposing the truth except for the fact that he loved her. She had brought him to the light.

Her Danai escort opened the door to a frigid chamber flanked by two other witches. An old woman sat erect in a chair. She wore a high-necked gown studded with emeralds at the collar. Rings glittered on her fingers. There was something rather frightening about her, Thena thought.

"Knock when you're ready to leave," her escort said, departing with some haste and closing the door behind him.

Daníel leapt to his feet when he saw her.

"Mistress," he murmured, his green eyes lighting up.

The old woman raised an eyebrow and Thena gave a quick shake of her head. *Not here.*

"Who are you?" she asked.

"Who the hell are *you?*" the old woman snapped. "This is *my* room."

Thena squared her shoulders. "I am Thena. An initiate of the Temple of Apollo."

The old woman bared her teeth in a ghastly smile. "A mortal. The final insult."

She was a Valkirin, Thena realized. And her door was guarded. So she had no authority in this place.

"Be quiet, hag," Thena replied calmly. "I'm here to see Daníel, not you."

"Hag?" The woman rose from her chair with surprising agility. "I'll make you choke on your own tongue, you little chit."

Heat flooded Thena's face. She'd like to see this creature with a collar on. That would teach her some manners.

"Stop."

They both turned and glared at Daníel.

"If you make a scene, the guards will come. And I wish to speak with her privately."

"I don't give a damn what you—"

Daníel stared at Gerda and the iciness of his gaze seemed to give her pause.

"Fine." The woman scowled deeply and slurped from a goblet. "But go into the corner. I don't wish to hear it."

Thena swallowed her annoyance and marched away, as far as she could get from the horrid old woman. The wall of ice followed the gentle curve of the tower itself. Gerda's chamber was large, and they managed to retreat far enough that she couldn't eavesdrop on their conversation.

Daníel waited for her to speak first, as was proper.

"Why did they put you up here?" Thena whispered. "Do they suspect?"

He gave a brief shake of his head. "They don't trust me because I'm a Valkirin. That's all. Victor Dessarian would have accused me otherwise. He's not a subtle man."

Her shoulders relaxed. "Good. Have you seen Rafel?"

"Twice. He told me a tunnel is being bored through the ice. They will seek a parley with the other holdfasts."

The politics of the witches was all new to Thena, but she knew it was critical to understand what the Danai intended.

"What exactly happened here?"

"House Dessarian of the Avas Danai managed to take Val Moraine from Eirik Kafsnjór. Eirik's son is alive but he was blinded in some kind of accident." His brow furrowed. "I don't know why he's free, but Gerda is a prisoner. The ice is a result of talismanic magic. A defense mechanism. The other holdfasts will be coming. There's an ancient hatred between our clans."

Thena thought on all this. "We have another problem," she said. "Andros. He knows who I am. Where do you think he would go?"

"Back to the forest, most likely."

"So we have to assume his people know. Would the Danai come here?"

"They might. But they wouldn't expect you to be here. Most likely they will attack Delphi directly."

She bit her lip. "We're running out of time. How long before the tunnel is finished?"

"Rafel said a week." His green eyes searched her face. "We could run, Mistress. You know where the Talisman of Folding is. Leave the guards to me."

"What about Korinna?"

"Leave her," he said without hesitation.

Thena had no qualms about that. But she very much feared returning to the Pythia empty-handed. They had been tasked with bringing back one of the daēva talismans. And there was a chance one of the Danai in this keep was the one they sought. She had to be sure.

"Not yet. Do you think Rafel is following his orders?"

"He hasn't betrayed us yet."

That wasn't quite the same thing.

"Do they trust him?"

"They seem to."

"Then we stay until the tunnel is complete. As long as no word from outside comes in, we're safe." She glanced at Gerda. "She might know something too. Be nice to her. See what you can find out."

"I miss you, Mistress," he murmured, and the heat of his gaze conjured a warm flush to her neck.

"I know, Demetrios," she whispered, showing her dimples. "When we return to Solis, we will be together again."

"You swear it?"

Anger deepened the heat in her face. How dare he ask her to swear! But it wouldn't do to upset him. She glanced at the old witch, who stared at them with glacial eyes. If Gerda weren't here, Demetrios might demand more. Desire and loathing made her shiver.

"I swear it," she said, touching his fingertips. "Walk in the light, Demetrios. And do not forget me when the time comes."

A muscle in his jaw feathered. "I couldn't if I tried, mistress," he said with despair.

FOR THE LOVE OF FAIR CAECILIA

The Kafsnjór ancestors who built Val Moraine were belligerent and frequently cruel, but they did like to throw parties. The dining hall was cavernous, with a hundred garish octagonal tables inset with gold and gems. It had a platform at one end where musicians performed and an open space at the other to accommodate the drunken brawls that inevitably ensued. Fortunately, the fuzzying effects of alcohol made it difficult to touch the Nexus, else the gatherings would have caused far greater destruction.

The hall had played host to weddings and wakes, victory celebrations and siege councils. During the Iron Wars, some of the Kafsnjórs had even flown their abbadax in circles through its lofty heights to keep the animals exercised—and themselves from succumbing to "ice fever," the skin-crawling sensation one developed after a year of being stuck inside the keep with three hostile armies camped on the adjacent peaks.

But never in its long and checkered history had the hall sat almost empty, as it did now.

Three of Victor's young Dessarians occupied a table near the stage. One of them made a jest and the others laughed loudly, turning to stare at the young man who sat on the opposite side of the hall, as far as he could get from his kinsmen.

Galen ignored them, biting savagely into a raw carrot. What he wouldn't give for a nice fat rabbit! But the thought of rabbits made him think of Ellard and Galen found he'd lost his appetite. He pushed the plate away and stared up at the gloom-shrouded ceiling. The dining hall sat in the heart of Val Moraine. This didn't make it any warmer, he reflected, but at least he didn't have to look at the outer wall. He spent all day, every day hacking away with a pick and would die a happy man if he never saw a single shard of ice again.

"You should eat something," Ellard said. "You've got to keep your strength up."

Galen turned so he could just see his friend from the corner of his eye. It was better not to look at him straight on. His face was intact, but his throat....

"I know," he whispered.

Ellard still came to him, but he wasn't so angry anymore. They talked of old times. Once, he'd let Galen hold his hand. It was warm. But that had made him weep and Ellard didn't do it again.

Now Galen listened to them talking at the other table. He couldn't help himself, although he knew what they were saying. *Traitor. Liar.*

Murderer.

The others had always considered him odd, but no one actively hated him before the whole disaster with Nazafareen. Mostly he was just ignored. Though they all belonged to House Dessarian, the daëvas naturally gravitated toward their own kind. The woodworkers were methodical and industrious. The arborists tended to be quiet and contemplative, like the the trees they tended. Some years back, Galen had joined the scouts, thinking it would get him away from the compound, but they were a cocky bunch, strong in earth power and eager to prove it. When Galen showed no interest in joining their contests, they thought him stuck-up and aloof. Worse, that he believed himself superior because his father was the notorious Victor Dessarian. He soon quit and joined the cadre who gathered food.

Galen knew the forest well from his own ramblings and had no trouble finding acorns, birds' eggs, mushrooms and the like. He even hunted a little, though the other daēvas found raw meat disgusting. Yet he'd never truly settled into this new life. Part of him was always waiting for something else. He couldn't shake the nagging feeling he was supposed to be another person entirely.

Galen blamed this alienation on the loss of his parents. Neither was dead, yet he was an orphan by any measure. The lonely child in him seized on the idea that if he had his mother back, she could fix everything. Tell him what to do.

Now he could hardly meet her eyes.

"I danced on this table once," Ellard said wistfully. "Drunk as a lord. Neblis played the zither. She was quite good before—"

His voice faded away as Galen sensed someone approaching from behind. He chomped on the carrot and refused to turn. He wouldn't give them the satisfaction of appearing afraid.

"Do you mind?"

Galen glanced up in surprise. Rafel stood there, a plate in his hands.

"Sure," Galen replied, trying to keep the pathetic eagerness from his voice.

Rafel took the chair across from him and set the plate down, though he made no move to eat. Galen's eyes slid over the iron collar. The silence lengthened.

"You were an arborist, right?" Galen asked, a little desperately.

"Yeah." Rafel stabbed a slice of pear with his fork.

"Which groves did you tend?"

"South from Alden's Glen to the border with Fiala."

"I know that area well. I used to swim in Long Lake."

Rafel smiled for the first time. "Me too. The place you can jump off the rocks?"

"That one." Galen grinned back. "I swam into the beaver dam once. But they had young and the female got mad. Almost slapped me with her tail." He laughed. "I brought them fish, though, and we made friends."

"There's an oak in that grove more than six thousand years old," Rafel said reverently. "It survived the great burning. One of the few that did."

"The great burning?"

"I guess only the arborists talk about it anymore. There was a wildfire hundreds of years ago. It destroyed most of the forest."

"Like the song, you mean." Galen hummed a snatch. Then Rafel took it up and they sang softly together.

> For the love of fair Caecilia
> For the heart of a fickle maiden
> The beeches mourn, bole and bough
> The larches blaze, ash and cinder
> Through the long night, through the red dawn
> Hot blows the Viper's breath
> For the hate of fair Caecilia
> For the hate of a Danai maiden
> Driven to the shores
> Of that windswept sea
> Into the dark waters, into the cold depths
> 'Twined forever drift the lovers lost

Their voices died away. It was a slow melody, with sweet high notes—like on the word *forever*—that sank to a dirge in the melancholy places. They were both tenors and Galen thought they'd made a fair job of it. He snuck a look at the other table. The three Dessarians were gone. Only a few lumen crystals remained lit and shadows cloaked the enormous hall.

"I always wondered who the Viper was," Galen mused. "Some jealous suitor, I imagine."

"It's a very old song, I think. My grandfather used to sing it. He'd get teary at the end sometimes but when I asked what it meant, he wouldn't tell me."

"It has to be made-up, don't you think? Even a daēva gone mad with jealousy couldn't start a fire. If there truly was such a catastrophe, it must have been a lightning strike."

Rafel shrugged. "Perhaps. Ysabel used to say——" He cut off and stared down at his plate.

"Your sister?" Galen asked gently. "She was always kind to me."

Rafel nodded, his eyes guarded.

"Is she...?" Galen fumbled for words. Alive? Dead? Still in Delphi?

"I have to go." Rafel abruptly pushed his chair back. "See you in the stables."

Galen watched him leave, wishing he'd never mentioned it.

"I like him," Ellard said thoughtfully. He'd returned the instant Rafel passed through the massive double doors. "I think he needs a friend almost as badly as you do."

"What do you think happened to him?"

"What do *you* think?"

"Something awful."

Ellard leaned back in the chair, crossing his legs at the ankles like he used to do. "Well, you're right not to ask him. He'll tell you if he wants to."

"Do you think he knows about me?"

"Of course."

"Then why doesn't he hate me?"

"Hard to say." Ellard mulled this over. "Maybe he hates someone else so much, he has no energy left to bother about you."

That made a kind of sense. Galen pushed his plate away. He hummed softly as he departed the gloomy hall, and the shades of past revelries gathered in the darkest corners to listen.

For the love of fair Caecilia
For the heart of a fickle maiden...

❧ 8 ❧

ASH VARECA

Javid strode up the broad stone steps of Izad Asabana's mansion, nodding at the young girl sweeping the entryway. She blushed and gave him a shy smile. All the servants knew his face now. He was Asabana's dashing new pilot, and rumors of his exploits in Delphi had turned him into something of a local legend. Like mushrooms after a hard rain, the tales grew thick and fast, each embellishing on the last. Some said he'd used spell dust to set the Pythia's hair on fire. Others that he'd led a revolt in the Assembly and fought his way free when the Polemarch's soldiers attacked, the only survivor of that bloody day.

Javid's silence on the matter just encouraged them. The truth, of course, was that he had done nothing but get himself arrested, hang around in a dungeon for a few weeks, and then narrowly escape being burned alive—not because he did anything brave, but because Nazafareen saved him. But he figured no one would believe the bare facts at this point, so he kept his mouth shut.

"Where's your master?" he asked the girl.

"Dining on the terrace," she replied.

"Thank you," he said courteously, giving her a small bow that made her blush deepen.

A brutal heatwave had smothered Samarqand for the last fortnight, so arid his sweat seemed to evaporate the instant it left his pores. Javid glanced longingly at a fountain spewing tepid water in the blue-and-white tiled entrance hall. He was tempted to cup a handful and splash it on the back of his neck, but the girl was watching from the corner of her eye. He thought of the iced wine Asabana would surely be enjoying on the terrace and swallowed. Javid usually declined his boss's offers of drink—it was best to keep one's wits sharp when dealing with Asabana—but Javid decided he would have a cup, not because it would quench his thirst—it wouldn't—but because he planned to ask a rather large favor and needed courage.

Sunlight smacked his face like an open forge as he stepped onto the balcony. The Zaravshan River had shriveled to a narrow ribbon of sluggish, muddy water, leaving the once green groves on either bank withered and brown. Asabana sat in the shade of a canopy erected above a table with a few simple dishes laid out, things Javid's mother might make. He smelled chickpea and tomato stew with hints of saffron. It wasn't the lavish meal typical of the Persian nobility, but Izad Asabana held open disdain for the plump aristocrats of the court. His birth had been even lower than Javid's and he had no shame of it. Quite the opposite.

Then Asabana leaned back and Javid realized he wasn't alone. His alchemist, Marzban Khorram-Din, sat to his left, along with Leila, the alchemist's daughter. Javid hesitated. He'd hoped to speak to Asabana privately, but at the same time, he didn't wish to wait any longer.

"My boy!" Asabana called, spotting him. "Come!" He waved one hand, rings winking in the sunlight.

Javid went to the table and bowed, much lower than he'd given the servant girl, to each of them in turn. The alchemist merely stared at him with his cool, piercing black eyes. He wore a long beard, as all in his profession did, and trousers secured by a wide sash that held several bags of spell dust. Leila looked modestly away, but he thought he saw a flicker of something cross her face. Curiosity? Amusement?

"My lord," Javid said.

Asabana beamed at him with his usual joviality and Javid thought of the pilot he'd replaced, who had skimmed spell dust from the shipments and tried to sell it on the black market. It was whispered he'd been thrown alive out of a wind ship over the Cimmerian Sea.

"We were just talking about you," Asabana said. "Sit down."

Javid chose a chair on the opposite side of the table, facing the three of them. The meal had been mostly eaten, and a wasp crawled over a skin of sticky sauce on one of the plates.

"Were you, my lord?" he asked lightly.

"Don't worry, I have no complaints. You've done well. Five runs to the palace so far?"

"Six, my lord," Javid replied, knowing full well that Asabana knew the correct number.

"Of course, six. And does the prince seem well?"

"I haven't had the pleasure of meeting him yet, my lord. A chamberlain takes the deliveries."

"Ah well, perhaps you will in time. I imagine you're here to get paid." He waved to a servant who waited in the shade of the doorway. "More wine. You'll have a cup with us, won't you? It's from the south. A bit rough, but it does the trick." Asabana laughed. "What else is there to do in this damned heat but get drunk?"

Javid smiled politely, noting that Asabana's eyes were clear and sharp.

"About my wages, my lord." He glanced at the alchemist, who was staring into the distance as though lost in thought. "I have a request."

"Not a raise already," Asabana growled.

"No, my lord. But I wish you to keep the money and spend it for me...elsewhere."

Asabana must have noticed his glances at the alchemist and

his daughter for he slapped a palm on the table. "Speak your mind, son. I trust these two with my life. They can hear whatever you have to say."

Javid drew a deep breath. Leila watched him closely, but he kept his eyes on Asabana.

"There's a prisoner in the Polemarch's dungeons. A Stygian thief. I want to get him out."

Asabana leaned back and took a long sip of wine. "That'll be tricky."

Javid remembered the last time he saw Katsu. Soldiers had come to their cell, wearing cloaks with the crossed-swords emblem of the Archon Eponymos. They'd escorted Javid past the dungeon guards and would have made it out to the street if the Polemarch's men hadn't arrived and dragged him off to the Acropolis.

"You attempted it once, my lord," Javid said.

"That was before the Polemarch declared martial law."

"Everything has a price, my lord. You told me so yourself."

Asabana gave a thin smile. "Yes. The question is whether you want to pay it."

Javid's father had always warned him about borrowing money, and this would be no normal debt. They both knew it. But for all his claims to being a soulless mercenary, Javid had a soft spot for the Stygian. He would likely be dead if their paths hadn't crossed. And *that* was a debt he wouldn't turn his back on.

"What will it cost?" he asked.

"A lot more than this purse." Asabana held up Javid's wages for the last two weeks.

"Then keep my wages for as long as necessary. I'll work overtime. Anything you want."

Asabana studied him with an inscrutable expression. "A loan, you mean."

"If you would indulge me, my lord."

Asabana tossed the purse in the air and caught it again. Then he poured out half the coins on the table and handed it back to Javid. "A man's got to have some spending money. I won't have my pilots going about in ratty clothes. I've got my reputation to consider. So I'll keep half your wages."

"Thank you, my lord." Javid sensed more coming. It didn't surprise him. Asabana was the kind of man who would take every ounce of leverage he could get.

"But when the time comes that I need a favor from you, I expect to get it, no questions asked."

"I agree," Javid said immediately.

"Good. What's this man's name?"

"Katsu, my lord."

"A thief, you say?"

Javid nodded.

"Who'd he steal from?"

"Just another man on the street," Javid lied. "He's a nobody."

"I'll see what I can do. Things are ugly in Delphi, son, and getting uglier. With the Ecclesia dissolved, the Pythia's pulling all the strings. I hear she kicked the Marakai out of the port. The emperor in Tjanjin won't be happy about that." He stood. "Don't you have a delivery today?"

"I do, my lord."

"Keep your eyes open. Word is King Cambyses is on his last legs. It won't be long now."

Javid felt relieved Asabana didn't ask why he wanted Katsu out of the dungeon. Apparently, that was immaterial.

He bowed to Asabana, and then Marzban Khorram-Din and his daughter. The alchemist gave the slightest nod. Leila gracefully inclined her head. Javid guessed she was about thirty years of age. Despite her cool demeanor, he couldn't help but admire her. Her father was training her to be the first woman alchemist in Samarqand. She was reputed to be brilliant, if standoffish.

So Javid respected her, though he didn't trust either of them.

They were all lackeys of Izad Asabana—and that went double for himself.

"Thank you for your gracious hospitality," he said, striding toward the door into the mansion.

"Son!" Asabana called. "Shall this thief be told who his benefactor is?"

Javid paused. "No, my lord. I'd prefer to remain anonymous."

Asabana nodded his approval. "Always better that way."

A WEEK PASSED. JAVID MADE TWO MORE DELIVERIES TO THE palace and felt confident of the routine now. He greeted the other pilots in the field and climbed the ladder into his assigned wind ship, the *Ash Vareca*, a phrase with several ambiguous meanings. The first was *most glorious*, but depending on the context, it could also mean *crafty* or *criminal*, which Javid thought rather apt.

Unlike his old ship, the *Fravashi*, she was a beautiful vessel, newly built and with every surface polished to a high gleam. He used a flint to light the burner that inflated the sack with hot air and cast off from the mooring. The ship rose slowly, finally catching an easterly current that carried him over the city wall and toward the Rock of Ariamazes. It occupied the center of the city and resembled a square boulder half a league across. The only openings were narrow slits at the top. Otherwise, it was all of a piece. Danai work, dating back to the days when Samarqand had close relations with the forest clan. The low angle of the sun from the west meant the streets on the eastern side were cast in permanent shadow. And since the sun never set, they were much cooler than the surrounding neighborhoods and extremely desirable real estate for well-to-do merchants and minor nobility who couldn't afford a large estate outside the city.

Javid used a pinch of spell dust to correct his course and alit in the field abutting the southern face of the Rock designated for wind ships. As usual it was a beehive of activity. The Rock of Aria-mazes was a small city unto itself, run by an army of bakers, cooks, wine stewards, cup-bearers, body servants, scullery maids and grooms. At a somewhat higher rank were the physicians, bureaucrats, musicians, scribes, messengers and emissaries, although they were still considered the "Outer Court." Javid knew the true power lay in what was called the Inner Court, the princelings and concubines and courtiers and eunuchs. This Inner Court was managed by a powerful official known as the Hazara-patis, which meant Master of a Thousand. And with the king on his deathbed, the Hazara-patis was the true power behind the throne.

Javid deflated the sack and tied down to the mooring peg. Despite the bustle of ships being unloaded, a pall hung over the Rock. There was a palpable sense of uncertainty in the hushed voices of the servants. He tucked the lacquered box beneath his arm and went straight to the side gate where he was accustomed to meeting the Chief Steward, who reported to the Hazara-patis, and handing over the dust. But this time was different.

The steward who awaited him gave a bow adequate to Javid's station, which was not high at all, so the man's next words came as a surprise.

"You are summoned," he said.

"To whom?"

"Prince Shahak."

Years of practice allowed Javid to mask his shock, but his stomach gave a slow roll.

"I am unworthy of this honor," he murmured fervently, knowing it would be the gravest insult to reveal how little he wished to meet his client in person. There was nothing for it but to follow the man into the torch-lit darkness of the great fortress.

The royal apartments were buried in the very heart of the Rock, and Javid used the journey to review all he knew about Prince Shahak. He was thirty-two years old and unmarried. He was also the eldest son of King Cambyses and thus next in line for the throne, but his mother, the Queen, favored her middle son and was scheming with certain sympathetic elements of the nobility to undermine Shahak's claim. The support of the Hazara-patis would be crucial, but Javid was unsure where the man stood. Personally, Javid didn't care who took the throne. One princeling was much the same as the next to him. But his boss, Asabana, very much desired Shahak to win his claim because Asabana had power over him: spell dust.

Prince Shahak purchased vast quantities of it on a regular basis. Clearly he had a strong interest in magic. He must have an alchemist who knew the language of spell dust, and if the man was anything like Marzban Khorram-Din, Javid shuddered to meet him. So they would probably both be waiting.

Javid had visited the palace many times before on business for the Merchants' Guild and the layout of the Outer Court was familiar to him: the squinting scribes hunched over their scrolls, the audience chambers with columns soaring up to the dim ceiling above, the murals and bas-reliefs everywhere of hunts and battles and processions of men bringing gifts to the king.

But he had never before been to the royal apartments—not even close. As they moved deeper into the Rock, the corridors narrowed into labyrinthine zig-zag patterns, the better to defend against attack. Javid saw far fewer servants, and they crept about on silk-soled slippers that made no sound. The air grew colder. It smelled of ancient stone and he shivered to think he walked in a place the sun had not touched in more than a thousand years. Three times he was wordlessly handed over to another servant of higher rank, who led him deeper still. His disquiet mounted with each step. Why did the prince wish to see him? Was he displeased with the last shipment? If so, what would he do? The nobility was notorious for punishing messengers, and that went triple for royalty.

Javid didn't bother trying to memorize the route. He would be escorted out with the prince's blessing, or not at all.

At last they reached two doors, each ten paces high and carved with fantastic beasts. Javid was given to the chamberlain waiting outside, who in turn gave three smart raps on the door and swung it wide.

Holy Father keep me, he thought.

Javid stepped through but saw nothing but the carpet because etiquette demanded a full prostration, which began as a bow that grew lower and lower until the knees bent and the forehead touched the floor, at which point one stretched out face-down with the arms reaching above the head. He performed it with great care and elegance.

"You may rise," a taut voice declared.

Javid waited another heartbeat, then stood but kept his gaze rooted on the carpet.

"What is your name?" the prince asked.

"Javid, your royal highness."

The prince must have made some sign, for the chamberlain withdrew, softly closing the great doors behind him. They were well-oiled and made only the gentlest whisper.

"You may look upon us."

Javid did as commanded. Prince Shahak was thin as a blade with large brown eyes and thick eyelashes. His face was narrow, his nose suitably aquiline. He wore his black hair loose and parted in the center. Slender fingers emerged from the sleeves of a heavy, embroidered robe in shades of green and purple. Javid had heard he was handsome, and the lines of his face suggested it as a possibility, but there was something a bit ghastly about the man lounging in a large plush chair. His skin had a gray cast and hung loose on his bones. The flickering light of a brazier in the corner did not flatter him. Javid felt a trickle of sweat run down his spine. After the corridor outside, the room was smoky and stiflingly warm.

"Where is it?" the prince asked.

His tone was offhand but his fingers had a slight tremor.

Javid stepped forward and knelt before him, offering up the lacquered box.

"Ah."

Prince Shahak snatched it from his hands and opened the lid. His whole body seemed to relax at the sight of the sparkling dust it contained. He produced a tiny silver spoon from the sleeve of his robe and scooped up a bit of dust. Unsure if he was supposed to retreat in the absence of a direct command, Javid stayed where he was, kneeling at the prince's feet. He heard a sharp inhalation followed by a sigh of pleasure.

"Come," the prince exclaimed in a different voice, this one full of life and good humor. "Have a cup of wine with me, Javid. I have company so rarely these days." He laughed. "Not honest company, at least. You wouldn't lie to me, would you?"

The sudden change—and the astonishingly familiar attitude, as if Javid were an old friend—caught him so off guard he merely blinked for a moment. Protocol was the lifeblood of the Persian court. If one wrote down every rule, every proper form of address, for every occasion, it would fill a hundred scrolls in the tiny, spidery lettering the scribes uses for long-distance messages. Each aspect of life at court required a flowery, elaborate ritual. And here was Prince Shahak staring at him frankly and inviting him for a cup of wine.

Not to mention the fact he had just *inhaled spell dust*. Javid couldn't begin to imagine what effect that might have on a person. He'd never heard of such a thing. Never even suspected it could be done.

"Your Highness," Javid managed. "You do me too great an honor."

"Oh, rubbish," the prince declared, bounding out of the chair with sudden energy. To Javid's complete and utter amazement, he seized another chair and dragged it over. "Sit."

Small tables scattered about the room held statues and other knickknacks. Javid's gaze desperately searched the room for the wine. He finally spotted it, in a golden decanter perched upon the hindquarters of a roaring griffin.

"Please, allow me to pour for you first, Your Highness," he said, more confused and unsure than he'd ever been in his entire life.

"Yes, do," the prince said, discreetly inhaling another spoonful of spell dust. The color had returned to his cheeks and his brown eyes shone with curiosity.

"I've heard about you," the prince said when Javid had sat down and offered him a cup.

"Indeed, your highness?" Javid replied, pretending ignorance. Who knew what rumors had reached the palace?

"You were captured by the Pythia."

"It was a piece of ill luck," Javid said smoothly, though his bowels instantly turned to water. Holy Father, how much did the prince know? His mission to the darklands had involved a scheme to evade the king's taxes. Javid could well imagine the hideous death he would face if the truth came out.

"Tell me about her. I wish to know everything."

"I only spoke with her once." Javid remembered every detail of that hair-raising encounter. "She's young, less than thirty I'd guess, although no one seems to know her age. She has a commanding presence. Lord Asabana says she's the true power in Delphi now. The Polemarch and the Archons do her bidding."

"I fear she will wait until we're all squabbling over my father's corpse to invade," the prince said darkly. "Why does she hate us so?"

"That I cannot say, your majesty. But I know she despises the daēvas with all her heart."

The prince barked a harsh laugh. "She simply fears what she does not have. Magic." He took a long sip of wine. "My mother and brothers are scheming against me," the prince said, his gaze growing distant. "She does not approve of me."

Javid said nothing. Who knew who was listening?

"She doesn't understand. Power is there for the taking. But one must be willing to take risks." He leaned forward, a gleam in his eye. "Give me your cup."

Javid did so.

"Watch." The prince closed his eyes. Then he tossed the cup into the air. Red liquid flew in an arc. Javid felt a sudden intense burst of heat and then he heard wingbeats. The goblet vanished and a white dove fluttered upward, frantic. The prince held out a hand and it settled on his wrist.

Javid realized his mouth was hanging open and shut it with a snap. It wasn't possible. He understood the basic principles of magic. The daēvas could directly work the three elements of earth, air and water. Only the Vatras had mastery over fire. Spell dust also had a variety of uses, but they were all similar to elemental magic. But what the prince had just done.... That was transformation of one object into another. A dead thing to a living thing. Even the daēvas couldn't do that, Javid felt certain.

Prince Shahak leaned back, weariness marking his face. A thin line of blood dripped from his left nostril.

"Leave us now," he said.

Javid made the prostration, his mind racing. No wonder the Queen didn't approve of her eldest son. He was dabbling in arts well beyond the bounds of prudence. And it was just as clearly taking its toll.

"Return in three days. You will come to me personally from now on."

"Yes, Your Highness," he murmured, backing from the room.

An elderly chamberlain with huge ears waited in the corridor to escort him from the Rock. Neither spoke a single word until Javid stepped into the sunlight and they uttered terse pleasantries. No money changed hands—that would be horribly crass. The prince had a credit line with Izad Asabana and his accounts were settled monthly.

But if he *had* been given a sack of gold...Well, Javid might have tossed it into the *Ash Vareca*, set a course for the darklands and never looked back.

༄ 9 ༄

NEW HOPE

Fingers of mist curled around the *Chione*'s square sails as she drifted into the fogbank. Nazafareen gripped the rail with her left hand, peering into the gloom. Darius stood next to her with a lumen crystal, but its blue glow hardly penetrated the dense mist. All was still except for the muffled slap of water against the hull.

As soon as they entered the fog, the wind died completely. If the Marakai hadn't summoned a current to carry the ship forward, Nazafareen doubted they would be moving at all. As it was, the pace seemed terribly slow. She burned with impatience to meet Sakhet-ra-katme, not only because she might know how to find the talismans. Of all the daēva clans, the Marakai were the strongest healers. Surely Sakhet would know how to fix the holes in Nazafareen's mind. And perhaps the knowledge would offer some clue as to why Nazafareen had this strange breaking power, and what it meant.

Everyone had gathered on deck, though her companions were no more than faint outlines in the mist. And then one of the crew gave a shout. The *Chione* glided through the last ragged fingers of fog into an open space. The stars reappeared overhead and

Selene's warm yellow light burnished water as calm as a mirror. Nazafareen gripped the rail tighter.

Then she saw something small and dark on the surface. The others saw it too. Immediately, four Marakai dove gracefully over the side and swam over to the piece of flotsam, examining it with grim faces. Without a word, they vanished beneath the surface for many long minutes. Finally, they emerged and swam back to the boat, climbing up a rope ladder.

"There's more wreckage at the bottom," one told Captain Mafuone. "The remains of a boat. Part of the hull is wedged in the rocks."

"And Sakhet?" the captain asked in a tight voice.

"We found no body. But the currents are strong in the depths."

He handed the captain a piece of wood. Most of it was charred, but Nazafareen could see traces of red paint on one side.

"Holy Father," Darius muttered.

Kallisto strode forward, tears springing to her eyes. "It cannot be," she said. She reached for the piece of wood, then drew her hand back as if she couldn't bear to touch it. "I recognize the color. It was her houseboat." Her mouth twisted in sorrow, and Herodotus put an arm around her shoulders, looking stricken himself.

Nazafareen realized at that moment she had not truly believed in the fire daēvas. They were bogeymen, a shadowy threat with no substance. Her hatred had focused on the Pythia. But here was evidence that at least one of them walked free in the world. She felt a flush of shame that she'd been thinking only of herself and what Sakhet could do for her.

"It was the Vatra," Kallisto said in bitter confirmation. "He found her first. And we must assume he learned what she knew before he killed her. He could be hunting the talisman at this very minute."

"Do you know what he looks like?" Captain Mafuone demanded.

"Not really. Just that he is red-haired, like all the Vatras. My visions come in flashes and they are veiled with metaphor."

The captain exchanged an uneasy glance with her current master. "In what way?"

"The Vatra has the face of a wolf, or sometimes a jackal. I've seen him savaging a Marakai girl with his teeth." Kallisto swallowed, her face pale. "But I've also seen her wearing the Blue Crown of the Khepresh." She raised a hand. "Don't ask what she looks like. I cannot see her face either. I think she must be warded and the spell is strong enough to cloak her even from Dionysius."

Darius stepped forward. "May I?" he asked deferentially.

Captain Mafuone handed him the piece of wood. He sniffed it and rubbed a bit of charcoal between his fingers.

"This happened recently," he said. "Within the last hour. He can't be far ahead of us."

Captain Mafuone nodded. "We'll make for the Isles. The others must be told what happened here. And it's the nearest land, this Vatra could be there." She paused. "Sakhet belonged to both the Selk and the Nyx. We must inform the viziers."

A gentle rain began to fall as the *Chione* set a new course. The fog thinned and began to break apart. Nazafareen sensed the magic shielding Sakhet's home was fading and she felt a deep sadness although they had never met.

"It's my fault," Kallisto muttered. "I failed to warn her in time."

"It is *not* your fault, my dear," Herodotus said sternly. "You know birds aren't always reliable. You did everything you could."

"If he finds this girl, what will he do with her?" Nazafareen asked.

"The talismans made the Gale. I imagine they have the power to bring it down."

"So he won't kill her?"

"I don't think so. Not until he's used her." Kallisto looked at Herodotus. "All may not be lost. There is the matter of Nabu-bal-idinna's scroll."

"Lest the power corrupt their hearts, they shall not know it nor touch it until the fourth talisman brings it forth," Herodotus recited.

"You mean he can't use her without this fourth talisman?" Darius asked.

"If the alchemist spoke truly." Kallisto sighed. "Sakhet might have known what it was. Or the Vatra might know already. But how can we protect the talismans when the only person who knew about them is dead?"

No one had an answer to this.

THE ISLES OF THE MARAKAI COMPRISED FIVE BARREN HUMPS OF rock where the waters of the White Sea and the Austral Ocean flowed together. They had formed millennia before from volcanic eruptions on the sea floor and although the fiery calderas were now dormant, sulfurous steam still rose through vents, making the climate around the Isles warmer than the surrounding ocean.

Captain Mafuone and her crew were Sheut Marakai, which meant *shadow*. Their home was the southernmost island, but the *Chione* sailed past it and made for the neighboring isle of the Selk.

Ships crowded the harbor beyond the breakwater. Most of the sails were emblazoned with the image of a gray-striped cat, though a few displayed the giant carp of the Jengu and the Blue Crown of the Khepresh. A ramshackle collection of mortared stone buildings sat along the shoreline. Herodotus said the town was called New Hope and had been built by the Stygians, the only mortals to live in the darklands. They eked out an existence fishing and diving for pearls, which they traded to the Marakai for fruits and vegetables from Solis, and items of wood or metal. The glow of lumen crystals spilled through the windows of the houses, blue and white and yellow, and Nazafareen's heart lifted to see land again.

Barking dogs ran up and down the long stone jetty. The *Chione* glided smoothly alongside the wharf and sailors leapt ashore to fasten the mooring lines. A few hopefuls from the town had gathered at the vessel's arrival, but the captain waved them off. There was no cargo to trade since they'd dumped it all overboard.

"Come," she said to Kallisto. "We'll go straight to the vizier."

Kallisto nodded. "I'd like to bring Nazafareen and Darius, if you'll permit it."

The captain hesitated. "It's forbidden for outsiders to enter the Mer."

"I am an outsider," Kallisto pointed out. "And I think the vizier would wish to hear Darius's story about the Oracle of Delphi. Nazafareen is a breaker of magic. She is also part daēva. So in fact, I am the only mortal among us."

The captain considered this. "I suppose things are changing, though the Selk vizier is a fussy man. All he cares about is pleasing Anuketmatma and hoarding the Selk treasure. Only the Sheut believe in the Vatras' return."

Kallisto snorted. "Whether he believes or not is immaterial. It is what he knows that we must discover."

"May I come too?" Herodotus asked eagerly. "I'm writing a history—"

"Oh, what the hell," Captain Mafuone muttered, striding down the gangplank.

"Was that a *yes*?" Herodotus whispered to Nazafareen.

She shrugged and they all hurried to catch up.

SUCH A CHARMING MONSTER

Nicodemus sipped his mug of bitter ale and watched the ships bobbing at anchor. One had just come limping into the harbor, minus both her masts, but his keen eyes noted the tentacled tattoos of the crew. Sheut. Not the one he sought.

As usual, the crowd in the tavern was a mixed bunch. Most of the mortals here had roots in the Isles going back generations to the first wave of refugees fleeing the war. They were close-knit and hardworking. The Stygian economy relied on the barter system and everyone knew each other. If you were a liar or a cheat, you wouldn't get away with it for long.

But there were always a few new faces. The Isles attracted a certain type of person, he'd found. They were almost all men, though a woman did turn up from time to time. Invariably, they were running from something. Life in the Isles was hard and cold and dark. You didn't come here unless you had nowhere else to go and nothing left to lose.

Like the pale-haired fellow at the next table. His clothes were far too well-made for a native and a sapphire ring glittered on his finger, but his eyes had all the empathy of a dead carp. They met Nicodemus's for an instant, then flicked away. Some minor noble from Solis no doubt. Nico had noticed him watching the young girl who swept the floor. She was a skinny thing in a shapeless tunic and trousers she'd probably inherited from one of her brothers. But her small breasts poked through the fabric and the man's eyes crawled over them like maggots.

Nicodemus smiled to himself. He leaned over.

"Who'd you murder?" he asked in a conspiratorial whisper.

The man's eyes widened. "I beg your pardon?" he said in a strangled voice.

"Must have been someone important, eh? Someone who mattered. Did they offer you exile? Or did you just jump on the first Marakai ship you saw?"

The blood drained from the man's face. Nico raised his own cup and downed its contents with a grimace. "Nothing like fermented kelp. We'll be shitting black for a week." He slid his chair closer. The noble inched back as if he had the plague. "Or maybe you liked to hurt little girls? Is that it?"

A muscle twitched in the man's cheek. How sadly predictable they were, Nico thought.

"I'll give you a piece of friendly advice," he said softly. "Whoever you used to be, you're nobody now. Just a piece of scum that washed ashore. Fuck with these people and they'll chop you up and feed you to the gulls."

The man stood so quickly he sent his chair tumbling over. He hurried out of the tavern without a backward glance.

Nico watched him disappear into the crowds swarming around the docks. He understood the instinct, even if he held such men in contempt. Nicodemus was a hunter too. But it wasn't his fault. It was *their* fault. The Kiln had made him that way.

His gaze settled on a boy of about twelve who was desultorily swiping the tables with a dirty scrap of cloth. A lock of hair fell across the boy's forehead and he pushed it away with the back of his hand. The resemblance was superficial, but something tightened in Nico's chest. A memory surfaced as often happened when he hadn't gotten enough sleep. He tried to shove it back down, but he knew it was already too late when instead of the rancid stink of the tavern, he smelled an earthen burrow deep underground, the air thick with dust and something worse....

ATTICUS MOANED IN HIS SLEEP. HIS COLOR WAS BAD, GHOSTLY white with patches of red mottling his neck. Nico crouched over him and examined the tiny puncture wounds on his brother's foot for the tenth time. As he feared, they were festering. The venom of a rock spider would eat through flesh and bone if it wasn't cleaned out thoroughly. He trickled the last precious drops of water over the ankle. It wasn't enough. The foot needed soaking or Atticus might lose it. Plus they had nothing to drink now. Nico licked dry lips. He'd have to go for water.

He crawled to the corner where he kept his gear. The burrow was about ten paces across, with a low ceiling and two tunnels leading out. He used the wider one when he had to go to the surface. The other was an emergency escape route. His mother had taught him that before she died. Never, ever dig a burrow with only one way out.

"I'll be back soon," he told Atticus.

His brother rolled over and opened his eyes. They were blue-black, the same as Nico's. Like the summer sea on a moonlit night, Domitia used to say when she was being nice. Nico had always liked the sound of the words *moonlit night*, though neither held any real meaning for him. And it had been a long time since Domitia was nice.

"I want to go too," Atticus said, brows drawing into a stubborn line.

"You can't walk," Nico replied wearily. "Just sit tight."

"I can walk."

"You can't." He felt frustration building and gentled his tone. "If I see a ship, I'll tell you all about it."

Atticus stuck his lip out but quit arguing. It was a game they played on the rare occasions Nico let him come along to the dunes where the water was. Sometimes they spotted Marakai vessels off in the distance and tried to guess where the ships might be headed. The world outside the Kiln was a great mystery. Only Gaius knew what it looked like—or what it used to look like. It could all be like the Kiln now, though Atticus refused to believe that. So when they were alone together, they gave their imaginations free rein to conjure the wonders it might hold.

"If trouble comes while I'm gone...." Nico looked at his brother's swollen foot. Could he even crawl out of the escape tunnel? "Never mind. It won't." He grabbed his gear. "Back in a few hours." He forced a smile. "Don't worry, I'll get you fixed up."

"Okay." Atticus drew the word out, his eyes already slipping shut again.

Nico turned his back. There was no point in worrying about what he couldn't control. That was another rule. Stay focused on the here and now. Get the water and come back, just as he'd done a thousand times before.

He crawled through the tunnel with the bundle of gear in one hand and three water skins in the other. It sloped steeply upward. The air grew hotter as he ascended. When he reached the exit, he paused and listened for a long moment. Nothing but the low voice of the wind. Nico unwrapped the bundle. Strips of cured hide wound around his nose and mouth. A knee-length cloak covered him to the knees. Both were made from the skin of a lizard that blended with the sand and rocks of the Kiln. It made him nearly invisible. He pushed aside the screen of thorny brambles and scrambled out. As much as he feared the surface, it felt wonderful to stand upright again. Atticus was still small, but Nico had reached his full height and the confined space of the burrow made him half-crazy after too many days inside.

His gaze swept the terrain, watchful for any sign of movement. Desert hardpan stretched in all directions. The unrelenting sun had baked it into a scaled pattern of cracks like the underbelly of a cockindrill. Nicodemus set out for the north coast, running at an easy lope. Waves of heat shimmered in the distance. He'd fill one of the skins with saltwater for the soaking. It was a waste, but he had no choice. Two skins of fresh might last them a week if they were careful. He still had a little meat left from the last hunting trip.

What if you're too late? What if Atticus loses the foot? Should have gone yesterday.

Nico silenced the voice in his head, but he ran a little faster.

After an hour or so, he heard the murmuring crash of the sea and knew he was close. The hardpan gave way to golden dunes with a few hardy grasses poking out. Even though Domitia had warned him, Nico once tried to dig a burrow here, closer to the water. It kept collapsing and he'd finally given up.

The sand was broiling even through the thick calluses on his feet. He ran pell-mell over the last dune and waded into the surf up to his knees. Waves thundered across the jagged offshore reef, aquamarine in the bright sunlight. He didn't know how to swim, but even if he did, the dark shadows cruising through the shallows would have warned him off.

Nico eyed the water with hopeless longing, then turned back to the sandhills. Using his hands, he started digging a shallow hole on the back side. The dunes trapped rainwater, which floated on top of the heavier salt water. Only the top inch or so was clear. The rest would be brackish. He filled the first two skins slowly and carefully, tasting each to make sure they weren't contaminated. The third he filled down at the sea. The salt and minerals would help leach the poison from Atticus's foot.

This task accomplished, Nico used strands of tough grass to tie the three skins into a bundle. The muscles of his neck flexed as he hefted them over one shoulder and started home. He could make a mud poultice. That should help too. A gust of wind whipped sand into his eyes as he topped the dunes, so he heard the crab before he saw it. The soft click of chitinous claws.

"Fuck," he spat, dropping the water and reaching for his tooth knife.

The crab must have sensed the vibrations of his digging. Its carapace was about two paces across and speckled grey and red. This one was a male, with one large foreclaw that ended in black-tipped pincers. The other seven legs were used for locomotion and Nico knew how fast they could go. It had stopped at the bottom of the dune, uncertain where its prey had gone.

"Fuck," he mouthed again, silently.

The sand seared his feet but he didn't dare run. The crabs had poor eyesight and hunted primarily by sound and movement. They usually stayed in the rocky tidal pools farther down the beach. Bad luck he'd run into this one.

Nico could feel the sand crumbling under his heels, trickling down the backside of the dune. The crab opened and closed its foreclaw in an almost thoughtful manner, as if pondering some question. A person scratching his forehead.

Where, oh where, can you be?

He eyed the water skins he'd thrown down. He couldn't leave without them.

Easy, he thought. Slow and easy. He flexed the fingers of his left hand, the knife firmly in the other.

Bursting into sudden motion that nearly made Nico piss himself, the crab scuttled a few paces to the side. Then it stopped. It was facing partly away from him now. But he could see five more coming up the beach, streaks of grey and red against the sand. The time for subtlety was over.

Nico made a grab for the skins. His fingers closed around the knot of grass just as the sand gave way beneath his feet in a silken sheet. With a yell, he went tumbling down the dune. He rolled to his feet, tangled up in the cloak, and saw the flash of many-jointed legs galloping down the treacherous sandhill with no trouble at all. He still had the knife—Rule Three: Never Lose Your Weapon—but he knew it wouldn't make a dent in the carapace. So he went straight to Rule Four: When in Doubt, Run for Your Life.

The crab caught him with the oversized claw mid-stride. He heard the tough hide of his cloak tear like a fragile bit of seafoam. The crab jerked him off his feet, then stunned him with a blow to the head. He sucked in a mouthful of bloody sand.

Not this way. Not with Atticus waiting. Alone.

The crab crouched over him. Its smaller foreclaw pinned his left hand, digging with agonizing weight into his palm. Nico looked into its tiny yellow eyes. He raised the knife in a futile gesture just as the crab's pincer opened wide.

And then it gave a convulsive shudder. A bare foot, small and delicate, kicked the carapace over so the crab lay on its back, twitching feebly. Before Nico could fathom what had happened, a hand seized his own and hauled him to his feet. Domitia's pale blue eyes regarded him dispassionately, so like her father's. Yellow ichor ran from the point of a crude flint spear lashed to a thigh-bone. A daēva thighbone. She must have scavenged it from a corpse.

"I told you, your knife's a piece of shit," she said contemptuously, tossing him the waterskins. With a hard jerk, she ripped off two of the dying creature's legs. "Want one? Good eating."

Nico gave the barest shake of his head. He thought he might throw up, not over the crab, not even over the spear, but because something felt broken in his head. He coughed and earned a blinding stab of pain. One of his molars felt loose. But he still had the knife, even if it *was* a piece of shit.

"Suit yourself." She glanced back at the dunes. "Better go."

Domitia turned without another word and loped off toward the hardpan, her crab legs dragging in the sand. After an instant's hesitation, Nico did the same. His skull throbbed but the bleeding had clotted by the time he reached the burrow.

In the end, Atticus kept his foot. But the healing made him thirsty so the water only lasted three days instead of a week. And Nico felt a new, unwelcome fear growing inside him. He said the same exact words every time he left for food or water or whatever it was they'd run out of. A magic spell of protection.

I'll be back soon.

And it worked.

For a while.

NICODEMUS SHOOK HIMSELF, REMEMBRANCE MERCIFULLY fading. It was so vivid sometimes, but he knew the reason. The memories came to him so he'd never forget. Every single thing in this shithole tavern would be a priceless luxury in the Kiln. The scarred wooden tables and chairs. The dented pewter mugs and bucket of water the boy was sloppily tipping onto a puddle of ale. *Water to wash the fucking floor.* It boggled the imagination.

Nico was about to order his third mug when he saw a girl dart past the mouth of an alley across the way. She was only there for an instant, but he felt an electric shock of recognition. He stabbed a hand into his pocket and tossed a handful of coins on the table. He strode outside and looked around.

There she was, slinking along in the shadows, eyes darting, shoulders hunched. A Marakai ship rat through and through. Could she really be the talisman? He'd seen her face clearly enough in the image he wrenched from the bird's mind. Long and dour, with skin so dark it seemed to glow. Scrawny as a scarecrow. Her hair was the biggest part of her. Nico knew it was the same girl. Or had Sakhet-ra-katme tricked him? The thought lit a blaze of anger in his gut, which was already queasy from the ale he'd been nursing while he watched the docks. His skin prickled with the heat of it. He wanted to burn something. Or better yet, someone.

Nico drew a deep breath, letting the excess bleed though the soles of his feet and into the rock. It glowed red for an instant, then subsided. His power had been weak inside the Kiln and even after two years of freedom, he sometimes had trouble controlling it.

Calmer now, he forced himself to slow down and think. The talismans bore no special mark. The power lived in their blood. Sakhet couldn't have known he would snatch one of her messenger birds. This girl had to be the one he sought.

A gust of wind made the tavern's sign—a striped grey cat—creak and clatter. Nico trailed her at a discreet distance through the miserable hovels of New Hope. Fortunately, the Isles were a stewpot of humanity and his red hair didn't attract undue attention. He watched as the girl went aboard a ship called the *Asperta*.

He considered taking her right then. An army of Marakai wouldn't be able to stop him. But there was no gate in the Isles and his little boat would never make it all the way to Delphi. No, better to go to Tjanjin, where there *was* a gate.

He hummed to himself as he headed down the hill to the *Asperta*.

MEB PERCHED IN THE CROW'S NEST, PICKING AT SCABS AND feeling sorry for herself. Since the disaster with Anuketmatma, her status had gone from *beneath notice* to *full-fledged pariah*. The little cat's pique had stirred up one of the worst storms in recent memory. The *Asperta* made it to port in one piece but just barely —and only because Anuketmatma allowed it. She'd snarled and spat when Meb tried to dry the milk from her fur, hence the long scratches on her arms and face. Captain Kasaika finally managed to appease her with a morsel of fish and two hours of chin scratching, but by then it was too late. The forces of destruction had been unleashed and Anuketmatma couldn't—or wouldn't—call them back.

Most of the crew had gone ashore to drink and gossip in the taverns, but Meb was confined to *Asperta*, except for the message she'd just carried from Captain Kasaika to the harbor master. What the captain would do with her now, she had no idea. Meb scowled and examined a particularly nasty welt. At least the cat was gone, handed over to another ship's care. *Good riddance*, she thought sourly.

"Excuse me!"

Meb peered down at the jetty. A tall man with dark red hair was looking up at her. He gave a low bow and she frowned. No one had ever bowed to her before.

"Is your captain aboard?"

"What do you want her for?" Meb asked suspiciously.

"I have business to conduct."

His smile made Meb uneasy. What if Captain Kasaika sold her to the mortals?

"She ain't—"

Meb cut off as the captain herself appeared. She was still in a temper about Anuketmatma and glowered down at the man.

"No trade today," she said curtly.

The man swept another bow, lower this time. "I am not here to trade captain. May we speak in private?"

Captain Kasaika turned away. "Later. I'm busy."

He produced something from his cloak and held it up. The captain frowned. She beckoned him up the gangplank and examined it.

"If you stole this seal, I'll have you arrested by the Medjay," she said coldly.

"I think you'll find it's legitimate," he replied, unruffled by her tone. "Will you invite me aboard? I have a business proposition."

Captain Kasaika looked him over. "Five minutes," she said.

The man gracefully leapt aboard and went below. Meb hesitated only an instant. She scrambled down from the crow's nest and followed. She might be weak in the power, but she had years of practice at eavesdropping. Now she pressed her ear against the door to Captain Kasaika's cabin, keeping one eye on the passageway.

"I'm on an urgent mission for the emperor and need to sail for Tjanjin right away," the man said.

"Why the *Asperta*? We just arrived. My crew needs a rest."

"I understand your cargo was damaged in the storm. I can help you make up the loss. Triple the usual rate." He paused. "I can also tell you that His Imperial Majesty stands in opposition to the latest decree of the Oracle. It's an outrage, and he intends to withdraw his ambassador from Delphi immediately."

Captain Kasaika was silent for a moment. "I'll need permission from the vizier. And to confirm you are who you say you are."

"Of course."

They haggled for a bit and finally struck a deal. Meb hurried back up to the deck just as the captain emerged.

"Mebetimmunedjem!" the captain bellowed.

"Right here," Meb said breathlessly.

"Fetch my wastrel crew from the taverns and tell them we're sailing in four bells."

"Yes, captain," Meb replied, bare feet slapping the deck as she ran down the gangplank.

She looked back once. The man was watching her. He gave a friendly wink. Meb scowled and turned her back.

11

A MEETING AT THE MER

Captain Mafuone led them to a road that wound past the town and into the barren hills beyond. There were no lumen crystals to light the way—apparently the Marakai saw well enough without them—but the stars shone bright overhead.

"What's the Blue Crown?" Nazafareen asked Herodotus, who walked at her side.

"A legend of the Khepresh Marakai," he said. "It supposedly came from the sea, brought in the teeth of one of the wave horses called the Nahresi. No one has ever worn it, but they say one day, the Marakai will unite under a single ruler who will wear the Blue Crown."

"How will they know who it is?"

He glanced at her. "Well, anyone has the right to try it on. But if you're not the chosen one, the Nahresi come galloping out of the sea and trample you with razor-sharp hooves. So such requests are rare." He cleared his throat. "According to a scroll I found in the library, *Sojourns Among the Stygians*, the last time it happened was the result of an ill-advised bet some fifty years before—"

The road topped a rise and Herodotus trailed off. Nazafareen's breath caught in her throat. An enormous structure dominated the center of the island, unlike any she had seen before. It had three sides rising to a point at the top and the whole thing was plated in gold that shone brilliantly beneath the moons.

"Ah, we've reached the Mer!" Herodotus exclaimed. "A construction peculiar to the Marakai. Apparently, the triangular shape is better suited to high winds. It's where they keep the Hin—the tenth of the cargo they deal in. And those are the Medjay."

Stern-faced men and women ringed the Mer, the half-human, half-daēvas hired by the Marakai to guard their wealth. They wore vests and pants of a mottled grey and carried short spears. Captain Mafuone stated their business and six Medjay escorted the visitors into the inner chamber of the Mer.

Lumen crystals glittered on a mountain of treasure. Gorgeously carved chests from the lands of the Danai overflowed with swords and carpets, ivory and carnelian and amber, opium and spell dust, silks, spices, ceramics and tapestries. Nazafareen felt her jaw hanging open and closed it with an effort. It was like some great dragon's lair, only instead of a dragon, a man with a pinched face and long braids stood in the center of the chamber, a stylus in his hand as he checked off items from a list. Captain Mafuone gave him a smart salute.

"Vizier," she said. "Forgive the interruption, but we bring grave tidings."

He looked up with a slight frown that deepened as he surveyed the group.

"Captain Mafuone," he replied. "Who do you bring to the Mer? This is highly irregular."

The captain made quick introductions, which the vizier acknowledged with a cool nod.

"That is all very well, but I fail to see—"

"Sakhet-ra-katme is dead," she interrupted. "We have just come from her houseboat, or what was left of it." She held out the piece of charred wood. "It was burned."

"Let me see." The vizier inspected the wood closely. "And where is her body?"

"The currents took it."

"This is all you have?" He shook his head. "Perhaps you've made a mistake. How could Sakhet's boat be burned?"

"There is no mistake," Kallisto said quietly. "She was killed by a Vatra."

"A Vatra?" His eyebrows rose. "Is she mad?"

"No," Mafuone said coldly. "I fear she is entirely correct. The Diyat must be convened right away."

The vizier returned to his list, making a small notation. "They're already meeting on the Isle of the Khepresh about the Oracle's pronouncement and can't be disturbed."

"What pronouncement?" Mafuone asked.

"You don't know?" He rolled his eyes. "Apparently, their sun god has decreed Delphi must go to war with Samarqand because it is a den of magical iniquity. There will be no more free trade with the *witches*. The *witches* must be subjugated and the god will provide a means to do so." The vizier laughed dismissively. "The Five will deal with her, have no fear."

Mafuone didn't smile. "She already has the means. The Oracle has somehow discovered talismans to bind a daēva. Darius saw them firsthand."

The vizier's thin lips pursed. "That *is* worrisome."

"Indeed. But the Oracle may still pose the lesser threat," Mafuone continued. "We believe Sakhet was murdered for what she knew."

"And what is that?" he asked with a touch of impatience.

"We believe her death is connected with the talismans who stopped the Vatras a thousand years ago. Their powers were passed on, vizier. Did Sakhet ever speak of it to you?"

He scratched his forehead with the stylus. "I haven't seen Sakhet in hundreds of years, captain. No one has." His tone softened a little. "I mean no disrespect, but I need proof of these claims before bringing them to the Five. I'm not about to start a panic based on a single piece of charred wood. This could have drifted from anywhere."

The captain sighed. "We will inform the Nyx."

"I would be most grateful," he said. "And truly, I hope you are wrong." He gave a weak smile. "Perhaps Sakhet simply sailed away!"

Mafuone gave him a last disgusted look and they started for the door. As they neared the exit, another Marakai captain entered the treasure room, a man at her side. Nazafareen's heart gave a sudden lurch. He had dark red hair tied back with a leather thong. He looked to be about thirty and wore a blue cloak with silver trim. Nazafareen felt Darius tense. The man noticed them all staring but simply gazed back with mild interest. She'd left her sword back on the ship, but there were many other ways to kill.

And then the vizier's thin lips parted in a welcoming smile.

"Nicodemus!" he said. "It *has* been a long time."

The man tilted his head gracefully. "Too long. But I've been occupied in service to the emperor. He sends his regards."

The man stepped forward, cloak sweeping back to reveal some kind of ceremonial knife in his belt. She saw it only for an instant and then he strode past her, exchanging small talk with the vizier.

Kallisto shook her head and they continued on, though Mafuone paused to clasp hands with the other captain, whom she seemed to know well. They made their way down the hill to New Hope in discouraged silence. The taverns were doing a brisk business, with Marakai and Stygians mingling freely over cups of foul-looking ale. Nazafareen was thinking of the red-haired man, and how close she'd come to attacking him and probably getting arrested by the Medjay, when a girl came hurtling around the corner of a squat stone building. She let out a yelp of surprise. They tangled together and Nazafareen sat down hard in a moist patch of earth that smelled like it was visited often by the patrons of the tavern next door.

The girl shot her a filthy look. She muttered something—not an apology, Nazafareen felt certain—then ran on toward the docks.

"What a little wretch," she muttered, eyeing her cloak with disgust. "Faugh!"

Darius laughed and pulled her to her feet. "I think you'd better swim to the ship," he advised. "And better yet, do it naked."

When they reached the *Chione*—and Nazafareen had hurled the offending garments overboard—they all retired to their cabins. Captain Mafuone said they'd repair the ship on her home island of the Sheut, where she hoped they'd receive a warmer reception.

"What a bloody horrible day," Nazafareen said to Darius as they lay under the covers, Hecate spilling like molten silver through the porthole. "How could that vizier be so blind?"

"Fear makes people blind sometimes," he replied. "And cruel. Humans and daēvas both."

Something in his voice made her sit up. "You're talking about *her*."

"Her?"

"Thena."

Darius's gaze shuttered. "How do you know that name?"

"You say it in your sleep sometimes."

He was quiet for so long she thought he was angry.

"I wish to forget it. But I can't." His voice caught. "She reminded me of the *ama* I had as a child. The one who taught us we were Druj."

Now she wished she'd kept her mouth shut. It had been stupid and impulsive and yes, cruel. What would the old Nazafareen—a superior version of herself, no doubt—have done to make Darius feel better? There was a new ease between them since he'd finally come clean, but it wasn't the same as knowing a person intimately for years. It was so frustrating! If only she could remember. Then an idea came to her.

"I could give you the water blessing," she suggested. "Like that time at the brothel. Marduk's Spear, wasn't it?"

Darius's gloom seemed to lift at this. He laughed long and hard.

"Holy Father, I think I've been blessed by water enough on this trip." He pulled her close and her heart beat a little faster. "But here's a counter proposal. Why don't we skip the blessing and go straight to what happened *afterwards?*"

Nazafareen smiled against his lips. "Certainly. But I'm afraid I've forgotten that part. You'll have to remind me."

His hands roved beneath the covers, eliciting a sigh of delight. "I may embellish on the original," he warned. "It would be tedious to simply repeat myself."

"Oh, you can repeat yourself all you like," she said lazily. "A man with a silver tongue like yours can ramble on for *hours* without ever becoming a bore."

And so they passed the evening in fond reminiscences and when Darius slept at last, it was with a peaceful smile.

12

KHAF-HOR

Nazafareen woke after a few hours and wandered up to the deck, a fresh breeze flapping her cloak. Kallisto stood alone at the rail. She looked bereft. Nazafareen hurried over, enfolding the older woman in her arms.

"I'm so sorry about Sakhet," she said. "I didn't know her like you did, but I mourn her too. We all do. Don't worry, we'll figure something out. Darius is a tracker. I'm sure he—"

"I must leave you," Kallisto interrupted, gently untangling herself from Nazafareen's embrace.

"Leave us? Why?"

"To seek out the other talismans. I'd left that task to Sakhet, but she's gone now and it's time we face it. Our paths must divide or all will be lost."

Kallisto's decision made sense, though Nazafareen didn't like it much. "Where will you go?"

"I'll take Rhea to Val Altair. Charis and Cyrene will go to House Dessarian. Darius's mother knows them, if she's still there. If not, they can tell Tethys we were friends of Sakhet. She should be informed of her death. And she may know something about the Danai talisman. At the least, she can bring the matter before the Matrium."

"I think Tethys would do that," Nazafareen said slowly. "But the Valkirins have less love of mortals than any other clan. They're a harsh people. Why will they listen?"

"I have the staff of truth. When I show them the talisman and swear on it, they must believe me."

"Perhaps," Nazafareen said doubtfully. "What about the rest of us?"

"You will stay here with Herodotus and Megaera and continue to look for the Marakai girl. Go to the Five. Captain Mafuone will take you." Kallisto patted her hand. "I know it's a great burden I leave you with, child, but there is no other to carry it."

"Then I will do all I can," Nazafareen said. She paused. "And if the Vatra has her already?"

"We mustn't give up hope," Kallisto said firmly. "I suspect Sakhet kept this girl well-hidden, but perhaps she revealed her identity to the Diyat. If you do find her, bring her to the Temple of the Moria Tree on the Cimmerian Sea. Megaera knows where it is. The Maenads there will keep the talisman safe. We'll do the same if we are successful."

"Does Captain Mafuone know?"

Kallisto nodded. "She agrees. Come, we must tell the others."

Selene had risen above the hills by the time Kallisto, Cyrene, Charis and Rhea packed their things and gathered on deck. Nazafareen hugged each of the Maenads fiercely. Darius hung back until they all swarmed on him at once, pinching his bottom and tickling his chin until he threatened to call a wind and throw them overboard. Herodotus wiped his eyes as he gave his wife a final kiss farewell. One of the Jengu ships was sailing to Val Altair and they watched until it dwindled to a speck on the horizon.

Nazafareen felt the weight of responsibility on her shoulders, and she could see the others did, too. She thought briefly of the girl who'd knocked her down, but there were Marakai girls everywhere, on every ship. Her gaze roamed across the jetty. Most of the vessels were Selk, bearing the image of the little striped cat, Anuketmatma. A few had the Blue Crown or the giant carp of the Jengu. And then she saw a single ship with a fanged eel on its sails. It stirred her memory.

"Which fleet worships the eel?" she asked Darius.

"Nyx, I think."

"Nyx." Nazafareen froze. "Wasn't that the other fleet of Sakhet?"

"Indeed it was," Herodotus said. "She was both Selk and Nyx, which is rare among the Marakai. The eel is named Khaf-Hor. He has all sorts of magical powers, including the ability to summon a dense fog." He scratched his beard. "I wonder if he made Sakhet's fog. Truly, it was very peculiar—"

"That man!" Nazafareen's heart raced. "The one we saw at the Mer. He wore a dagger with the hilt of a fanged eel."

Darius frowned. "Are you certain?"

"I only saw it for a moment, but I noticed because it was so unusual."

They stared at each other. "You think he took it from Sakhet."

Cold certainty gripped Nazafareen as she remembered his bland expression. *Too* bland. "Yes. I think he did."

Megaera swore a vile oath.

They hurried to find Captain Mafuone, who was in her cabin sorting through a mess of waterlogged records and splintered wood.

"At the Mer, you greeted another captain," Nazafareen said breathlessly. "What ship does she command?"

"The *Asperta*," Mafuone said. "She sailed for Tjanjin late last night."

Nazafareen told her what she'd remembered. Mafuone looked troubled.

"But that man was an emissary from the emperor. The vizier knew him personally."

"With all respect, captain, he didn't have the look of Tjanjin," Herodotus pointed out. "I know merely having red hair does not make one a Vatra, but where did he come by a Nyx knife?"

Mafuone's lips thinned. "All right. I'll go back to the Mer and ask the vizier how long he's known this man. But if you intend to pursue the *Asperta*, we'll have to get my ship seaworthy. The journey to Tjanjin takes three days and we won't make it in this condition. I expected to repair her in the port of the Sheut."

"How long will it take?" Nazafareen asked, burning with impatience.

"Depends. Replacing the masts is the main problem. The rest can be done at sea."

"I have some skill with wood," Darius offered. "I could speed up the work."

Captain Mafuone didn't hesitate. "Do it," she said. "My crew will help you."

She barked out orders and they set about nursing the poor *Chione* back to life. A group of Marakai sailors went to the harbor master and returned with two tall trunks of bonewood. Within an hour, Darius made them into gleaming spars, his strong hands shaping the wood like a sculptor with a lump of wet clay. The second had just been mounted and the new sails rigged up when Captain Mafuone returned.

"Three ships came into the harbor since we arrived, but other than the Jengu vessel bound for Val Altair, only the *Asperta* sailed in the last day," she reported. "The emissary's name is Nicodemus. The vizier vouched for his character, but admitted he met him two years ago. He delivered trade contracts from the emperor to the Five."

"Two years," Herodotus said thoughtfully. "That's about the same time the new Pythia came to Delphi."

Nazafareen and Darius exchanged a look.

"Do you think there's a connection?" Darius asked dubiously. "It doesn't seem likely."

"I don't know. Either way—"

"There's more," Captain Mafuone interrupted, her onyx eyes glittering. "When I asked if there were any young girls aboard, the vizier hesitated." Her lips curved in a half-smile. "Apparently, he thought I was angry about the storm and wanted to demand reparations from the Selk."

"Reparations?" Darius asked, as confused as the rest of them.

"The *Asperta* was carrying Anuketmatma."

Herodotus raised an eyebrow. "The mother of storms?"

"The very same. Someone failed to care for her properly and she grew angry."

"You mean the cat?" Nazafareen asked. She pointed with her stump to the broken masts that still lay on the *Chione*'s deck. "A cat did *that*?"

"She is more than a cat," Mafuone replied wryly. "In any event, it seems the blame fell on a girl of twelve who does grunt work on the ship." She shook her head. "Why Captain Kasaika trusted her with Anuketmatma is beyond me, but there it is."

"What's this girl's name?" Nazafareen asked, a tingle of excitement running down her spine.

"The vizier had no idea. She's known as Mouse on the docks." Captain Mafuone sighed. "If she is the talisman, I should tell the Five. They can send a fleet after her."

"But by the time you talk to them, it will be too late," Nazafareen exclaimed. "Aren't they busy worrying about the Oracle? And what if they don't believe us, just like that fool vizier?"

Mafuone raised an eyebrow.

"It is your decision, of course, captain," Herodotus broke in hastily. "But I'm afraid Nazafareen may be correct. If a Vatra is indeed on that ship, there's no time to waste."

Captain Mafuone turned away for a moment, studying the *Chione*.

"You did well with the masts," she said at last. "Normally, it would take us a week or more." She glanced at Darius. "If the Five finds out what I've done, I could lose her. But I suppose that's better than losing our only chance to avenge Sakhet. And perhaps to save a young girl. So I will take you to Tjanjin."

Mafuone's eyes flew wide as Nazafareen embraced her.

"Thank you, captain," she said fervently.

"I do this for the Marakai, not you," Mafuone said sternly. Her voice softened a touch. "But you're welcome. As I reckon it, we're half a day behind. As long as we don't run into Anuketmatma again, I think we can make up the difference." Her strong voice carried across the deck. "Raise the sails!"

A flurry of activity ensued. The crew had just cast off the mooring line when a man came hurtling down the wharf, panting like a blown horse. He had the native Stygian look, with dusky skin and dark curly hair to his shoulders. A beard covered gaunt cheeks. At first glance, Nazafareen thought him some kind of mad beggar. The soles of his boots were loose and flapped like tongues. A ragged cloak streamed out behind him.

"Captain!" he cried, running alongside the *Chione*, which had begun its slow glide along the pier.

Mafuone leaned over the rail and grinned. "By the Mer, look what the tide carried in," she called back. The ship had nearly reached the end of the pier. "We'll have to chew over old times later, my friend. The *Chione* is sailing for Tjanjin."

"Will you...grant me...passage?" he gasped.

Captain Mafuone hesitated only a moment. She swore softly under her breath and beckoned to him. A quick nod and one of the sailors tossed a rope over the stern rail. The Stygian dove gracefully into the water just as the *Chione* cleared the jetty and swam to the rope. In short order, he'd been hauled dripping onto the deck.

Nazafareen frowned as he shook himself all over like a dog.

"Who is he?" she asked, her mind suddenly full of suspicion.

"A thief catcher," Mafuone replied. "I know him well. He's a good man from an old family. And I owe him a debt."

Their new passenger approached the captain with a very wide, very white grin that made him almost handsome despite the sorry state of his clothing. They gripped forearms.

"Where've you been hiding?" she asked with an answering grin.

He pulled a strand of seaweed from his hair and flicked it into the water. "I ran into a spot of trouble in Delphi. All the ports are closed so I took a horse to the Twelve Towers and caught a ship from there. Just arrived an hour gone." He glanced back at the shanties of New Hope. "But you know me. Can't get out of this hellhole fast enough. I need to return to Tjanjin." His face darkened for a moment. "I have business to conclude there."

He glanced at the others gathered on the deck, his keen gray eyes lingering on Megaera's staff and Nazafareen's sword. Then he noticed Darius and gave a little start.

"You're Danai," he said.

Darius nodded amiably. "House Dessarian."

Nazafareen suppressed a scowl. This man seemed to know an awful lot. But if he *was* an enemy, better to keep him close. She seemed to remember Victor saying that once.

"I'm Nazafareen," she said, stepping forward with a big, fake smile. "You're lucky you caught us." She winked. "We're in a bit of a hurry."

The *Chione* slid past the breakwater and met the chop of the White Sea. Immediately, she surged forward as the crew worked together to summon a powerful northerly current.

The man smiled back, lazily, as if he knew what she was up to and found it amusing.

"A pleasure to meet you," he said, giving a low bow. "My name is Katsu."

THE LANGUAGE OF DUST

Javid left the wind ship moored at the Abicari and made his way home on foot, still unnerved from the encounter with Prince Shahak. His family lived nearby in a small mudbrick house with a low wall to keep the neighborhood dogs out. Chickens scratched in the dusty yard. They eyed him hopefully and he paused to pluck a tomato from one of his mother's beloved plants, which the hens fell upon like a pack of jackals. One of them seized the biggest chunk in its beak and ran off with the others in hot pursuit. At least some things never changed.

Javid's youngest sister Bibi, who was only ten but fancied herself wise in the ways of the world, greeted him at the door with a kiss on the cheek.

"So you're a dust dealer now," she said matter-of-factly, stroking the embroidery on his collar with fingers that held sticky traces of dates.

Javid batted her hand away. "Who told you that?"

"Ma. She says you're working for a lord." Her brown eyes glinted with mischief. "Give me some. Just a wee little pinch." She held her fingers a hair's breadth apart to illustrate how modest this request was. "I need to put a spell on Farima. She hid my doll again."

Javid regarded his sister with amusement. Farima was a year older and the two of them had been at war with each other since the cradle. "What kind of spell would you put on her?"

"I was thinking more of a curse," she whispered. "Something to make her nose hairs grow real long."

He nodded. "Yeah, that's a good one. But you have to know the right words to say or it won't work."

"Oh." Her face fell. "Can you find them out for me?"

Javid's lips twitched. "I'll ask Marzban Khorram-Din. He's Lord Asabana's alchemist and he's ever so nice and kind. I bet he knows."

Bibi shot him a sideways glance. "Don't tell ma. She might not like it if I did magic."

"It'll be our secret." Javid frowned at the unnatural silence in the house. Usually, it was full of shrieking, bickering girls. "Where is everyone?"

She started hopping up and down on one foot. "They went to see Baraz. He's making Golpari's wedding dress."

"And they left you here?"

"I'd rather stay home." She scowled and switched feet. "That stupid wedding is all they talk about. I don't ever want to get married." Her face took on a hunted look. "And I don't want kids neither. I want to be like you."

Javid raised an eyebrow.

"Not a boy, silly," she added. "Just free to do what I like."

He almost told her about Leila, but it would be cruel to get her hopes up. Marzban Khorram-Din could do as he pleased. If he wanted to thumb his nose at tradition and train his daughter as an alchemist, no one dared stop him. He had power, of a sort. But Javid's family was poor. Poor girls didn't go to school. They didn't learn a trade, not even a lowly one. They got married.

Bibi might change her mind when she discovered boys. He

studied her, so fierce and determined. Or, knowing Bibi, she might not.

"Maybe you can work for me when I get my own wind ship," he said.

Her face lit up and she ceased her hopping long enough to give him another sticky kiss.

"Where's da?" Javid asked. "At work?"

"Upstairs." She lowered her voice. "His hands are bad again."

They were both silent for a moment. Bibi was only ten, but knew what it meant if da couldn't work anymore.

"I saw Farima out by the chicken coop this morning with a sneaky look on her face," he said. "You should check the nesting boxes."

Bibi's black eyes narrowed and she was out the back door in a flash. Javid climbed the stairs to the warren of tiny bedrooms on the second floor. In just the few months he'd been away, his father had somehow grown old. He'd never been a big man, but he always radiated energy and vitality. He made the ropes for the wind ships and had a grip like an iron band. Javid had seen his father crack chestnuts with his bare hands. But something was happening to his joints. When the weather changed, they would swell up and turn red. And it seemed to be getting worse.

Seven of Javid's older sisters were already married, but there were still four to go and they would need dowries. He'd been slipping most of his wages to his mother, but there wasn't much left over after Asabana deducted Javid's debt—which he'd be paying off for the foreseeable future. Javid knew she was worried. They all were.

"Hi, da," he said, sitting on a chair next to the bed.

His father smiled warmly. He'd had white hair since Javid could remember, but his face was tanned dark from the sun and he still looked ruggedly handsome. His hands rested on the blanket. Javid tried not to wince at the sight. They looked like misshapen claws.

"Son." He glanced at a bowl of foul-smelling yellow liquid on a table. "Pass me that, would you?"

Javid sniffed the contents and grimaced. "What is it?"

"Some brew your ma made. Holy Father, it's nasty, but it helps."

Javid helped him drink it down, which he did without complaint. Ma still called him Yasmin, but his da never forgot. Javid had been terrified when he first told them he wanted to live as a boy, but his da had warmed to the idea immediately. By the twelfth girl child, he'd given up on the idea he'd ever have a son and was willing to take what he could get.

"How's the new job?"

"Good." Javid paused. "I met Prince Shahak today."

His father raised a bushy white eyebrow. "Holy Father," he muttered. "Shahak's next in line, isn't he?" He paused. "And King Cambyses. He's still alive?"

"Yes, but no one knows for how much longer." Javid trusted his father to keep a secret. "The prince is Izad Asabana's biggest client."

"You're moving in illustrious circles these days."

Javid shrugged. "I'm just a delivery boy."

"We're talking about spell dust."

Javid nodded. "I always figured Shahak had an alchemist. But the prince...he takes it directly. Inhales it."

His father gave a low whistle. "Holy Father," he said again.

"Yeah. Listen, I don't know what's going to happen. But if I can keep my head down, I might earn enough so none of us have to worry ever again."

His da covered Javid's hand with his own. The skin felt feverishly warm. "You're a good son. But I'll get better. Your ma's remedy just needs a little time to work."

Javid didn't challenge this lie. His da was a proud man. "I know. But Asabana hinted he has a bigger run for me, once the prince takes the throne."

"Risky?"

"Probably. But I intend to take it. Make a pile and get out."

"That's what all gamblers say." His father took his hand away and winced in pain.

"You need a magus."

"Bah. They charge a fortune and half their cures are worse than the disease."

Javid had to admit there was some truth to this. But he also knew his da couldn't afford a magus.

He gave Javid a hard look. "Watch your back with Asabana. Does Savah know what you're up to?"

"He's the one who got me the job."

"Hmmm. Well, I never trusted Savah either, even if he is my cousin. He only cares about his own skin. You should do the same."

"I have to go, da. Lord Asabana's expecting me."

His father nodded. "See you at supper, son."

Javid grabbed a piece of bread and ate it on the way to the palace grounds. He retrieved the *Ash Vareca* and flew it back to Asabana's estate. The perpetual haze blanketing the blacksmiths' quarter mingled with low, dark clouds moving in from the Umbra. He wondered if the heatwave was finally about to break.

He found his employer in a glass-enclosed solarium, floating on his back in a large tiled pool. Marzban Khorram-Din and Leila sat on a bench surrounded by lush potted plants. The smell of jasmine hung heavy in the air.

"What's happening at the Rock?" Asabana asked lazily. "Is our client happy?"

Javid related the encounter with Prince Shahak, leaving nothing out. Asabana clearly already knew about the prince's peculiar habit because he chuckled and shook his head when Javid described the silver spoon. But Marzban Khorram-Din scowled and Leila simply looked horrified.

"So he likes you," Asabana said, paddling over to the edge of the pool.

Unlike the other lords of the court who believed a bulging gut to be a status symbol of the highest order, Asabana was lean as a grizzled wolfhound. Javid felt mildly shocked he would appear half-naked before Leila, but then nothing about their arrangement was normal.

"The prince was not what I expected, my lord."

Asabana winked. "Turn on the charm, boy. We need to keep Shahak close and make sure he takes the throne when the time comes." He made the sign of the flame, brushing forehead, lips and heart. "Samarqand needs a strong leader to deal with the Greeks, and the Guild agrees with me."

Privately, Javid wasn't at all certain Prince Shahak would be a strong leader, or even a sane one, but he kept his mouth shut.

Asabana made a face. "And watch out for the Queen. She's a real priss. If she gets herself named regent, she'll put us out of business. No more spell dust, no more money."

"Yes, my lord." Javid hesitated, glancing at the alchemist and his daughter. "I was wondering about the other matter we spoke of. In Delphi?"

"Ah yes." Asabana rolled to his back again and closed his eyes. "Taken care of, my boy."

Javid felt a weight lift from his shoulders. "You mean the thief is out?"

"Free as a swallow."

"Was he.... How was his condition?"

"My contact said he had scars on his hands. Otherwise intact."

Javid smiled, mainly because it confirmed Asabana spoke the truth. "He had those before he was arrested."

One debt is paid, he thought. Now for the next.

"How much do I owe you?" he asked, dreading the answer.

Asabana frolicked in the pool with the carefree zest of a river otter. "Things are complicated in Delphi. Our ambassadors packed up and left last week. The usual channels are all buggered up. I had to pay six...." He considered for a moment. "No, seven separate bribes, each more outrageous than the last." He ticked the items off on one hand. "Plus the cost of a horse and saddle. Three days' provisions for the Umbra. Passage on a Marakai ship. A few other sundry expenses."

Javid suppressed a sigh. "Whatever it amounts to, I'll pay you back, my lord."

"I'm sure you will." He spread his arms expansively. "Come join me for a swim, kid. You're sweating like a donkey."

The clouds broke open at that moment and rain began pattering down on the glass roof.

Javid gave a feeble smile. "I'm afraid I never learned how."

"Nonsense, I'll teach you. Come on, jump in. We don't stand on ceremony here." He grinned, revealing gold teeth. "You can leave your smallclothes on if you're the modest type."

Javid frantically tried to think of another excuse when Leila, who had risen to study one of the plants, gave a sharp cry.

"Are you all right, my dear?" the alchemist asked, his stern features creased with concern.

It was the first time Javid had ever heard the man speak. Despite his fierce appearance, his voice was gentle.

"I've tripped over my gown," she said with an embarrassed laugh. "I told the seamstress the hem was too long." She leaned heavily on the back of the bench. "Perhaps your pilot would be kind enough to escort me to my chambers."

"Want me to summon a magus?" Asabana asked. He didn't sound thrilled at the prospect. Spell dust hadn't been deemed heretical, not explicitly, but Javid doubted the priests approved of it either. It was a source of power they didn't control and thus a threat to their influence.

"I'm a clumsy cow," Leila said lightly. "But I'll be fine. I just need a strong arm to lean on." She cast Javid a coquettish glance that seemed utterly out of character.

"Of course," he murmured, stepping to her side with relief. "I'll have the servants fetch ice for the swelling." He paused. "Do you require my services any further today, my lord?"

"Nah. Go on home." Asabana floated away on his back, dark hair fanning out like a bat's wings. "Take care of her. She's valuable."

Javid nodded politely to Marzban Khorram-Din and helped Leila to the door. As soon as they turned the first corner, her limp vanished and she strode off. He jogged to catch up with her.

"I thought you hurt your ankle," he said.

She cast him a flat look. "I saved you back there. You should thank me."

Javid feigned ignorance, but his heart sank. "What do you mean?"

Leila turned to him. "You know very well what I mean."

They stared at each for a long moment. Javid finally looked away.

"How'd you find out?" he asked, folding his arms defensively.

"I can just tell. Your throat is too smooth, for one thing. And you should have a beard by now."

"Maybe I shave twice a day."

She made a face. "Please."

"Are you going to tell Asabana?"

Leila snorted. "Of course not. Why do you think I helped you? We have to stick together."

"We? I consider myself a man."

She examined him with curiosity. "It's not just so you can be a wind pilot?"

"That was part of it at first," he conceded. "But I just...I've never felt like a woman."

"Fair enough." She smiled suddenly. "I like you, Javid. You have balls."

He couldn't help but laugh. "So do you."

Something shifted between them in that moment. They might not be friends yet, but they weren't enemies either.

"Let's walk in the garden," Leila said.

"You're supposed to have a sprained ankle," he pointed out.

"They can't see us from the solarium."

"It's raining."

"Then there won't be any gardeners or servants about." She dropped her voice and glanced around. "Don't trust anyone in this house. They're all spies for his *lordship*." Her lip curled a little at the word.

Javid's new coat would get soaked, but he could dry it by the kitchen fire later. He'd never had a chance to talk to Leila alone before. She and her father had managed to stay on Asabana's good side and Javid desperately hoped to do the same.

"At least hold my arm until we're out of view of the house," he said.

She inclined her head in assent and laid a hand on his proffered elbow. They headed around to the back of the mansion where the long veranda looked over the river. A flight of stairs led down into the manicured gardens.

"How long has your father been with Asabana?" he asked as they took one of the winding paths into a grove of orange trees that offered some shelter from the rain.

"Nearly ten years now."

"Why do you work for him if you don't like him?"

Leila made a rude noise. "Why does anybody work for him? He pays a lot. And once you're in, it's not easy to get out." She plucked an orange from one of the low branches and started peeling it. "My father chose Asabana because he was the only patron who agreed to permit a woman apprentice. None of the nobles would have us, not together."

"They're fools then."

"Without a doubt. As you can see, Asabana's fortunes have flourished thanks to my father." She offered Javid half the orange.

"I see no reason to be especially grateful to our employer. He worships gold before all else, so he had no difficulty putting aside his prejudices against women when there were astronomical profits to be made. It was a business decision, not a moral one." She spat out a seed. "I don't think Asabana has any morals. He is a creature driven entirely by greed."

Javid shrugged. "At least you know where he stands." He glanced at her. "I'll admit, Asabana isn't the only one who scares me."

"You mean my father? He scares most people. That's the point. But he's a decent man." She stopped beneath the low, dripping branches and turned to face Javid. "Asabana is testing you. Our supplies are running low. He's going to need a pilot to sail north pretty soon."

"I'm counting on it," Javid said grimly. "Have you been there? To the source?"

Her face grew shuttered. "Perhaps."

Leila's obvious reluctance to discuss it piqued his curiosity, but Javid knew better than to push her. He supposed he'd find out for himself soon enough. They reached the end of the walk and turned back. The rain turned into a downpour. They didn't speak again until he'd escorted her to her chambers on the top floor. She paused in the open doorway and he caught a glimpse of the room beyond, tables piled high with scrolls and complex mechanical devices and murky glass jars with pale things floating inside. One of the walls bore a starburst pattern of scorch marks and he wondered what sort of experiments she conducted in there.

"You owe me a favor now, flyboy," Leila said. "Don't forget it."

Javid brushed rain from his coat and gave her a jaded smile.

"I owe everybody," he replied.

OVER THE NEXT WEEK, JAVID MADE FOUR DUST DELIVERIES TO

the palace. It was the same routine each time. They would drink a cup of wine and Prince Shahak would perform some trick. He made a chair vanish and reappear on the other side of the room. He disgorged colored ink from his mouth and painted a self-portrait with it. He made an apple feel as heavy as a lump of iron and a solid gold statue seem light as a soap bubble. As he performed these minor miracles, the prince would watch Javid closely, gauging his reaction.

Javid always expressed awe and delight, which was clearly what the prince desired. Shahak seemed lonely—and probably afraid of what would happen when his father died, although he never spoke of it. He admitted he used to have an alchemist named Yarlaganda, but soon outgrew the man's instruction. Yarlaganda was reluctant to further his studies so Shahak dismissed him, which Javid took to mean the alchemist was appalled at the prince's habit of ingesting the dust directly.

"They are too cautious and bound by the restraints of tradition," Shahak said dismissively. "But I am living proof that magic is an organic thing with limitless possibilities, if one has an open heart and mind."

The prince told Javid of his grand plans to restore Samarqand to its former glory. To reclaim the desert as far as the Gale and turn it into a lush, green oasis. He seemed unconcerned by the nosebleeds that always followed his displays, but Javid wondered. Despite his misgivings, he'd grown to like the prince. He seemed to mean well. Yet the signs of his addiction were manifold. He was wan and listless until he inhaled the dust, and then he would be seized with a kind of manic energy that dissipated into lethargy by the time Javid left.

What could he do? Absolutely nothing. If Prince Shahak desired to kill himself with spell dust, it was his royal prerogative. He hadn't listened to his own alchemist and he certainly wouldn't listen to Javid.

He confided all this to Leila when he met her in the garden of

Asabana's mansion. In their spare time, she'd been teaching him some of the language of spell dust beyond what he already knew for navigational purposes, and he conveyed whatever gossip he gleaned at the Rock. She'd never heard of anyone taking dust directly and seemed deeply disturbed by it, though she wouldn't say why.

"The source is Asabana's secret and I am sworn to keep it," she told Javid as they sat on a bench, watching the river flow by. "But I doubt the prince will live long. And that is perhaps for the best."

"He wields a sort of magic I've never even imagined," Javid said. "So I understand the appeal. But he seems blind to the side effects."

"That is the way of all power," Leila replied. "We see only the rose and forget the thorn." She cocked her head. "And what of this thief you indentured yourself for? Do you love him?"

It was a very frank question and Javid felt himself flushing. He'd hoped Katsu might turn up at the Abicari asking for him, but it was a foolish wish. Of course, the Stygian had gone home. Javid wondered briefly if he still sought the talisman that had been stolen from the emperor of Tjanjin. He had a feeling a little time in the dungeons wouldn't put Katsu off the hunt.

"*Love* is a bit strong," he said. "We hardly know each other."

"But you prefer men to women?"

Javid nodded.

"Have you ever—"

"No."

"Don't be reticent," Leila said with annoyance, when he failed to elaborate. "I prefer women and I've had several lovers. One simply has to be discreet."

Javid glanced at her. "I've admired a few of the other pilots, but nothing could ever come of it."

"Why not?"

"Because men who like other men undoubtedly want something I lack."

"You mean a penis?" She sniffed. "They're overrated."

"Easy for you to say. There are plenty of women who share your preference. But I don't fit into either world."

"Don't you have...urges?"

Javid sighed. It felt strange to be discussing these things with Leila, but in truth, it was good to talk to *someone*.

"Of course I do. But I don't see any solution."

Leila nodded slowly. "So you prefer to live on your own terms, even if it's lonely, than pretend to be someone you aren't."

"More or less. I won't put on a dress just to get laid."

She laughed. "And you shouldn't have to. You're handsome enough. I hope you find this thief who stole your heart."

Javid rolled his eyes, but their conversation was still tumbling around in his head as he approached the Rock later that morning, so he paid little attention to the fact that the steward who met him at the door was not the usual one. And he failed to notice that the route they took was different until it was too late and they stood before two enormous bronze doors. A phalanx of guards—the royal kind, with roaring lions emblazoned on their red tunics and sharp swords in their scabbards—stood watch outside.

The throne room, Javid realized with a start.

He had no sooner processed this unwelcome piece of information when two of the guards grabbed him by the arms and dragged him inside.

A thousand candles lit the cavernous room in wavering light. King Cambyses lay on a stone slab, his arms crossed across his chest. Linen wrappings concealed his body, but his head had been left bare. The king's face held the usual masklike aspect of death, made even more gaunt by the ravages of the pox, but that wasn't the worst of it. His flesh seemed to be melting from his bones. Some distant part of Javid knew it was a bad idea to stare, but he couldn't wrench his eyes away from the ghoulish sight. Then the guards drew him closer and he realized the corpse had been coated with wax that was melting in the warmth of the candles.

The teachings of the magi forbade burial in the earth as repulsive and unclean. Ordinary people were left out in the desert for scavengers to pick the bones clean, but kings received fancier treatment. There was an arid valley near the shore of the Austral Ocean where their tombs could be found, all the way back to Cyrus the Great who'd built the Rock of Ariamazes. Cambyses would soon be shipped off there. Judging by the smell, which the wax did little to improve, it wouldn't be long.

"So," a woman's voice said coldly from the shadows. "It is Lord Asabana's dog."

The guards released Javid's arms, seizing the lacquered box of spell dust as they did so. He made the prostration and tried to keep from trembling. His mind raced. The King must have died overnight and the Queen had somehow managed to keep the news a secret.

"You are here to see Shahak."

Not "the prince" or "my son." Shahak.

"Yes, Your Illustrious Majesty," Javid informed the marble floor.

"I'm afraid you're too late." Her voice sounded well satisfied. "He's fallen ill. I doubt he shall last the day."

Poisoned? Javid wondered. Or sick from cravings for the dust? In truth, there was only a breath of difference between the two.

"Bring me the box," the Queen commanded her guards.

Footsteps scurried to the throne. Javid heard faint sounds as the hinges opened.

"As I thought," the Queen said. "Your master is a trafficker in degradation. The degradation of the soul." Her tone softened. "Under normal circumstances, I would have you dipped in boiling oil, your tongue torn out with hot pincers and your eyes removed. But this has been a trying day already, with much yet to do. So I will show you mercy. A clean stroke to the neck." She sighed audibly. "Do it over there. I won't have blood on my husband's body. It would be unseemly."

Javid heard the rasp of swords whispering from their scabbards. In the corner of his eye, he saw a flicker of movement.

Now or never.

Javid scrambled to his feet. He hadn't risen through the ranks of the Merchants' Guild without learning some hard lessons about politics. Variations of this exact scenario had kept him awake at night for the last two weeks. Javid reached into a secret compartment sewn into his coat. There was no time to judge precise quantities. He seized a generous handful and threw it into the air. The dust formed a glittering cloud that seemed to hang suspended over the king's corpse.

Holy Father, please work.

"Peta habannatu!" Javid roared, pointing at the lacquered box. *Close for me.*

The lid slammed shut and the Queen gave a little scream.

"Alka!" *Come.*

The box flew into Javid's hands, knocking him back a few steps. He clutched it to his chest with the ferocity of a mother defending her newborn infant.

The Queen half-rose from the throne, one hand at her throat. A veil covered her hair but Javid saw her face clearly for the first time and felt a moment's surprise at how beautiful she was. Then a guard slammed into him from behind. Hairy arms enclosed him in a bear hug. Javid felt a rib snap as the rest of the royal guard surged forward, swords raised.

The Queen! a voice in his head shrieked. Do something to her! Distract them!

Half the dust disappeared when he'd used it to call the box, but a few motes remained, shimmering in the candlelight, enough to cast another spell. Yes, he would dangle her upside down! Leila had taught him the phrase for that.

"Sarratum," he began with a hoarse gasp.

The word meant *queen* but Javid never got any further because a perfect hush descended over the throne room. The heavy, garlic-tinged panting of the guard, the furious mutterings of her royal highness, the thud of boots on stone, even his own stuttering heartbeat....all gone. The guards skidded to a stop, superstitious fear on their faces. Javid felt panic grip him in icy fingers. Holy Father, I've gone deaf! he thought wildly.

The last of the dust vanished. And then he understood.

It was funny, in a way.

Sarratum meant queen. But he hadn't pronounced it right. He was too winded and it came out as suharruru, or close enough.

Quiet.

As a test, he opened his mouth and tried to speak the proper spell. Nothing happened. He felt the breath exit his lungs, felt his lips and tongue form the words, but the sound simply dropped away like a stone into a well.

The Queen's soldiers were still stunned, but spells only lasted a few minutes.

Javid threw an elbow at the mountain of flesh behind him, low enough to catch its soft nether regions. The guard keeled over, mouth working in what Javid suspected would be high-pitched shrieks if he'd had the capacity to make sound. Wasting no time, Javid darted for the doors and leapt like a jackrabbit past the startled guard outside the throne room.

As he galloped through the palace, the lacquered box clamped in one sweaty hand, he regretted not paying closer attention when he was being led to Prince Shahak. The corridors zigged and zagged like a maze and the eerie silence muted any sounds of pursuit. It all had a nightmarish quality. Every time he turned a corner, he expected to run straight into the arms of a dozen soldiers.

I'll never make it out of the Rock, he thought, taking yet another random turn that led to yet more corridors and locked rooms. Five hundred guards and stewards and chamberlains stood between the inner and outer courts. But if he could find the prince, if Shahak wasn't dead, if they hadn't confined him to the dungeons....

Sound came roaring back as he skidded around a corner—shouts, the thud of boots—and Javid saw the heavy carved doors of the prince's chamber just ahead. Six soldiers stood ready before it, swords drawn. Their heads swung toward him in unison.

Javid opened the box and tossed a pinch of dust into the air with a badly trembling hand.

Don't muck this up, he thought.

His chest heaved but he sucked in a deep breath of air and managed to speak the words with precision.

"Ina etuti asbu."

Dwell in darkness.

Swords clattered to the ground as the soldiers clutched at their eyes. He'd used the imperative tense of the verb, so his own sight remained unaffected. Javid bolted past them into the room beyond. He slammed the doors shut and threw the inner bolt. Prince Shahak rose to his feet, pale and wasted. In truth, he didn't look much better than his father, though at least his nose was still intact.

"Take it, Your Majesty," Javid hissed, thrusting the box toward him. "They're coming to kill us both!"

The prince snatched the box from Javid's hands. He didn't bother with the little silver spoon. He just seized a handful of spell dust and snuffled greedily until it was all gone. A moment later, raised voices erupted in the corridor. Something heavy crashed into the doors. It sounded like reinforcements had arrived and they could see perfectly well.

"Your Highness?" Javid ventured. "I've exhausted my repertoire of spells. I'm sure you know far more than I do. They're here, just outside actually, and I don't mean to overstep myself, but I think you'd better do something about it."

Prince Shahak stood there, staring blankly down at the box. A thin line of too-dark blood trickled from his right nostril.

Oh, Holy Father. He's overdosed.

Two more tremendous blows and the doors gave way. Four soldiers burst into the room, although they stopped just over the threshold. They were wary, Javid could see it, but they were also disciplined and ready to die. Dozens more packed the corridor outside. The orange light of the braziers glanced off their naked swords.

Prince Shahak raised his head. A muscle fluttered in his jaw.

"Eli baltuti ima idu mituti," he said softly.

It took Javid a moment to work out the meaning. Once he did, he dove behind the nearest piece of furniture—a writing table—and curled into a tight ball. He wanted to close his eyes, but some perverse curiosity drove him to witness what would happen next.

Eli baltuti ima idu mituti.

The dead will outnumber the living.

Prince Shahak gave a ghastly smile. His cheeks flushed with feverish life. He did not raise a hand or make any sort of dramatic gesture. But words spilled from his mouth, a torrent of jagged, harsh syllables that lifted the hair on Javid's arms even if their meaning was beyond him.

Pressure built in the room, electric and painful to the ears. Shahak fell silent, but his eyes shone with a hellish light. The soldiers began to twitch. Coarse hair sprouted from their skin. Garments tore and fell away. They dropped to all fours, jerking as limbs shortened and rearranged themselves into a semblance of dogs, though with too many joints and in mostly the wrong places. Grotesque red tongues lolled from open mouths.

"Shall we keep them as pets?" the prince murmured. Then he shook his head. "No, they are *anzillu*. Abominations. And they betrayed us." He waved a hand. "Daku." *Kill.*

Javid watched in horror as the dog-soldiers turned on each

other with low, rumbling growls. Muscled bodies crashed together, jaws rending and snapping, until all that remained was a heap of bloody fur.

A moment later, the soldiers in the corridor outside burst apart in a crimson spray, like melons dropped from a great height. The sound of it was horrendous. Javid gagged as a single hazel eye rolled past his foot.

Without turning around, the prince said, "Alka." *Come.*

Oh, how Javid wanted to ignore that command! But it seemed unwise. So he rose on watery legs and followed Shahak into the corridor. The prince walked ten paces ahead with the relaxed gait of a man taking an evening stroll. It gave Javid plenty of time to second-guess every decision he'd ever made in his nineteen years of life. True, he had urged the prince to do something, but he hadn't expected *that*.

He'd never seen Shahak consume so much dust. What if he intended to kill everyone in the palace? Their blood would be on Javid's hands too. He stifled a groan.

At last, they reached the throne room.

An elderly man waited outside. He had sharp black eyes and a head as bald as an egg. The sigil on his robe marked him as the Hazara-patis. The Master of a Thousand. He clearly understood which way the wind was blowing for without hesitation, he bowed and pointed to the door.

"They await you, Your Highness," he said.

Javid hesitated, hoping he might manage to slip away, but Prince Shahak beckoned him forward with the twitch of one finger.

Inside the throne room, the Queen cowered behind her own royal guards with two boys who must be the Prince's brothers. One was quite young, no more than five. He had dark hair and his mother's delicate features. She clutched him to her breast. The other was older, thirteen or fourteen, and stood apart. He stared at the prince without flinching. His face was taut with terror, yet he showed courage. Javid could see a bit of his father in the jawline, but he lacked Cambyses' reckless arrogance. This boy looked both sensitive and intelligent.

Javid's remorse deepened. He would have made a better king. But it was too late now.

Shahak paused in the center of the chamber and studied his father's body without expression. In the wavering candlelight, his face appeared about as lifelike as the corpse. Finally, he turned to his mother and brothers. The little one began to cry.

"Go ahead," the Queen spat. "Kill us all. When your soul tries to cross Chinvat Bridge, you will fall into the abyss." She surveyed his blood-spattered garments. "Or perhaps you already have."

"You tried to take what was mine by birth and law," the Prince replied evenly. "And you failed. Make the prostration and I will spare you."

The Queen turned her face away.

For an instant, Shahak's mask of composure slipped. He gnashed his teeth. They clacked together and he spat three little misshapen pearls on the ground.

"Rabum," he growled.

The Queen and children quivered, their limbs jerking about like puppets in a grotesque mockery of fear. Javid wanted to run from the room, but he inexplicably found himself at the prince's side, speaking in low, urgent tones.

"Stop, Your Highness, please stop. Please."

The prince's empty eyes swung towards him. "Why?"

"Because...because it's indecent," Javid said helplessly. "They are human beings, Your Highness."

"Are they?" He laughed. "We shall see."

More words slid from his throat. Essuru. *Bird*. Kalbi. *Dog*. Usemi. *Change into*. Others Javid didn't know.

The results were immediate. The Queen and her children became mismatched beasts with fur and feathers, scales and skin, beaks and snouts, just like the carvings on the door to the prince's chamber. This task accomplished, Shahak seemed to run out of steam. He staggered to the throne and collapsed into it with a heavy sigh.

The Queen's royal guardsmen threw themselves to the ground in a full prostration.

"Long live the new king!" one cried hoarsely.

The others took up the chant.

Javid looked at the three piteous creatures who used to be the royal family. The Queen's beak opened and closed, exactly like his ma's chickens did on hot days. Her children pressed their scaled bodies together, tails low in submission. But it was the eyes that transfixed him. Yellow and filled with all too human terror.

Javid felt Shahak's gaze boring into him. He realized he was the only one still standing.

"Long live the new king," he mumbled, dropping to his knees, which gave way with very little effort. "Long live King Shahak!"

✦ 14 ✦

BLACK PEARL

Meb tossed a fish head over the rail and dropped the rest in a bucket. She used a flat stone as a chopping block, arranged on the small patch of deck near the bow she always claimed for herself. She'd tried to make herself as small and insignificant as possible, and it seemed to be working. The rest of the crew had gone back to pretending she didn't exist, which was fine by Meb. Her strong hands performed the work by rote as her mind drifted, the stars twinkling pinpoints overhead.

She was glad they'd left the Isles behind. Word of her disaster with Anuketmatma had doubtless spread to all the other fleets by now. At least Captain Kasaika hadn't kicked her off the *Asperta*. She glanced up at the moons. Selene had set and Hecate smiled in a silver crescent low on the horizon. It was Artemis that filled her with dread. The vagabond moon was already nearly the same size as Hecate. When she reached her full splendor—twice the size of Selene, the second-biggest moon—Meb would turn thirteen. Usually, a birthday governed by the house of Artemis was considered auspicious. Thirteen was the age at which a young Marakai was formally inducted into the fleet and received their first tattoo. But Meb couldn't work water. Who would want her? She'd probably be gutting fish for the rest of her life.

She bit her lip against a savage rush of anger and self-pity. Maybe she should run away and save everyone the trouble. Where would she go? Certainly not Solis. The Pythia seemed like a horrible woman. But Tjanjin.... Meb adored the capital of Chang'an. All the interesting smells, prickly spices and incense. The mortals there didn't mind daēvas. Maybe she could get a job working for the emperor, like their illustrious passenger. Even if it was just carrying messages, that would be better than gutting fish or rinsing kelp.

She lost herself in a pleasant fantasy as the waves lapped rhythmically at the hull. She would have nice clothes to wear because the emperor would never let his personal emissary go about in rags. And she would have days off to go exploring. The other Marakai would have to treat her nice because the emperor would be cross with them if they shouted at her....

"Need a hand?"

Meb jerked in surprise. It was their red-haired passenger. He looked down at her with a solemn but polite expression that made Meb feel strange. Like he really *saw* her. But she must have misheard. Captain Kasaika would snort and say she'd let her line out too far, which Meb knew meant daydreaming when she should be working.

She pulled a fish from her bucket, hoping he'd go away. But he was still standing there and seemed to be waiting for an answer.

"Are you talking to me?" she asked in a small voice.

"I don't mean to interrupt. But my cabin is stuffy. I'd rather make some use of myself during the journey and the crew hardly needs my help to sail the *Asperta*."

Her hands fell to her lap, twisting in embarrassment. "But I'm gutting fish." She glanced at his fine silver-hemmed cloak. "It's *dirty*."

"I have my own knife. And I've done it plenty of times before."

Meb shrugged and returned to her work, though she watched him warily from the corner of her eye. Why anyone would *choose* to gut fish when they didn't have to was a mystery. But he had an aura of mystery, no doubt about it. For one thing, he wasn't clumsy like most mortals. He moved well on deck, confident and light on his feet like a dancer. Meb figured he'd probably been on lots of ships in his service for the emperor.

The passenger settled himself across from her, pushing his cloak back and out of the way. He wore a plain black woolen coat underneath with a high collar. Meb snuck another quick glance. He must come from somewhere else. Red hair and blue eyes was an unusual combination, and almost unheard of in Tjanjin, where the people were small and dark, with tilted eyes. He didn't look old, but his face had a hard edge that made her think he'd seen a lot. In truth, Meb found him both intriguing and a bit frightening. He must be some kind of high-ranking courtier. If she offended him, even by accident, she'd be in even bigger trouble.

"My name is Nicodemus," he said, lining up his knife with the gills of a lungfish and slicing its head off with practiced efficiency. "What's yours?"

"Mebetimmunedjem," she muttered.

"That's a mouthful."

She thought she heard a trace of mockery in his tone, but his face looked friendly.

"I guess it is. Most call me Meb."

"I'm glad to meet you Meb. You can call me Nico if you want."

She gave a sharp nod. She was so unused to talking, it made her nervous. But then he went quiet for a while and she began to relax. The work passed quickly with two people. When they finished the first bucket, he slid the next one over and started on it without being asked. A few of the crew glanced over with raised eyebrows, but no one interfered.

"That's a fine knife you have," he said admiringly.

The blade was a mess, all covered in blood and scales, but Meb felt a flush of pride. It *was* a fine knife. Made by the master smiths in Samarqand, with a hilt of jade and carnelians. Too nice for gutting fish, but she couldn't help showing it off.

"I bought it for a black pearl," she blurted. "It was inside a fish and I found it. That's why I always check the guts."

Discovering the pearl was the only piece of good luck Meb ever had and she felt inordinately proud about it.

He gave a low whistle. "A black pearl? I've never even seen one. The gods must favor you."

"Not really," she muttered. "I never found nothing so good again."

He blinked, seeming to sense her change of mood. "Well, you never know what could happen," he said lightly. "Life is full of possibilities."

Not for me, Meb thought, but she kept her mouth shut. He had a way of drawing her out, getting her to talk, that she instinctively distrusted. Why had she told him about the pearl? Because she wanted to impress him, that's why. Oh well, she thought. It's not like he's going to steal my knife. He's probably rich as a vizier.

She watched his deft hands and noticed his own blade for the first time. It had a fierce-looking eel wrapped around the hilt.

"That's Khaf-Hor," she exclaimed, despite her vow to stay quiet. "Is it a Nyx knife?"

He gave her a conspiratorial wink. "I won it gambling in a tavern. Do you like it?"

"Yeah. But mine's better."

He laughed, a pleasant, unselfconscious chuckle like they were old friends. Meb felt a smile curling at the corners of her mouth. It was nice to laugh *with* someone.

"You're honest." His eyes grew distant. "Too many people tell you what they think you want to hear."

Meb was not familiar with this concept—more like the opposite—but she nodded anyway.

"I suppose you've done a lot of traveling," he said. "With the *Asperta*."

She shrugged. "I guess."

"Have you ever seen the Kiln?"

She glanced at him. "Just the coast and from afar. Captain Kasaika says there are dangerous reefs offshore the whole way 'round."

"I've heard that too. I've always wondered what it's like there. My mother used to say I had too much imagination. Always daydreaming."

That she understood. "Captain Kasaika says the same thing about me."

She almost, *almost* asked him about a job then, but couldn't work up the nerve. If that pleasant laugh turned mocking, she'd just die of humiliation.

"I suppose it's very hot there," he ventured. "And bright."

"I s'pose," Meb replied absently, poking through the innards of a cutthroat. It would be just perfect if she found another pearl *right now*. Then he might not laugh if she did ask for a job. He would see that she was lucky. But of course there was nothing but more guts. She tossed it aside.

"Do you think anything lives in the Kiln?"

Meb looked up. Truly, this was the strangest conversation she'd ever had with anyone.

"Don't imagine so. How could they?" She gave the matter serious consideration. "Monsters maybe."

"What sort of monsters?" His dark blue eyes caught the starlight like dusty sapphires.

"Oh, I don't know, all sorts," Meb said, warming to her subject. "Not like Khaf-Hor or Sat-bu or Them, though. 'Cause there's no water, obviously. These would be landbound monsters."

His lips twitched. "Indeed."

Meb had little experience of land and the creatures that dwelt there, but lying came like second nature to her and what is imagination but a splendid lie?

"Big teeth, for sure, and claws too. They'd shit sand—"

She slapped a hand over her mouth, leaving a bloody smear across her lips.

"Your pardon, my lord," she stammered, a panicky heat spreading through her chest. "I meant—"

"I know what you meant," he said with amusement. "And I'm not a lord. So they shit sand. What else?"

Meb clamped her lips into a line to keep from laughing. When she'd quite recovered, she gutted a dragonet. "I think they'd have great scales like mirrors to reflect the sunlight and blind their prey."

"And what would the prey be?" he asked softly.

"Dunno. Something weaker but smart enough to survive. Something good at hiding."

Nicodemus studied her for a moment. He wiped his knife clean on the cloak, heedless of the gore that stained it. "Such a perceptive child," he said. "I think—"

The cook's bellow wafted up from the open hatch beside her. "Mouse!"

Meb sighed. "Thanks for helping," she muttered. "Gotta go."

"The pleasure was mine," he replied courteously.

Nico lay on his bunk, fingers laced behind his head. If he could manage to gain the girl's trust, things would go easier when they reached Tjanjin. If not, he could always take her by force. He didn't care much either way, except that it would be simpler if she went along willingly.

A bitter smile touched his lips. She had come close to describing a wyvern, except for the part about shitting sand. That was all wrong. The children of the Kiln didn't eat sand. They ate each other.

It was why Gaius insisted the women had as many kids as possible. So their race didn't go extinct before they got their revenge on the ones who'd put them there.

And if a girl didn't find a mate quick enough, Gaius made sure she got pregnant one way or another. Even girls as young as Meb sometimes, as long as they had their first blood. It made Nico sick to think about it. When he was old enough to understand what was going on, he'd felt a shameful surge of relief that Atticus was a boy. One less thing to save him from.

Domitia was the only childless woman he knew. He wasn't sure how she'd managed it, if she was barren or what, and the one time he asked she got that look in her eye that made anyone with half a brain beat a quick retreat. But he wondered if that's why she got the idea to hunt for the gates. To get away from her father, even though she worshipped the ground he walked on.

Above all else, Domitia was a survivor. Nico couldn't fault her for that. He didn't think she disliked children. He saw her playing with the others' babies sometimes. But being pregnant slowed you down. Made you tired. And after it was born, you had to be responsible for a loud, smelly creature who attracted unwanted attention for leagues around.

And that's how you got killed. Just ask his mother.

Nico took out the globe and blew on the runes. This time he found Domitia in her personal chamber, bent over a table piled with parchment. Records about the war and the various daēva dynasties, no doubt. She still believed she could find the other talismans by tracing their family trees across a thousand years. It seemed a futile endeavor to Nicodemus, but it kept her busy.

"Where are you?" Domitia demanded with her usual lack of civility.

"I'm with the girl." He couldn't keep a hint of smugness from his voice. For all that she'd hounded him, he was the one to finally succeed. "On the way to Tjanjin. We'll come to Delphi by gate—"

"The one at the temple was broken by that stupid woman," she snapped. "Don't forget."

"I hadn't," he said tightly.

Nico harbored a deep wariness of gates since their companions had died trying to pass through from the Kiln. He'd heard the noise it made when it collapsed, like the buzzing of a thousand wasps. If Domitia hadn't been right behind him, she would have died too.

Sometimes he wondered if it wouldn't have been for the best.

"There's another gate in the Umbra, not too far from Delphi. I'll take that one." He paused. "And I think I saw the Breaker. At the Mer on the isle of the Selk."

"Missing a hand?"

"That's the one."

"You should have killed her," Domitia grated.

She clearly bore this woman a personal grudge—and Domitia never let go of grudges. She'd nurse them for years. And then, once you'd forgotten all about whatever it was you'd done to her, Domitia would fuck you over in some spectacular, merciless way.

"I didn't want to risk losing the talisman," he replied. "Burning her in the middle of the Mer in front of the Selk vizier and the captain of the ship I'd commissioned didn't strike me as the wisest course of action."

She began pacing up and down, her pristine white gown swishing against the stone floor. Nico still found it bizarre to see Domitia dressed in soft linen. To see her *clean*. They'd all been half-wild, but Domitia was the most feral of them all.

"She was with a Danai and the woman with the staff. I don't doubt they're looking for the girl, but only Sakhet knew her identity. And I killed every bird she sent out."

"Are you sure? Every one?"

"Yes," he replied, irritated. "I'm sure." He frowned. "And what have *you* managed to accomplish, with all your scheming?"

Domitia shot him a flat look. "I'm glad you found the girl, but there are larger considerations."

"Like what?" he laughed. "Getting the Greeks to invade the Persians?"

Her stony face confirmed his suspicions.

"What, exactly, is the point? When the rest of us are free, we can do whatever we like. What use is a mortal army anyway?"

"I'm following Gaius's command," she said stiffly.

Nico shook his head. Domitia's blind faith in her father never wavered, even after all he'd done to her. "He would make the whole world into the Kiln, you know that, don't you?"

"And what if he does?" Her voice dripped with contempt. "We'll survive. The others won't."

"Perhaps. But it doesn't sound like much fun," Nico observed, knowing it would irritate her beyond all reason.

"Fun?" she echoed. "Is this all a jest to you?"

Nico watched her wind herself up. Domitia was tough as nails, but her temper had always been her weak point. That, and a total absence of anything resembling a sense of humor.

"Or are you soft from consorting with mortals for too long?" she persisted. "Drinking their wine, bedding their women." She leaned into the globe, the glass distorting her face like a fishbowl. "Have you forgotten where you come from? A little burrow snake who used to beg me for food. I saved your life a hundred times over by the time we were ten."

Of course, he'd saved *her* a hundred times too, but she never mentioned that.

Nico smiled. "Fuck off, Domitia," he said mildly.

"Bring me the girl," she hissed. "You—"

He released the flows of air from the globe and her voice mercifully faded away.

He should have brought Atticus. How many times had he

wept with regret that he'd left his brother behind? But there was no guarantee of success. In truth, he had fully expected to die in the attempt. Gaius insisted the gates were all broken beyond repair, though he hadn't stopped them from trying.

If Atticus were here, Nico might seriously consider leaving the rest of them stuck behind the Gale, if only so Gaius didn't get out. The old bastard would have to die sometime.

But Atticus was still in the Kiln. So he would bring Meb to Delphi, but not for Domitia and certainly not for Gaius. Gaius was, as his new friend Gerda might say, batshit crazy. Nico had seen Gaius tear the legs from a shadowtongue while the creature screeched and squirmed and then eat the whole thing raw. They all thought he'd drop dead from the venom. A single drop of it would eat through stone and the cheek pouch held at least an ounce of poison. Gaius was puking sick for a couple of days.

Then he got better.

There were a thousand stories like that and Nico believed them all. Gaius had survived a millennium in the Kiln when most of them didn't live past the age of twenty. He'd taken hideous wounds, suffered through wracking fevers, been buried in the mudslides that came every decade or two after a violent rainstorm. None of it did the trick. He always reappeared, looking like shit but miraculously whole.

Gaius also taught the orphans how to get water, how to make weapons, how to dig a burrow. Gaius claimed none of them would be alive without him and he was probably right.

But Nico still hated him.

HE FOUND MEB THE NEXT DAY, PRYING WHELKS FROM A LONG length of rope that dangled over the edge of the ship. Her hair stuck out in all directions and was so stiff from salt, it barely moved in the steady wind filling the sails. She wore a leather vest that just covered her flat chest and baggy no-color pants. The child had the most spectacularly ugly feet Nico had ever seen. Her toes were long and simian, with ragged nails that looked *chewed*.

"Hello," he said, leaning against the rail.

Meb gave a brief nod. She was wary again, like a stray dog who wasn't sure if it would get a pat or a kick.

"Fine weather," he observed. "Will it last?"

"Dunno," she said in a surly tone. "Ask the captain."

"But you're Marakai—"

"I *said* I dunno," she muttered savagely, then clamped her lips together in that peculiar way as if she was vowing to never utter another syllable.

"Wait!" Nico said as she rose to leave. "I'm sorry." He reached into his pocket. "I have something for you."

She watched him, tense and ready to bolt. He opened his hand slowly and made a show of unwrapping the bit of cloth.

"See? It's a little piece of the sun."

She peered at the glob of sticky golden wax, its hexagonal cells only slightly mushed from his pocket. "A what?"

"A honeycomb. It's sweet."

She wrinkled her nose.

"Try it," he urged.

The Marakai diet was restricted to raw fish and black kelp— and the nasty little whelks she was prying from the rope. Nico had been told mortal children liked sweets. It couldn't hurt to bribe her with some candy.

Meb stuck out a grubby hand and shoved it into her mouth. A long moment passed as she held it on her tongue. Her eyes widened....and she spat it out, retching.

"Gah!" she exclaimed. "That's the most disgusting thing I ever tasted." Her lips pursed and wriggled, as if she wanted to spit some more but didn't dare. "I mean, thanks," she added. "It was nice to offer. But by the Mer, it's awful!"

Nicodemus stifled a smile. She acted diffident, but there was pride lurking in this girl and he knew she wouldn't like it if he laughed at her.

"Mortal children love it," he said with a shrug. "But I suppose the Marakai are different."

"Yeah." She gave him a level look. "How come you treat me like this?"

"Like what?"

She searched for words. "Like a real person."

Suddenly, Nico couldn't meet her eyes. "Just bored, I guess," he said.

She nodded, in no way offended. Actually, she looked relieved. It was an explanation that made sense to her. He watched her hurry away. Then he nudged the soggy remains of the honeycomb with his toe. They fell without a splash into the dark sea.

BREATH OF THE NAHRESI

The *Chione* raced across the waves, swept along by a powerful northwesterly current. The Marakai crew were working vast amounts of water power to close the distance with the *Asperta*. If she concentrated hard, Nazafareen could feel an echo of it, like the whispering of distant voices. Her own blood hummed in response.

Crack!

Her eyes flew open, the fragile connection shattered. Twenty paces off, Darius was sparring with Megaera. Once her seasickness passed, she'd offered to teach him the staff and Captain Mafuone gave them a space on the stern deck.

It hadn't taken Darius long to outpace his tutor. He was stronger and faster, with feline reflexes. The Maenad was doing her best to match his blurring slashes and spins, but she was clearly hard-pressed. Nazafareen had the feeling Darius was holding back so as not to humiliate her. Surprisingly, Megaera didn't seem to mind. She was quite taken with him, and Megaera rarely liked anybody.

When he wasn't in one of his black moods, Darius could be enjoyable company. He had a quick wit and enjoyed trading barbs with her. After Megaera teased him about his beard, which she compared to a moth-eaten fur slipper, he'd borrowed a knife from one of the sailors and managed to shave it off with only a few nicks. But he hadn't cut his hair, which was almost to his shoulders now. It had a nice wave to it, Nazafareen thought idly, and slid through her fingers like silk.

Darius pivoted on the ball of one foot, bringing his staff overhead and offering a tantalizing glimpse of bare hip. Nazafareen's cheeks warmed as she remembered the previous evening, soft kisses in the hollow of his throat, strong hands cupping her—

"She's brave to fight him," Katsu observed, dropping easily to the deck beside her. "I have no fear of any man—or woman—but only a lunatic would take on a daēva."

Nazafareen gave a guilty start. The Stygian wore a half-smile as if he could read her thoughts. He wasn't old, but the fine lines around his eyes—and their haunted look—made her think he'd suffered some recent hardship.

"Must one be insane to be fearless?" she said lightly.

Katsu shrugged. "Only the very young or very old are truly fearless. The rest of us scrape together our courage and do what we must knowing the consequences."

She looked at him askance. "You speak like a soldier."

He smiled. "More like a mercenary."

Nazafareen's suspicions deepened. "Ah, yes. The captain said you were a thief-catcher. How does one fall into such a profession?"

"I trained in the fighting arts at the Temple of the Four Winds, but I didn't wish to become a warrior-priest." Katsu grinned. "Too much of a sinner, I suppose. But I may go back there when we reach Tjanjin. The brothers would take me in."

"And how did you end up in Delphi?" she persisted.

He glanced at her. "I was looking for something."

"Did you find it?"

His expression darkened. "No."

Nazafareen was just conniving to squeeze more information from him when one of the Marakai sailors sauntered up. Like the captain, she wore a dozen silver bracelets on each arm. They jingled as she stuck her hands on her hips.

"Katsu!" she said with a wicked smile. "You're looking disreputable as ever."

He eyed her slowly up and down. "And you, Nefertnesu, are a lotus blossom drifting on a still pond, each drop of dew a shining jewel."

She laughed. "Very pretty. You might be a Stygian, but you have the poetic soul of the Tjanjinese." She winked. "Come to my cabin. I would hear more verses."

Katsu leapt to his feet. "It would be my greatest pleasure. And yours as well, I hope."

Nazafareen watched them go below with irritation. She wasn't entirely sure what she suspected him *of*, but it seemed a mighty coincidence he'd sought passage the very moment they left port. And he had come from Delphi. A creature of the Pythia? He didn't seem like the fanatical sort, but looks could be deceiving.

Nazafareen looked up as Megaera approached and dropped to the deck beside her.

"What do you think of the Stygian?" she asked in a low voice.

"I'm not sure." Megaera scowled. "He did come from Delphi though. He told me the Pythia razed all the temples of Dionysius and put a death warrant on anyone caught worshipping him." She glanced at Nazafareen. "Don't worry, I didn't mention what you did to the gate or anything of importance. But I swear, I'll see that woman brought low, one way or another." Her mouth drew into a line. "I just hope Stheno got away before they put our temple to the torch."

"Stheno?"

"The snake." Megaera smiled fondly. "Rhea named her for one of the Gorgons. She could be touchy about strangers, but she kept the place free of vermin."

Nazafareen remembered Stheno well. The creature had given her a bad start the first time she'd slithered out from the bull's head altar. She didn't especially like snakes, but it saddened her to think she'd met a lonely end.

"I'm sure she's fine," Nazafareen said consolingly. "And we'll rebuild the temples someday. Even bigger and better than they were before."

Megaera sighed, laying her staff across her knees. "Our cult has been in decline for a long time now. The Pythia merely delivered the final blow."

Nazafareen tipped her head back, studying the river of stars above. She recalled what Rhea told her when they followed the Stork's unfaithful wife. How the Vatras were the children of Apollo and the Maenads were the children of Dionysius. The gods were brothers, both sons of Zeus, but where Apollo stood for logic and order, Dionysius governed the realms of instinct and magic. The light and the dark. Yet one could not exist without the other.

"The Pythia is not all-powerful," Nazafareen said. "She's just a greedy woman with too much ambition. But the Maenads answer a higher call. And I'm certain Dionysius watches over us."

"It is so," Megaera said. She gave a crooked grin. "Your temper may actually be worse than mine, but you do speak sense from time to time."

Nazafareen grinned back. "Only occasionally, and usually by accident." She clapped the Maenad on the shoulder. "Just ask Darius. He says my mother used to compare me to a barking dog. Lots of noise but very little sense."

Megaera laughed. "Your mother had a sense of humor too."

"I suppose she did." Nazafareen's laughter died. "If only I could remember her."

Megaera was saved from replying by the arrival of Herodotus, who stooped over them like a wading bird.

"Captain Mafuone wishes to see us," he said, lowering his voice. "I think she wants to know what our plan is."

"Plan?" Nazafareen asked, glancing at Megaera.

"Yes."

"Do you have one?"

He tugged at his beard, leaving a smudge of ink. "I thought *you* did."

"Yes," Nazafareen said hastily. "Of course I do."

Once they'd gathered in her cabin, the captain cut straight to the point.

"We're pursuing a Vatra," she said. "I don't want the *Chione*, nor my crew, to meet the same end Sakhet-ra-katme did. How do you intend to take Meb back, assuming we find her?"

"I can break his flows," Nazafareen replied.

"If you are in Solis. But half of Tjanjin is covered by the Umbra."

Nazafareen hadn't realized this and the thought made her deeply uneasy.

"If we find him in the twilight, I'll manage him," Megaera said. "His magic is nothing to me."

Mafuone raised an eyebrow. "Really? And why is that?"

"Dionysius blessed us with an immunity to fire. I would demonstrate, but fire isn't permitted in the darklands."

"No, it is not. For a good reason. Which is why you cannot take Darius with you, nor any of my crew. It's too dangerous."

"I won't let them go alone," Darius said immediately.

"And how will you resist reaching for the flames?" the captain demanded. "The urge is instinctual. The blood will boil in your veins!"

Darius glanced at Nazafareen, who nodded. He let his sleeve fall back.

"This cuff is a talismanic device. Nazafareen wears its match. She can sever me from the power if needed."

Again, provided they were in Solis. But Darius did not mention this.

Captain Mafuone looked at him with something close to horror.

"Why would you wear it?"

"I have my reasons," Darius said stonily.

She shook her head. "It is your choice. And if it saves you from burning, I suppose it has its uses. But we have another difficulty. If Nicodemus is truly friends with the emperor, he has an all-powerful ally."

"He won't stay in Tjanjin," Nazafareen said. "His plan must be to bring Meb to the Gale. To force her to break the barrier. That's what Kallisto believed."

"Then why did he want the *Asperta* to sail to Tjanjin rather than Delphi?"

"Because the ports there are closed to the Marakai," Herodotus suggested.

"Which leaves him with the same problem."

"What if he doesn't go to Tjanjin at all?" Nazafareen said. "What if he takes her as a hostage and forces them to sail directly for the Kiln?"

Mafuone shook her head. "There's nowhere to land. I've seen the whole coast." She spread her hands on the table. "So. The question remains whether we assume they are going to Tjanjin or somewhere else. I know Kasaika though. She'd put up a fight if she knew."

"Would he risk burning a ship in the middle of the ocean?" Darius wondered. "He'd die too. And Meb would be lost."

They were all quiet for a moment, mulling over the possibilities.

"Is there a gate in Tjanjin?" Nazafareen asked.

"Not that I know of," Herodotus said. "But the scholars keep their secrets close. What I wouldn't give for an hour in their library! It's one of the largest and oldest collections in the world. Strictly closed to outsiders, unfortunately."

"So there may or may not be a gate." Nazafareen looked at the others. "I vote for Tjanjin. He could have taken Meb by force on the Selk island, but he didn't. That means he's cautious, to a degree. He won't risk her without a good reason."

"I agree," Captain Mafuone. "Tjanjin then."

Darius and Megaera nodded in assent, though Herodotus still seemed lost in wistful thoughts about the forbidden library. Nazafareen had to tug his hand.

"What? Yes, Tjanjin," he said. "The reasoning seems sound to me."

They rose to leave. At the door, Nazafareen turned back. "You won't tell Katsu any of this?"

The captain frowned. "No. But you have nothing to fear from Katsu. I told you, he's an honorable man."

Nazafareen forced a smile. "Of course."

THE *CHIONE* SAILED ON. SHE SAT ON THE DECK, LISTENING TO Herodotus and Darius discussing the constellations and how they differed in the world of the Empire. The Archer existed in both places, and so did the Queen, though Herodotus called it Cassiopeia. But others seemed unique to Nocturne, like the Maze and Pan's Flute, a line of bright stars that always pointed north.

She'd grown fond of the old scholar and his childlike curiosity. He was always asking questions of the crew, about their habits and customs and the stories their mothers told them and how they chose their captains and a hundred other things. The Marakai were suspicious at first, but his obvious sincerity and diffident manner had won them over and most of them indulged him when they weren't busy working. He'd accumulated reams of parchment, purchased in Susa before their departure, that he kept in waterproof oilskin packages. Nazafareen thought it would be worth learning to read if only so she could enjoy the books he intended to write.

She hugged her knees deeper into the cloak, squinting as a blue light appeared on the horizon. The ship drew closer and she saw luminous streaks within the water, like swarms of blue fireflies.

"What is that?" Nazafareen wondered aloud.

"The Milky Sea," replied one of the sailors. He wore heavy lines of kohl around his eyes in the style of the Marakai men. "You'll only find it on the way to Tjanjin."

She stood and leaned over the rail as the swarms surrounded the ship until the entire surface seemed lit from below.

"But what is it?"

"Some say the Blue Crown of the Khepresh came from these waters. That it's the breath of the Nahresi as they gallop along the ocean floor." He smiled and pointed to the horizon. "I think you bring us good luck, for here comes the Aurora as well. Never have I seen the two at once."

As if in answer, curtains of magenta and green and crimson descended from the heavens, like a hole had been torn in the sky and was bleeding pure light. Nazafareen stood transfixed at the spectacle. It seemed driven by an invisible wind, unfurling in ribbons of shimmering color that looked alive.

She leaned against Darius and they watched without speaking as the light from the sea joined the light from the sky. It was a cold, unearthly power. Her own magic didn't stir, yet it touched something deep within her, something human but magical nonetheless.

When it finally faded away, Nazafareen realized her face was damp. And she thought of the man with the scar, the Valkirin named Culach Kafsnjór, who was blind and would never see such marvels.

Something shifted in her heart then. A small thing. So small,

Nazafareen barely noticed at the time. She dried her face and they went below and she didn't think of Culach again. Not for days.

But when she did, this small shift would have large consequences.

❧ 16 ❧

MEB THE SHARK

Nicodemus gave Meb a casual wave as he disembarked from the *Asperta*. Her mouth formed an odd grimace he suspected was a smile. Then she slithered into one of the open hatches leading below. He'd managed to speak to her twice more during the journey, but the cook had scolded her for slacking off and Meb mostly disappeared after that. Perhaps it was better. He'd planted the seed. She didn't yet trust him, but she liked him. And he still had a final card to play.

No, you're hopeless at cards, he thought. Let's call it a final roll of the dice. *They* always fall your way.

The port of Tjanjin sat just past the edge of the Umbra. Eternal twilight cloaked the eastern side of the island, with a few smoky blue mountains visible in the distance. By contrast, the capital city of Chang'an basked in low-slanting sunlight from the west that gilded its scarlet pagoda-style rooftops. Silken banners with bold black glyphs rippled in the breeze, advertising everything from fireworks to teahouses—half of which were illicit gambling dens. Nico stretched like a tiger, relishing the warmth on his skin. He wasn't built for the dark and cold. They dulled his blood.

He'd decided to capture the girl someplace quiet. Years of tracking dangerous animals in the Kiln had instilled a healthy sense of caution. Move too soon and you might find yourself the hunted rather than the hunter. Not that he believed Meb to be dangerous. If she could use her power, the others would hardly treat her as they did. But he had no wish to kill Captain Kasaika and her entire crew. It would be pointless bloodshed.

So he politely thanked the captain, paid the balance of his passage and melted into the crowds clogging the harbor. Then he found an alley with a clear view of the *Asperta* and sat on a barrel to wait. Nico had long experience at waiting. He could lie half-buried in sand for hours, the sun pouring down in molten waves, watching the burrow of a bush-rat. One of the few creatures in the Kiln you could actually eat, bush-rats were also extremely paranoid—probably for the same reason—and difficult to catch. But starvation was a great motivator.

A stillness settled over him. Part of him floated in the oneness of the Nexus. The other part remained quietly focused on the *Asperta*.

After a while, Meb emerged from below decks and spoke briefly with Captain Kasaika. The girl's body language was skittish and hangdog as usual, but when the captain gave a brusque nod, she brightened. He watched Meb slip like a shadow along the pier. No one gave her a second glance. She meant nothing to anyone, except for him. He hardened his heart against a tiny mote of pity. This girl was heir to the power that had imprisoned his people for a thousand years. Whether she knew it or not was immaterial.

He thought of Atticus, whom he'd found screaming over the corpse of their mother at the age of two. The memory was dim and fractured—Nico himself was five or six—but he remembered the blood on the walls of the burrow, and Gaius's strong hands closing around his arm and dragging him away. Later, Gaius had hunted the wyrm that got inside. He brought Nico the head, grinning like a lunatic.

Present for you, boy. Eat the eyes and you'll have a hard-on for a week!

Nico hadn't. He'd buried it in the sand so it wouldn't attract predators and then he'd set out to dig a new burrow for him and Atticus. Even if Gaius had offered, the thought of living in his burrow made Nico faint with fear.

If his brother wasn't dead himself yet, he had a chance at a real life. And Gaius.... Well, Nico would worry about him later.

He stood and chose a course to intercept her when two men tumbled out of a tavern door ahead, grappling drunkenly. A crowd of onlookers spilled out behind them, offering shouts of abuse and encouragement. Nico heard bets being placed in the harsh, rapid tongue of Tjanjinese. One of the combatants reeled into him and Nico shoved the man away. His gaze swung back to the pier. Meb had vanished.

Nicodemus's mouth thinned. He walked over to the brawling men and kicked one of them viciously in the head, knocking the man senseless. There was a moment's hush. Then the crowd erupted in outraged cries. He spat out an oath in Tjanjinese and stalked off. No one tried to stop him.

It didn't matter. Nico guessed where she was going. Meb might be the talisman, but she was also a child. She wouldn't have money for a tea house.

And there was a much more interesting place on Tjanjin that cost nothing at all.

Darius leapt to the pier before the *Chione*'s mooring rope was even secured. He scanned the crowded port, searching for Selk ships. Nazafareen's boots thumped down beside him a moment later.

To her great relief, the port lay on the sunlit side. Her power had returned the moment the sun peeked over the western horizon—along with the bond and Darius's infirmity. He kept his withered hand hidden in the sleeve and Nazafareen avoided looking at it, not because it repelled her, it didn't in the least, but because it made her feel guilty.

"Do you see the *Asperta*?" she asked.

"Not yet. We should split up and search."

Tjanjin was easily five times larger than the Selk port. It had six main jetties, countless smaller ones, and besides the Marakai ships, there were fishing vessels and pilot boats and swift passenger ferries with water wheels that appeared to be powered by spell dust.

"Come with me," Megaera growled, seizing Herodotus by the sleeve and hauling him off down the jetty. "We'll take the east side," she called over her shoulder.

"Poor Herodotus," Nazafareen murmured. "She bullies him terribly."

"Only because he lets her," Darius observed. "Let's go."

They dove into the controlled chaos of the port with Captain Mafuone. Voices jabbered in a dozen different dialects. Sewage and sawdust mingled with rotting fish and smoky joss sticks. Nyx vessels nudged shoulders with Sheut and Khepresh. It looked haphazard, but Mafuone seemed to know where to go and led them straight to the farthest pier.

"Over there," she said, pointing into the forest of masts at an older vessel with the volatile gray cat flying from its masts, her tail lashing in the wind.

The ship was still being unloaded. It must have just arrived. But there was no sign of the red-haired man, or a girl either.

"Captain Kasaika," Mafuone called out when they reached the *Asperta*.

The captain glanced up from a piece of parchment where she was ticking off items of cargo. She was short and buxom, with a closely shaved head. Unlike Mafuone, she wore no jewelry, but every visible inch of skin bore colorful tattoos, fantastic scenes of storm clouds and shipwrecks, frothing smashers and flocks of birds flying for cover. The scenes were so painstakingly lifelike, Nazafareen could almost hear rolls of thunder in the distance.

"Mafuone." Kasaika looked surprised. "I didn't know you were behind us."

"A last-minute decision," Mafuone replied. "You carried a passenger. Where is he?"

"Gone ashore an hour or so ago," Kasaika replied, returning to the parchment. "Why?"

"I'll explain in a moment." Mafuone shot a quelling look at Nazafareen. "But we're also looking for a girl."

"By Anu's whiskers, what's she done now?" Kasaika demanded in exasperation.

"Nothing," Nazafareen said quickly. "But we have to find her. Did she go somewhere with the man named Nicodemus?"

Kasaika looked her up and down. "Whoever you are, I'll not hand Meb over—"

"We don't wish to harm her," Mafuone interrupted. "The opposite. She's in grave danger."

"I gave Meb leave to go ashore," Kasaika said after a pause. "She usually visits the aquarium. It's open to the public."

"How do we find it?" Darius asked.

Nazafareen felt the urge to run, to hunt and track, rising in his blood.

"It's next to the palace. The main entrance is just up the road, past the fish market." She pointed toward the city. "That way. But—"

"What does Meb look like?" Mafuone asked.

The captain of the *Asperta* threw her hands up. "She must have done something, you want her so bad. Did she steal from you?"

"Please, Kasaika. We've known each other a long time. I'll tell you everything, but they need to find that girl."

"Meb? Skinny, wild hair. Acts like the Five put a blood bounty on her head. She's a skulker and a sneak. Lazy, too." Kasaika's words seemed unkind, but Nazafareen sensed a gruff fondness. "Not many Marakai go to the aquarium so she'll stand out— though if there's a shadow in fifty paces, Meb'll lurk in it." She drew a breath and began rolling up the parchment. "If that girl's in trouble, maybe I better go with you."

"No time," Mafuone said. She turned to Darius and jerked her chin toward the city. "I'll stay and talk with Captain Kasaika."

Nazafareen and Darius set off, pausing every now and then to ask directions. Most of the residents were fluent in several tongues and happy to offer help. Soon they reached a pair of tall wrought-iron gates with fanciful sea horses clinging to the finials. Nazafareen caught the crisp scent of cedar and pine trees. Beyond the gates, rolling wooded hills, each with a red-roofed pagoda on top, stretched into the distance. Shallow pools shimmered between them, connected by rope bridges.

"If he uses fire, you'll have to sever me," Darius said. "Don't hesitate."

Nazafareen nodded tensely. "I'll never let you burn, Darius. And I know I can break his flows. I did it with the Valkirin. He won't have her."

They ran through the gates and into the aquarium.

MEB PERCHED ON A LOW STONE WALL, WATCHING A DOZEN dark shapes cruise through the large saltwater pool beside her. Every now and then, a curved fin broke the surface, leaving a wake of ripples. The emperor used a clever system of locks to raise vast amounts of water up the hill from the port below. It was almost feeding time and the shapes circled in mounting excitement. Meb reached her hand out as one slid past, fingertips brushing its rough hide. She gave a little shiver of pleasure. The pool was her favorite exhibit, and the aquarium was her favorite place in the whole world.

At the aquarium, she wasn't Meb the Mouse. She was Meb the Shark.

Two workers with buckets walked to the middle of the rope bridge suspended over the pool and started tossing chunks of fish into the water. Meb thrilled at the ensuing frenzy. She watched the ragged jaws gnash and tear, the mighty tails whip to and fro, and felt a surge of savage admiration. She clacked her teeth together experimentally. She might pretend to be a shark at supper and eat her own fish that way, though she'd have to make sure the cook didn't see. He already thought her table manners abominable.

It was still early and the aquarium was deserted, just how she liked it. She rose to leave—Meb always visited the exhibits in exactly the same order, and the octopi pagoda, her second favorite, was next on the list—when she saw a man and woman on the far side of the pool. They seemed to be looking for something, a particular exhibit perhaps. The woman shaded her eyes and suddenly Meb recognized the chin-length light brown hair and bold nose. It was the one who'd bumped into her back on Selk.

She instinctively sidled away to one of the mermaid statues ringing the pool and peeked out from behind a fin. Meb noticed things about people and she saw the man had some kind of injury to his left arm. He was trying to hide it with long sleeves, but it hung dead at his side. And the woman was missing her hand. What an odd pair, Meb thought. They started to turn her way when a hand clamped over her mouth. She struggled wildly. She owned nothing worth stealing, but she had a dim notion there were bad people on the Umbra side who trafficked in children.

"Hush, Meb," a voice whispered in her ear. "It's me."

The hand relaxed and she found herself looking into a pair of kindly dark blue eyes. It was the passenger from the *Asperta*.

"Why'd you grab me?" she demanded.

"I need you to listen closely, Meb," he said softly, drawing her deeper into the shadow of the statue. "Those people are looking for you."

"For me?" She frowned.

"They've been sent by the Oracle of Delphi. Do you know her?"

Meb nodded suspiciously.

"She captures daēvas and forces them to do her bidding. She arranged for the capture of your parents. But they're alive. I can take you to them."

Meb felt a terrible coldness grip her. The man was lying. Her parents were dead.

"Let *go*," she hissed, pulling at her arm, which he held in his strong hand.

To her surprise, he did let go. "You don't believe me and there's no reason you should," he said evenly. "You have every right not to trust me. But I can prove it."

Meb wanted to run, but her feet didn't move. She could hardly breathe.

"Your mother's name is Ahset. Your father is Sendjemib. He used to call you Jem because it's part of his name too and he said you were precious. He taught you how to catch driftfish with your bare hands when you were six. Your mother has a scar on her left forearm. A line caught it and nearly took the limb off but your father cut it with his knife before—"

"Stop," she whispered, heart pounding. "Just stop."

The day her parents vanished, Meb had gone to New Hope to buy a new net for her mother after a huge tigerfish swam into the old one and shredded it to bits. She'd never let Meb do that before, but Meb had begged and pleaded and she'd finally relented. Meb had sworn not to speak to anyone except the Stygian who made the nets, who her mother said was an honest man. When she'd returned, flushed with newfound confidence and a beautiful flaxen net in her hands, she found the house empty.

They lived in a stone dwelling with four rooms and a roof of woven kelp, on the remote, unsettled side of the Selk Isle, and were the only Marakai she knew who didn't live shipboard. When Meb asked her parents why, they hugged her and said it was because she was special. Meb knew they meant her disability, but she wasn't lonely for the company of other children. She passed her days swimming and fishing and combing the shore for interesting things the sea heaved up, and altogether felt quite happy and loved.

That awful day, Meb had waited and waited, but they never came back. Sometimes she wondered if a rogue smasher had come along and swallowed them whole, but there was no sign of it on the beach of their quiet lagoon. She'd finally returned to New Hope and told the captain of the first Marakai ship she found, who happened to be Kasaika. After long months of fruitless, painful hope, she'd resigned herself to the fact that their deaths would remain a mystery.

And now Nicodemus was telling her they were alive, after all this time.

"I know it's hard to believe," he said gently. "But I helped free them. The emperor hates the Pythia too. That was the mission he sent me on. They're waiting for us, but we have to hurry."

"How come you didn't tell me before?" she asked in a daze.

"I wasn't sure who to trust so I waited until we arrived in Tjanjin." He sighed. "If you don't want to come, I won't make you. But it's a chance that won't come again. I'm meeting your parents and we're leaving Tjanjin. Right now. It's not safe here."

Meb wasn't stupid. She had a thousand questions. And she sensed holes in his tale. But she wanted to believe him. So badly. She glanced around the edge of the mermaid. The man and woman were gone.

She thought of the *Asperta* and Captain Kasaika. She thought about endless buckets of fish and the long nights when she lay in her hammock, listening to the crew laugh and joke together. They *belonged*. She didn't belong anywhere. They *hated* her. Even if Nicodemus was lying, what could be worse than her life now? He didn't seem the type to traffic in children. He'd given her honey-comb—even if it was disgusting.

"All right," she said decisively. "Let's go."

He gave a grave nod and they set off across the rope bridge.

NICO FELT A THRILL OF ALMOST SUPERSTITIOUS DREAD AS THEY left the bridge and entered a cedar forest. He couldn't believe the pair from the Mer had managed to track them here. Domitia claimed the woman could wield huo mofa, but what if she had other powers they knew nothing about?

He insisted on holding Meb's hand. She didn't like it, he could tell, but she allowed him to lead her away. He hadn't clasped a child's hand in his own since Atticus. Meb's felt damp and grimy, where his brother's had always been hot and dry. They couldn't be more different. Atticus was good-natured and cheerful, whereas Meb was a nasty little thing. He'd give her to Domitia and walk away. She was one of *them*. Nothing more.

They passed through one of the long pagodas, which held great glass tanks filled with darting rainbow-hued fish. Lumen crystals inside the tanks lit Meb's features in a greenish glow, as if they were walking together on the bottom of the sea.

"Not much farther," he whispered, giving her hand a reas-suring squeeze.

They crossed rope bridges and took more winding paths. The gate lay inside the aquarium, but on the far eastern side. They were nearly there when Nicodemus heard a shout. He spun and saw them. The Danai and the woman. He shoved Meb away and unleashed a gout of flame, but it evaporated like mist a pace away.

The woman stared at him, triumph and fury mingling on her face.

"Let her go!" she yelled, drawing a sword. "Let her go, you bastard, or I'll—"

The rest of her words were snatched away by a ferocious gust of wind that knocked Nicodemus from his feet. The *Danai*.

He felt everything slipping away. Domitia was right. He should have killed them when he had the chance. This wasn't a fight he could win.

Nico cursed his own stupidity. But there was always a way out. Always. He hadn't survived the Kiln for thirty-one years without taking that lesson to heart.

NAZAFAREEN REVELED IN THE DARK POWER OF THE VOID. IT was different this time. She didn't feel sick at all. She felt *wonderful*. Black lightning sizzled in her veins. When the negatory magic filled her, the holes in her brain didn't seem to matter. She was a creature of pure instinct. Delilah had called her reckless, but she felt entirely in control. As if she was born to use it.

She'd released Darius from the cuff once she realized she could smother the Vatra's flames with ease. Half the aquarium sat in the Umbra, but they'd crossed the line to the sunlit side. Here, she could do as she pleased. And no one could stop her.

Now the Vatra was on the run. He crawled toward a wooden door set in the high stone wall encircling the aquarium.

She ran across the swaying rope bridge, Darius on her heels. Bottle-nosed porpoises darted through the pool below in agitation. The girl clung to the trunk of a pine tree, clearly terrified. Nazafareen felt Darius release the flows of air. The wind died.

Fifty paces. She readied herself to snap any flows the Vatra tried to weave. Daēvas were hard to kill, but they bled like anything else.

Nazafareen squinted at the girl and realized she'd seen her before. It was the same one who'd knocked her to the ground in New Hope. She'd literally had Meb in her arms.

"I won't lose you again," she muttered.

Then the Vatra beckoned. And the girl ran toward him.

"No," Nazafareen screamed. "Don't!"

She felt a tiny burst of power and shattered it, but she was an instant too late. The wooden door opened. The two of them slipped through.

Nazafareen didn't pause, slamming into it with one shoulder, but it was locked tight again. She gazed up at the wall. Twenty paces of stone stretched above her head.

"Damn," she growled, glaring at her stump.

"I've got it," Darius muttered. Even with his withered arm, he managed to find tiny hand and toeholds. A minute later, he was peering over the top.

"Do you see them?" Nazafareen called.

He looked down at her. "Yeah. And about a hundred of the emperor's guards."

Nazafareen kicked the door in frustration.

"What are they doing?"

"The guards are escorting them toward the palace. They know the Vatra."

"Damn!"

He dropped to the ground, landing lightly on his feet. "Too many to fight." He paused. "And a bunch of them are headed back this way."

"I'm not leaving without Meb!"

"We'll come back. But we need a plan."

They heard voices on the other side of the door. Nazafareen raised her fist to pound on it, but Darius grabbed her arm.

"Holy Father, listen to reason. If we get arrested, there's no chance. We'll come back. Tonight. But we need help."

Calm determination flowed into her through their bond.

Nazafareen swore again but followed him into the trees. As they passed the spot where the Vatra had fallen, a faint pulse of talismanic magic snapped her head around like a hunting dog catching the scent of a hare. She slowed and crouched down. A glass object lay under a bush. It was shaped like a globe and had strange runes carved into the base. Storm clouds roiled in its depths. The Vatra must have dropped it when Darius knocked him down. Nazafareen picked it up, fighting the urge to shatter the magic inside.

"Hurry," Darius yelled over his shoulder.

"Coming!" She pocketed the talisman and sprinted to catch up.

17

THE TRAVELER

Captain Mafuone leaned back in her chair and regarded the group assembled in her cabin.

Nazafareen sat next to Megaera, who was still grumbling under her breath at being left behind in the harbor. Darius leaned against the door, one knee bent. Herodotus had found a dark corner for himself, where he surreptitiously scribbled on a bit of parchment, determined to record the proceedings for posterity. Captain Kasaika sat directly across from Mafuone, tattooed arms gripping the sides of her chair.

Word had been sent to all the Marakai ships that a Selk girl was missing and they should watch for her. Mafuone also dispatched her own crew to keep an eye on the palace gates. No one would leave Tjanjin without them knowing about it.

"You should have told the Five," Kasaika said for the third time.

"There was no time," Mafuone replied. "If we'd waited, the Vatra and Meb would already be gone."

"And you think he can use her to break the Gale?" Kasaika ran a hand over her gleaming scalp. "By the Mer, this is some crazy shit."

"How are we going to get her back?" Nazafareen burst out. "That's what we need to be talking about."

"Quiet, girl," Kasaika growled. "I'm thinking."

"How many Marakai are in the harbor?" Nazafareen persisted. "Two hundred? More? If you call them together and march on the palace, I can't imagine the emperor's guards will stop you!"

"It's more complicated than that," Kasaika snapped. "Think for a moment. If this man is truly a Vatra, he's holding Meb hostage. And I will *not* mount an invasion of Tjanjin without the explicit consent of the Five!"

"You're both right," Darius said quietly. "We can't afford to wait, but we can't risk Meb either."

"I still can't believe Sakhet-ra-katme is dead," Kasaika muttered. "She asked me look after Meb when her parents disappeared. Sakhet said she had a disability, but she never mentioned a word about talismans. That Meb is one of them.... The girl can't work a drop of water!"

"It's one of the signs." Herodotus's mild voice drifted over from the corner. "A weakness in the element of their own clan."

"But why?" Kasaika demanded.

"We don't know," Darius admitted.

"And Nicodemus had Sakhet's knife?"

"I saw it myself," Nazafareen said. "At the Mer on Selk. But if that's not proof enough for you, he tried to work fire right in front of me."

"How do you know he didn't use spell dust?" the captain of the *Asperta* asked with an edge of skepticism.

"He wove the flows directly. I saw them."

Kasaika gave her a hard stare. "You can *see* elemental flows?"

"And break them."

Her brown eyes slitted. "Show me."

Kasaika's gaze turned to the cup of wine braced in Megaera's lap. An instant later, a crimson globule of liquid floated in the air. Megaera's mouth fell open as it quivered in the air before her face, forming a perfect sphere. Nazafareen smiled. She slashed at the web of power and it splashed onto Megaera's boots. The Maenad swore under her breath.

Kasaika stared, shock on her face. "How...?"

"She killed two chimeras on my vessel," Mafuone put in. "She is a Breaker of magic."

"Huo mofa?" Kasaika muttered warily. "I've heard of this. Very dangerous."

"I've learned to control it," Nazafareen lied. "If you send your people to the palace, they wouldn't be in danger from the Vatra."

Kasaika's jaw worked for a long moment. "I still can't approve an attack on the palace." She held up a hand. "But neither will I abandon Meb, whether or not this man is truly a Vatra."

"You don't believe," Mafuone said flatly.

"I know all about the Sheut prophecy," Kasaika replied. "That the time of Isfet will return. But it's a belief of the Shadow Marakai, not the Selk. I don't rule it out, but I need more proof than the word of a mortal."

"I have daēva blood," Nazafareen said heatedly.

"Whatever." Kasaika turned to Mafuone, ignoring the others. "We must demand an audience with the emperor first. Tell him his emissary lured one of our girls inside and we want her back. He's always been our staunchest ally among the mortals. Delphi has declared us enemies, and who knows what will happen to Samarqand? We must tread carefully. You know I'm right, Mafuone."

The captain of the *Chione* gave a reluctant nod.

"I want to go too," Nazafareen said, her head swinging back and forth between them.

Kasaika laughed. "Not a chance. This is a Marakai matter. And you squawk like a drunken gull."

Nazafareen opened her mouth, then shut it with a snap. She remained silent, but gripped her sword hilt with white fingers.

"If we're unsuccessful, I'm willing to consider other proposals," Kasaika said. "By the Mer, that's my final word."

Nazafareen grumbled something unintelligible. She reached into a pocket of her cloak.

"I also found this. I think the Vatra dropped it."

She held out the globe. Captain Mafuone took it in her hands and studied it for a moment. Then she passed it to Kasaika.

"A talisman," Kasaika murmured. "Any idea what it does?"

"None. Can't you tell?"

"Reading talismans is not a Marakai talent." She shrugged. "It's a curious object." She peered at the clouds speeding past in the globe's depths, as though driven by hurricane winds. "Perhaps something to do with the weather?"

A little flicker of lightning from inside the globe lit her features.

"I'll keep it," Nazafareen said. "Maybe we can learn something."

She held out her hand for the globe just as a shadow passed the square porthole. She turned to see Katsu staring into the cabin, his gray eyes fixed intently on the globe. Then he gave a start and smiled, raising his hand in a wave. She watched him amble down the gangplank and vanish into the crowds. He didn't look back.

"Why is he still on board?" she asked. "We've been docked for hours."

Mafuone raised an eyebrow. "Saying goodbye to Nefertnesu, I imagine. They've been down below together. She always did have a weakness for Stygians."

The two captains rose to their feet. Mafuone stood more than a head taller, but Kasaika exuded a brute authority that wasn't in the least undercut by the angelically smiling cat inked on her cheek. The globe emitted another flicker of lightning and for an instant, Darius could have sworn he saw the massive wave on

Kasaika's forearm curl and foam. He blinked. Hadn't the sinking ship been on her *other* bicep before?

"Stay here," Mafuone ordered, eyeing them all sternly. "There's no danger they'll leave the port. And there's a good chance we can handle this diplomatically. If you do anything to foul it up—"

"We won't," Darius said quickly. "Good luck."

When they were gone, Herodotus rose to his feet. "I think I'll retire to my cabin for a spell. Unless you need me?"

Darius waved a hand. "No, we should all get some rest."

Megaera downed the dregs of her wine and followed Herodotus to the door.

"Wake me as soon as they return," she said with a warning edge. "The very minute!"

Darius assured her he would and Megaera stomped off, her boots leaving a faint trail of wine on the floor.

"Rest?" Nazafareen muttered with a hint of outrage after the door closed. "While Meb is in the clutches of that Vatra?"

"You can't do everything," Darius pointed out reasonably. "Give the captains a chance."

She opened her mouth.

"We promised."

"*You* promised."

"For both of us."

She gave a noncommittal grunt.

"If they fail, I promise to storm the castle with you," he said with a wry grin. "But you'll be no use if you're exhausted."

She suppressed a yawn. "I'm fine."

Darius shrugged. "All right then." He lay down and closed his eyes. "Ah, so comfortable."

Nazafareen grumbled. After a minute or so, she curled up next to him.

"Darius?"

"Mmmm?"

"I'm worried."

He sighed and rolled over to face her. "I know."

"I have a feeling." She paused. How to explain? "I know you told me everything about our past. But it's not the same as knowing for myself."

He smoothed her hair back. "I'm sorry."

"No, it's all right. I suppose I've accepted it. I might never remember. But *you* do." She lay her hand on his. "And that helps." She paused. "The thing is, all I have is my instinct. That's all I can trust."

He nodded slowly. "I think I understand."

"I was right about the Vatra before. And now my instinct is telling me Meb is in terrible danger. It's telling me I ought to be *doing* something."

Darius was silent for a moment. "When you joined the Water Dogs, you did it for your sister. To avenge her death. But you didn't trust me. You used to hold onto my power when we both needed it. It took a long time for you to learn to let go."

She frowned. "Are you asking me to trust you again?"

He searched her face. "No. I think you already do."

Nazafareen smiled. "I love you, Darius."

"And I love you, North Star."

He kissed her temple and closed his eyes.

Her thoughts still whirled on for a while, but using the negatory magic must have tired her more than she thought because the gentle rocking of the ship and the weight of his arms around her finally lulled Nazafareen into sleep.

A MUFFLED OATH ROUSED HER SOME TIME LATER. NAZAFAREEN sat up to find Darius grappling with Katsu on the floor of her cabin. He sat astride the Stygian's chest, pinning his limbs down. But Darius only had one good arm, and Katsu twisted and bucked with inhuman strength. She leapt out of bed and put the edge of her sword against his throat. Katsu immediately ceased struggling, but cold fury burned in his eyes.

"I caught him trying to steal the globe," Darius said, leaning forward so the weight of his knees dug deeper against the Stygian's arms. "Mafuone said he was a thief catcher. More like a thief, I'd say."

"You are the thieves!" Katsu burst out.

Nazafareen pressed the tip of her sword deeper and a bead of blood welled around the point. "You're in league with the Vatra, aren't you? I bloody knew it!"

The thief regarded her with icy disdain, heedless of the blade. "You stole that talisman from the emperor. I've been hunting it for nearly a year. I'm surprised you would return to the scene of the crime, but—"

"What's he yammering on about?" Nazafareen asked Darius, who shrugged. "The globe belonged to a daēva who kidnapped a young girl. We just took it from him today. Or yesterday. Whatever day it is."

Katsu blinked in confusion. He appeared about to reply when Megaera came bursting through the door, Herodotus blinking owlishly at her heels. She took in the scene and stepped forward, staff raised to crack skulls. "We heard fighting. What's the Stygian doing here?"

"He tried to steal the globe," Nazafareen said.

"Steal it *back*," Katsu said tightly. "Did you know there is a bounty of thirty thousand *yi* on that talisman?"

Herodotus's eyebrows shot up to his forehead. "Thirty thousand *yi?*" he repeated faintly. Ink-stained fingers tugged at his beard. "Why, that would be fifty-two thousand drachmas, or eighty thousand siglos, if one were in Samarqand. That is to say, a fortune!"

The commotion drew the *Chione*'s watch, who poked his head in.

"Trouble?" he asked.

Nazafareen hesitated, then shook her head. She wasn't ready to reveal what they'd found to the crew. "A minor disagreement. Let him up," she told Darius, who eased his knees from Katsu's arms and backed away, though he looked wary.

The Marakai shrugged and withdrew.

"Talk," she said to the Stygian. "And no evasions this time. What is this bounty?"

Katsu wiped the smear of blood from his throat and sat heavily on the bunk. They listened in silence as he related how he'd gone to Delphi in search of the talisman and been arrested outside the palace of the Archon Basileus, when he fought off a rival who thought Katsu had found the globe and hoped to seize it for himself. How he spent months in the Polemarch's dungeons, with no hope of release. He told the story without a shred of self-pity. That more than anything made Nazafareen believe he spoke the truth.

"Someone bought my way out," Katsu said finally. "I've no idea who. When I find out, I will have to repay the debt." His gaze fell on the talisman. "I returned to Tjanjin intending to start the search anew. Perhaps there was a clue I overlooked the first time. The bounty still stands. If I won it...." He trailed off. "Well, there it is. You have it all now. And you say you took it from a *Vatra?*" White teeth flashed. "Really, where did you find it?"

"Do you know of a man named Nicodemus?" Nazafareen asked.

"Of course. He's an advisor to the emperor." Katsu's eyes widened. His hand curled into a fist and thumped the bunk. "It makes sense. The talisman vanished the day before the Greek ambassador left for Delphi, so he was the obvious culprit. But Nicodemus must have framed him and taken it for himself."

"What else do you know about him?" Darius asked.

"The courtiers call him the Traveler. No one knows where he came from—some say Delphi, some Samarqand, others the lands across the White Sea—but he supposedly has great skill at deciphering talismans and he's helped the emperor identify the uses of many in his collection that were previously unknown."

"He's a Vatra," Nazafareen said grimly. "This we know for certain."

"The Vatras forged all the talismans in the world," Herodotus put in. "When they were vanquished, the art was lost. But Nicodemus might have an innate understanding of them."

"The emperor is obsessed with talismans," Katsu said. "Collecting them is his passion. Some can be used by mortals, but others require power to work. He buys anything and everything. To be honest, I think half the objects down there are clever fakes. Until Nicodemus came along, he had no one to curate his collection. The emperor values him highly."

"So the emperor wouldn't hand him over?" Megaera asked. "For any reason?"

Katsu laughed. "Without absolute proof, he'd never believe a word against Nicodemus. The whole court fears his influence."

"We have a problem then," Nazafareen said, rubbing her stump. "A big one."

"Oh, for the Gods' sake, just tell him," Megaera burst out. "It can't get any worse."

So Darius and Herodotus quickly explained why they had come to Tjanjin. The Stygian gave a low whistle.

"What will you do now?" he asked.

"Find a way into the palace," Nazafareen said, her jaw setting. "And get Meb back ourselves."

Megaera gave a firm nod and poked Herodotus, who looked up from his scroll. "What? Oh yes, certainly. Get her back ourselves. That's what Kallisto would want, I'm sure."

"Agreed," Darius said, blue eyes glittering. "The question is how."

They all stared at Katsu. He scrubbed a hand through his wispy beard.

"I don't know," he said slowly. "It's heavily guarded. And the soldiers are trained to use spell dust. Even with a Danai, you don't stand a chance. Besides which, the palace is huge. The part you saw is the tip of the iceberg. Most of it lies underground, dug into the mountain. Even if you managed to get inside, a search could take days."

"What if we offered to trade the globe for Meb?" Megaera asked.

"The emperor will simply take it from you, and likely have you arrested. He's not an evil man—I'm certain he doesn't know what Nicodemus truly is—but he is the emperor. In Tjanjin, that makes him a godlike figure. It would humiliate him to be forced to negotiate. His pride would not allow it."

"What does the globe do?" Darius asked.

Katsu shook his head. "No idea."

There was a long, despondent silence.

"May I see it?" Herodotus asked diffidently. "I have made a small study of talismans. Perhaps I can discover its purpose."

Nazafareen gave him the globe. He turned it this way and that, eyes bright with curiosity, then examined the runes on the base for several long minutes.

"Ah," he said at last. "It is the language of the Vatras."

"Can you read it?" Nazafareen asked eagerly.

"Not all, but some." He pointed to the runes. "This means *summon* or *call*, and the other means *search*. I don't know that one, but this is *air*, and that *water*....and *warm wind*, I think."

"Give it to me," Darius said.

Nazafareen felt him seek the calm of the Nexus. Then he wove fine, probing strands of air and water into the globe. Nothing happened. Darius gave a long sigh and the runes glowed blue.

"Not *warm wind*," Herodotus cried. "*Breath*! Oh, I should have seen that. Now look for something. Hold the image in your mind."

Darius closed his eyes and the view inside the globe changed.

It soared across the White Sea and entered a great, dark forest. Greenery blurred past, faster and faster. Finally, the view slowed and fixed on a clearing. Ranks of Danai filled it from edge to edge. Delilah stood on a spur of rock, flanked by Tethys and six other Danai women with ageless faces. She drew her sword and raised it into the air. Five hundred bows were raised in answer.

"The Matrium," Darius murmured in wonder. "She's reached them."

They watched for a while more but couldn't hear what anyone was saying. Darius released the flows and the runes faded, the view inside settling into clear blue skies this time.

"Use it to find Meb," Megaera urged.

Darius activated the globe again but instead of a rapid transformation, the view changed sluggishly, almost reluctantly, settling on roiling fog. He made a noise of frustration.

"What's wrong with it?" Nazafareen asked, poking at the glass until Darius lightly slapped her hand away.

"Kallisto could never see the girl's face in her visions," Herodotus said after a moment. "She might be warded. But perhaps we could try the Vatra?"

Darius nodded. This time, the change was instantaneous—perhaps because he was so close by. An elderly man sat on a throne. He had a very long mustache that reached nearly to his lap. Beside him stood Nicodemus. The view closed in on the Vatra's face and Nazafareen saw him clearly for the first time. He was staring straight ahead with the ghost of a smile playing on his lips. The Vatra had a webbing of fine lines at the corners of his eyes, which were a blue so dark as to appear almost black. He looked somewhere in his middle years, healthy and strong. Yet there was something about the way the flesh sat on his bones—as though a different man lurked just beneath the surface and this vitality was recently acquired, like new boots that didn't fit quite right.

The emperor appeared to be speaking to someone out of sight. He did not seem pleased.

"Do you think the captains are in there?" Megaera whispered.

Nazafareen realized they'd all fallen silent—eavesdroppers who feared getting caught.

"Can they hear us?" she mouthed at Herodotus, who shrugged.

"I doubt it," he replied in a normal tone that made them all jump. "If we can't hear them, it stands to reason they can't hear us."

"I suppose," she said. "Darius, can you make it so we see the whole room?"

"I'll try," he replied.

An instant later, the view jerked backwards as though tied to a string and hovered above the palace.

"Too far," he muttered to himself. "Gently, now."

It swooped in nauseating jerks back into the throne room, but this time he managed to hold it some distance away. Captain Mafuone and Captain Kasaika were indeed there, and both women scowled deeply.

"Told you," Katsu murmured.

Nazafareen barely noticed the dozens of black-armored guards, the simpering courtiers and haughty purple-robed alchemists filling the chamber. She only had eyes for the emperor and the Vatra beside him, who leaned over every now and then to whisper in the emperor's ear.

"That bastard," she said. "Go closer to the Vatra. Maybe we can read his lips or something."

Darius appeared to be gaining control of the talisman, for he managed it fairly smoothly. The view again closed on Nicodemus's face. Suddenly, he turned and looked straight at the globe, eyes narrowing. Darius hastily pulled back again but the audience appeared to be at an end. The emperor gave a peremptory wave of his hand. Captain Mafuone and Captain Kasaika stalked out of the chamber with stiff backs.

Nicodemus turned away and gave the emperor a low bow. He made some sort of flowery speech. The emperor nodded and the Vatra withdrew through a door behind the throne. The globe pursed him along a corridor and down a long flight of steps that wound into the mountain. All of them leaned over it, hardly breathing, as he entered a series of dimly lit galleries with objects displayed on pedestals and inside glass cases, though he strode past too quickly to tell what they were. At last, Nicodemus reached a door standing partly ajar. He stared at it for a moment, then threw it open. The color drained from his face. A flash of rage contorted his features. The room beyond was empty.

MEB CROUCHED BEHIND ONE OF THE DUSTY GLASS CASES. SHE was in a huge room with a high ceiling and every tiny sound seemed to echo and amplify itself. She breathed through her mouth, perfectly still, pretending she was just another one of the curious objects on display.

She could hear Nicodemus cursing nearby. It had been a very close thing. He'd left her in the room and said he had business to attend to, but would return shortly. Meb had played along. He was big and strong and she'd seen him work *fire*.

When he'd taken her knife away and locked the door behind him, she knew. Nicodemus was a liar. She couldn't imagine what he really wanted her for and didn't want to find out. She just wanted to go back to the *Asperta*. So she'd picked the lock with a fishbone. She always kept a few in her pocket. They were useful for all sorts of things. Digging dirt out from her toenails, for example, or scraps of kelp from her teeth.

But she'd never picked a lock before and it took a long time. Her hands were shaking so badly at the end she almost gave up.

But she understood the basic idea of tumblers because Captain Kasaika kept a strongbox in her cabin and Meb had watched her open it a hundred times. So she'd kept at it and finally she heard a click and the door cracked open. She'd made it to the end of the corridor when she heard footsteps coming. So Meb ducked behind the glass case and saw him walk by, close enough to touch.

"Meb!"

She squeezed her eyes shut. The voice drew closer. He'd entered the gallery.

"Come on out! I won't hurt you."

She didn't know what he was, but it wasn't human and it couldn't be daēva. Maybe he was one of them alchemists. The cook said they did magic with spell dust.

His footsteps grew closer. Then they stopped. "Your parents are waiting!"

The silence stretched out.

"I know you're here somewhere." His voice changed. It wasn't so friendly-sounding anymore. "You'll never find your way out, Meb. I know every inch of this place. It's dangerous down here. And if I have to hunt you down, I'll be angry."

And then the footsteps passed. She counted to one hundred and crept out of her hiding place. Strange masks peered at her from the cases, alongside bits of jewelry and daggers and other queer relics. Meb dimly sensed power lurking inside some of them, but she had no idea what they did or how to use them.

She crept from shadow to shadow. He was lying again. There *was* a way out. The same way they'd come in, if she could find it.

You're Meb the Shark, she thought, biting her lip hard to keep from crying. If he does catch you, he'll regret it. And when Captain Kasaika finds out, she'll chop him up for fish bait.

But in her heart Meb knew better.

She dropped to her knees again and started crawling.

18

MEGAERA'S EVEN STUPIDER PLAN

"Clever girl," Nazafareen whispered, as they watched Nico stalk through a long gallery chock-a-block with objects of all shapes and sizes. "It looks like she's escaped him somehow." She turned to Katsu. "Where is he?"

"*That* is the emperor's talisman collection," Katsu replied. "But it's a labyrinth down there."

"We have to help her," Nazafareen said at once. "And *you* have to get us inside."

Katsu laughed. "It's impossible."

"Nothing is impossible."

"This thing is."

Nazafareen sighed. "What if we give you the globe?"

He raised his eyebrows.

"I don't want to part with it. It's obviously invaluable. But Meb is more valuable."

Katsu shifted uneasily. "So you really think she has some kind of special power?"

"Yes. I do. And this Vatra certainly does." Nazafareen stared at Katsu with reproach. "Even if she's not the talisman, I wouldn't leave her to *him*."

The Stygian thought for a moment. "When the globe was first stolen, I tried to discover if someone from outside the palace could have gotten in. I'm friends with some of the imperial guards and we discussed it over a few cups of wine. In the end, we decided it couldn't be done. That the culprit had to be someone on the inside. And indeed it was."

"Get to the point," Megaera growled.

"The entrances to the palace are heavily guarded at all times. But there's an ancient system of aqueducts beneath the grounds. The largest ones carry the water for the aquarium."

"Keep talking," Darius said.

Katsu scratched his beard. "I suppose a person could swim through one of the aqueducts. But they don't really lead anywhere."

Darius nodded slowly. "I could use earth to punch a hole into the talisman collection, once we were beneath it."

"It's...conceivable," Katsu said doubtfully. "Of course, there are iron bars over the outlets. And the only one large enough to fit into runs from the shark pool."

"Sharks?" Megaera murmured. "What is a shark?"

"A fish with big teeth," Katsu replied. "Very big."

"Leave the sharks to me," Nazafareen said carelessly. "I am not afraid of fish."

Katsu smiled. "You haven't seen one yet."

Herodotus paused in his scribbling and looked up. "I never learned to swim," he said with regret. "But perhaps you could tie me to Megaera? She wouldn't mind, would you, dear?"

The Maenad patted his hand absently. "Of course not. And it's a fine plan. Truly well thought out." Her eyes glimmered with amusement. "But I have another proposal. It's a lot simpler." She leaned forward. "How about you just set me on fire?"

❧ 19 ❧

SUNCUPS FOR JULIA

Time was a peculiar thing, Culach thought.

Once it had held meaning. A day, a week, a year. These were real and measurable. But since the coming of the ice, it seemed to have ground to a halt. He slept and woke, and made love to Mina, and ate when he felt hungry, but he couldn't say how long it had been since that day in the stables when Victor found Eirik's diamond.

Mina kept him apprised of what was going on in the keep, which turned out to be not much. She barely saw Galen anymore. Apparently, he was Victor's mole, digging a tunnel to the outside. Victor himself had withdrawn to Eirik's study. The other Dessarians played dice and took turns guarding the mortal women from Delphi, but they were getting restless.

Earlier, Culach had gone to the stables to visit with Ragnhildur. She emitted a doleful cry when she saw him. He'd inspected her claws with his fingers and offered her a potato, which she wouldn't deign to touch. But he knew she must be starving. The mounts needed meat. They needed to hunt.

After Mina, Ragnhildur was the one creature Culach would trade his life for. Eirik had given him the abbadax on his thirteenth birthday—one of the few acts of generosity towards his son—and they'd been together since, through hunts and battles and long, glorious flights over the sea. They didn't need words to understand each other, though he often spoke to her anyway.

"I wish I could give you Victor Dessarian," he whispered. "He'd tide you over for a while."

Ragnhildur expelled a hot breath and leaned against him.

He'd heard Galen and the other Danai chopping away at the ice down at the far end of the stables. Every few seconds, there would be two dull cracking sounds, almost overlapping, as they worked in rhythm with each other. He'd wondered how they managed not to go mad.

Now Culach lay in bed, listening to Mina's soft breathing next to him.

Time. They had so much of it now, oceans of time, but once that tunnel was finished, it would run out abruptly.

So perhaps it was a gift, he thought drowsily. A last precious gift.

His eyes closed and he slid seamlessly into the dream.

Into the Viper.

A small mudbrick dwelling in the desert. The sun was setting behind the dunes and he could feel the first hints of evening in the cool breeze lifting his hair. He hadn't been to see Julia in months. Not because he didn't want to. He thought of her often. But he'd been putting it off. Part of him still resisted what had to be done.

She must have seen him coming through the narrow window, for now she stood framed in the doorway, auburn hair brushing her shoulders. A hesitant smile lit her elfin features.

"It's good to see you," she said, stepping back.

Farrumohr ducked his head beneath the low lintel and followed her inside. It was little more than a hovel, but Julia had swept the floors and placed a vase with golden suncups on the table. Lumen crystals were neatly stacked to one side, next to bowls of sand and water. The tools of her trade.

"Sit down," she urged. "I'll find you something to eat."

He watched her slender back as she bustled around, digging through the meager larder for fruit and bread.

"I watch the new city rise every day," she said, setting plates on the table. "It will be wondrous when it's completed. King Felix says there will be a place for all." She took a bite of bread.

"Felix is an old fool," he said quietly.

She frowned. "Why do you dislike him? He's a good leader."

"He's weak. He overpays the Danai—"

"Not that again." She pushed her plate back. "The past is dead, Farrumohr."

Silence lay heavy between them.

"And how is Gaius?" she asked, obviously hoping to change the subject.

"He won a seat in the Senate."

"So I heard." She tilted her head. "I always expected it to be you, Farrumohr. You understand the currents of power better than most of them."

His mouth twisted. "They don't like me. Never have."

She sighed. "And so you put your ambitions in *him*."

Julia was clever. It was one of the things he respected about her.

"I offer him advice, yes."

She laughed. "More than that, I think. Gaius may be well-liked, but he's hardly the sharpest tool in the bin. Even when you were little boys, you let him believe he was the leader of your games, when in fact he was doing precisely what *you* wished." She studied him. "So what is it your puppet will do now, Farrumohr? What is the game this time?"

Her tone was light, but he sensed seriousness beneath it.

Farrumohr shrugged, though his heart beat faster. "Gaius will make a far better king someday. He'll unite all the clans under one ruler. It is our birthright, Julia. Fire is a higher power. The only element that cannot be polluted."

Her face hardened. "You know I don't like that kind of talk. The others help us. The new city—"

"Why should we pay them anything for their shoddy work?" Farrumohr knew his voice was rising, but he couldn't stop himself. "They're liars and thieves, all of them."

She took his hand. "Don't. Please. Can't we just have a pleasant visit?"

He mastered himself with effort. "I'm sorry."

And he was. He knew he was an awkward man. Only Julia had ever cared for him. And Gaius, of course, but Farrumohr had worked very hard to cement their friendship. What he lacked in charm he made up for in an innate understanding of others' character flaws, their innermost desires. And for all his handsome looks and easy laughter, Gaius was vain. He craved flattery and approval.

Farrumohr swallowed a lump in his throat. Yes, only Julia treated him with kindness, despite everything. She was the only person he'd ever truly loved.

They talked for a while and she showed him some of her work. Julia made talismans, simple lumen crystals and the like, which she traded for food. The items were serviceable, but she'd never understood the subtleties of the art the way Farrumohr did.

The shadows lengthened as night fell. Finally, he stood.

"I should go."

Julia smiled and rose. "I'll see you at the Feast of Artemis, but I hope you come again sooner. It gets a bit lonely sometimes."

Farrumohr knew the others avoided her because of him. The answering smile on his face felt stiff, though she didn't seem to notice. His stomach churned. "Of course I will. It's a long time away still." He held out his arms and she stepped forward, embracing his tall, thin form. He smelled her hair, familiar and comforting.

Has to be. No other way.

All for the greater good.

The narrow blade hidden in his sleeve slid into her back, piercing her heart. She stiffened and he twisted the blade before she could seize fire. He'd learned this by practicing on animals first, mostly stray cats. One had to twist the blade or the dying took too long.

Farrumohr held her close, tears streaming down his face. To his great relief, she passed without speaking.

He took Julia out to the desert, to a solitary place far from the house. He lay with her there for a time, stroking her cold flesh. Then he buried her deep in the sands and returned to her workshop.

In its most basic form, a talisman was simply an object imbued with power to perform a specific function. Their forging required flame, so only the Vatras had the talent. But the most powerful talismans were bound up with the creator's emotions, unique to that particular Adept. The chimera, for example.

But what he had in mind required an even greater sacrifice.

Farrumohr sat down at Julia's table and channeled his grief into the making of Gaius's serpent crown, even as King Felix continued work on the great capital whose completion he would never live to see. His dark act provided the seed, but the talisman still needed to be refined. Guided to its singular purpose. The crown needed hatred and fear and pain, *wanted* it, and Farrumohr held this goal in mind as he brought the lash down again and again, sweat and blood streaming from his back, whispering the names of his enemies.

And the crown took shape, its gold glowing more richly with each stinging crack of the whip.

Danai. Marakai. Valkirin.

Liars and thieves.

When it was done, he returned to Julia's grave one last time, where he wept a bit and promised her vengeance. He left the bunch of wilted suncups on the spot as they had always been his sister's favorite flower.

CULACH SHUDDERED IN HIS SLEEP AS THE REST OF THE VIPER'S short and vicious life unfurled before him. The murder of King Felix. The placement of Gaius on the throne. The feast of Artemis and rejection of Gaius by Caecilia. The destruction of the Great Forest. And finally, the shattering of the heavens and the Vatras' desperate flight from the capital. Farrumohr's slow descent into the sands.

And for the first time, even though he felt each moment of agony, Culach welcomed it.

The monster was dead at last.

20

WE ALL GO A LITTLE MAD
SOMETIMES

Galen raised the pick and slammed it into the wall of ice ahead. A few splinters flew off. He raised it again, muscles trembling with fatigue. Another dull crack, followed by tinkling shards. It was like hacking through granite. But if he stopped to rest, he'd have to turn around—and Galen didn't want to do that.

"Why don't you just kill yourself?" Ellard asked softly over his right shoulder.

Galen raised the pick.

He'd hoped digging the tunnel would offer a distraction, but the punishment proved to be a constant reminder of what he'd done. And now Ellard had grown vengeful again. The specter followed him everywhere—awake or asleep. He raged about the fact that Galen had abandoned his body inside Darius's house. By now, Tethys would have arranged for Ellard to be buried in the woods, a tree planted in his name. He was a hero, after all. But Valkirins were supposed to be laid to rest in the crypts beneath their holdfast.

Ellard had told Galen about them. Except for those who'd died during Culach's Folly, every one of Ellard's ancestors was preserved in the chill heart of the mountain. He'd gone down there on a dare when he was young—a common rite of passage among Valkirin children. Ellard said some of the corpses had ghastly wounds from the fighting during the Iron Wars, before Eirik sealed the keep.

"You failed once, but there are other ways," Ellard whispered, his warm breath lifting the hairs on Galen's neck. "That pick, for example. Duller than a knife, but I'm sure it could open a vein."

Galen surveyed the tunnel. It was about fifteen paces deep now and six wide, just enough for an abbadax to creep through with its wings folded. He had no idea how much farther the ice extended. Ten paces? Fifty? He was starting to wonder if it had any end.

"Or you could throw yourself into one of the wells. Drowning's still better than I had it." A low, mirthless laugh. "Getting gutted by a chimera is a messy way to die. It's ridiculous, really. Me, a Kafsnjór, dying to save your miserable house, while you betrayed them all to Eirik. And now he's dead too. I can't say I miss him, but—"

"I told you I was sorry. A thousand times."

Galen stamped his feet to get the blood going. He didn't want to lose any more body parts to frostbite. Ellard didn't reply, but Galen could feel him there, so close.

"I loved you," he muttered. "That's what I regret the most. That I never told you."

The specter fell silent for a moment. "I loved you, too."

Tears froze on Galen's cheeks. Ellard always knew where to land the blow. The precise weak point.

Because he's not real. Because he's you.

Galen felt himself fracturing into jagged splinters.

"If I die…would we be together?" he managed, turning around at last. "I'd do it in a heartbeat then—"

His words trailed away and a flush of embarrassment crept up his face.

"Who are you talking to?" Rafel asked.

Galen hadn't heard the Danai come into the stables. He was quiet as a cat.

"No one." Galen tried to lift the pick again, but it slipped from his numb fingers. "Damn," he mumbled.

Rafel bent down and picked it up, but made no move to return it. The hood of his coat had fallen back and frost rimed the iron collar around his neck, glittering in the dim light of the tunnel.

Rafel studied Galen with a worried frown. "How long have you been here?"

"I don't know." It was the truth. Galen had no idea.

"Did you even rest at all? Did you eat?"

Galen reached for the pick. "I'm fine."

"Well, you look like shit." He paused. "Don't let Victor get under your skin. We've all made mistakes."

So Rafel knew everything. Well, of course he did. To his relief, Galen found he lacked the energy to care.

"I doubt yours compare to mine," he replied.

A shadow crossed Rafel's face. "You don't know what mine are."

"Fair enough. I just wanted my mother back. That's all." He gestured to the tunnel. "And now none of us can leave until I break through this fucking thing."

Rafel nodded slowly. "So you're doing it for her?"

"I'm doing it so I don't have to think." He studied the Danai with open curiosity. They'd spent most of the last week together and Galen still barely knew him. "Why are *you* here?"

"Same reason."

Rafel looked as though he might say something else, but then his expression turned inward. Galen had seen it before, in the handful of terse exchanges they'd shared. As if he was there but not there. As if part of him had gone somewhere else.

"Better get back to it," Galen said. He grabbed the pick and the scabs on his palm broke open. A trickle of blood ran down the handle.

"Wait," Rafel said.

He used a knife to cut a strip from his own shirt and wound the makeshift bandage around Galen's hand.

"Sure you don't want to take a break?" he asked. "I don't mind."

Galen shook his head. Rafel still held his hand and suddenly, Galen didn't want him to let go.

"One of the daēvas killed by the chimera was a Valkirin," Galen blurted out. "His name was Ellard."

Rafel looked at him for a long moment. "You cared for him."

"Yes."

"I'm sorry."

"I see him sometimes." Galen could hardly get the words out, but when he did, it felt like a great burden had been lifted.

"Is that who you were talking to?"

Galen nodded. "You think I'm mad, I suppose."

"I think you're lonely."

Galen's breath hitched as Rafel stepped closer. They were almost exactly the same height. Their eyes met and Galen saw sorrow, but not pity.

"I think you've done terrible things for love." He pressed Galen's bandaged hand to his cheek. "But I have too."

And then Rafel's lips were on his, the radiant heat of his body like a furnace through their heavy layers of clothing. Galen smelled leather and the clean scent of his skin. He grabbed Rafel's coat and dragged him closer, inflamed with despair and desire both.

In truth, Galen had wanted him from the moment he laid eyes on him, but he'd refused to acknowledge it. He'd been afraid of what Ellard would say. It seemed like a final betrayal. And part of him believed no one would ever want him again.

Now Rafel's fingers twined in his hair and Galen felt himself grow painfully aroused.

"What do you want me to do?" he whispered, unsure.

Rafel pushed him against the tunnel wall. "I'll show you," he said raggedly.

A small noise made Galen turn. He cursed.

They broke apart as the door flew open and Victor strode into the stables. Galen grabbed his pick with a shaking hand. His mouth felt swollen and bruised.

"How's it progressing?" Victor demanded.

Rafel had already returned to his end of the tunnel. Galen could hear him chipping away.

"See for yourself," he snapped, in no mood to grovel.

Victor gave the tunnel a cursory glance. Galen hadn't seen him in days and was shocked at the change. His father looked thin and wan, with streaks of white at his temples.

"You have two more days to break through. Two days. Or I'll do what I should have done in the first place." He turned toward Rafel. "You're free to go. This is *his* problem."

Galen heard the pick fall. Rafel stalked back out of the tunnel and walked up to Victor.

"I'll stay until it's finished," he said coldly. "And you don't have to be such a bastard about it."

Victor's black eyes flared in anger. Then he laughed. "My son doesn't deserve you. But you'll discover that eventually."

Rafel shook his head and went back to work. Galen did the same, though he was acutely aware of the other Danai. He wanted to kiss him again, but he sensed Rafel's mood had soured. Two days, Victor said. And what then? Would they ever see each other again?

A reckless impulse seized him. He didn't care what Rafel had done. It couldn't possibly be worse than Galen's crimes. But he didn't want to lose him. And he was done keeping secrets. Galen laid a hand on Rafel's shoulder.

"There's another way out," he said quietly. "One no one knows about."

Rafel lowered his pick. "What?"

"It's below the keep, in the tunnels. We were supposed to collapse them all, but I...I couldn't. I'm too weak in earth. So I left one open." He paused, heart racing. "Maybe we could go together."

Rafel just stared at him. He looked stricken. Galen turned away, cursing his own stupidity.

"Never mind. I'm sorry I said anything."

"No, it's not—"

"Just forget it," Galen said savagely, bringing the pick forward in a mighty blow. He stumbled as it caught. Galen yanked it back and stared at the ice. A ray of pale moonlight illuminated the tunnel floor.

They'd broken through.

IN HER REMOTE TOWER TWO STORIES UP, GERDA WATCHED Daníel sleep. He curled up on the bare stone floor and didn't seem to mind in the least. Like he was used to it.

Her lips thinned. She could still scarcely believe the heir to Val Tourmaline had been chained like an animal by the Oracle of Delphi. The world truly was hurtling toward the Pit. Well, her new friends would take care of them all. If Culach behaved himself, she'd see to it that they let him live. And Lord Idiot? Gerda smiled. Her holdfast might be gone, but at least she could have the satisfaction of watching the invaders burned alive. When the other Valkirins got here, it was crucial they understood the situation. She eyed Daníel speculatively. Perhaps he could be of some use to her cause.

He gave a faint snore and she crept over to the place she stashed her globe. She'd been dying to contact Nicodemus for days, but Daníel's presence complicated matters. Now that he was sleeping....

She fed air and water into the talisman and breathed softly on the runes.

"Find me the Gambler," she whispered.

The leaden skies inside the globe faded and she saw him, stalking through some dimly lit chamber. The last they spoke, he said he'd found one of the talismans. Soon, he would free the others from the Kiln. They would sear a path through the Great Forest straight to Val Moraine.

She moved closer until his face filled the globe. He looked angry. And he didn't see her. He must have left his globe somewhere else. Gerda gritted her teeth in frustration. She wanted to tell him about Daníel.

She reluctantly released the flows. If she couldn't talk to the Vatra, she could at least collect information for the next time he contacted her. Gerda pursed her lips in thought, then directed the globe to move from room to room in the keep. There was Victor Dessarian, sitting in Eirik's chair with a broody look on his dumb face. And her great-great-grandson Culach, tossing and turning as if in the throes of a nightmare. Her eyes narrowed. Was that the *Danai* hostage in bed next to him?

"What are you doing?"

Gerda gave a little shriek and clutched her chest.

"Blind me!" she snapped. "I thought you were sleeping."

Daníel regarded her with cool green eyes. They didn't seem so vague anymore.

"You're spying," he said. "With a talisman."

"Spying?" She snorted. "It's just a little bauble. And mind your business."

His features softened with longing. "I want to see someone."

"No."

Daníel jerked his head toward the door. "Or I'll tell them you have it."

"You ungrateful little shit," Gerda murmured. "I give you my dead husband's clothes and this is the thanks I get?"

He stared at her, unmoved.

"Oh, all right," she grumbled. "Who do you want to see? Halldóra, I suppose."

"The mortal girl I came with."

"The one that called me a hag?"

"She didn't mean it."

"Like hell she didn't!" Gerda fingered the globe. "You're as bad as the rest of them. Fine. But no touching."

She blew on the runes and the globe entered a small chamber.

"I learned a new trick," she admitted, activating another set of runes on the bottom. "We should be able to hear as well as see now. Ah yes..."

Daníel leaned forward.

THENA KNELT ON THE COLD STONE, HER LIPS MOVING SILENTLY in prayer. Days had passed since her encounter with Daníel and the nasty old witch woman. She hadn't seen him again, nor had she or Korinna been summoned for questioning. They had simply been left to rot.

In the long, dark hours, she occasionally thought of her family and the farm she'd left behind. If Apollo had not called her to a life of devotion, she would be a wife and mother by now. Would she have been happy? It was a baffling question and one she didn't dwell on. There could be no looking back now. She had chosen a higher purpose—or been chosen. Yes, she liked to think of it that way. The three Fates, the Moirai, had marked out her thread at birth and woven it into a greater pattern Thena could only guess at. The betrayal of Andros and her imprisonment in this cruel fortress were simply part of the tapestry.

It was through such trials that one discovered one's true character. Thena's faith had only strengthened. She felt the weight of destiny on her shoulders. The god had named her as his instrument on earth and she would not fail him.

But Korinna was made of weaker clay.

"We have to get out of here," the yellow-haired girl muttered for the thousandth time. "We've achieved nothing. Nothing!"

Thena looked up but didn't reply. Korinna pulled the blanket tighter around her shoulders. Dark circles shadowed her eyes. She refused to bathe in cold water and Thena could smell the sour odor of her body.

"Please," Korinna said softly, fever-bright eyes fixed on Thena's face. "I want to see the sun. This endless night is like death. I want to be warm. To feel the light on my face, to see the blue sky again."

The pain of her half-healed blisters helped Thena stay awake. She hadn't slept in a long time. She was waiting. Waiting for a sign.

"Apollo's light shines on us no matter where we are."

"The old Pythia used to say that." Korinna looked wistful. "I wish.... I wish she were still with us."

The previous Oracle of Delphi had been a stout, middle-aged woman with the soft hands of a wealthy noble's wife—which is precisely who she'd been. Both Thena and Korinna learned their duties as novices under her tutelage, which was strict but kind-hearted. She had begun the tradition of feeding the poor on feast-days. Thena had loved and feared her, though not nearly to the same extent as the current Pythia.

"Do not presume," Thena snapped. "If your heart is no longer loyal, at least have the decency to keep it hidden."

Korinna scowled. "I know you have the Talisman of Folding," she said bitterly. "You concealed it somewhere near the well."

Thena rose to her feet, her legs stiff from kneeling. "Our work is not done here."

"Our work?" Korinna sneered. "You're obsessed with that

blue-eyed witch you freed. Well, you have his name now. Go hunt him down if you wish. Or seduce his father. Perhaps that will cure you."

"Watch your tongue."

"No." Korinna lifted her chin defiantly. "I'm leaving, with or without you. And you're going to tell me where you hid the talisman."

Thena's head ached, a dull throbbing behind her temples. "Or what?"

"Or I'll tell them everything." Korinna's eyes were wild. "I'm going to die either way. At least it will be on my own terms. I'll throw myself on their mercy—"

Korinna's voice muted to a toneless buzz. Thena saw her mouth forming words but they no longer held any meaning. Poor thing. Her mind had gone, just like Maia.

"Of course," she said soothingly. "Of course, you're right. I'm sorry."

She walked toward Korinna, slowly, as one might approach a timid animal. Her head ached terribly, but she kept her face smooth.

"I have an idea. We'll tell them we wish to look for the talisman again so they bring us down below. I'll sneak away and fetch it and we can go home. How does that sound?"

Korinna backed into the corner. She didn't seem to believe it. Thena felt betrayed that Korinna had so little trust, but then her mind was gone, wasn't it? She couldn't be blamed.

"It will all be over soon," Thena murmured. "I promise."

She felt the righteous power of the sun god as the pain in her head suddenly vanished. But my, all that yammering and buzzing! If Korinna wasn't quiet, the guards might hear.

I must show mercy, she thought. Just like I gave Maia.

"Hush," she said. "Hush, now."

And then the pillow was in her hands and that blankness came over her, and Thena went away for a time. When she returned,

Korinna lay on the bed and her face was soft but her eyes were bloodshot and the buzzing had stopped. Thena fixed her hair—it had gotten awfully mussed—and drew the cover up to her chin. She gently touched Korinna's mouth, forming her lips into a smile, though it wouldn't stay put.

"Fevers are terrible things," she said aloud. "And poor Korinna was already weak from the cold and damp. She succumbed so quickly. I had no idea she was even *ill*." Tears formed in her eyes. "She was my dearest friend. If only she'd told me!"

She thought for a moment and nodded. Yes, that sounded right.

Thena moved to the door and began to scream for help.

THE GLOBE DARKENED TO A RAINSTORM AS GERDA RELEASED the flows of power. It was so quiet, she fancied she could hear the ice shifting against the walls of the keep. She leaned back in her chair and looked at Daníel.

"Wow," she said. "That's your girlfriend?"

Daníel sat immobile, staring at the globe, his fists clenched.

Gerda poured herself a large cup of wine. She sipped it with relish. Her skin had crawled watching the flaxen-haired girl's terrible end and the wooden expression of her killer, but Gerda welcomed chaos in the keep. The idiot's pile of woes couldn't be large enough.

"Well, I have to say, Daníel, she's quite a piece of work. Who's the dead one?"

"Korinna," he mumbled.

"You poor boy. I think you've fallen in with some very bad company."

Daníel said nothing, but emotions warred on his face.

"I wonder what Korinna was going to tell the Dessarians, eh?" Gerda said.

"You misunderstand," he replied curtly. "Korinna is the unstable one. She was always jealous—"

"Spare me the bullshit. I'm almost six hundred years old." She looked at him through narrowed eyes. "Perhaps I should call for Victor."

"Don't do that!" He seized her sleeve in abject misery. "Please."

Gerda pursed her lips. Something was wrong with him. Not just blind love of a cursed mortal. Something *unnatural*.

A long time ago, Gerda had been the most skilled healer at Val Moraine. It was a talent of all the Kafsnjór women. But when she'd failed to prevent Ygraine from dying in childbirth, she'd given it up. Culach's mother was one of the few people Gerda truly liked. She blamed herself—and so did Eirik—though she had known from the start that it was a dangerous pregnancy. Twins, and tangled together in a fatal embrace. She'd barely managed to save the infants. Ygraine had died in her arms minutes after their delivery.

But looking at Daníel, she decided it was time to come out of retirement. He needed her help, and she needed an ally. She needed his *loyalty*. And she wouldn't let that black-haired chit have it.

"I'll keep my mouth shut if you let me examine the collar," she said.

He shrank back. "No."

"Oh, stop fussing. I just want to see it."

Daníel tensed as her gnarled fingers brushed the iron. Oh yes, a very nasty ward. And behind it, a darkness clouding his mind.

Gerda wove delicate strands of air and water and cast a shimmering net around him. He resisted, every muscle contracting, his pupils dilating to black discs, and Gerda cinched the net tight. It wouldn't harm him, just make him pliable and calm.

Now for the heart of the matter.

"You don't really love this mortal girl, do you?" she asked gently.

"I do."

Daníel stared at a fixed point over her shoulder, his voice a monotone.

"But why?"

"She freed me. Brought me to the light."

"What light?"

"I am a witch. My soul is stained."

Gerda snorted. "Bah! You're a Valkirin prince. She should grovel at your feet. Did Thena tell you this nonsense?"

"She brought me to the light," he repeated stubbornly.

"Heed me now," Gerda said in a stern and commanding tone. "You are not a *witch*. You come from an ancient, noble race. Magic lives in your blood and marrow! We are Valkirins. Masters of the open sky! You will still be young and handsome when this little murderess is moldering in her grave."

Daníel didn't speak, but he gripped the arms of his chair with white fingers.

"Whatever foul spell she has cast on you, the cage is not locked, Daníel. If you stay, it is of your own accord."

She let that sink in. Now to discover what sort of plot these mortals were hatching. She would have it out of him, one way or another.

"Thena spoke of *our work*. What did she mean by that?"

Sweat trickled down his brow despite the icy cold. His mouth twitched. "The talismans—"

Gerda leaned forward eagerly, just as the door flew open. With a muttered oath, she shoved the globe under her skirts.

"Wake," she hissed at Daníel.

Green eyes blinked into full awareness as Mithre strode into the chamber. He wouldn't remember any of it, not consciously. But Gerda hoped her words had penetrated to the place where that darkness lived.

"You're wanted," Mithre said to Daníel.

He stiffened. "What for?"

"A parley." The Danai paused. "Your grandmother is here."

"Halldóra?" Daníel sprang to his feet.

Gerda watched them leave with narrowed eyes. *Parley?*

The moment they were gone, she took out the globe again.

21

LORDS OF SKY AND STONE

Thena pounded on the door until two young witches came.

"What is it now?" the first demanded. He looked like a barbarian, with a feather earring and the pelt of some white-haired animal slung across his shoulders.

"My friend Korinna," Thena wailed. "She's dead."

They pushed past her and hurried to the bed. As they examined the body, she told her story with new embellishments—Korinna's appetite had been poor lately and her breathing heavy and labored. It was too cold in the keep, and her delicate constitution must have succumbed.

"I told you we needed more blankets," Thena said, heaving a piteous cough. "I feel a touch of fever coming on myself."

"What happened to her eyes?" the first witch asked in a hard voice.

Thena peered down at Korinna, pretending confusion. "Her eyes? I don't know. I suppose they are a little red, but—"

They'd barely begun to question her when shouts erupted in the hallway, followed by the sound of running feet. One of the witches stuck his head out the door.

"What's happening?" he called.

"Galen and Rafel broke through!" a voice replied. "Halldóra of Val Tourmaline is coming in."

The two Danai looked at each other.

"I'll wait outside," the first witch said to his companion. "They might need you for an escort."

He took up a post in the corridor just as Rafel entered. When he saw Korinna, he stopped and looked at Thena. They gazed at each other for a long, wordless moment.

The witch standing guard clapped him on the shoulder. "I'm sorry, cousin," he said. "I understand you cared for her."

Somewhat belatedly, Rafel adopted an expression of grief. "Oh gods," he whispered.

"A fever, the poor thing," Thena said, drawing him away to the far corner.

Rafel glanced down at her hands, taking note of the scratches before Thena could cover them with her sleeves.

"What did she do?" he asked, all traces of sympathy gone.

"It's not your place to question, *Nikias*," Thena replied. "And she died of a fever."

His mouth twisted. "Of course she did." He glanced over his shoulder. The guard had returned to the corridor. "I need to know where you hid the talisman."

"And why would I tell you that?"

"Because I found him."

Was he lying? Thena felt the pain behind her eye again. "Who is it?"

"Victor's son, Galen."

Thena never suspected Darius had a brother. Or that he was *here*. Her pulse raced.

"He's weak in earth power," Rafel said. "It's the sign, yes?"

For a brief moment, Thena wished Korinna was still alive just so she could prove how wrong the girl had been. But her thread had been snipped short, as the Moirai decreed.

"We have to get him out somehow," she said, tapping a tooth with one ragged nail. "Daníel can help—"

"I can handle it," Rafel interrupted. "But I need to know where you hid the Talisman of Folding."

Thena smiled serenely. "You see? The God's hand arranges things even in this forsaken realm of darkness. He has not abandoned us, *Nikias*."

The witch's lips tightened at the use of his slave name. "Where is it, Thena?" he demanded, his voice ragged.

She studied him. She could see the hatred in his eyes, though he tried to conceal it. Rafel wasn't broken in the least. She'd always known it.

"Wait until everyone is sleeping tonight," Thena said. "Then come get me. Kill the guard if you must. We'll all go together."

For an instant, she thought he might strike her. But the guard waited just outside the door. Rafel's fists relaxed.

"What about Daníel?" he whispered. "They've taken him away to be part of this parley with Halldóra of Val Tourmaline."

"I'll manage Daníel," she replied. "Off with you now." She glanced over at the bed. "I must see to Korinna. She shall have the proper rites, as befits an initiate of the Temple of Apollo." Thena gave him a gentle smile. "One must always show mercy, Nikias. Don't forget that."

KATRIN LEANED FORWARD IN THE SADDLE, THE LOW CEILING OF the ice tunnel nearly brushing her head. Halldóra's abbadax crept along just behind, along with Frida and Sofia. They'd been camped across the valley, preparing for a long siege, when sentries spotted a dark spot in the unbroken carapace of ice surrounding Val Moraine. Katrin had flown with Halldóra to investigate when a Valkirin appeared at the entrance, waving his arms. Halldóra swooped down, her face pale with shock. He'd called to them, saying Victor Dessarian wanted a parley. Then he disappeared into the tunnel.

Katrin knew Halldóra's grandson Daníel had gone missing over a year before, though she couldn't imagine why he'd turned up at Val Moraine. She somehow doubted Eirik had been holding him prisoner all this time, although it might be possible. No one ventured down to the cold cells without a good reason, and they'd been empty for years before Victor Dessarian took the keep and tossed her and Culach inside. She told Halldóra all of this as soon as they returned to the camp.

Katrin admired Halldóra. She was clearly overcome with emotion to find her grandson alive, but she maintained her composure and consulted calmly with the others before reaching a decision. She wanted to know what Katrin thought of Victor Dessarian. Could he be trusted to keep a pact? Did he have honor? Katrin wasn't sure how to respond. He hadn't killed his prisoners, while Eirik most certainly would have. And he kept his bargain with Culach. Katrin was living proof of that. But then again, he was Danai, and Danai were all cowardly dogs at heart.

In the end, Halldóra decided she would meet with Victor, but she would not cede him the Maiden Keep under any circumstances. The Dessarians had to go.

Katrin was relieved to hear this. As promised, she'd put in a word for Culach, though she hadn't received any guarantees. In Halldóra's view, he was a traitor through and through.

Now she found herself in the stables, with ten Danai stiffly flanking the door to the keep. Katrin slid from her mount and eyed them with disdain. In a moment, the others stood beside her.

"Told you I'd be back, assholes," she said.

Halldóra drew herself up, tall and fierce. "Where's Victor?"

A slender man with dark skin and vulpine features stepped forward and gave Halldóra a polite nod. "I'm Mithre, Victor's second. Thank you for agreeing to come, Halldóra of Val Tourmaline. Victor awaits you inside. He thought the stables a bit chilly for conversation."

Halldóra didn't move. "Where are we going? And where's my grandson?"

"Daníel is with Victor. He's not our hostage. Not precisely," Mithre added, as though uncertain how to explain. "But I give you our oath no harm will befall any of you—or Daníel—while you're our guests here."

"Guests?" Halldóra snorted. "We shall see. But lead on, then." She glanced back at the tunnel mouth. "I have a hundred riders out there and if I don't return to my camp within the hour, a tenth of them will go to Val Petros and Val Altair, after which they shall return with a *thousand* riders. The rest will storm this keep, so they don't get bored while they wait."

Mithre's lips twitched but he nodded again. "The situation is perfectly clear. This way, please."

He turned and strode inside, his Danai trailing behind. Halldóra shared a quick look with Katrin and followed.

Victor waited in Eirik's old study, sitting at the head of an ornate iron table that must have broken a few backs to drag in. Katrin was delighted to see he looked awful. Red-rimmed eyes gazed at them from a hollow face that had lost none of its arrogance. The diamond was hidden inside his coat, but she could see a glint of the chain around his throat. Just like Eirik.

Mithre took a chair to Victor's left. Daníel sat at the opposite end of the table, where an empty chair waited for Halldóra. She made no move to sit. Instead, she surveyed the assembled Danai, all clad in fur-lined white leathers and half with swords at their hips instead of bows.

"I wonder if you've truly conquered Val Moraine, Victor Dessarian, or if the keep has conquered *you*," she observed.

Frida and Sofia laughed at this. The young Danai shot them dirty looks, though Victor gave no reaction.

"You can play at being a Valkirin," Halldóra continued dryly, "but without our blood, I'm afraid you won't last long in these mountains."

"I've lasted long enough," Victor replied. "And your emissaries couldn't tell the difference, could they?"

Frida scowled. Katrin heard she'd fallen straight into Victor's trap, barely escaping with her life. The emissaries from Val Petros and Val Altair weren't so lucky.

"But don't worry," Victor added with a faint smile. "I've no wish to be your king."

Katrin's hand fell to the hilt of her blade. "How dare you—" she hissed.

"We will discuss terms in a moment," Halldóra snapped, her voice like steel again. "But first I wish to know how Daníel came to be here—and why he wears an iron collar around his neck." She turned to her grandson. "Did the Dessarians take you for a hostage?"

Daníel returned her level gaze. The whole room seemed to hold its breath.

"No," he said at last. "It was the Oracle of Delphi."

A minor pandemonium erupted among the party from Val Tourmaline at these words.

"Quiet!" Halldóra shouted. She waited for perfect silence before speaking. "The *mortals* caught you? How?"

He touched the collar. "This is a talisman, grandmother. Like none I've ever seen before. It allows them to control a daēva. The Oracle has others. Danai too."

Now Halldóra did take the chair, sitting heavily. "I'd heard she was stirring up trouble, but we pay little attention to such matters." She turned an accusing eye on Victor. "You knew this. What have you done about it?"

"Daníel arrived just after I deployed the ice defenses," Victor said. "There's been no way to get word out until today."

"So no one else knows? The Matrium?"

Victor shook his head.

Katrin snuck a look at Halldóra's heir, her skin crawling. A talisman to bind a daēva? What an obscenity!

"How did you escape?" Halldóra asked Daníel.

"A mortal helped me. She's here too."

Victor pointed at two gold bracelets lying on the table. "Those are the match of the collars. When a mortal wears one, it gives them control over the Nexus. We cannot touch the elements without permission. The bond can also be used to cause severe pain. I would have destroyed them, but they're warded—just like your grandson's collar."

Everyone in the room stared at the bracelets with disgust and, Katrin had to admit, a touch of fear.

"You're welcome to Daníel," Victor continued with a wave of his hand. "And I've no wish to remain indefinitely at Val Moraine. But nor will I let you have it. So here are my terms. We unite to destroy the Oracle and liberate her prisoners, and you leave Val Moraine an icebound tomb. With assurances that there will be no repercussions for my ridding the world of Eirik Kafsnjór."

Halldóra considered this for a moment. "I don't like the second part much. But I do agree Delphi must be dealt with, swiftly and severely." She drew a deep breath. "It has been a long time since Danai and Valkirin fought side by side. A thousand years, by my reckoning. The other holdfasts might not accept it, even if they believe me."

Victor appeared to listen but his expression grew vague, one hand slipping inside his coat to grasp something. Katrin's green eyes narrowed. She'd seen Eirik perform the same gesture count-less times.

"I would speak," Mithre said, rising to his feet and addressing the Valkirins. "I followed Victor into the shadowlands. We found a new world on the other side. There were no daēvas, only mortals. We were the first. The mortals there discovered a similar talisman, but they called it a bond. We were slow to react, slow to *unite*, and they enslaved us all. Forced us to be soldiers. To kill each other."

Daníel listened closely to his words, Katrin noticed, though it was hard to tell what he thought of them.

"You think you're strong and the mortals are weak, but they're not. If they can take one, they can take us all." Mithre sat down.

Frida and Sofia were no longer smirking, nor was Katrin. Halldóra nodded slowly.

"I'll leave it to you to inform the Matrium," she said to Victor. "I'll tell Runar of Val Petros and Stefán of Val Altair. We can meet on the plain outside the city, in the Umbra. But I have not yet agreed to the final disposition of Val Moraine. That will be taken up again once the Oracle has been dealt with." She gave Victor a grim smile. "And any new treaty will include your mother. Or do you rule House Dessarian now?"

Victor's gaze slitted but he gave a brusque nod.

"Done," he said.

GERDA CLENCHED HER TEETH, LETTING THE GLOBE FALL INTO her lap. Before she could stop herself, she'd hurled her goblet of wine across the room, thin arms quivering with rage. It shattered against the wall in a scarlet stain.

An alliance between Danai and Valkirin? Curse Halldóra to nine hells! This simply wouldn't do.

She looked around at the dismal chamber where she'd spent the last century waiting to die. Before she found Nicodemus, there'd been little to live for. She passed the long, lonely hours drinking and talking to ghosts. But the return of the Vatras changed everything. Together, they could restore the Valkirins to their former glory. Masters of the air! Lords of sky and stone! Her pulse quickened. Yet again, the Avas Danai stood in their way. Well, she wouldn't let history repeat itself.

Gerda ran to the door and pounded on it with both fists.

"What now?" a voice on the other side asked wearily.

"Open up, boy!" Gerda said her most commanding tone. "This instant!"

The bolt was thrown and the door cracked open. A young Danai stood on the other side. He barely looked old enough to shave. Even in her fury, Gerda felt insulted they'd given her the runt of the litter.

"I demand to see Halldóra," she said imperiously.

He sighed. "Look, I can't leave my post—"

"Listen, you little weasel. Do you have any idea who I am?" She struck her breast. "The oldest living Kafsnjór! I was hunting icebjorn five hundred years before you crawled from your mother's miserable womb. Halldóra of Val Tourmaline is one of my dearest friends. If she finds out you've kept me hidden away, *abused* me, you can kiss that treaty goodbye. And Victor will nail your hide to the wall. You'll be despised by every—"

"All right, all right." He did look a little worried now, which pleased her. "But you have to wait here."

Gerda clenched her teeth as he shot the bolt. Long minutes crept by. Then she heard footsteps in the corridor. The door swung wide.

Halldóra of Val Tourmaline had aged since Gerda last saw her, but she was still a handsome woman. The light blue gems of her holdfast's namesake gleamed in her silver hair.

"Gerda," Halldóra said, eyebrows lifting in surprise. "I didn't even realize you lived."

"Please, for the love of all that's decent, take her away with you," muttered Victor Dessarian, who stood behind Halldóra.

"I will speak with her alone," Gerda said haughtily.

Victor laughed. "Not likely." He shouldered his way inside.

Three other Valkirins provided an escort and Gerda was delighted to see one of them was Katrin. They shared a warm smile. She'd always liked Katrin. A proper Valkirin, that girl was.

Daníel hovered in the background, his expression shadowed.

"Wait outside," Halldóra told them.

Katrin didn't look happy about it, but she nodded. Four Danai gathered down the corridor, whispering among themselves.

Gerda closed the door and stared at Victor, who lounged in her favorite chair. Well, let him stay. What did she care?

"I'm sorry about Eirik," Halldóra said. "He will be sorely missed."

"No, he won't." Gerda drew Halldóra aside. "There's no need to pretend. Everyone hated him, even his own children."

Halldóra didn't bother disputing this. "You're more than welcome at Val Tourmaline," she said. "The ultimate fate of Val Moraine remains undecided, but be assured—"

"That is not what I wish to discuss," Gerda interrupted, glancing at Victor. "This is an ill-conceived alliance."

"I don't require your blessing," Halldóra replied stiffly. "I understand you bear the Danai a grudge, but Eirik is dead now. And we have a common enemy that is far more dangerous."

"The mortals?" Gerda sneered. "Pah! A bugbear, conjured to distract you from the truth." She drew herself up. "Heed me now, Halldóra. War is coming, but not the one you think." She paused. "The Vatras will return. They aren't all free of the Kiln yet, but they will be."

"The Vatras," Halldóra said flatly.

"I can prove it to you. But first you must understand what really happened." She pointed to Victor, who watched them with hooded eyes from across the room. "It was all the fault of the Danai. They betrayed the Vatra king and drove him to a blind rage. And our ancestors made the mistake of sheltering his enemies. We chose the wrong side! But now we have a chance to choose again."

Halldóra studied her with an unreadable expression. "Why do you think they're free?"

"Because I've spoken with one. Seen him work fire with my

own eyes. He promised to liberate Val Moraine from the invaders. But if you ally with the Danai now.... We will burn. All of us."

"The woman is mad," Victor muttered.

Gerda smiled grimly. "Am I? Or do you have doubts in your heart? What if I speak the truth? If I were you, I would dig myself a very deep hole to hide in when the Vatras come. And they will come. Make no mistake—"

"Enough," Halldóra interrupted with a touch of impatience. "What proof do you have?"

"I will give you proof." Gerda retrieved the globe, blowing on the runes. "Show me the Vatra," she whispered.

A man appeared in the depths. He crouched over a glass display case.

Victor leapt to his feet and hurried over, his face a thunderhead. "What is this?" he demanded, peering at the glass orb. "Some trick?"

Gerda smiled. "It is no trick, you fool. His name is Nicodemus."

"I had these rooms searched! You lying old—"

Victor reached for the globe and Halldóra laid a hand on his arm.

"It is hers," she said sternly.

Victor grumbled but dropped his hand. "This is ridiculous."

"He's in Tjanjin, I think. But he escaped the Kiln, with one other."

Halldóra watched him for a moment, then sighed.

"Why don't you come with me and we can discuss this further at my camp?"

"No!"

"She's not taking that globe," Victor growled. "It's spoils of war and belongs to me now."

"Over my dead body," Gerda hissed, clutching the talisman.

She willed Nicodemus to take out his own globe, but as

before, he didn't seem to see her. She felt Halldóra's interest waning.

And then...a sudden flame erupted from the man's palm, illuminating his features in flickering red light. The shadows fled before the sudden light. He appeared to be standing in a windowless chamber cluttered with objects of every description.

Halldóra gave a low gasp. She leaned forward.

"I cannot believe it," she whispered. "After all this time."

"You see?" Gerda said in satisfaction. "We must do all we can to help him break the Gale." She let the image vanish. "A new age will come! The lost art of forging talismans will be restored. Air and fire are sister elements. Of all the clans, we were always the most alike." Gerda touched Halldóra's arm. "I know you want vengeance for Daníel, but the Vatras will punish the mortals, do not fear. And if you are the first to forge a pact, I am certain they'll reward you with Val Moraine and all her riches."

Halldóra stared at the globe, which had grown cloudy. She drew a deep breath and looked up.

"We must tell the Marakai," Halldóra said—to Victor.

He nodded, face white with shock.

Gerda scowled. "Why do you speak to him? He is our enemy. I will inform Nicodemus the holdfasts stand behind the return—"

"You *are* mad," Halldóra snapped, eyes blazing. "Ally with the Vatras? They have no allies! They despise us all. *We* helped imprison them, in case you've forgotten. Do you think they would overlook that now?"

Gerda recoiled. "Don't be a fool!"

"Give me the talisman," Halldóra growled. "You shall not work any more mischief with it."

She reached for the globe and Gerda yanked it back. "You're making a terrible mistake!" she screeched.

"No, it is you who've made the mistake. You are either a monster or an old fool, I care not which." Halldóra's grey eyes hardened to flint. "But I would see my whole holdfast burn before I grovel to the Lost Clan."

Gerda felt everything she'd worked for slipping away. A terrible, black grief descended on her. First, she had mourned the dead of Culach's Folly, their corpses left to rot in some foreign land. Then, only months later, the Dessarians came to finish the job. Gerda could have endured the horror of losing her entire holdfast if she knew the Valkirins as a race would be saved. But even that was not to be.

Gerda's mouth set. Her thin white hair lifted in a sudden whirlwind. Halldóra sensed it and reached for air herself—too late. Gerda lifted her like a child and hurled her at the wall of ice, a hundred times harder than she'd thrown the goblet. There was a terrible crack as her skull struck. Halldóra hit the ground in a broken heap.

Gerda spun to Victor, teeth bared, and saw the shining edge of his sword sweeping toward her.

Albert, she thought, and nothing more.

22

LEAP OF FAITH

The sudden explosion of power in Gerda's chamber caught the Valkirins waiting outside by surprise. Katrin had been listening to their muffled voices, soft at first but increasingly heated. She couldn't make out what was being said, only that they were arguing about something.

"Gerda must be ripping Victor up one side and down the other," she'd observed.

"Good for her," Sofia said. She reached up and rewound her tight bun, holding the silver pins between her teeth. "They say Gerda Kafsnjór could skin an armored cockindrill with her tongue. I'm not surprised the Dessarians failed to kill her. The woman's bloody immortal."

Katrin hadn't realized Gerda was alive either—not until a Danai youth had intercepted them outside the stables and pulled Victor aside. He'd hesitated, then told Halldóra the matriarch of Val Moraine wished to see her, although that wasn't the word he'd used.

Now something had gone terribly wrong. Katrin kicked the door open and froze in horror. Daníel drew a sharp breath beside her.

Halldóra lay on her side against the far wall, head twisted around. The quantity of blood pooled beneath her left no doubt she was dead. Victor stood over Gerda, gore-stained sword in hand. He looked up at Katrin with panicked eyes.

"It's not what you—" he began.

"Treachery!" Katrin cried. "Murder in the keep!"

She lunged forward, intending to take the wretched Dessarian's head from his shoulders, but Frida grabbed her arm.

"The heir," she hissed. "We must get him out before they seal us in again. There's no time!"

Daníel still stood in the doorway, rigid and aghast, staring at his grandmother.

Katrin swore and the three of them swarmed down the corridor with Daníel in the middle, cutting straight through the startled Danai who stood in their path.

"Follow me!" she yelled. "I know the shortest way to the tunnel."

They pounded down corridors, the lumen crystals embedded in the walls flickering fitfully in the darkness, and finally reached the door to the stables. Katrin yanked it open and stopped as she realized one of their party was missing.

"Where the fuck is Daníel?" she demanded.

"He was next to me a moment ago," Frida panted.

Sofia cursed. "He must have slipped away at that last crossing." Her eyes glistened with unshed tears. "We have to go back—"

"Damn him." Katrin heard shouts, growing louder. A dozen Danai rushed down the corridor, murder on their faces. She ducked as a rain of arrows whooshed past. The stone beneath their feet began to tremble and crack.

"Those bastards," Frida muttered. "They must have planned it from the start."

"Shit," Katrin said. "*Shit.*"

"Go," Frida urged. "We'll get Daníel later."

There was no time to mount the abbadax, which were tethered in the farthest pens. So Katrin sheathed her bloody sword and ran full tilt into the ice tunnel. The exit loomed ahead, a circle of starry sky, and without breaking stride she threw herself into the void. The valley rushed up to meet her, a thousand paces of air, five hundred, two, the wind flaying every inch of exposed skin, and then she felt a wrenching shock as a rider swooped down and caught her arm. Katrin grabbed a fistful of leather and hauled herself up behind him.

Two more riders dove for Frida and Sofia. The abbadax screamed, wings beating hard, as they banked sharply and flew into the night.

GALEN CREPT THROUGH THE DESERTED CORRIDORS OF THE KEEP, darkness pressing hungrily at the edges of the light cast by the lumen crystals. Some kind of ruckus had erupted on the levels above. He'd heard distant shouts and the ring of swords, but they'd faded away and now an ominous silence hung over Val Moraine. Galen didn't know what had happened, nor did he intend to find out.

He reached the kitchens and cautiously peered inside. They were dark and empty. He found a crate of apples and threw some into his leather satchel, along with potatoes and turnips. Enough to keep him alive until he got out of the mountains.

He wished he could bring Mina, but it had become obvious she loved Culach and wouldn't leave him. Galen wished them whatever happiness they could find. He was a grown man. It was past time to face the truth. To take charge of his life and whatever he could salvage of it.

Perhaps he'd go to the Isles of the Marakai. That's where people went when they didn't want to be found. And then...who knew?

Galen turned to leave when a shadow detached itself from the doorway.

"I was afraid you'd gone."

He peered into the gloom. "Rafel?"

The Danai had slipped away in the commotion that ensued after they broke through to the outside. Galen considered looking for him, but in the end he decided he'd embarrassed himself enough already. Better to leave quietly and spare him another awkward refusal. Now Rafel moved closer. He looked shaken.

"Your father killed Gerda. Halldóra too. It's madness. The holdfasts will destroy him utterly now."

So that was the fighting he'd heard.

"I don't care," Galen said. "I'm leaving. Now."

"Then I'm coming with you." Rafel's voice sounded strange.

Galen wanted his company, wanted it desperately. But he needed to be sure Rafel knew what he was getting into. "It will be a hard journey. And that's assuming we even find our way out of the tunnels. They could still be blocked deeper into the mountain. I'm not sure."

Rafel stepped closer.

"I know a better way," he said softly.

Galen slung the satchel over one shoulder. "What way?"

"A Talisman of Folding. The mortal woman called Thena claimed she lost it, but she lied. I'm certain she hid it somewhere close by the well. We just have to find it. It will take us a thousand leagues in an instant."

"I thought she helped you escape."

"She's not what she seems." He paused, a naked plea in his eyes. "I'll tell you all of it, I swear. But we don't have long before they notice we're missing."

Galen didn't move. "Where would we go?"

"I'll take you somewhere safe first. Anywhere you want. Then I'll use it myself."

Understanding dawned. "You're going after Ysabel."

Rafel nodded.

"And she's in Delphi?"

"A captive of the Pythia. She... She tortures us." He touched the collar. "With this. But it doesn't work in the darklands. If I can get Ysabel to Nocturne, they can't hurt her anymore. They can't hurt either of us."

Galen didn't hesitate. "I'll help you."

"No," Rafel said immediately, his face darkening. "It's too dangerous."

"Because I can't work earth? I can still fight!"

"That's not it."

"What then?" Galen demanded.

"I can't tell you now—"

"Then I'm coming," Galen said firmly. "Please. I'm a better man than you think." He swallowed. "Or I want to be."

"You're already better than I am," Rafel said hoarsely.

Galen smiled. "I wasn't looking forward to climbing the mountains again anyway." He glanced at his foot. "They took a bite out of me last time."

Galen held out his hand. After a moment, Rafel took it.

NO, THAT WASN'T RIGHT, THENA THOUGHT TO HERSELF.

She wound a strand of Korinna's flaxen hair around one finger so it made a curl, then arranged it against her pale cheek. The girl's features had begun to harden in death, but Thena could still try to make her look pretty for the afterlife. She studied her work with a critical gaze. She'd decided to leave Korinna's eyes open since they were her best feature. Blue, with flecks of hazel. The whites had turned red, but there was nothing Thena could do about that.

"You ought to have listened," she said, her lip quivering. "You really ought have."

Korinna said nothing. Of course she didn't. Thena rested her aching head in her hands.

Oh, but it was all a distraction, wasn't it? Rafel had abandoned her, that much was clear. He wasn't coming back. He intended to take the talisman for himself.

Thena had called and banged and wept, but no one came, not a single guard. They were going to leave her to die here in this lonely chamber.

"I told you he wasn't broken," she said to Korinna. "In fact, he hated you. He only kept his mouth shut for his sister's sake."

I've done my duty, she thought as a worm of despair wriggled into her heart. I've been steadfast. What more can Apollo ask of me? Perhaps this *was* Tartarus. A chill, lightless abyss where the worst sinners were cast. Apollo himself had nearly been imprisoned there when he killed the Cyclops who forged Zeus's thunderbolt, though Zeus had relented in the end.

After Rafel came, she had imagined their return to the temple in triumph with the Danai talisman. The Pythia would praise her bravery for saving their fair city from the witches. Her redemption would be almost complete.

Almost.

For what Thena wanted more than anything was to take some Shields of Apollo and hunt the one who had gotten away. To hunt Darius. His treachery still haunted her.

Surely, the Pythia would grant her that.

But only if Thena brought her the talisman.

Feeling listless and drained, she curled up next to Korinna, pulling the blanket over them both. She began to sing softly, a hymn as old as the bones of the earth.

> O, Delian king, whose light-producing eye
> Views all within, and all beneath the sky
> Whose locks are gold, whose oracles are sure,
> Who, omens good reveal'st, and precepts pure:

Hear me entreating for humankind,
Hear, and be present with benignant mind;
For thou survey'st this boundless Æther all,
And every part of this terrestrial ball.
Abundant, blessed; and thy piercing sight,
Extends beneath the gloomy, silent night;
Beyond the darkness, starry-eyed, profound,
The stable roots, deep fixed by thee are found...

Thena's head jerked around as she heard a creak.

"Rafel?" she cried, leaping to her feet.

The door swung open. It was not Rafel, but her heart soared just the same.

"Demetrios," she whispered. "Oh, you've come for me!"

He regarded her for a long moment, his eyes gathering up the dim light. Silver hair fell unbound across broad shoulders that filled the doorframe. After all her suffering, Thena felt an upwelling of emotion. She knew Demetrios would never abandon her.

He strode into the room, kicking the door shut behind him. A second later, he loomed over her, gripping her arm. Thena winced in pain.

"You're hurting me," she hissed.

"Pain purifies the soul," he replied. "Didn't you used to tell me that?"

Sea green eyes regarded her with controlled fury. This was not the Demetrios she knew, Thena realized with an unpleasant jolt. This was someone else entirely.

"Demetrios—"

"Don't call me that," he snapped.

"Daníel, then," she said quickly. "What's happened? Oh, we must flee from this place! Rafel has taken the talisman—"

"I heard what Korinna said."

"What?"

"You let the Danai go. *You let him go.*"

She shook her head. "No, Daníel. No, I never—"

"Why?" His fingers squeezed harder. "Do you love him?"

Tears sprang to Thena's eyes. "I saved you, Daníel! Purged you of your wicked nature. Everything I did was for the good, for the light! Deep down, you know it's true. Korinna was a liar—"

He put a large hand on her mouth, his jaw working. "Be quiet."

Thena tried to speak, but his hand was clamped over her lips. With the other, he seized her throat.

"I am nothing to you." A storm of emotions broke across his face. The hand tightened and she gasped for air. "A plaything."

Her toes left the floor, kicking futilely. The edges of Thena's vision began to blacken. She felt the scissors poised to snicker shut. To sever her thread from the pattern forever. Her fists pounded at his chest, but it was like hitting a stone wall.

And then he drew a shuddering breath. Thena tumbled to the floor.

"Get out," he spat. "Before I change my mind."

She clutched her throat. The pain was distant. More than anything, she felt bereft. "You are more than that," Thena whispered hoarsely. "Much more. We belong together. Come with me, Demetrios. Please."

He turned away, tears shining on his cheeks. "Just go!"

Thena fled.

There were no guards outside her room. She hoisted her skirts and made straight for the hidden door leading down to the enormous caverns in the heart of the mountain where the Valkirins grew their food. But as she passed the chamber where the black-eyed witch, the father of Andros/Darius, used to question her, Thena paused. The door sat ajar. She peeked inside.

There was the long table, covered in maps. There was the thronelike chair he would sit in, along with a dozen others. And there.... A gleam of gold.

Sol Invictus. The Conquering Sun.

The god spoke to her, telling her what to do, and Thena obeyed.

A minute later, she was racing down a series of cramped, winding staircases. The warp and weft of the pattern was clear now. Thena could hear the humming rattle of the great loom as it spun out her destiny.

∾

GALEN BREATHED DEEPLY, SEIZED BY A SUDDEN AND unexpected yearning for the forests of his home. How long had it been since he smelled something living? Val Moraine was metal and stone and ice. But now the scent of loamy earth mingled with the spice of citrus and sweet tang of rotting apples. It reminded him of Tethys's night garden where he used to play as a child, a sanctuary of exotic hybrids that thrived on moonlight. The garden was beautiful and complex, with hidden traps capable of drawing blood—just like his grandmother.

She'd caught him lingering at the gate once. He would sometimes sneak off and look at it, fantasizing about running away and searching for his father in the shadowlands, or imagining Victor stepping through it and sweeping him up in a hug. Tethys had scared him half to death, looming out of the darkness. She wasn't angry—not precisely. But she told him the gates were locked and warded. He'd stopped going after that.

Then Nazafareen had blown them all wide open.

I'm sorry, he thought. So sorry....

"Nearly there," Rafel whispered.

Galen blinked, scanning the dim interior of the cavern. Large open cisterns irrigated the crops via a clever system of stone channels. Rafel stopped at one draped in hart's-tongue moss.

"This is where we came through from Delphi," he said, pointing into the cistern's inky depths. "Talismans of Folding use liquid as a passageway. Thena had it. She slipped away for a minute, but she couldn't have gone far. She may have left a marker. Look for anything out of place."

Galen moved slowly through the trees, scanning the ground. The cavern had been designed to feed hundreds, and most of the crops sat decaying on the ground. He used his feet to shuffle through the layer of dead leaves and plant matter, uncovering worms and beetles that fled from the sudden light. They searched in concentric circles outward from the cistern. Galen plucked an apple but found he was too nervous to eat it. He slipped it into his pocket and frowned. The earth at the roots of the tree looked disturbed.

He crouched down and began to dig. A few inches beneath the soil, his fingers touched something hard.

"Rafel," he hissed.

The Danai came running over. Galen pried a disc from the ground and brushed it off. One side depicted a tower, the other a man and woman in profile.

"That's it," Rafel breathed. "I have to be the one to use it." He gave a shaky laugh. "I assume you've never been to Delphi."

Galen shook his head. "I've never been anywhere outside the forest, except for here."

Rafel glanced at him. "You're not missing much."

They clambered over the edge of the cistern.

"The talisman creates a shortcut," Rafel explained. "Through some...nether plane. I'm not sure how to describe it. It feels likes water, but don't worry, you'll be able to breathe. Thankfully it's brief."

Galen's stomach tightened. "Understood. So it will take us straight into the temple?"

"I know where they keep her. We get in and out. Kill anyone you see, especially if it's a girl wearing a bracelet. You can't hesitate." He paused. "They have torches on the walls. Don't look at them. Just stay well back. Can you do that?"

Fire.

"Yes," Galen said. "I can do that."

"The Pythia has some Valkirins too, but we can't worry about them now." He sounded sad. "But once the clans get word, they'll go in force." He touched Galen's cheek. "Thank you."

Galen kissed him to cover his embarrassment, a lovely lingering kiss that left him light-headed. "Ellard likes you," he blurted, and instantly regretted it.

But Rafel just smiled. "I'm glad," he said. "Ready?"

Galen nodded. They clasped hands again.

"Don't let go," Rafel said.

They leapt into the cistern. Chill water enveloped Galen as he sank down. But instead of growing colder in the depths, the substance warmed and thickened. Rafel drifted forward. It was hard to see because a reddish mist covered everything, but Galen had the sense of a vast space around him, of a dull, lifeless place beneath a yellow-grey sky. On and on they swam. His lungs screamed for air and he finally gave in, inhaling the reddish substance with panicky gasp. The pressure in his chest ceased, although it wasn't an entirely pleasant sensation. It had a distinct taste, of dry bones and dusty riverbeds and charred wood. Galen jerked in alarm as something brushed his foot, but then it broke free and they were ascending again.

Light struck his face. A different kind of light than he'd ever seen before. Not the silver of Hecate nor the buttery yellow of Selene. Not the cool blue of a lumen crystal. This was orange and fierce. Galen blinked and crawled from a sticky pool covering the floor of a stone chamber that reeked of wine. He was still getting his bearings when a plump girl sitting in the corner squawked in surprise. Before she could make another sound, Rafel was on top of her, slamming her head into the wall until she went limp.

"This way," he hissed, hauling Galen to his feet.

They ran into a hall and up a flight of stairs. Galen clenched his teeth against the dancing, flickering energy he sensed all around, but he kept his eyes on Rafel's back. And then they stood before a wooden door and Rafel kicked it down and a girl looked up, his twin, Ysabel, her body so wasted Galen could hardly believe she wasn't dead, and Rafel heaved a sob. Galen ran to the wall and tore her chains loose from the mortar. Rafel lifted her in his arms. They'd turned back to the door when he fell to his knees with a scream so terrible Galen's heart literally stopped.

A woman stood there, her white gown stained red from hem to neckline, her hair plastered in snakelike tangles across her face. She wore a gold bracelet around her wrist.

"I followed you, *Nikias*," she said, a hellish light in her eyes. "Deceitful little witch."

Galen threw himself at the woman, Rafel's screams filling his head, and he would've torn her apart, but a sparkling dust filled the air and he suddenly couldn't see. Galen fought anyway, calling a whirlwind, punching and kicking and biting like a wild animal.

Until the iron closed around his throat, and he knew they'd failed.

23

SHADES OF THE UNDEAD

Nazafareen peered up at the palace wall, one boot tapping out a jittery rhythm on the carpet of pine needles. It seemed like hours since Darius had clambered over.

"What if they caught him?" she whispered to Megaera, who sat cross-legged on the ground, unconcerned by the gentle rain pattering around them.

The Maenad shot her a look. "Darius? He makes a mouse sound like a rampaging bull."

Nazafareen knew she was right, but it didn't stop her worrying. He'd already suffered unknown tortures at the hands of the Pythia. The psychic wounds of his captivity lingered, though Darius did his best to bury them. When their bond was weak or absent—as it was now, in the shadow of the Umbra—Nazafareen felt a fierce protectiveness and hated to let him out of her sight.

Finally, a head popped over the edge and a coil of rope tumbled down. Nazafareen realized her fist was clenched tight and loosened it, the fingers stiff.

"All clear," Darius called softly.

She grabbed the rope with her left hand and used her toes to dig for purchase as he hauled her up. She rolled over the top and dropped to the earth. It was soft from the rain, but she still felt a hard jolt in her knees.

"*That* hurt," she muttered, limping into the concealment of a bamboo grove.

They were in the Garden of the Golden Valley, which lay in a remote part of the palace grounds at the edge of the Umbra. Nazafareen peeked through the tall stalks. Velvety twilight cloaked a landscape of artificial mountains and lakes, circled by gravel pathways. Their graceful curves drew the eye to a series of miniature gardens, each scene artfully composed of unique trees and flowers. Small viewing pavilions with wooden benches enticed visitors to pass the time in serene contemplation of nature.

It was the sort of place Nazafareen would have enjoyed wandering through with Darius, while they talked of inconsequential things. But now she kept thinking about how weak she was in this half-light. Her breaking power flickered like a dying torch. She wondered uneasily if the Vatra knew, too.

A moment later, Herodotus landed inside the wall—he had the sense to keep hold of the rope, Nazafareen noticed—followed a moment later by Megaera. Katsu made his own way over without aid, landing on his feet as light as a cat.

They all huddled together in the shelter of the bamboo.

"A patrol just passed," Darius whispered. He turned to the Stygian. "Which way now?"

"Check the globe first," Katsu replied.

Darius took it out and blew on the runes. Immediately, the Vatra appeared. He stood in the center of a large chamber, cluttered with objects of every description. There was an intense, predatory stillness to his posture.

"Oh dear," Herodotus muttered into his beard. "He's hunting her."

Darius released the flows and the image disappeared.

"He's still down there, all right," Katsu said. "But the only way inside is through the palace itself. We'll get as close as we can, then split up. I know the routes the patrols usually take. We should be able to avoid them."

They crept deeper into the grounds, keeping to the shadows. The gentle rain helped, muffling sound and raising a fine mist in the hollows. Once, they startled a doe nibbling on some bushes. It stared at them and bounded into the woods, white tail flashing. The peaceful beauty of the scenery seemed at odds with the company's dire purpose, and Nazafareen felt a growing sense of unreality, as if she had slipped into a pleasant dream. They passed through the Garden of Solitary Joy, and the Garden of the South, and the Valley of the Blue Wave. Several times, Katsu led them to a hiding place moments before a patrol passed—but even that felt almost like a game.

The imperial gardens had their own magic, she thought. The sort that lulled you into complacency with droning bees and petal-strewn ponds. Luckily, the Stygian seemed immune, perhaps because he was familiar with it. She'd worried he might back out at the last moment, but Katsu was as good as his word. Nazafareen could tell he didn't like the idea of betraying the emperor, but he wanted the globe even more.

At last, the imperial palace appeared through the trees, not nearly as large as the Rock of Ariamazes but much more pleasing to the eye. It was made of red-lacquered wood, with three tiers and a pointed roof that curved upward at the corners like a boat. Not a single tree or shrub stood within five hundred paces of its walls.

They followed Katsu to a bridge arching over a meandering stream and studied the palace from the concealment of the supports. Two dozen soldiers in belted black robes stood rigidly before the main entrance.

"You're sure about this?" Katsu asked doubtfully.

Megaera merely grinned and handed her staff to Darius.

"Give it back in one piece," she said. "You carry the honor of the Maenads now."

He inclined his head. "Thank you, dáskalos," he murmured, a Greek word which meant *teacher* or *master*, and she nodded in satisfaction.

Megaera slipped some distance away with Herodotus, who carried an unlit oil lamp. He upended the contents over her head.

"Even if this works, we won't have much time," Katsu said. "A minute perhaps. I hope you can run fast."

Darius smiled. Nazafareen drew a deep breath. She made a sign to Herodotus.

He took a flint from his pocket and struck it. Once, twice. A spark flew from the stone, arcing through the air like a firefly. With a whoosh, Megaera erupted in flames. Nazafareen tensed. She'd seen Rhea hold a tiny flame to her arm once with no effect, but that was very different.

Megaera turned to them, a blazing torch from head to toe. She gave a little wave.

Herodotus lifted his robes and started running for the palace, skinny legs pumping.

"Vatras!" he hollered at the top of his lungs. "The Vatras are here!"

Megaera followed at a leisurely pace, arms swinging by her sides.

Nazafareen poked Katsu in the ribs. He stood there with his mouth hanging open.

"Go!" she urged.

The Stygian shook himself. The ranks of imperial guards in front of the palace were running forward now, shouting the alarm. They wore a sort of long, belted black dress, with scaled leather coats on top. Herodotus veered away to the left, towards the aquarium, and the guards followed.

"By Babana, the oyster king, I've never seen the like," Katsu murmured. He began to run, leading them in the opposite direction. They turned the corner of the palace unseen and had nearly reached a side door when it burst open and more guards poured out. They held wickedly curved blades and moved more like daēvas than humans, with fluid, predatory grace.

"No killing blows," Katsu growled. "They're good men."

"Well, *that* makes it trickier," Darius muttered, blue eyes coolly assessing the armed horde running toward them.

"They're not our enemies," the Stygian insisted, dropping into a loose-limbed fighting stance. "Their duty is to protect the emperor. They would fight on our side if they knew the truth. It's dishonorable to take an innocent life."

Darius and Nazafareen exchanged a look. "He's right," Darius muttered. "Use the flat of your blade."

Darius met the first one with a flurry of cracks from Megaera's staff that ended moments later with the man's sword in his own hand. He looked at it with longing for an instant, then tossed it aside.

"To me, Nazafareen!" he cried.

She swept her own blade from the scabbard and the melee began.

MEB CRAWLED THROUGH A NARROW TUNNEL BETWEEN TWO heaped piles of junk. Decades worth of dust lay on the objects, tickling her nose and coating her palms. Nico's voice was distant now, though he'd nearly found her the last time. He was getting angry. But she'd never come out. Never. And someone would come looking eventually, wouldn't they?

Or maybe they wouldn't. No one knew she'd gone with him. And it didn't seem like people came down here much. She wiped a filthy hand across her nose, then pinched it hard to stifle a sneeze.

Well, there had to be a way out. She tried to remember what she'd seen when he brought her, but she'd been crawling around in circles and it was all running together in her mind.

"Meb!"

He was definitely in the next gallery. His voice echoed hollowly through the spaces.

"Do you know what a lich is?"

She peered between two crates. His back was to her, but she could see his face in profile. A flame danced over his open palm, casting wild shadows on the ceiling. She quickly retreated.

"They're very nasty. Shades of the Undead whose touch means death. Several of them live inside the talisman I have in my pocket right now."

A long silence.

"I don't want to summon them, Meb. Once freed.... Well, they're not easy to unknit. But liches have a special talent. They can sniff out living flesh."

Lying. He's a liar, she thought. He just wants to trick me into coming out.

"It would be much easier if you cooperated, Meb."

The voice was moving away now and she took the opportunity to squeeze into a crooked space flanked by tall headless statues. Clay masks leered down at her from a glass cabinet beyond, the faces contorted in grimaces of laughter or pain, she couldn't tell which.

"Tell you what. I'll count to ten. If you haven't come out, I'll have to free the liches."

She moved backwards, retracing her path deeper into the collection.

Nicodemus started to count.

I've never even heard of no liches, she thought. They ain't real. Just some made-up thing. And who's to say they wouldn't get *him*, anyway?

She moved faster now, her surroundings looking more familiar. She was sure she'd seen that jade dragon before. And that funny gourd-shaped instrument with strings, half of them snapped. But when? Was it when she first came in? Or after?

"Seven...six...five..."

Meb skittered like a beetle underneath a table piled high with tottering tea sets. Her shoulder brushed a leg and she heard the pile shift, ever so slightly. Her heart froze. Then it settled again.

"Two...and one. Well, that's it then." He almost sounded sorry, which made it worse. "Here come the liches, Meb!"

She gritted her teeth and pushed onward. And then, by some miracle, she saw a door ahead. It was just across the room. Twenty paces. She bit her lip.

Don't go belly up now, she thought. You're fast. Just do it.

She burst from her hiding place and rushed toward the door. Then she caught movement in the corner of her eye. A shadow, but darker than those surrounding it. Darker than the darkest starless night. Darker than the bottom of the Great Green. A low moan came from her throat.

It drifted along, trailing ragged streamers at the edges. She wanted to run but her legs wouldn't move. A feeling of dread stole over her. The lich had no face, but she could feel its gaze fix on her.

Meb screamed. She screamed and screamed.

A wind rose, tearing at her hair. With a hideous cry just on the edge of hearing, the lich blew apart like smoke.

"Ah fuck," Nicodemus muttered behind her. "That was close."

More were coming. Meb could see them. The Shades of the Undead.

She didn't resist when he seized her arm and dragged her through the door.

MANY CENTURIES BEFORE, THE GROUNDS SURROUNDING THE palace of Xun Lai Xiang, the Son of Heaven, Keeper of the Nine Ecstatic Mysteries, and thirty-third emperor of the island-state of Tjanjin, had been razed of all vegetation that might offer concealment for an assassin. A special kind of grass was planted, a gift of the Avas Danai. It was plush as a Susan carpet and only grew two inches high. Many picnics and games were enjoyed on this vast emerald lawn, including a form of badminton where the shuttlecock was a clever mechanical bird.

Unfortunately, the current emperor's great-grandfather turned out to be allergic to the grass, so he'd torn it up and ordered five hundred cartloads of crushed pink and white seashells to be hauled up from the shore and raked into pleasing patterns.

They crunched under Nazafareen's boots as she parried an overhead blow from one of Xiang's imperial guards. She floated serenely in the Nexus, which sharpened her senses to a deadly degree. Although the guardsman was formidable, she had little trouble anticipating his strategy.

Behind her, Megaera's staff whirled in Darius's hands, stunning his opponents and breaking a few bones, though he seemed to be keeping his word to Katsu. A few lay unconscious, others moaned weakly, but none appeared dead.

Nazafareen's guard feinted to the right, trying to draw her off-balance. She swept her blade around, aiming for his sword arm, and drew first blood. The man didn't even flinch. He redoubled his attack with a flurry of blows and though she managed to skip out of reach, her left arm trembled with effort. That was the problem with fighting one-handed against a two-handed opponent.

If she could knock him off balance for an instant....

It was time to cheat, she decided, letting her awareness roam into the earth even as she parried another vicious blow that nearly took her head off. She felt the roots of the grass below the layer of shells, sleeping but alive, and the blind creatures delving in the soil, and the echo of the humble beings who had built the shells and called them home.

She put aside thoughts of how weak she was in earth power. *Don't snatch at it*, Darius always told her. *Let it flow into you naturally*.

So Nazafareen did that and the shells trembled, rippling outward in gentle waves like a pebble thrown into a still pond. The guard wasn't knocked down, the effect was more subtle, but his eyes widened in confusion and Nazafareen punched him in the temple with the hilt of her sword—though not quite quickly enough.

He was right-handed and saw it coming. As she stretched forward, his blade slipped into her, just beneath the armpit. Then her own devastating blow connected and he dropped like a stone.

Nazafareen turned her back to Darius and Katsu, fingers quickly probing the cut. The blade had nicked a rib. It didn't feel deep, but wetness soaked her side. She pressed her palm against the wound and let her cloak fall closed. She didn't want the others to know, especially Darius. They needed her. And there was no time to fuss over an injury.

She sheathed her sword and looked around. The rain had stopped. She saw no sign of Megaera or Herodotus. In fact, the grounds were eerily quiet. To her relief, neither Katsu nor Darius appeared to have taken a single scratch. How the Stygian managed it without any weapon besides hands and feet was something she intended to ask him about later. But now she felt time seeping away with every heartbeat.

"That was *you*?" Darius asked, leaning on Megaera's staff.

Nazafareen nodded.

"You're learning," he said dryly.

"Move," Katsu barked, starting for the door to the palace. "More guards will be here any minute. I can lead us down to the collection, but we have to get inside before we're seen."

"Wait!" Nazafareen cried. "See exactly where the Vatra is first," she told Darius. "Quickly."

He pulled out the globe and the runes ignited in blue fire. The scene inside changed instantly, but it wasn't the gloomy galleries of the emperor's talisman collection. Sunlight painted the Vatra's copper hair. He was dragging Meb across a rope bridge. Statues of frolicking porpoises ringed the turquoise pool beneath them.

"He got past us," Darius growled. "They're in the aquarium."

"I recognize the place," Katsu said. He paused. "There's a gate nearby."

Nazafareen seized a handful of Katsu's coat. "You never mentioned that!"

"And you never said he might use it," Katsu replied flatly.

"How close are they to the gate?" Darius asked.

He shook his head. "Very. We won't—"

"Don't you dare say it," Nazafareen pressed harder against the wound. "Just show us the way."

They took off running for the western wall. Nazafareen was grateful her bond with Darius lay dormant else he'd know she was leaking like a sieve. She fixed her eyes on the wall ahead, stoking her anger and hatred.

Sometimes that was all you had left.

❧ 24 ❧

THE DROWNED LADY

"Where are we going?" the girl demanded, stumbling to keep up as Nico hauled her across the rope bridge.

He didn't reply. Summoning the liches had left a bad taste in his mouth. When he used the talisman, he could feel the veil tearing open to some forsaken abyss of the Dominion where the restless dead clung to a crude semblance of existence. Nine-tenths of the emperor's collection was junk, but that last tenth... There were objects whose purpose even Nico couldn't divine, though he felt their power.

"I ain't walking if you don't tell me," Meb said stubbornly, dragging her feet as they neared the end of the bridge.

A little pavilion sat on the island beyond, with a bench carved to resemble a giant clam shell. A nice middle-class family from Chang'an sat on the bench, enjoying the view of the harbor. The mother wore a silk robe with an elegant crimson sash. Her lustrous black hair was swept into a loose bun held in place by four jade dragonfly pins. The children, a boy and a girl in matching silk coats and trousers, looked over with curiosity. The girl, who was about Meb's age, tugged at her father's sleeve.

"Help!" Meb cried, trying to yank herself free of Nico's grip. "He's a child stealer!"

The father stood up, frowning. He was a distinguished gentleman, probably a merchant, with exquisite posture and diction. "Excuse me, sir, but I think you ought to—"

Nico sighed. He raised a hand and flicked it. A swarm of yellow sparks cascaded from his fingertips. They guttered in the grass like dying fireflies. The mother gasped, her perfectly painted lips forming an oval of surprise.

"I can do worse," Nico told them.

Beside him, Meb stiffened. "Yeah," she muttered. "He can. I seen it. Better run away."

The father hesitated, but when Nico glanced at his wide-eyed children, he hunched his shoulders. The family hurried off and Nico dragged a somber Meb to the island.

He could see the gate just ahead. It sat at the bottom of one of the pools, marked by a stone pillar with weathered engravings. Most were in languages long dead, including his own. According to the scholars of Tjanjin, the gates were incredibly ancient, perhaps tens of thousands of years old. No one knew who made them, not even Gaius. Most of the markers had been lost to the ravages of time. But the mortal culture here was the oldest in the world, predating both the Greeks and Persians, and they had preserved their gate—though its existence was a closely held secret. He could see the glow of it in the water like a fallen star.

"Why won't you *say* anything?" Meb persisted. "Just tell me. It's worse not knowing. I'll go along quiet if you tell me."

Nico glanced at her. Grime streaked her face and her eyes were red, but she wasn't crying or whining. If she had, it would have been easier to despise her. But she was tough. Maybe even tough enough to survive the Kiln. So Nico decided he wouldn't lie to her. He'd give her that much.

"You're wrong there, Meb," he said. "In this case, knowing would be worse."

She bit her lip and yanked with surprising strength, unbalancing him. His other hand held a leather script filled with talismans—the cream of the emperor's collection. Nicodemus had no intention of returning to Tjanjin and during his studies of the talismans, he had noted those that could be of future use. The one to summon liches, for example, and others of a similarly dark nature.

He had to let go of her or drop the bag in the water. So he let go. But it only took an instant to steady himself on the guide rope. He caught her again within two strides. She kicked him in the shin and Nico laughed.

He shouldn't have. His earlier instinct about her pride turned out to be entirely correct. A maniacal light entered Meb's eyes. Quick as a sand snake, she sunk her teeth into the back of his hand. Nico let out a mighty roar of pain. Meb dodged past and raced ahead.

Straight for the gate.

Nazafareen stumbled up to the wall. It looked very high. Much higher than the last time she climbed it. Katsu was already halfway up. She pulled her hand out from underneath the cloak and examined it. It was stained crimson.

"You're hurt," Darius said reproachfully.

She waved the hand, trying to catch her breath. "Not really," she said, and the ground tilted and she found herself staring up at him. "Well, shit."

"Holy Father, how bad?" he demanded. Darius pulled her cloak aside and gave a sharp hiss.

"Don't think it punctured anything important," she protested weakly. "Just a little blood loss."

"More than a little," he growled, his eyes searching her face. "Keep pressure on it."

Nazafareen obeyed, ignoring the dull ache in her ribs.

"Can you hold onto me?"

She nodded and sat up. The world spun for a long moment, then righted itself. Darius helped her to stand and used one end of the rope to tie them together around the waist. Then he tossed the other end to Katsu. The Stygian caught it and dropped down on the other side. Nazafareen laid her head against Darius's back.

She felt him climbing and the tension of the rope as Katsu reeled it in from his side. Things greyed out for a moment. When she came back to herself, she stood on a gravel pathway facing the placid pools of the aquarium. Darius untied the rope, peering at her with a worried expression.

"Katsu says it's not far now. Can you walk?"

They must be near the edge of the Umbra for she saw brightness ahead. This part of the aquarium was nearly all water, with little islands connected by rope bridges. It sat on the highest point and all of Tjanjin spread out below. She could see the tall Marakai ships lying at anchor alongside the stone piers. A patchwork of jaunty red and blue rooftops descended in terraces down the hill. Beyond it all lay the White Sea, undulating in long, slow swells that broke against the harbor mouth.

The whole world seemed to stretch out before her, vast and unknowable. It made Nazafareen afraid. If Nicodemus took Meb into the Dominion, she would be lost forever. They would vanish without a trace. Nazafareen knew this in her bones.

She drew a shallow breath. "I can do better," she said to Darius. "I can run."

Before he replied, she dashed toward the first bridge, clumsy and tired but too stubborn to quit. A fresh breeze struck her face and her head cleared a bit. Katsu was already at the next island.

"Hurry!" he yelled back. "They're at the gate!"

She could feel her power stirring as the glow on the horizon brightened. It gave her strength to cross the bridge. And then she saw them, a hundred paces away. The Vatra and his prisoner. They were wading through waist-high water toward a tall stone pillar. Meb dodged to the side and Nicodemus leaped for her, snagging her hair. She cried out as he wrenched her head back.

Nazafareen reached for her breaking power but it slid away. Not strong enough yet.

"Help me over the line," she cried to Darius.

He understood instantly, scooping her up and sprinting in a mad blur across the next rope bridge. A molten sliver of sun broke the horizon. The moment its warmth touched her face, Nazafareen's bond with Darius came to life. She felt the deep reservoir of his elemental magic churning in a corner of her mind. At the same instant, her own power broke loose of its fetters. She lashed out wildly, without thought, throwing it all at the gate. It left her in a sheet of black lightning that seemed to bleed the color from the world.

In the moment before it struck, some instinct made the Vatra turn. His eyes widened. He shoved Meb away—directly into the crackling lance of negatory magic. Her back arched in a ghastly bow. One arm flung out, the fingers splayed wide. Terrible pain etched her face, but then it softened. The whiplash of power dissipated, releasing its hold on her, and she slipped beneath the waters.

It all happened in the barest instant. Nazafareen stared at the spot where Meb had vanished, unwilling to believe what she'd just done. She felt Darius's shock, like a slap to the face.

I've killed the talisman, she thought, the anger that fed her power turning instantly to horror and grief. I've killed a *child*.

The Vatra turned on her and unleashed a gout of flame. Katsu threw himself to the ground. Nazafareen barely managed to clamp down on the bond before it seared past them, inches away, like the door to a white-hot forge had been thrown wide. Seconds later, the rope bridge caught fire.

Darius dragged her away from the flames to the next island, his face a grim mask. He couldn't touch his own power. She couldn't let him. But she could sever the Vatra's flows. She could finish it. Finish *him*.

"Wait here," she told Darius, and something in her voice made him obey. He stepped aside without a word.

Nazafareen couldn't meet his eyes. She was too afraid of what she might find there.

Perhaps it takes a monster to fight a monster, she thought bleakly, dropping into the pool and wading forward.

Nicodemus backed toward the gate as the Breaker bore down, her amber eyes fixed on him with single-minded intent. He couldn't sense her magic at all. It was a void in the world, tangible only by its devastating effects. Every time he reached for fire, the power fizzled and died.

He hadn't meant to push Meb into the path of it. His reaction was purely instinctual. In fact, he'd been trying to *protect* her.

And now she was gone.

He fumbled in the script and took out the clay scarab to summon the liches, but it splintered to fragments in his hand. And then she was on him, her sword whistling through the air. He dodged right, shocked at her speed. It blurred past his face and bit into his arm. Nicodemus spun away, a thread of heat stinging his flesh.

Her face was expressionless, her eyes empty of any recognizable emotion.

The blade slashed again, two strokes in rapid succession, and he knew he was bleeding freely now, he could see it swirling in the water, though he didn't yet feel the pain. Nicodemus howled and lunged forward, hoping to use his size and strength to overwhelm her. He'd taken half a step when a vise closed around his heart. The pain made his eyes water. Every muscle seized.

"Do you see now?" she asked softly.

The pressure eased for a moment, and he drew a shuddering breath, but then it increased again. Squeezing and releasing. Making him suffer, like a child tearing the legs from a bug.

Her face changed, and a kind of sick joy came into it. Her pupils shrank to pinpricks.

Nico knew that look. He'd seen it before.

The day Gaius threw the wyrm's head at his feet.

Nico felt a hot jet of urine trickle down his leg. The agony was so bad he would've begged her for death if he had breath, not that he expected it to do much good.

And then a dark shadow passed over the sun. Her pupils dilated. She blinked rapidly, the cruel light fading to confusion.

The vise fell away and Nico fell with it.

~

MEB DRIFTED LIKE A RAGDOLL. WATER POURED INSIDE HER nose and mouth. Crept deep into her lungs. But for some reason, she wasn't afraid. She let it fill her. If this was death, it came to her peacefully, as a friend.

Deeper she went, toward the greenish glow. Tall gray reeds swayed in an invisible current. And then Meb saw a doorway, standing alone. It was giving off the light. A woman waited just inside, dark hair fanning out around her. She was corpse-pale and Meb could see the water filled her too. She beckoned with open arms.

Meb's toes dragged through soft mud as she drifted forward. It felt pleasantly cool and squishy. She hadn't thought much about dying before. The Marakai returned their dead to the sea, and this wasn't exactly the sea, but it was water so maybe that was proper enough. She wasn't quite sure how she'd died, but she'd felt something break inside her. Like a whole other set of bones she didn't even know she had. They'd snapped, and that part hurt for an instant, but it passed. And then she was in the water and the water was in her. So yeah, drowning, most likely. Except she hadn't choked or spluttered or ached for a breath of air, which did seem odd.

Done is done, Meb thought. I'm dead. Best get used to it.

She thought she would pass straight through the doorway but the woman blocked her way.

"Mebetimmunedjem of the Selk Marakai," she said, though to be precise, Meb heard the words in her head because nothing came out of the woman's mouth except a small silver fish.

She drew Meb close and gave her a kiss on her forehead. Her lips were cold.

"Who're you?" Meb asked, and a fizz of tiny bubbles drifted upwards.

"Some call me the Drowned Lady."

Meb nodded. "Guess I'm coming with you."

A school of minnows darted from the Lady's mouth, which Meb knew was laughter.

"You ain't dead, Meb," she said. "Not for a long while." Her dark eyes turned up to the surface far overhead. "You have to go back up there. Give 'em a show." Her mouth curved in a sly smile. "Go on."

The Lady gave her a little push.

Meb drifted up and up, lazily. She was glad not to be dead, but Nicodemus was up there. The water felt safe. But the Lady said she had to and Meb wasn't about to cross her. She'd be back someday, even if it was a long time from now, and she had a feeling the Lady would remember if she'd done what she promised.

When her head broke the surface, she saw people. Meb watched, feeling curiously disconnected, as a naked mortal ran up the hill, an older bearded man in a robe at her side. They were followed by a large number of the imperial guard.

Across the pool, she saw the one-handed woman standing over

Nicodemus with an expression Meb didn't much like. It was real mean—even though he probably deserved it.

Meb opened her mouth and the water poured out. It didn't hurt. The water was part of her now, but up here she would breathe air. She paused for a moment, listening to the song of the ocean all around. She's never been able to hear it before. Or she *had*, very faintly, but it was in a language she didn't understand.

Now she did. The song wasn't a single melody, but many woven together. She heard the shimmering notes of tidal pools and the deep resonance of riptides and the breathy whisper of spindrift and a thousand other subtle sounds. Like a great orchestra playing just for her.

Then she spoke to it.

The waters began to rise, playfully at first but growing in power. The ships in harbor sank lower and lower, until their hulls rested on the mud. And still Meb spoke to the sea, calling it to her for a thousand leagues, until a wave bigger than the tallest mountain in the world trembled over Tjanjin, casting all of the isle in its shadow. Meb held it there, pleased at her handiwork.

She thought this was what the Lady wanted her to do.

Or did she want *more*?

The people all stood frozen, gazing up at the wave, except for one. The woman with a missing hand. She stared at Meb for a long moment and Meb felt a twinge of unease, but then she rubbed her stump with bloody fingers and that seemed to calm her. She waded forward, keeping an arm pressed against her side as if she had an injury there.

The woman stopped a few feet away and regarded her.

"Hello, Meb," she said quietly.

"Who are you?" Meb asked.

"My name is Nazafareen." She glanced up at the wave, poised on the very brink of surrender. Fish swam up and down the face of it, but they didn't fall out. "That's impressive. But maybe you should put it back."

Meb frowned. "Why?"

"Because if it falls, it will kill a lot of people."

"I won't let it fall."

The woman nodded. "I have power too, Meb. I don't understand it and I'll confess, it scares me sometimes."

"I'm not scared."

But Meb *was* scared now. Just a bit. All the people were staring at her, and the old Meb, Meb the Mouse, Meb the Shadow, who was still in there, itched to skulk away.

"Do you think you can put it back carefully?" the woman asked.

"Yeah. I think so."

"Do that then," she said firmly.

Meb whispered to the sea again, telling it to behave itself and go where it belonged without a fuss, like Captain Kasaika might have done. The wave trembled, then slid back on its haunches, surging into the harbor with the liquid thunder of a waterfall. She did try to be careful, though many of the mooring ropes snapped and some of the smaller vessels capsized.

"Well done," the woman pronounced in a pleased tone. "Very well done." She glanced around and frowned. "He's gone," she murmured.

A Danai waded toward them now. The one with the withered arm. He had a kind face and bright blue eyes and Meb liked him instantly. He broke into a wide grin, kissing the woman on the mouth and then cupping his gentle hands around Meb's face.

"Are you all right?" he asked her, his voice a little hoarse.

Normally, Meb wouldn't suffer to be grabbed by a stranger. But she knew he meant well.

"I'm okay." Meb glanced at the soldiers, who were on their knees, staring at her in fear and awe. "Can I go back to the *Asperta* now? Captain Kasaika will have my hide for this."

The woman—Nazafareen—gave a fragile smile. "Sure, Meb. We'll go together."

25

LOOK ON MY WORKS, YE MIGHTY, AND DESPAIR!

The Zaravshan River unspooled in a gleaming ribbon as Javid guided the wind ship due north. A week of steady rain had revived the parched crops on either side. Green fields followed her winding course, tended by teams of oxen and laborers in broad straw hats. The weather had changed just that morning. Two hours into the flight, the *Ash Vareca* glided along under ideal conditions—blue skies with a light, fresh breeze from the south. And yet the knot of apprehension in Javid's gut cinched tighter with every league.

On the one hand, he was glad to put Samarqand at his back. Shahak seemed to regard Javid as his savior and demanded his presence at all hours of the day and night. The king had mellowed a bit since the bloody day he took the crown, but he was mercurial and frankly, terrifying. He consumed spell dust at such a fantastic rate, Izad Asabana's stores were nearly depleted. And so Javid's big commission had finally come along. The prince didn't want to let him go, even for a day, but he accepted that Javid was the only pilot skilled enough to be trusted with the run.

That was the rub. Javid knew Asabana would never be paying him so much if it wasn't dangerous. And he still didn't know exactly where they were going. His boss referred him to Leila, who had been cagey, saying merely that the source of the dust lay to the northwest.

"How much further?" he asked her.

She stood next to him, amidships beneath the air sack, her long hair unbound.

"Another few minutes."

"Holy Father, just tell me," he snapped. "I'm not turning back now. But I *am* the pilot of this ship and I'd like to have some idea of our destination. Is it Delphi?"

She glanced at her father. Marzban Khorram-Din sat on a stool among piles of empty silk-lined bags, hands folded in his lap and eyes closed, appearing deep in meditation.

"You flew across the Umbra?" she asked innocently.

Javid sighed. "You know I did."

"So you've had experience with extreme conditions. That's good." She paused. "You'll need it."

It came together in that moment and Javid gave a low groan.

"The Gale," he said. "You want to cross it, don't you?"

"I've done it before," she said quickly. "Many times. We just have to get high enough."

"How high?"

"Very high."

Javid thought of the pile of gold he'd been promised. His father hadn't worked in weeks. He probably never would again. They were barely surviving on the few coins Asabana gave him after withholding the debt payment, and his sister Golpari's wedding was two weeks away.

But the *Kiln*. Holy Father. Javid thought of the scorched stone of the Rock. Of the glimpse through the gate of a shimmering desert when he and Nazafareen traveled through the shadowlands. Like everyone else, he'd grown up on stories of the war. The Gale existed for a good reason and crossing it seemed the height of madness.

"You have to trust me," Leila said, studying him with her clever brown eyes.

"What about the fire daēvas?" he asked uneasily. "I heard they were still alive in there."

Leila smirked. "Who told you that?"

"A friend. She heard it from some Maenads."

"Well, I've been inside the Kiln and I can assure you it's deserted." She peered at the map in her hand and checked it against the path of the river. "It's time. We must start gaining altitude."

Now would be the moment to refuse, a sensible voice informed him. Before it's too late.

But another part of him—the one who'd volunteered to cross the Umbra, the one who used to sneak into the palace grounds to steal figs, the one who loved his family and felt responsible for them—stayed silent.

Leila produced a pouch of spell dust and tossed a handful into the air. It hung suspended in a glittering cloud for a moment as she whispered some words. Then the ship gave a mighty lurch and began to climb. Javid grabbed a cable.

"You don't have much finesse, do you?" he muttered.

Up and up the *Ash Vareca* soared, until the river dwindled to a fine artery. The air grew thin and cold. Javid had flown up to three leagues before, but they were easily twice that height now. Thin wisps of cloud shrouded the ship and the fields gave way to tawny sand as they veered away from the river.

Javid stood at the port rail, gaze fixed on the western horizon. The sky took on a strange greenish cast. After a few minutes, a line of black clouds appeared, hanging like a curtain across the desert. Lightning flickered in their depths. Cone-shaped funnels trailed from the underbelly, reaching in long, ragged fingers toward the ground. They swayed like cobras and where the fingers touched the earth, the force of the wind tore loose spinning clouds of sand that made the most horrifying sound he'd ever heard.

The funnels raced toward them. Javid carried out a swift calculation based on their current trajectory. Then he made the sign of the flame, touching forehead, lips and heart.

"We're not high enough," he called to Leila.

"Father," she said calmly. "Perhaps you could increase the altitude while I maintain the bubble of vapor? I think it will need to be fortified."

Of course, she would have to conjure air to breathe. They were far too high. Javid realized she was handling at least five complex weavings of power alone and felt both impressed and unnerved.

Marzban Khorram-Din opened his eyes. He reached into his own pouch and pulled out a pinch of spell dust.

"Hold on to something," he said in that austere, croaking voice.

Javid had just wound a rope around his hand when the *Ash Vareca* hurtled upwards like a boulder shot from a trebuchet. The anvil-formed thunderhead loomed just ahead...and then they soared over the top of the Gale, the flat bottom of the cloud beneath and blinding sun breaking through overhead. He felt a moment of raw, tingling exhilaration before they were plummeting down the other side, buffeted by strong gusts that tore at the air sack.

Javid let out a whoop that earned a disapproving scowl from Marzban Khorram-Din and an indulgent smile from Leila.

"I'll handle it from here," he said smoothly, taking a pinch of his own dust. Javid spoke a few words of command from his admittedly far more limited repertoire, but nothing happened. He frowned and tried again. Still nothing.

"Spell dust doesn't work in the Kiln," Leila said. "Magic seems to be dampened by the wards on the Gale."

Javid had his second unpleasant revelation. "So that's why you brought me along."

"See?" She turned to Marzban Khorram-Din, who had resumed his meditative posture on the stool. "I told you he wasn't stupid."

Fickle crosswinds still battered the *Ash Vareca*, the ropes creaking as she swayed back and forth. Javid hurried to light the burners and arrest the ship's too-fast descent. The sacks began to swell with hot air and he watched the scrap of red silk tied to one of the cables. Accurately judging wind direction was one of a pilot's most important skills since the ships had no independent means of propulsion—except for dust. The moment it caught a westerly current, he stabilized their ascent and they left the churning monster behind.

"I thought I might manage it without his help this time." Leila looked annoyed at herself. "Father says I must if I'm to take over once he's gone."

"You almost did. It's still more than ten wind pilots together could have done."

Leila smiled. "We still have to do it again to get home."

He grinned back. "I don't mind. What a tale! My sister Bibi will wet herself." His smile faded. "I can't tell anyone, can I?"

"Only if you want to end up like Asabana's other pilots," she replied dryly.

Javid studied the landscape below. Wind-swept dunes stretched in all directions like a sea of golden sand. As they descended, he could feel the intense heat radiating from the desert. Combined with the unrelenting sun, it felt like a blacksmith's forge. Sweat popped out from every pore. He imitated Leila and donned a white linen head wrap doused with water.

"Why did you come here in the first place?" he asked. "You couldn't have known about spell dust then."

She glanced at the alchemist, who opened his eyes and gave a brief nod. "My father is a great admirer of Nabu-bal-idinna, an explorer of the golden age. Just as Nabu-bal-idinna sought to map the shadowlands, we wanted to map the known world. Including the Kiln. He talked Izad Asabana into funding an expedition. I think Asabana liked the boldness of the proposition. It appealed to his vanity. He wasn't a lord then, but I suspect he secretly wanted to be. All he risked was a wind ship, which was no great price. He'd already made a fortune smuggling."

"And you found no sign of life?"

"None. We didn't get far in our explorations though." She leaned over the rail. "Once we discovered the spell dust and how to use it.... Well, there was no point in continuing, was there?" Leila sounded a bit wistful. She stared out at the horizon, shimmering with liquid waves of heat, her eyes distant.

"How far does the desert extend?" Javid asked.

"I don't know. Hundreds of leagues."

"Do you think it's all like this?"

She turned to him. "No," she said softly. "I imagine most of it's worse. The farther west you go, the stronger the sun will be."

Javid surveyed the blasted landscape. Worse? Surely nothing could survive out here.

Leila leaned over the rail, and when she spoke, her voice was cool and collected as always. She pointed. "Do you see it?"

It took him a moment. Javid shaded his eyes against the glare. Then he spotted something, like a glint of sun striking a mirror. As the ship neared it, his breath caught. The ruins of a glass city lay ahead. Some of the buildings appeared intact, if half-finished, with lofty towers gathering all the hues of the rainbow and throwing them back like prisms. But other parts showed the ravages of a terrible fire, the glass blackened and melted.

At Leila's direction, he landed the ship in a huge open plaza flanked by statues half-buried in the sand. They were made of stone and depicted men and women whose smiling faces struck him as tragic and macabre amid the silent ruins.

"What is this place?" he asked Leila.

But it was Marzban Khorram-Din who answered.

"This was Pompeii," he said. "The capital of the Vatras."

Javid felt no fear. He could see it had been deserted for long centuries, though it must have been a marvel before its destruction. They made their way into the city, passing dry fountains full of dust and empty gaps that looked like parks judging by the benches and graceful arches. If ever there had been gardens or trees, no sign remained. An eerie calm hung over the place, with not even a breath of wind to stir the sands.

But still he saw no evidence of spell dust. Each of them carried ten of the silk-lined sacks. They passed down a street with smaller dwellings that might have been homes or shops. Leila and Marzban Khorram-Din halted before one of them.

"You can go in if you like," Leila said softly. "It's better alone, the first time."

He gave her a questioning look, but she merely waited.

So Javid ducked through the low doorway. He stood in what must have been the kitchen. A table had been set with plates and goblets, now covered in a fine white ash that looked iridescent in the dim sunlight.

Around the table sat a family of four. Two adults and two children. The fire that claimed their lives was so fierce and sudden, it had charred them instantly in the exact poses they'd held in life. Javid hesitated for a long moment, grim doubts filling his heart. Then he reached out and touched the nearest corpse. His fingers brushed the shoulder, light as a summer's breeze, but even that was too much. The unnatural stillness preserving the body was a fragile thing. The figure collapsed into a pile of glittering dust.

Javid stumbled out of the house, breath coming in nauseated gasps.

"Holy Father. I can't...."

"You must," Leila said firmly. There was pity in her eyes, but hardness too. "They are dead and can't be brought back. But if we do not return with these sacks...."

Javid squatted on his haunches, head in hands. "Holy Father," he muttered again.

"War is coming," she went on relentlessly. "King Shahak must save us from the Pythia. He is a flawed man, but he is all we have. This is just a commission, Javid, like any other."

He shot her an appalled look. "How can you—"

"*Like any other*," she repeated. "Except that you are being paid an obscene amount of money to do it." Leila paused. "Think of your family."

She didn't elaborate. Javid understood all too well. As repugnant as it was, if he failed to return, they would be good as dead. If King Shahak didn't kill them, Asabana would.

He laughed, a ghastly sound. Holy Father, the king was snorting the bones of dead daēvas. Dead Vatras! And Javid had made himself Shahak's pet. His father was right. He never should have started working for Asabana. But it was too late now.

He stood and took a long drink of water from the skin Leila offered him. It revived him somewhat.

"This is easily the worst thing I've ever done," he said in disgust.

"You'll get over it," Leila said.

He looked at her. "I really hope I don't."

Javid closed his eyes, praying for forgiveness from the souls whose grave he was about to rob. Then he shook the bag open and went back inside.

26

A TOAST TO THE DEPARTED

Culach sat in Gerda's favorite hard chair, thinking about his great-great-grandmother. Mina had told him the news and, at his insistence, accompanied him to Gerda's chamber. He still wouldn't believe she was dead until he touched her fine, silken hair and felt the coldness of her hand. Then he'd broken down and wept, to everyone's surprise—Culach's most of all.

Gerda could be selfish and cruel, but she was one of the few people who had showed him kindness as a child. Well, her own brand of kindness at least. She wasn't the type to coo or cuddle, but she would tell him stories about his mother, which Eirik never did. If not for Gerda, Ygraine would be a faceless ghost.

Personally, Culach believed Victor's claim that Gerda had murdered Halldóra. She was entirely capable of it, and he knew how much she would have loathed the thought of an alliance between Valkirin and Danai. But Victor was the only witness and he didn't deny killing Gerda. Any chance of peace between the clans was destroyed. The holdfasts would unite against Val Moraine now. There would be no more parleys—not after the last one ended in a bloodbath.

So Culach sat in Gerda's chair, his eyes dry if a bit puffy, listening to the swish of Mina's skirts as she paced up and down. He might have wept for Gerda, but Mina was preoccupied with one thing: her son, Galen.

"That mortal took him, I know it," Mina burst out.

"He might have gone willingly," Culach said. "I bloody would have, if I were him."

"She's a maniac. She murdered the other girl. I saw the body. It was no fever! Who knows what she wanted with my son?" She paused, her voice full of foreboding. "You don't think—"

"No, I don't." He held out a hand and she drifted over, leaning against him. "Be glad Galen got out. I'm hard-pressed to think of a worse place to be right now than the Maiden Keep."

The surviving Dessarians, who numbered less than a dozen after Katrin carved a swathe through them on her way out, were taking turns guarding the ice tunnel. The moment the holdfasts attacked, they would use earth power to collapse it again. But they hadn't done it yet—Mithre wouldn't allow it. He held out some naïve hope they could still cut a deal, though Culach knew better.

"Rafel is missing too," Mina said. "I don't understand it. I've searched the keep from top to bottom. *How* did they escape?"

Culach sighed. "I've no idea. If you find out, let me know so we can go too."

"How can you be so cavalier?" she demanded.

"I'm not," he muttered. "Have you spoken with Victor?"

"No. Mithre told me what happened."

Culach took the end of her braid, stroking it gently. "I passed him in one of the corridors earlier. He didn't speak, but I know it was him." Culach hesitated. "He didn't smell right, Mina."

"What do you mean?"

He wouldn't say it to anyone but her. It sounded crazy.

"He smelled like my father, at the end. Bitter and old."

She let out a breath. "That's not good."

"No," Culach agreed. "Not good. But he's all I've got. Halldóra might have seen her way to letting me go, but Runar and Stefán?" He laughed. "I'm sure they'll devise a most unpleasant end for me."

She touched his face. "But they can't get in, can they?"

"Hopefully not."

She kissed his lips. "They won't. But I don't want to stay in this room. You can't see it, but there's blood.... It's awful, Culach."

"I have to take Gerda and Halldóra down to the crypts," he said. "We can't leave them here."

"I'll help you." Mina moved away from him, her footsteps receding to the far corner of the room. "I won't pretend I liked Gerda," she said quietly. "But I understand. She was your last living relative." He heard her poking around. "Would you like a keepsake? Something to remember her by?"

"That would be nice. She had a spinelstone she used to show me as a child. It turns colors in the starlight. Not that I'll ever see the stars again, but—"

"What's this?" Mina muttered.

"What's what?"

"I think...it has power in it, Culach. A talisman of some kind. It rolled under the cabinet."

She came over and pressed an orb into his hands. It felt smooth, like glass. Culach turned it over and ran his fingers across faint ridges that might have been carved runes.

"A globe?" he asked.

"Yes, it has that shape. But I see clouds inside...They're moving!"

Culach felt a sharp pang at the loss of his elemental power. He tried not to dwell on it. But if Mina hadn't told him, he would never have suspected it was a talisman.

"Keep it if you want," he said roughly, thrusting it back at her. "I prefer the spinelstone."

"Of course," she said. "But I'll study it. Perhaps it can be of some use."

Culach rose, suddenly weary to the bone. "Let's get this done with. I'll take Gerda first."

He shuffled over to the place where Gerda lay and lifted her in his arms. She felt as light as a child.

"Are her eyes open?" he asked Mina.

"No."

"Open them then. Valkirins face death with courage."

Mina did as he asked. Culach was turning to the door when he heard heavy footsteps in the corridor. He knew the tread—and the scent. Iron and leather and old sweat. Mina placed a tense hand on his arm.

"What are you doing?" Victor asked.

"Laying my great-great-grandmother to rest," Culach snapped. "You'll not be feeding Gerda Kafsnjór to the abbadax—"

"I had no intention of it," Victor replied evenly. "I came to see to their bodies."

Culach bit back a cutting response. What was the point? As much as he despised Victor, it was a long way to the crypts and he didn't relish making the trip twice. As long as he didn't lay hands on Gerda. It might have been self-defense, but he wouldn't let her killer touch her again.

"You can take Halldóra," he said. "Treat her gently. She was among the best of us."

Victor paused. Culach could hear him pacing the room.

"Did you find anything with Gerda's body?" he asked.

"Such as?"

"A talisman. It's shaped like a glass orb."

Culach scratched his head. "Sorry."

"She used it to... Oh Gods, never mind. It must have been a trick."

"To what?" Mina asked.

"She claimed it summoned one of the legendary fire daēvas." He gave a mirthless laugh. "Halldóra saw him too. It's why Gerda.... Forget it. I'll search later."

The three of them repaired in a grim procession down to the lowest levels of the keep, and from there to the catacombs. Gerda probably had a prime spot picked out for herself, but Culach didn't know where it was. The crypts were simple rock shelves, so he directed Mina to find an empty space and arranged Gerda on it with her arms at her sides. Her limbs had just begun to grow stiff. Soon, the bitter cold would petrify her completely and preserve her from decay.

Victor laid Halldóra out in similar fashion on the next shelf.

"Do you speak some words over the bodies?" he asked in a strangely deferential and un-Victor-like tone.

"No," Culach said. "Normally, we would have a feast to celebrate their lives. But under the circumstances, I think I'll just get quietly drunk."

"I'll join you," Mina said, taking his hand.

They started down the tunnel. Culach expected Victor to follow, but he stayed where he was.

"I'll come up in a while," he said vaguely.

"Why?" Culach snapped. "What do you want with them?"

"I won't interfere with the bodies, I swear it on my honor. I just want to think." Victor paused. "Alone."

Culach disliked the close feel of the tunnels and decided not to stay and argue the point. Victor had kept his word so far.

"Suit yourself," he said. "I suppose it's as good a place as any to meditate on your mistakes."

Victor didn't bother responding.

So Culach and Mina left him alone there, among the generations of Valkirin dead with their frost-rimmed eyes and white skin, and returned to Gerda's chamber, where Mina found the spinelstone and also three bottles of terrible wine.

They toasted Gerda and her late husband Albert and, by the end of that long night, even Eirik Kafsnjór, who no one liked but was rich as sin and did know how to throw a party.

❧ 27 ❧

MAGNUS THE RATHER
UNPLEASANT

Victor stayed with Halldóra until the blood matting her hair froze to shards of crimson ice. He no longer felt the cold, or much of anything except a sickening sense of betrayal.

How badly he'd underestimated Gerda Kafsnjór. He'd thought of her as a nuisance, a sad old relic, but in a single stroke she'd managed to destroy any chance to avert all-out war. Victor found it small comfort Gerda was dead, and smaller comfort still that Culach seemed to believe his story. In truth, he found it implausible himself. Fire-working daēvas? No, the globe "talisman" must have been a hoax—Gerda's final ploy to turn Halldóra against him.

Runar and Stefán are the ones I should be worrying about, he thought bleakly. And that maniac, Katrin.

Though he didn't like to admit it to himself, Victor had been relieved when she turned and ran. The look on her face when she saw him standing over Gerda's body still haunted him.

So many enemies, all waiting for a single moment of weakness to strike. But he wouldn't give it to them. He'd endured worse. And Val Moraine still had plenty of food, although the thought of eating made him queasy.

What if the Valkirins find my wife? She was supposed to return. She won't be able to get inside, and the things they'll do to her....

Victor stamped the thought down, but it echoed through his mind, a poisonous whispering. He tried to picture Delilah's face and found he couldn't. He knew she had Darius's blue eyes, but the rest was a blur. He rubbed a hand across his forehead.

Just tired, he thought. I ought to sleep for a bit.

But that was another thing he'd been unable to do lately.

Unready to face the other Danai, Victor wandered aimlessly through the catacombs. Dusty jewels shone in the faint light of his lumen crystal, rings and brooches and chains of woven gold. The Valkirins had no gods that he knew of, but they were vain to the end. There must be a king's ransom down here. He gave a mirthless laugh.

Most of them kept their broadswords too, great iron blades a mortal could barely lift. The sight of them stirred a distant memory.

Tall, pale warriors with silver eyes, tearing up out of the earth as the necromancers called lances of black lightning from the sky. The screams of horses and men. The gates of Karnopolis buckling before the boiling mass of Druj....

Victor gripped the diamond beneath his shirt, its chill facets reassuring against his palm. His imagination was conjuring up ghosts. It was time to quit this place and find Mithre, see what could be salvaged. He strode through the tunnel, turning left, then right, then left again. The route should have brought him back to the staircase leading up, but Victor found he didn't recognize his surroundings. If anything, he seemed to be in an even older part of the catacombs. The frost on the corpses lay thick as cobwebs and their garb had an antique look, adorned with odd buckles and embroidery he'd never seen before.

Just what I need, he thought sourly. To get lost in the crypts.

He went back and tried a different turning. It led to a dead end. Muttering in irritation, Victor retraced his steps again, searching for Culach and Mina's footprints in the fine layer of dust. He began to have the unpleasant sensation that the dead were watching him. Or worse, that they weren't really dead after all.

It was the open eyes. The Valkirins stared at the ceiling, but each time he passed one, the hair on the back of his neck tingled as if its gaze had subtly shifted. Victor cursed himself for a fool. They were frozen lumps of flesh, that's all. Some of them had been here for a thousand years, perhaps more. They weren't going anywhere.

But then he began to notice gaps on the slabs. Places that should have held a body but didn't.

Victor refused to walk faster, though he wanted to.

I am the lord of Val Moraine now, he thought savagely, the diamond biting into his palm. I fear no part of this keep.

He rounded another corner and stopped. The dust ahead looked undisturbed. Victor was about to turn away when he noticed something thirty paces farther on. A jagged opening in the tunnel. He frowned. If it was a way in, he needed to close it immediately.

His boots rang softly against the stone as he went to investigate. Part of the wall had been knocked down from this side, revealing a chamber beyond filled with rubble. Runes covered the walls in some language he couldn't read but that might have been Old Valkirin. The room contained only scuffmarks in the dust, but when Victor checked the Nexus, he sensed empty space beyond the far wall. A second secret chamber, undiscovered by those who had come before him?

He drew deeply on earth, grimacing at the strain in his bones, and sought out the minute weaknesses in the rock. Rivulets of dust trickled down as the stone cracked. One good kick and it fell away in chunks. He held up his lumen crystal and peered into the darkness.

It was a tiny crypt, built for a single occupant. He lay on a narrow shelf, Valkirin by his features but wearing a dark coat and brown wool trousers. One eye was a startling robin's egg blue, the other a murky green. His hands lay across his breast, clasping something. Victor moved into the cramped chamber, breathing shallowly. The air had a taint to it, stale and damp.

The object clutched in the Valkirin's frozen fingers appeared to be a horn, curved like a fang and about the length of his forearm, but made of some metal Victor had never seen before. Smooth and jet black, it absorbed the light like a well of impenetrable shadow. An object of power, he sensed that right away.

Victor caught himself reaching for it and pulled his hand back at the last moment. What had possessed him? He knew enough about talismans to have a healthy respect for ones of unknown origin. The diamond was different. He knew exactly how to use it and what effect it would have. But there was likely a good reason this one had been walled away. From the looks of the man who held it, the horn had been here a long time indeed.

Victor shook his head to clear it. He surveyed the chamber and noted no other entrances. With a last glance at the man on the shelf, he passed through the outer chamber and back to the main tunnel. A few minutes later, he found the staircase leading to the upper reaches of the holdfast.

The diamond pulsed in his fist. He'd thought to find Mithre, but now he hesitated. Could the man really be trusted? Victor was no longer sure. From the beginning, Mithre had questioned every decision. Gorgon-e Gaz made me stronger, he thought, but it left Mithre weak. *I will have to watch him carefully.*

In fact, Victor was certain of just one thing.

He would never give up Val Moraine now.

Never.

✻ 28 ✻

DAUGHTER OF STORMS

M eb sat in her usual spot on the deck of the *Asperta*. She missed her knife. It was a fine knife and she'd bought it with the black pearl, which represented good fortune. Captain Kasaika had given her another knife, but it wasn't the same. She still wanted her old knife back. If she ever saw Nicodemus again, she'd make him give it to her.

The crew of the *Asperta* was preparing to depart, unfurling the square sails and casting off mooring ropes. Across the harbor, every Marakai ship followed suit. They would provide an honor guard all the way back to the Isles, where Meb would be hauled in front of the Five.

She scowled. They'd argued over her. The mortals wanted to take her somewhere on the Cimmerian Sea, but Captain Kasaika and Captain Mafuone wouldn't hear of it. The woman named Nazafareen had gotten quite angry, which made Meb smile a little remembering. She'd never heard anyone talk that way to the captains. Finally, Nazafareen had squatted down in front of Meb and asked what *she* wanted to do.

Mostly, Meb just wanted them to stop fighting over her. She hated it. She hated the way they looked at her, like they were all a little scared, except for Nazafareen, who didn't seem scared, just pitying.

Meb didn't want to go to the Five, but she wanted less to go with mortals, so she chose Captain Kasaika, who nodded approvingly. It was all a whirlwind from there. Nazafareen had hugged her and said goodbye, and now they were leaving.

Meb told Captain Kasaika she just wanted to get her tattoo and be crew like everyone else.

"We'll see," the captain said, which Meb knew meant no.

What the Five would do with her, she had no idea.

She poked the empty buckets with a toe. Captain Kasaika said Meb didn't have to clean fish anymore if she didn't want to, but it was all so strange and overwhelming that for once, Meb actually looked forward to getting some fish to gut, even if her new knife wasn't half as good as the old one.

The emperor's youngest daughter was traveling with them too, a girl about Meb's age. Captain Kasaika said Princess Pingyang was to be Meb's companion, but the girl had barely glanced at Meb before retiring to her cabin. She was either snooty or scared or both. This came as a relief since Meb hadn't a clue what to say to a princess. With any luck, she could be avoided during the journey—another reason Meb intended to stick to her old job. No princess worth her salt would be caught dead gutting fish, or talking to someone covered in blood and guts. Plus the princess already had her own attendant, named Feng Mian. They'd arrived with a spectacular amount of baggage, including colorful birds in cages that Meb was already scheming to set free. If there's one thing she hated, it was seeing a bird in a cage.

But now everyone had finally settled in and she was eager to leave. At least the sea no longer frightened her—not the way it used to. It flowed in her blood now. She thought briefly of the Drowned Lady.

Go back up there and give 'em a show.

Well, I guess I did that, she thought.

Meb squinted down the pier as six Marakai approached, bearing a velvet cushion. She groaned inwardly. Riding on the cushion was a small gray cat with stripes and slitted green eyes. No one told Meb they had to carry Anuketmatma.

Again.

The sailors boarded, but they didn't take the cat below, as was customary. They set the cushion on the deck and stepped back, studiously ignoring Meb. The Mother of Storms gave a languid stretch and yawn, baring her sharp incisors for all to admire. Then she slunk across the deck, making straight for Meb. She halted a few paces away and sat with her tail curled around her paws. They stared at each other for a long moment.

"You just try me, cat," Meb muttered.

She opened herself to the sea, just a teensy bit, to give herself the courage not to blink, which was fatal with cats.

Finally, Anuketmatma gave another ostentatious yawn. Then she padded over and rubbed against Meb's leg. Meb scratched her behind the ears.

"All right then," she said.

A breeze came, bellying the sails, and the *Asperta* raced for the harbor mouth, a dozen Marakai escort ships fanning out in her wake and the Mother of Storms settling peacefully in Meb's lap.

❦ 29 ❦

WHAT ROUGH BEAST?

The Pagoda of Waving Willows offered a perfect vantage point to observe the grand procession leaving the harbor. Nazafareen watched the Marakai go with warring emotions. Happiness for Meb, that she was free and alive. Lingering awe of what the girl had done. Anger—naturally—at the Vatra. And something else that felt unpleasantly like guilt.

"Kallisto won't like it," she said. "But Meb *is* Marakai. I suppose she belongs with them."

Megaera gave one of her fatalistic shrugs. "I don't think even you could have stopped them, Nazafareen."

"If Meb had wanted to come with us, I would've tried anyway."

"You did your best, my dear," Herodotus added, absently patting Nazafareen's hand. "Kallisto will understand."

She smiled at him. "I hope so."

They watched as the ships turned toward the darklands. From so high up, Nazafareen could clearly see the line of the Umbra's shadow. To the east, the sky and sea grew darker and darker, as though a storm was coming. To the west, bright sunlight burnished the cobalt waves.

"She'll be fine," Darius said. "Even without the fleets protecting her, Meb is quite capable of taking care of herself now. And there's no gate in the Isles. Wherever the Vatra went, it wasn't there."

"Well, that's the question, isn't it?" Megaera said. "He won't just give up. There's two more talismans. He'll go after one of them. But which?"

Nazafareen rubbed her stump in thought. "I also wonder if he's truly alone. We don't even know how he escaped the Kiln in the first place. How can we be sure there aren't more of them running loose?"

"We can't," Darius agreed. "But I think it's safe to say most of the Vatras are still imprisoned. First, because they would have overrun us by now. And second, because Nicodemus needs the talismans—one or all—to bring down the Gale. If there was another way through, it wouldn't matter."

Herodotus nodded in approval. "Sound logic."

"The other thing in our favor is *you*, Nazafareen." His blue eyes studied her with great fondness, although she sensed worry as well. Only Darius knew what she'd done to Nicodemus. Or if he didn't *know*, he suspected. He hadn't said anything though, and she hoped he never would. It wasn't her finest moment.

"Your negatory magic broke Meb's wards. I assume the same is the case for the others."

"True, but I may not be the only Breaker." She sighed. "So many ifs and maybes." Nazafareen took out the globe. Katsu eyed it hopefully. "May we use this one more time before you return it to the emperor? It might help us decide what to do."

He nodded his assent. "Of course."

Megaera shot her a look. "We're supposed to meet Kallisto and the others at the Temple of the Moria Tree."

"Only if they already found the talismans," Nazafareen replied. "What if they haven't? I'm not going all the way there for nothing. And if Nicodemus is hunting one of the others, we have to warn them."

"I suppose that makes sense," Megaera conceded.

Nazafareen gave the globe to Darius. "Look for Nicodemus first."

They all crowded around. He fed power into the runes, but instead of glowing a steady blue, they flickered. His brow furrowed in concentration. The scene inside the globe—of thin, wispy clouds drifting across a washed-out sky—seemed to take forever to change. And instead of showing them Nicodemus, it grew darker and darker, finally settling on impenetrable blackness. The runes flashed fitfully. Darius released the flows with an oath.

"He must still be in the Dominion. And talismans don't work there."

"Damn. Look for Kallisto and Rhea then," Nazafareen suggested.

The view sped over the sea and entered a realm of jagged peaks that could only be the Valkirin range. A formation of winged shapes appeared, grey phantoms amid the howling blizzard.

"Heavens, they're traveling by abbadax," Herodotus exclaimed.

It was impossible to make out their features, for the women had their faces down and hoods cinched tight, but two of the riders had passengers clinging to their backs. They swept past, fifty at least, and vanished into a dark pass.

"Where are they off to?" Darius wondered uneasily.

"Well, they must have made it to Val Altair," Nazafareen said. "Try Charis and Cyrene."

The scene raced with dizzying speed through the mountains and into the Great Forest. A mighty host marched among the towering trees. They carried yew bows and quivers of arrows that glinted in the shafts of moonlight filtering through the thick canopy. The globe swooped down to reveal the two Maenads, who were using their staffs as walking sticks. Although the scene was silent, they appeared to be singing, to the amusement of the Danai trotting to either side.

Megaera gave a fond snort. "I suppose they're off to finish the Pythia." She glanced at Nazafareen with an eager light in her eye. "Perhaps we should—"

"I would see one other," Nazafareen said quietly.

The Valkirin range had made her think of him, but in truth she'd been stewing about it for a while.

Darius raised an eyebrow.

"Culach."

He frowned. "Why?"

"Please. Just find him."

Darius sighed and the globe sped north again, passing through a wall of ice into a darkened stone chamber. Her breath caught as it settled on a man with short white-blonde hair. She'd expected to find him in a prison cell, but the chamber held furnishings fit for a king—if a bit austere for her taste, which preferred wood to silver and gold. He sat on a large bed, chin propped on his fist, appearing lost in thought. His green eyes were half-closed and roamed around the room in random patterns. A wicked scar bisected his jaw, though his face was otherwise almost angelically beautiful.

Yes, she thought. This is Culach Kafsnjór.

Nazafareen studied him. He looked troubled, but there was no sign of the greedy flame-eyed creature she'd seen before. She dimly remembered Culach carrying her in his arms when she couldn't walk anymore. She remembered his laugh, wry and self-aware. He was bent on invasion, but he hadn't seemed truly evil. Just cocky.

Then they had reached the gate.

"I'm glad Victor doesn't have him in chains," she said softly.

"Do you think he's the Valkirin talisman?" Herodotus asked.

She shook her head. "No. That's not it." And here the seed of compassion that planted itself when she watched the Aurora took root. "I want to speak with him."

"Why?" Darius burst out, letting the image in the globe fade away. "He tried to kill you."

Nazafareen returned his heated gaze. "Because when we were in the Dominion, Kallisto told me another Maenad had the gift of foretelling." She struggled to remember the exact words. "She said there would be war and strife among mortals and daēvas both, and we will be at our weakest when the beast comes to the door."

Darius remained silent, but she could sense his tangled emotions through the bond.

"Don't you see? I'm the reason for it. I want to tell Culach what I know. That I...I didn't mean to hurt him."

"You want his forgiveness?" Darius demanded. "He should be begging for yours!"

"There can be no more bad blood between the clans," she replied firmly. "All this nonsense must end. And if we go to Val Moraine, we can try to find Kallisto and Rhea. They're somewhere in the Valkirin range. Perhaps they already know who the talisman is."

As Nazafareen spoke the words, she knew they felt right. But Darius clearly thought she was mad.

"Megaera," he said, turning to the stocky Maenad. "She never listens to me. But *you* can dissuade her from this feckless course."

Megaera laughed. "She doesn't listen to me either. And I wouldn't try because she's making sense for once."

"Herodotus?" Darius said, an edge of desperation in his voice.

The scholar gave a weak smile. "I'm afraid I am not impartial in the matter. Whatever choice takes me closer to Kallisto is the one I favor."

Nazafareen kept a satisfied smile from her face with great effort. Darius would dig his heels in deeper if she gloated.

"I want nothing more than to see the Oracle of Delphi set down hard," she said. "Going to your people would be the easy choice. But I have a gut feeling it's the wrong one, Darius. A blind desire for revenge won't serve the larger cause. The Danai are united, but the Valkirin holdfasts are isolated and vulnerable. Look at the way he tried to take Meb. It wasn't by force, but cunning and subterfuge."

Darius looked away, unhappy.

"The talismans must join forces, and to do that, I have to get the Valkirins to trust me. Please." She paused and let her feelings flow through the bond. "I need to."

Nazafareen wouldn't say it, not in front of the others, but she was more than a little afraid of returning to Nocturne. Besides Darius, her breaking magic was all she had. Her entire identity.

Once she'd feared the huo mofa and the way it changed her. Now she feared the dark. But she had to face Culach. There was no way around it.

"We only go if my father still holds the keep," Darius said after a brittle silence.

It took an instant to confirm this. Victor sat with Mithre, poring over maps spread across a long metal table. Grey winged the dark hair at his temples and lines of care creased his mouth. One hand rested inside his coat, clutching something.

Darius released the flows of power and handed the globe to Katsu.

"Val Moraine." He turned to Herodotus. "For the record, I have a bad feeling about this. Write that down."

Herodotus dutifully obliged. "I've always wanted to visit the Valkirin range," he said. "And to see an actual holdfast! I might be the first mortal to set foot in one."

"Kallisto and Rhea already beat you," Megaera pointed out.

"Oh, yes, I suppose they have. The first scholar, then. That counts for something, doesn't it?"

The Marakai fleet had vanished over the horizon by this point. A few fishing boats and ferries dotted the harbor, but it looked strangely desolate without the great ships.

"I must leave you," Katsu said, rising to his feet. "May Babana bless your journey."

Nazafareen glanced at the red roof of the palace. Like every other soul on Tjanjin, the emperor had witnessed the rising of the great wave. When it became clear one of his closest advisors was in fact a fire daēva, he had immediately pledged his full allegiance to the Marakai in the struggle that was sure to come and gifted the fleet with fifty chests of pearls and jade as a token of goodwill. Tjanjin had been the only land spared the first time around, but the emperor had no illusions this good fortune would repeat itself if the talismans were not gathered to repel the Vatras.

"What will you do with the bounty?" Nazafareen asked.

Katsu smiled, teeth white against his scraggly beard. "I might head to Samarqand. There's someone I'd like to look up there."

"I wish you well." Nazafareen said with a grin. "I thought you were a lying rogue at first, but you turned out to be a hero."

He laid a hand over his heart in mock distress. "Not that, I think. Let's say a rogue, but an honest one."

Megaera poked him with her staff. "Take care, thief catcher."

The others made their farewells and Katsu ambled off toward the palace.

"There's a gate not far from Val Moraine," Herodotus said. "Now that we can read the signposts, it should be no great feat to find it."

The emperor had indulged his request to visit the palace library, and Herodotus spent the last day poring through its collections, hardly pausing to eat. Megaera had finally been forced to drag him away, muttering under his breath about *one more hour* and *chance of a lifetime*. But he'd discovered some useful things, including charts showing the relative location of gates in both this world and the Dominion.

"The Valkirin range." Megaera sighed. "We couldn't be going someplace warm, could we?"

Nazafareen picked up her rucksack. They each carried one,

packed with food and other sundries. "The gear we used to cross the White Sea should be adequate for the mountains," she said. "Don't you want to see snow?"

"Not particularly. But I'll save my complaining for later." She grinned. "Do you remember Diogenes of Sinope? That mad old philosopher who made misery an art form? I once saw him begging for alms from a statue. He said it was to practice being refused." She chuckled. "Herodotus, you knew him, didn't you?"

"Oh yes." The scholar sounded amused. "A great enemy of Plato. We were in a tavern once and they began arguing over the cups, and whether in fact they really existed. Nearly came to blows." He stood and shouldered his own rucksack. "Plato claimed a cup is merely an idea, and this concept of cupness precedes the existence of all particular cups. Diogenes rejoined that he could see the cups on the table, but not this *cupness*. Plato grew quite smug and explained that while Diogenes had eyes to see the cup, he lacked the intellect to comprehend *cupness*."

Herodotus shook his head. "Of course, we'd all had a few at this point. I had no idea what he was talking about. Plato's bad enough when you're sober. But Diogenes, that old provocateur, held up his own mug and innocently asked, 'Is it empty?' Plato nodded. 'So where is the emptiness which precedes this empty cup?' asked Diogenes." He grinned. "Well, Plato was trying to come up with a response when Diogenes reached over and, tapping Plato's forehead with his finger, said 'I think you will find here is the emptiness.'"

Nazafareen and Darius followed Megaera's laughter across a rope bridge from the Pagoda of Waving Willows to the next island. The pool beyond had a tall stone pillar at its center, ancient and weathered. They waded into the tepid water. When it reached her waist, Nazafareen paused. Captain Mafuone had healed her wound and she felt good as new. Better even. She squinted into the sun. It was low and weak, yet the power throbbed inside her, reaching for the light.

What would it be like in the Kiln?

"Don't," Darius said, reading her thoughts.

"How do you *do* that?" she replied with a frown. "And I wasn't."

Nazafareen tweaked his chin and dove toward the green glow of the gate.

❧ 30 ❧

THE LAST LAUGH

Acrid vapors rising from cracks in the ancient stone floor mingled with the heavy scent of burning laurel leaves, and Galen, who had been kneeling for hours, felt his eyelids grow heavy. He drew a deep breath, though it made him light-headed, and fought to stay awake. If he fell asleep, Thena would punish him. If he looked at his captors before they spoke to him, Thena would punish him. So he kept his eyes fixed on the ground.

But he could still hear. Now he listened closely to the murmured conversation on the far side of the chamber.

The Oracle perched on a three-legged stool, leaning toward two men. One was very fat, with small, vicious eyes and a helmet that squished his face like a sausage. The other wore a scarlet cloak and had dark hair swept back from his high forehead like a raven's wings. They were talking about Galen.

"Have you determined the nature of the block?" asked the man in the cloak. "Is it real or is he faking it?"

"I think it's real," the Oracle replied slowly. "He seems genuinely unaware of it."

For the past two days, she had asked him questions. About his parents and his abilities, and *their* abilities. She seemed to believe he had some kind of extraordinary power. Again and again, he had told her he didn't. That in fact, the opposite was true. She had never raised her voice, but her hatred was palpable.

Thena had aided her in the questioning. He felt her smugness through the vile collar around his throat. She believed she'd brought a great prize to the Pythia. The woman was mad. Some horrible mistake had been made. But now, kneeling in this inner sanctum deep beneath the Acropolis, Galen felt a new sense of purpose. He would find a way to kill the Pythia, or die himself in the attempt.

"What do you intend?" the man in the red cloak asked.

"I cannot test him yet because he cannot be trusted with the power. He will have to be broken first, Archon. Turned to our cause."

"With all respect," the fat man said, "you'd best do it quickly, Oracle. I sent four wind ships to scout the Umbra. They spotted a large force of daēvas massing at the edge of the forest. They'll be here in a matter of days. The one who escaped must have sounded the alarm."

Galen could hear the fear in his voice. The Danai were coming! For Rafel and Ysabel, if not for him. Assuming they were still alive. He hadn't seen either since he was collared. But the clan had found out somehow. Galen bit his lip to keep from whooping with joy. His grandmother Tethys would see Delphi leveled to the last stone—and the Pythia whipped naked and howling into the desert.

"It is no more than I expected, Polemarch," she was saying. "Leave them to me. But I agree it would be best to break this one without delay. It's usually a prolonged process, but there are ways to accelerate it. Thena, who wears his bracelet, has proven herself quite adept at—"

The Oracle twisted around as the door to the chamber flew open. Startled, Galen looked up. He heard Thena's indrawn hiss of air. A man strode inside, his mud-covered boots leaving streaks of dirt on the floor. He had coppery hair and a glower on his face.

"How dare you?" the Polemarch demanded, purple suffusing his jowls. "There are no public audiences today!" He sneered at the man's dusty traveling cloak. "If you're looking for a bowl of gruel, you'll find it in the dungeons." He turned to the Pythia and adopted a groveling tone. "When I discover which of the Shields allowed this filthy—"

The man raised a hand. Blue flames shot from the Polemarch's eyes and mouth and the stink of burning flesh filled the chamber. The inferno devoured him so quickly and thoroughly, he didn't even have time to scream. Two seconds later, a helmet with a smoking horsehair crest bounced off the stone and rolled away. The rest was a greasy smear.

The Archon swayed on his feet. Thena gave a shriek. Galen frantically probed the collar with his mind, hoping she might release his power, but met a wall. He'd seen fire dancing from the torches lining the temple's corridors—the first time he'd ever encountered the forbidden fourth element—but this was something else. He had no doubt the man could burn them all up in a single instant.

The Oracle showed no sign of emotion as the man approached her. He stopped a few paces from the tripod and the two stared at each other for a long moment.

"That was my general you just immolated," she said in an annoyed tone.

"He should have guarded his tongue."

They spoke as if no one else existed.

"Where's the girl you promised me?"

"I don't have her."

"Then it's a good thing I caught another." She pointed at Galen. "He is the Danai talisman."

"And can he use his power?"

She frowned. "Not yet."

The man started to laugh then, and seemed unable to stop. The Oracle's lips thinned as she beckoned to the Archon and Thena, who skirted the remains of the Polemarch and crept forward on unsteady legs.

"Well," she said. Her slender fingers touched the serpent brooch at her shoulder and her hair, which had been a lustrous, silken black, changed to the deep, violent red of a poppy.

"I am still the Oracle of Delphi," she intoned, letting small flames writhe over her fingertips. "The Sun God lives in me. I speak for him." Her voice lowered to a gentle murmur. "Do either of you doubt me? If there are objections, I would hear them now."

The silence in the chamber was absolute. The Archon fell to his knees and kissed the hem of her gown with bloodless lips. After a moment, Thena did the same, but Galen felt her shock and confusion. It mirrored his own. What *were* these creatures?

"Good." The Pythia smiled, though it soured when her gaze fell on the stranger. He'd finally mastered himself, wiping tears of mirth from his eyes with a corner of his cloak.

"You make a fool of yourself, Nicodemus," she said coldly.

"I'm sorry." He gave a last rueful chuckle. "It's just...I'll try to put it succinctly. That daēva over there?" He pointed at Galen, who tried not to shrink beneath the man's gaze. "He won't do you a lick of good. Not without the girl who broke your gate." Laughter threatened again, but he managed to suppress it. "The one who was just here a few weeks ago. The one you wanted me to kill."

The Pythia's eyes narrowed. "What are you talking about?"

Nicodemus smiled but it was a grim thing, and Galen realized his amusement masked a deep, implacable rage.

"She broke the Marakai girl's block," he said. "She's the fourth talisman."

EPILOGUE

The abbadax shifted on their newly-built dung nests, hungry and irritable. There had been strong differences of opinion when the two-legged creature-without-feathers came creeping into the stables. Three had wanted to devour him on the spot. But Wind from the North had accepted his blood-scent and hissed at the others until they backed away. Wind from the North was vicious. She did not suffer fools and the others feared her.

They were also anxious and uncertain because their own riders had left them behind in this strange icebound place.

Now she cradled the two-legs close to her body, keeping him warm, their hearts beating together. She remembered his smell from her home in Val Tourmaline, though she had not smelled him in a long time. But he used to come to the stables there, grooming and bringing treats. He had been kind to Wind from the North and she would be kind to him in turn.

In the recesses of her ancient mind, she even recalled his name.

Daniel.

ABOUT THE AUTHOR

Kat Ross worked as a journalist at the United Nations for ten years before happily falling back into what she likes best: making stuff up. She's the author of the dystopian thriller Some Fine Day, the Fourth Element fantasy series (The Midnight Sea, Blood of the Prophet, Queen of Chaos), the Dominion Mysteries and the new Fourth Talisman series. She loves myths, monsters and doomsday scenarios.

Sign up for her newsletter to get new release alerts so you don't miss *Nemesis*, the next installment in the series. And if you have a moment to leave a review, they're a huge boost for authors and so appreciated. :)

www.katrossbooks.com
kat@katrossbooks.com

CHARACTERS IN THE SERIES

Mortals

ARCHON BASILEUS. The head of civic religious arrangements in Delphi.

ARCHON EPONYMOS. The chief magistrate of Delphi.

HERODOTUS. A Greek scholar and former curator of the Great Library of Delphi.

IZAD ASABANA. A wealthy merchant and dealer in spell dust.

JAVID. A wind ship pilot from the Persian city of Samarqand.

KATSU. A Stygian thief-catcher.

KORINNA. An acolyte at the Temple of Delphi.

LEILA. Marzban's daughter.

MARZBAN KHORRAM-DIN. Asabana's alchemist.

NABU-BAL-IDINNA. An eccentric alchemist of the golden age of Samarqand who claimed to have traveled in the Dominion and met the Drowned Lady.

NAZAFAREEN. A wielder of negatory magic.

THE POLEMARCH. The commander of Delphi's armed forces.

PRINCE SHAHAK. Heir to the crown of Samarqand.

SAVAH SAYUZHDRI. Javid's old boss at the Merchants' Guild.

THENA. An acolyte at the Temple of Delphi.

Daevas

Avas Danai (Children of Earth)

DARIUS. A daeva of House Dessarian who was born in the Empire on the other side of the gates.
DELILAH. Victor's wife and Darius's mother.
GALEN. Victor's son with Mina. Half-brother to Darius.
MITHRE. Victor's second in command.
MINA. A Danai hostage at Val Moraine. VICTOR. Darius's father.
RAFEL/NIKIAS. A daeva who was kidnapped by the Pythia.
TETHYS. Victor's mother, head of House Dessarian and one of the Matrium.

Avas Valkirins (Children of Air)

CULACH. Once the heir to Val Moraine, he was blinded and lost his power.
DANIEL/DEMETRIOS. Halldora's grandson and heir, he was abducted and brainwashed by the Pythia.
EIRIK. Culach's father and the former lord of Val Moraine.
ELLARD. Galen's friend. Raised as a hostage at House Dessarian in exchange for Mina.
FRIDA: Halldora's second in command.
GERDA. Culach's great-great-grandmother.
HALLDÓRA. Mistress of Val Tourmaline.
KATRIN. Culach's former lover.
PETUR. Culach's best friend. He tried to kill Nazafareen and was killed by Galen.
RUNAR. Lord of Val Petros.
STEFÁN. Lord of Val Altair.
SOFIA: One of Halldora's riders.

Avas Marakai (Children of Water)

KASAIKA. Captain of the *Asperta*. Selk Marakai.

MAFUONE. Captain of the *Chione*. Sheut Marakai.

MEBETIMMUNEDJEM, a.k.a. Meb the Mouse. A 12-year-old orphan of the Selk who does grunt work on the *Asperta*.

SAKHET-RA-KATME. The oldest Marakai and one of the original talismans. A distant ancestor of Meb.

Avas Vatras (Children of Fire)

ATTICUS. Nicodemus's younger brother.

DOMITIA, a.k.a. The Pythia, a.k.a. the Oracle of Delphi. Gaius's daughter.

FARRUMOHR, a.k.a. the Viper. Gaius's advisor. Haunts Culach's dreams.

GAIUS. Former king of the Vatras.

NICODEMUS. A survivor of the Kiln.

Maenads

KALLISTO. Head of the Cult of Dionysius, she seeks to protect the talismans from harm. Her followers are RHEA, CHARIS, CYRENE and MEGAERA. Two others, twins named ALCIPPE and ADEIA, were killed by the Pythia's soldiers.

GLOSSARY

Abbadax. Winged creatures used as mounts by the Valkirins. Intelligent and vicious, they have scaled bodies and razor-sharp feathers to slash opponents during aerial combat.

Adyton. Innermost chamber of the Temple of Apollo, where the Pythia issues prophecies and receives supplicants.

Anuketmatma. Worshipped by the Selk Marakai as the spirit of storms, she takes the form of a small grey cat with dark stripes. The Selk carry her on their ships and lull her with milk and honey.

Avas Danai. Children of Earth, known for their dark hair and eyes and strength in earth power. The Avas Danai are divided into seven Houses located in the Great Forest of Nocturne. Their primary trade commodity is wood. Qualities of earth: Grounded, solid, practical, stubborn, literal, loyal.

Avas Marakai. Children of Water. Dark-skinned and curly-haired, they are the seafaring daēvas. They make their home in the Isles of the Marakai and act as middlemen between the mortals and other daēva clans. Their wealth derives from the Hin, equal to one-tenth of the goods they transport. No one else has the skill to navigate the Austral Ocean or the White Sea, so they enjoy a monopoly on sea trade and travel. Qualities of water: Easygoing, free, adventurous, cheerful, cunning, industrious.

Avas Valkirins. Children of Air. Pale-skinned and silver-haired, they live in stone holdfasts in the mountains of Nocturne. The Valkirin Range is the source of all metal and gemstones in the world. Qualities of air: Quick to anger, proud, changeable, passionate, ruthless, rowdy, restless.

Avas Vatras. Children of Fire. Red-haired and light-eyed. No one has seen the Avas Vatras for a thousand years, since they tried to burn the world and were imprisoned in the Kiln. The only clan with the ability to forge talismans. Qualities of fire: Creative, ambitious, generous, destructive, curious, risk-taking.

Bond. The connection between a linked pair of talismans that allows a human to control the power of a daēva. Can take the form of two matching cuffs, or a bracelet and collar. A side effect of the bond is that emotions and sensations are shared between human and daēva. A bond draws on fire and will only work in Solis, not in Nocturne.

Breaker. See *negatory magic*.

Chimera. Elemental hunting packs, they're made from water, earth and air, seasoned with malice, greed, sorrow and fear. Chimera cannot be killed by any traditional means and will track their quarry to the ends of the earth.

Daēva. Similar in appearance to humans with some magical abilities. Most daēvas have a particular affinity for earth, air or water and are strongest in one element. However, they cannot work fire, and will die merely from coming into close proximity with an open flame. Daēvas can live for thousands of years and heal from wounds that would kill or cripple a human. Regarding clan names, *val* means mountain, *dan* means forest, *mar* means sea, *vat* means fire. *Avas* means children of.

Darklands. The slang term for Nocturne.

Diyat. "The Five." The governing body of the five Marakai fleets.

Dominion, also called the gloaming or shadowlands. The land of the dead. Can be traversed using a talisman or via gates, but is a dangerous place for the living.

Druj. Literally translates as *impure souls*. Includes Revenants, wights, liches and other Undead. In the Empire, daēvas were considered Druj by the magi.

Ecclesia. The popular assembly of Delphi. Open to all male citizens over the age of twenty. Elects the Archons and votes on matters of law and justice.

Elemental magic. The direct manipulation of earth, air or water. Fire is the fourth element, but has unstable properties that cannot be worked by most daēvas.

Empire. A land reached through gates in the Dominion, it is a mirror world of Solis and Nocturne in many ways. Nazafareen and Darius come from the Empire. It is the setting of the Fourth Element Trilogy.

Faravahar. The symbol of the Prophet, revered by the Persians. Its form is an eagle with outstretched wings.

Gale. The impassable line of storms created to imprison the Avas Vatras in the Kiln.

Gate. A permanent passage into the Dominion. Temporary gates can also be opened with a talisman.

Gorgon-e Gaz. The prison on the shore of the Salenian Sea where the oldest daēvas were held by the Empire. Victor Dessarian spent two centuries within its walls before escaping.

Great Green. What the Marakai call the collective oceans.

Hammu. A giant carp that causes undersea earthquakes and tsunamis. Worshipped by the Jengu Marakai.

Infirmity. Called the *Druj Curse* in the Empire, it is the physical disability caused to daēvas by the bonding process.

Khaf-hor. Giant fanged eel with slimy, viscous skin. Worshipped by the Nyx Marakai.

Kiln. The vast, trackless desert beyond the Gale where the sun sits at high noon. The prison of the Avas Vatras.

Lacuna. The period of true night that descends when all three of Nocturne's moons are hidden. The timing of the lacuna varies from seconds to an hour or more depending on the lunar cycle.

Magi. Persian priests who follow the Way of the Flame.

Moons. Selene, Hecate and Artemis. Selene is the brightest,

Hecate the smallest, and Artemis has the longest orbit, taking a full year to complete. The passage of time in both Solis and Nocturne is judged by the moons since they're the only large celestial bodies that move through the sky.

Matrium. The seven female heads of the Avas Danai houses.

Nahresi. Skeletal horses that gallop across the waves. Worshipped by the Khepresh Marakai.

Negatory magic. A rare talent that involves the working of all four elements. Those who can wield it are known as Breakers. Negatory magic can obliterate both elemental and talismanic magic. The price of negatory magic is rage and emotional turmoil. It derives from the Breaker's own temperament and is separate from the Nexus, which is the source of all elemental magic.

Nocturne. The dark side of the world.

Parthenoi. Virgin warriors. See *Maenads*.

Rock of Ariamazes. The fortress-palace of the Kings of Samarqand. It was scorched in the Vatra Wars but never destroyed.

Sat-bu. Like the mythological monster Charybdis, she makes a whirlpool in the deep ocean that sucks ships down. Tentacled and faceless, she is worshipped by the Sheut Marakai.

Shadowlands. See *Dominion*.

Shepherds. Hounds of the Dominion, they herd the dead to their final destination at the Cold Sea. Extremely hostile to anything living, and to necromancers in particular.

Shields of Apollo. The elite unit of Greek soldiers that hunts and captures daēvas.

Solis. The sunlit side of the world.

Spell Dust. A sparkling powder; when combined with spoken words, it works like a talisman to accomplish any number of things. Only trained alchemists are fluent in the language of spell dust. Extremely addictive when consumed directly. Source unknown (except to the Persian merchant and dust dealer Izad Asabana).

Stygians. Mortals who dwell in the Isles of the Marakai. They're the only humans to live in the darklands, surviving by fishing and diving for pearls. The Stygians worship a giant oyster named Babana.

Talismanic magic. The use of elemental magic to imbue power in a material object, word or phrase. Generally, the object will perform a single function, i.e. lumen crystals, daēva cuffs or Talismans of Folding.

Talismans (*three daēvas*). They ended the war with the Vatras by creating the Gale and sundering Nocturne into light and dark. Their power passed on through the generations.

Umbra. The twilight realm between Solis and Nocturne.

Water Dogs. Paramilitary force of bonded pairs (human and daēva) that kept order in the distant satrapies of the Empire and hunted Undead Druj along the borders.

Way of the Flame. The official religion of the Empire, and also of Samarqand and Susa. Preaches *good thoughts, good words and good* *deeds*. Embodied by the magi, who view the world as locked in an eternal struggle between good and evil. Fire is considered the holiest element, followed by water.

Wight. A Druj Undead with the ability to take over a human body and mimic the host to a certain degree. Must be beheaded.

Wind Ship. A conveyance similar to a hot air balloon, but with a wooden ship rather than a basket. Powered either by burners or spell magic.

ACKNOWLEDGMENTS

As always, all my gratitude to Deirdre, Christa and Laura, for pointing out mistakes and showing me how to make the story stronger. What would I do without you?

And a big shout-out to the fabulous team at Acorn Publishing and all my fellow authors there. So proud to be part of the family!